POLITICAL GAIN

SARAH WYLAND

Cover Photo Copyright © 2020 by Charles Parker

Line edits and proofread by Caitlin Lengerich, @chronicledbycait

Paperback ISBN: 979-8-9924173-1-9

www.sarahwyland.com

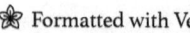 Formatted with Vellum

*For anyone who has ever felt like they
had to earn their worth.*

1

LYLA

This is an incredibly bad decision.

I *know* this is a bad decision.

I don't make bad decisions.

Yet here I am, wrapped in a tiny dress and dangerously high heels, my long hair falling in waves, and wearing more makeup than I have in a year.

I am a walking bad decision.

But tonight, and tonight only, I do not give a fuck.

Tonight, I am not *Lyla Adler*, dutiful youngest daughter of Senator Veronica Adler.

Tonight, I am *Lyla*, a woman wronged and looking for revenge sex. Or something. I don't know what the hell I'm doing. All I know is that when I was seething mad and ready to burn something down earlier, my sister's suggestion to get under someone new to get over my ex sounded like a good idea.

So, here I am, dressed in something I forgot I owned until I was packing up my closet, sitting at a bar, and nursing a martini. I ignore the *"What if?"* voice in my head. The one asking, *what if the press gets wind of me being here? What if they photograph me?*

It will be front page news for sure.

The youngest Adler—gone wild.

Mom would shit a brick.

So would her aide, Cosse. Might be worth it to piss him off, honestly.

Except . . . I hate the attention. I hate it more than I hate my ex, and that's saying something. My sister tolerates the attention, while my brother downright thrived in it before he defected from the family. He keeps himself out of the spotlight these days. He also doesn't speak to Mom.

God, I envy him.

Goosebumps erupt along my arms without warning.

Someone is watching me.

I don't know how I know, I just . . . know. Life in the public eye instills a certain need to be aware of your surroundings so I *always* know. I force myself to take another sip of my drink so I don't look paranoid, then shift on my stool for a better look at my surroundings. It's a dive, chosen specifically because, surely, said press has better things to do than track me down to it. It's also close enough to my brother's place that I can walk if I really want to, or fork over a few dollars to Uber if I can't or don't want to walk.

I chose Uber to get here. These shoes are *not* made for walking.

My eyes sweep the bar from right to left, and then I see him.

The most beautiful man I have ever seen.

He's leaning on the bar at the far end, dressed in dark jeans and a black Henley, the sleeves pushed up to his elbows. One arm has an intricate tattoo that starts at his wrist and disappears into his sleeve. His hair is dark and styled to look messy, and even from this far away, I can tell his eyes are as dark as his hair.

He's looking at me like he's the predator and I'm his prey.

Fuck. Me.

Literally.

Please.

Fuck me.

He sends a smirk my way, and my entire body heats. I look away, face flushed. It's been so long since I've been "on the scene," and despite my bravado tonight, the hot stranger's attention disarms me. I don't get attention from men who look like that. It's the button-downs-tucked-into-khakis-with-a-respectable-pedigree type that usually go for me. Safe, sensible options. Definitely not the ones who look like every bad boy stereotype I've ever read about.

I pick up my martini and down enough of it to need a new one, stat. I look for the bartender, but she's occupied with closing a group's tab about halfway down the bar. The other bartender, a man, is busy mixing drinks.

I chance a glance back at the handsome stranger. He's talking to the female bartender now, giving her an easy smile and a nod, then he takes the beer she places in front of him and joins a table tucked in a corner. Apparently, he only hangs out with beautiful people because every single person at that table is stunning.

There's the blond guy, his hair coiffed, his eyes so blue they almost glow in the dark bar, and another guy who looks the part of "the muscle"—big, broad, and heavily tattooed. Then there's a near carbon copy of Mr. Beautiful himself. His hair is a little longer and features softer, but there's no doubt they're related.

The one woman at the table is striking. Her hair is icy blonde, cut sharp at her chin. She looks like she was born wearing the leather she's dressed in. I want to be her friend and never cross her path at the same time. Mr. Beautiful looks over his shoulder, catching me staring again. I look away fast.

No more staring.

Besides, he's way out of my league.

I check for the bartenders.

Still busy.

I pick up my phone to mindlessly scroll so I don't look like a loser sitting at the bar alone, with an empty cocktail, which is, ironically, exactly what I look like as I scroll. I'm typing out a comment on my friend Heather's latest post when a large shadow falls over me a moment before a fresh martini appears in front of me. I startle as I look up and into the very chiseled face of Mr. Beautiful. He smirks at my response and something akin to electricity races along my spine.

"You looked thirsty."

"Thank you," I manage as I reach for the drink so I have something to do with my hands because I'm suddenly very unsure about what to do with said hands.

"I haven't seen you here before," he says as he leans on the bar top.

"You come here often?" I counter. Could be useful information if he's a regular and I decide to make this my neighborhood bar.

He shrugs. "Often enough that I would have recognized a woman as beautiful as you."

"I'm new in town."

"Welcome to New York," he says, smirk growing.

"Cheers." He clinks his beer against my glass. "Best fucking city in the world."

He takes a swig, and I watch his biceps flex while he does it. This man cannot be real. *Cannot.* He looks to have been carved from marble. Michelangelo himself couldn't have done better.

"In the world is a stretch," I say, because I can't help myself. "But it's all right."

"Pray tell, gorgeous. What's the best fucking city in the world in your eyes?" His eyes dance in amusement.

"I don't know." I shrug. "I haven't seen them all yet."

He smiles, and *ugh*, he's even more beautiful. He meets my gaze, his brown eyes as deep as I thought they were. He blatantly rakes his eyes down my body. I try to act unbothered, like I don't care if he likes what he sees, but the flushed skin under my dress would give me away.

"I like this dress." He reaches out and runs a thumb along the short hem, which has ridden up my thigh from how I'm sitting with my legs crossed on this stool. Heat flares and settles directly between my thighs. I squeeze them together to try to alleviate some of the sudden need flaring through me. He's bold as hell as he lets his fingertips ghost down my leg, barely touching me, until he reaches the strap of my shoe, looped around my ankle. "The shoes, too."

"Do you always go around touching things you like?" I ask. He leans in and *damn* he smells good. Like sandalwood, leather, and bad decisions.

"Only things that want to be touched." He traces the strap of my shoe, his touch feather light but blazing. "Be honest with me, gorgeous. You came here tonight in hopes of being touched, didn't you?"

I could say no. I could do what Lyla Adler, senator's daughter, would do and politely make an excuse to go anywhere else. I'm tired of doing things her way, though. This Lyla wants this man's hands on her again.

"I came here tonight in hopes of being thoroughly fucked." Who the hell has taken over my body and made those words come out of my mouth? I do not say things like that. "Know anyone who can help with that?"

"Turns out, I do." He leans closer, moving his hand to cup my cheek. He looks into my eyes like he's searching for something, and I stare right back. A nagging voice in the back of my mind tells me this is reckless—wonders if he will recognize me. I tell that voice to shut the hell up. "And I would love to see what's under that dress." He leans in closer, his lips a breath away from mine. "You want it, it's yours, gorgeous. But you're going to have to make the next move. Consent is a thing, after all."

I recklessly seal my lips over his and oh.

OH.

He tastes like mint, beer, and danger.

And bad decisions.

Definitely tastes like a bad decision.

One I'm about to make the hell out of.

He deepens the kiss, and I part my lips to give him more. His tongue slides over mine, and my hands curl into his shirt to draw him closer. His whole body molds to mine as one of his muscular arms wraps around me, pulling me against him.

"What's your name, gorgeous?" he asks when we part to catch our breaths. There's next to no room between us, but what is there is too damn much.

"No names." I shake my head. "They aren't necessary."

If he has no idea who I am, he can't take it to the press.

"I accept those terms." He kisses me again, letting it linger before he pulls away. "I need to close my tab and tell my friends goodbye. Meet me at the door in five minutes." He signals for the nearest bartender who appears right away. "Close out my tab." Then he brushes my hair over my shoulder, looking at me like he intends to devour me. "I'll be covering the lady's, too." I open my mouth to protest, but he stops me with another smoldering kiss. "Five minutes," he says, then he's gone as suddenly as he appeared.

Whoa.

Whoa.

I'm disoriented.

I just agreed to go home with a stranger.

A stranger who looks like *that*.

Such an incredibly bad idea.

That I'm absolutely going to follow through on because why not?

Five minutes, he said. I check the time. I can finish this martini before I go. I may need the liquid courage if the way just kissing him made me feel is any indication of how the rest of the night is going to go.

I look across the bar again. He's with his friends, but on his feet, talking to the group, all eyes on him. The one that looks like him catches my eye this time. He gives a little grin then looks away, like he's been let in on a secret he now needs to keep.

"Here's your card," the female bartender says as she stands in front of me. She's pretty, with her braids pulled into a ponytail and brown eyes that radiate warmth. "Tall and handsome covered your tab."

"Thank you," I say, taking the card from her.

"Take this, too." She holds out a scrap piece of paper. "It's my number. I'm Cecily and, well, you're obviously going home with him." I don't deny it. "He's a regular." I catch her drift—he doesn't leave alone often. "He's never caused trouble, but there's something about you I like, and you know, women supporting women, or whatever."

Okay, she's badass.

"I'm Lyla," I say as I take her number, giving her my real name and everything. "I appreciate this." I worry my lip. "I don't do this often."

Not *never*, but certainly not often.

"Hey, I do it all the time." She shrugs good-naturedly. "Nothing wrong with needing the peen or the tongue or whatever you're into. This"—she motions to herself—"is a no-judgment zone." Someone approaches the bar a few stools down and signals for her. She winks at me as she turns away. "Don't be a stranger, Lyla."

I won't be. Not if the men in this bar look like Mr. Beautiful and his friends.

I polish off my drink and slip off the stool. I'm not entirely convinced he's going to follow through, but he's at the door, leaning against the wall beside it, watching me with that predatory gaze again.

"You're fucking gorgeous," he tells me when I'm close enough.

"Right back at you," I reply. He smirks and pushes off the wall. Holy shit, he's tall. He's well over six feet, dwarfing my five-foot-two stature. He's as wide as two of me standing side by side and all muscle. He must do bicep curls in his sleep.

His hand catches mine.

"Let's get out of here." He tugs me through the door and outside into the humid night air.

"I hope you have a place we can go to," I say. "We're not going to mine."

"Let me guess. Bitchy roommates?"

"Very much so." I refuse to think about the dad-like disappointment that would roll off my brother if he knew I was willingly following a handsome stranger down a Brooklyn sidewalk with every intention of letting him do whatever he wants to me, so long as it ends in an orgasm.

"I have us covered." He smirks again. "Literally. Got a condom burning a hole in my wallet."

"That's the details, then," I say. He chuckles.

He still has my hand in his as we walk down the sidewalk. I assume he's leading me to an apartment, or maybe one of the brownstones around here, but then he stops at a black vintage Bronco parked on the street. I know very little about cars, but I know this one is sexy, expensive, and entirely impractical for New York City. It's also, somehow, the perfect extension of this man.

He opens the passenger door and gets in. I stand on the sidewalk with a raised eyebrow. He looks right back at me.

"You want to get fucked, or you want to stand on the sidewalk making me daydream about fucking you?" he asks. "Because I can promise you, gorgeous, that in the thirty-or-so minutes it's been since I first saw you, I've already had at least five fantasies about the ways I can take you."

"You want me to . . . drive?" I ask.

He snorts. "No one drives my Bronco but me," he states. "We're fucking in the passenger seat. I'm too tall to get in the back, and the steering wheel is in the way on the other side." He jerks his head. "Climb in."

I have to literally climb in. The Bronco is lifted, and he ends up hauling me into his lap in an incredibly ungraceful manner. My embarrassment is forgotten the moment I'm straddling his lap, however. I can feel him through his jeans, and I'm confident his cock is proportionate to his size.

He slams the door shut and gives me his undivided attention. "Fucking stunning," he says as he takes me in.

"You sure you don't want to trade names? I think I'd like hearing you scream mine."

"No names," I insist as my hands drift down his hard chest. "Just bodies."

He wastes no time. He buries a hand in my hair and pulls me in for a kiss while his other hand slides under the hem of my dress. He groans into my mouth, and his tongue asks for entrance that I gladly grant.

"Fuck, you taste good," he says between kisses. He hikes my dress up to my waist, giving me more freedom to move. I grind against him, working to push his shirt up. I want to see just how many abs he has under there—definitely six, probably eight—but the space is too tight for me to gain much leverage.

His hand moves from my hair to cup my cheek as he kisses me with bruising depth. His other hand wanders my body, never quite getting where I want him. I whine and rock against him. A deep chuckle leaves him.

"You're a needy little thing," he says. "Betting there's an ex-lover who didn't satisfy your needs?"

Correct, but I'm too busy exploring his neck and jaw with my lips while rocking my core against the bulge under me to answer.

He locates the zipper at my back, pulls it down, and finds my lips again. I'm groaning now, and any thoughts about being spotted, or the fact that I am very much about to have sex in the passenger seat of a vintage Bronco, are out the window. He pulls the zipper the rest of the way down, then pushes my dress from my shoulders. I'm wearing petals over my nipples and nothing else.

"Fuck that," he half growls and tears one off. His mouth latches on, and he's right. Fuck. That. The only thing I want on my nipples is his mouth.

"Oh, God," I breathe as I arch my spine, throwing my head back. He fumbles for the other petal without ever taking his mouth out of the action.

"It's just us here," he says as he switches nipples. "Give me your name and I'll give you mine. Then you can go hoarse from screaming it."

It's so tempting, but I won't. I'm going to remain a mystery.

"Shut up and suck," I order. He chuckles again.

"Bossy," he says. "I like it."

He also takes it as a challenge.

He's everywhere. His mouth, his hands. *Everywhere.* How does he do it? How does he seem to know exactly what I like? Like he's proving it, he finds a spot on my neck that drives me insane.

"Your mouth is brilliant," I breathe.

"Wait until you have my cock in you," he boasts.

Speaking of . . .

I reach for the button of his jeans. It's like he's been waiting for me to breach that barrier because his hand slides between my legs. I gasp as his fingers rub over me, using what little fabric my thong provides for friction.

"Damn, you want me." I look up from where I'm attempting to free him. I must be imagining the look of wonder in his features. It's dark, we're in the passenger seat of a Bronco, and I'm lust-addled; I can't be trusted to think straight. His fingers slip inside the fabric, and he groans as his other arm tightens where he's wrapped it around my waist. "So wet."

"You said you have a condom?"

"I do," he confirms. "You'll see it soon."

He gives no warning before sinking a finger into me. I gasp in surprise, despite being more than slick enough for the intrusion. He watches me, making sure I'm okay, before beginning to move it in annoyingly slow circles.

"So tight," he observes. A second finger slips inside. "You're going to feel incredible around me."

"Is that so?" I manage. I want to ride his fingers, but I can't quite manage it in this position.

"Very much so." He shifts forward so he can kiss me. His thumb finds my clit at the same moment his lips touch mine. I whimper against him. "You're going to have to come on my fingers first, gorgeous. You're much too tight to take all of me."

He fucks me with his fingers.

It is *fantastic*.

He finds the right rhythm, the right angle. When he crooks his digits just so, I mewl, rocking my hips, desperate for more. I cling to him, try to kiss him—to feel him—but he's got me so spun up that all I can focus on is his fingers buried in me.

"Go on," he coaxes as he moves his fingers a little faster and increases the pressure on my clit with his thumb. "Let's see you break."

I clench around his fingers as pleasure rocks through me like one big tidal wave. I cry out and tighten my hold on his shoulders, but his fingers keep going even after my orgasm wanes.

"I think you have one more in you before you get my cock. Let's get another finger in you." A third digit enters me and I lose what little rational thought I have left. "That's it," he praises. "Good girl." *Oh*. He's that guy. A little dominant, a lot dirty. I'm into it. "Come on my fingers one more time, then we'll get me in you." He kisses me. "I can't fucking wait to be balls deep in you."

He brings his mouth back to my breasts, and I fall to pieces. This man's fingers are *magic*.

"You." I breathe as he pulls his fingers from me and my orgasm fades. "Are way too good at that."

"Wait until you see what I can do with this."

He reaches to unbutton his pants, but I stop him to do it myself since he distracted me earlier. I help him shove his pants down enough to free him, and . . . *Oh. My. God.* How in the *hell* is he going to fit all of that in my small body? His smirk tells me he knows what I'm thinking, then he wraps his arm around my waist again and lifts his hips so he can reach into his back pocket for his wallet.

"Don't worry, gorgeous," he drawls. "We'll go slow. I'll only give you as much as you want."

And I realize I trust him. I trust a complete stranger not to take it too far.

I take the condom, tear it open, and roll it on. I lift to my knees as much as the roof of the Bronco allows and position myself over him. His hands are on my hips, and his eyes are on me. I slip down, take the head, and let my eyes close. He stops me by tightening his hands on my hips.

"Open your eyes, gorgeous."

I flutter them open. He's looking at me with so much intensity I think it makes me even wetter.

"There you go." He gives a single nod of approval. "It's suddenly the most important thing in the world that I look you in your eyes while I take you."

He can have whatever he wants.

He loosens his grip and lets gravity do the rest, staying true to his word to go slow. I take him inch by inch. The stretch, the feel of him, is *incredible*. His eyes never leave mine and it intensifies everything. I can't look away.

He gives me time to adjust before he starts to move.

Oh.

My.

God.

Each thrust goes a little deeper as my body opens more for him. We're all hands and limbs and moans and need as his thrusts grow harder, more demanding. I find myself wondering what he would be capable of in a bed with space to move, but I abandon that thought so I can focus on right here, right now.

The reality where I am being thoroughly fucked in the passenger seat of a Bronco parked along the curb in Brooklyn where anyone could see.

Best. Night. Ever.

"God, you feel so good in me," I moan in his ear.

"You should feel how you feel around me," he counters. "Tight, hot, wet perfection." He thrusts harder. "I want you to come all over my cock." His hand slips between us. "I want to see you fall apart again."

His wish, my command. Or something. Because the moment he stimulates my clit, my walls tighten around him, and my orgasm is imminent.

"More." I breathe. "Just ... A little ... More ..."

"You look so fucking good on my cock," he says as his thrusts grow harder, his touch firmer. "Now, come for me."

My body unleashes and I cry out as the coil snaps. I'm all pleasure as my rhythm falters and I lose all sense of time and space. I have never felt anything like this. I have never fallen apart so completely. I want to do it again and again. If this is sex, what in the hell have I been having all these years?

"So fucking good," he says as he keeps going. "Almost ... There ..."

Three more thrusts into my now pliant body and he

comes with a shout, his head thrown back, pure bliss in his features. I feel him pulsing in me, feel the warmth of him as he releases, even through the condom that catches him. It sends aftershocks through me, and I let out another breathy cry before I collapse against him.

For a few minutes, there is nothing but me, him, and this Bronco. He softens inside me as I rest on his chest, with both of his arms around me, smoothing his hands up and down my back. There's a part of me that could stay right here forevermore. The rest of me—the part that sounds and acts a lot like Senator Adler's daughter—starts to come to her senses, and I make myself sit up.

"That was sensational," he says, eyes on me as I fumble to thread my arms back through my dress sleeves. "Right now, in this moment, I think the sole reason I bought this Bronco is so I could fuck you in the passenger seat." He squeezes my hip. "Give me a minute, and maybe we'll tackle the backseat. Might have to get creative—" He frowns as I zip my dress. "What are you doing?"

"Going home," I say. "I told you I wanted to get thoroughly fucked tonight. Mission accomplished."

"But . . ." His frown deepens.

"I'm not looking for anything past right now," I tell him.

"Me the fuck either," he says. "I don't see what the harm is in going again before morning, though." He rocks his hips almost like a reminder that he's still in me. "Maybe I can get you all the way naked. At least take your panties off." It's only then that I realize he'd just pushed them aside and had me. God, that's hot.

"I appreciate the offer, but I've had all the orgasms I can take for one night," I say.

"Lies." He calls me out, and he's not wrong. I could absolutely have several more orgasms, whether on this man's fingers or cock, I'm not picky. Bet he would give me his tongue, too, if I asked. Except, I need to be smart. One night stand. One time only. He slips out of me as I reach for the door, intent on making my exit. His hand closes around my wrist and I look at him. "Let me at least take you back inside, buy you another drink."

"You trying to get me drunk so you can fuck me again?" I ask.

"Not so drunk you lose your agency, but perhaps tipsy enough that the cacophony of thoughts racing through your mind slows down long enough for you to let me have you one more time like I know you want to."

His offer is tempting. And how does he know my thoughts are racing?

"Listen, you are fantastic at this," I begin. "But I'm not interested and . . ."

He shuts me up by kissing me.

Shit.

Never stood a chance, did I?

"Fine," I breathe when he pulls away. My traitorous body wants him again, logic be damned. "One drink."

He grins like he's won the lottery and buttons himself back up before we're out of his Bronco and walking back the way we came. His friends are gone when we return to the bar, but he claims their same table and orders our drinks. He asks me for my name a few more times, but I refuse to give it to him. I figure out quickly that if I keep my lips on his, he can't do a whole lot of talking.

Then, I let him fuck me in the women's bathroom.

He locks us in, removes a condom from his wallet—how many times was he planning to have sex tonight?—and takes me from behind while I brace against the sink. I vaguely wonder if tonight will ruin me for other men as I climax on his cock once more.

Last call has long passed when we stumble out of the bar. Neither of us is drunk, but we're not sober, either. And a good amount of my high is directly related to the orgasms Mr. Beautiful has wrung from my body over the last few hours.

"Let me give you a ride home," he says, placing his hand on my lower back as I fumble with my phone to summon an Uber.

"I'm calling an Uber," I tell him.

"No." He shakes his head. "I don't like putting beautiful women into a stranger's car late at night."

"I literally got into a stranger's car and let him absolutely wreck me with his cock," I remind him. "So, pot? Meet kettle."

He grins. "I wrecked you, huh?" I roll my eyes at his over-inflated ego. "And I don't have a car. I have a vintage Bronco. Very different."

"Thank you for the offer, the drinks, and the sex," I say. "I have a car on the way." I give him a look that says "leave."

"Do you seriously think I'm going to leave you standing on a sidewalk by yourself to wait for a stranger to take you wherever the hell you're going?" he questions.

"I can take care of myself."

He gives me a once-over from head to toe. "You're tiny."

"Your point?"

"Just stating the obvious."

I glare at his implication, which isn't exactly wrong, but whatever. "You're a lot less likable when your cock isn't in me."

"Let me take you home, and maybe it will be in you again," he counters.

Like I'm going to show up at my brother's place, with a stranger, at three in the morning. "My Uber is three minutes away."

"Then I'll stand on this sidewalk and let you think about my cock inside you for three more minutes." He pushes his hands in his pockets, intent to do just that, while I decide to ignore him, which is definitely easier said than done. I check my notifications while we wait.

Shit.

I have a dozen missed calls from my brother, and an embarrassing number of texts from him, asking where I am. There are a few from my sister, too, saying she hopes I'm too busy getting laid to read them, but if I could just let our brother know I'm not dead, that would be great.

I was, in fact, too busy getting laid to read their texts.

I fire off a "Fine. On my way home," to my brother, then let my sister know that her suggestion proved excellent. I can't say I'm not thinking about my ex anymore, but I can't say I am, either.

"This is stupid," Mr. Beautiful says, unable to keep quiet for the full three minutes. "Cancel your car and let me take you home."

"It will be here in"—I check my app—"one minute. Sorry, handsome, but this ride is closed for business."

"Pretty sure I was the ride in this situation," he volleys. "At least trade numbers with me. Maybe shoot me a text the next time you're planning to go drinking alone."

"Shoot you a text?" I parrot. "You sound like my dad."

Dad.

The pang in my gut isn't as strong, but it's definitely there.

He holds out his phone. "Put your number in my phone."

He's not asking. I'm not caving. "I told you. No names. Just bodies."

"Your body is the reason I want your number in my phone," he pushes. "Hell, I don't even need your real name. Put yourself in there as 'Bronco Hook Up.'"

"Charming."

"Got to keep my contacts straight somehow."

I make a face and he realizes what he said.

"Shit. Now I sound like I fuck random women on the regular."

"According to my sources, you do." I see my car at the end of the block.

"I have a healthy sex life," he states. "Your bartender doesn't know shit." I give him a look, wondering how he knew I gleaned that info from the bartender. "I'm not looking for a commitment—fuck that and fuck your sources, too. But I do like the female body, and yours is exquisite. If you're not looking for serious, I wouldn't mind you riding my cock a few more times."

His offer is tempting. The sex was phenomenal, and this Lyla wants to agree. But Lyla Adler, Senator's Daughter, knows it's a bad idea. She's not a one-night stand woman, not really. She's a relationship woman, and this man is not the monogamous type.

"No." My car pulls up to the curb. "My ride is here." I reach for the door handle, and damn if he doesn't swoop in and open it for me. I don't get him. Blasé as hell about sex, but also a gentleman? Sort of? "Don't worry. I did all the safety checks." I quickly flash my screen at him. "Same car, same license plate." I peek into the car and see a tired-but-kind-looking woman behind the wheel. She looks exactly like her Uber profile photo. "Same driver—even has the Uber light in the window. We're good."

"Last chance," he replies.

"I'll tell you what," I say as I slide into the car, eyes still on his. "If we cross paths again, maybe I'll consider it."

I pull the door shut and leave Mr. Beautiful on the sidewalk.

"It's not my business," my driver says as she pulls away from the curb. "But I hope you fucked the shit out of that tall drink of what has to be a very strong cocktail."

"I did," I admit, because why not? "Totally worth it."

I chance a glance out of the back window for one last look at him.

But Mr. Beautiful is already gone.

"**Y**ou can't do shit like this, Lyla!"

Bradley Adler has gone full-dad mode.

I sip my not-strong-enough coffee because I forgot my brother makes his weak as hell and try to ignore the way my head pounds as he lectures me for my very late return home last night, or this morning, such as it was. It's all white noise, really, because I'm an adult and can do what I want, including consent to a very tall, very handsome stranger perhaps ruining me for the rest of men in existence.

"Are you even listening?" He runs an exasperated hand through his hair.

"You're just repeating yourself now." I shrug and cut into my French toast—the frozen kind, because if there is one thing the Adlers have in common, it's that none of us can cook.

"And, technically, she *can* do shit like this," my sister Alice pipes up. She's on speaker phone, and I don't think her presence is going the way Bradley intended it to when he called her and demanded she help him "talk some sense into our baby sister" a half hour ago. "She's an adult. She went out. She had fun. She's back home, hungover, and probably pissed at you."

"What she said," I echo as I take another sip of coffee and cringe. "Would it kill you to use like two more scoops of coffee grounds?"

"My god." He pushes back from the table and starts to pace. I watch him, amused. I wouldn't say I'm hungover, exactly, but I definitely feel the impact of having more alcohol than usual, and the headache is probably directly related to my lack of water intake over the last eighteen or so hours. I also very much feel the reminder that I had sex with a bigger cock than I'm used to last night.

"You just moved to town, Lyla." Bradley marches around his kitchen like he was born to lecture me. "You don't know this neighborhood. You could have gotten hurt. Lost. Kidnapped. Killed. The list is long!"

"That's dramatic." He's acting like there are trained assassins on every street corner of his Park Slope neighborhood.

"Where the hell were you?" he presses. "And why do you have your location sharing turned off? I need to know where you are."

"Why do you need to know where I am?" I question. "Again, adult. Can go to bars alone. Can pay for my own Uber. Also very capable of using public transportation when needed. It might surprise you, but I've even walked down a sidewalk all by myself a time or two. I'm not the helpless teenager you left behind when you decided to tap out on family time."

A low blow, but if it lands, Bradley doesn't show it.

"I'm trying to look out for you," he says. "People worry, Lyla."

"I'm sorry you were worried," I say. "I don't plan to make going out to a bar alone and staying out until the early morning hours a regular thing. Deacon and I had a heated argument yesterday. I needed a distraction.

"You had an argument?" he asks. "About what?"

"Yeah, about what?" Alice asks. "You two are broken up." A pause. "Aren't you?"

I get why she paused. We've broken up and gotten back together a few times now, but this time, it's for good.

"We are absolutely broken up," I confirm. "I sent him the signed paperwork removing me from the lease we shared. He called to make a play for me to come back. I told him I moved in with Bradley. He freaked out."

"Why did he freak out?" Bradley demands. "He's the one—"

"Well aware of what he did," I cut him off. Though Bradley doesn't even know what exactly he did. "He's just having a hard time letting me go. He didn't realize I had moved to a new state. That's all."

"I don't like the sound of that," Alice frets.

"He's harmless and officially hours away now," I remind them. "On to bigger and better things. Whatever those may be."

"Any chance what kept you occupied last night was bigger and better?" Alice inquires, already less worried because, unlike our brother, she trusts me to handle my shit. It's always been like this. Bradley, overprotective. Alice, protective but also willing to let me try things and be there to pick up the pieces if it doesn't go well, or high five me if it does. Me, the good little sister who only recently stopped trying to please every single person in her life.

"Substantially," I confirm, and she wolf whistles. It takes

Bradley a moment to register what we're talking about, but then he blanches.

"You were off having a one-night stand while I was worried sick about you?" he demands.

"He used a condom," I offer as I cut another piece of French toast as casually as if we're discussing the weather, which, judging by the light pouring in through the window, is absolutely lovely today. "Twice."

Alice howls. Bradley lets a string of curse words fly. I smirk, proud of myself for riling my big brother. Honestly? I'm pretty proud of myself, too. I stepped so far out of my comfort zone last night, and the ache between my legs proves it was worth it.

"Lyla, you absolutely cannot . . ." His fresh round of lecturing is cut off by a loud noise on Alice's side.

"Sorry," she apologizes. "Gotta go. Time to do Air Force shit."

"You were completely unhelpful," Bradley informs her.

"You're completely overprotective," she fires back. "Lyla, I'll call you when I can. I need to hear all about Mr. Used-A-Condom-Twice."

"I fucking hate sisters," Bradley declares.

"It's a worthwhile story," I tell her, ignoring Bradley. "Call when you can."

"I will," she promises. "Sorry to abandon you with Big Dad Energy."

"I can handle him," I reply just before she hangs up. Bradley glares at me.

"Are you insane?" he asks. "Fucking random strangers? Going out to bars by yourself? That's not you, Lyla. That's not what you do!"

"It's not like he was my first one-night stand." Bradley looks ill. "And you know what, Bradley? Doing things how

I've always done them hasn't gone all that well in recent months. I didn't drop my life in D.C. to move here and repeat the same old life I was living. If I want to go to a bar and have sex with a stranger, I'm allowed to do that."

"Sex with a stranger—Lyla, you cannot . . ."

"Look me in the eye and tell me you haven't hooked up with a stranger," I challenge. He glowers because he knows damn well he has. I know he has, too. I've caught them trying to sneak out of the house. "This won't be a regular occurrence, but I assure you, I have no regrets about what I did last night."

None whatsoever. Except . . .

Maybe the phone number exchange wouldn't have been the worst idea.

"Ground rules," he decides. "You have to be home by—"

"You are not about to give me a curfew," I cut him off. "Let me say it again, I'm an adult."

"Fine, fair." He gives in. "How about this? If you're still out at midnight, you send a courtesy text so I know you aren't dead."

"Fine," I agree after taking a moment to consider. If the shoe were on the other foot, I'd want to know he was okay, too. I'll let him have this one.

"And share your location," he continues. "Just in case."

"I'll share mine if you share yours," I volley because I'll be damned if he's going to get to track my whereabouts without me tracking his. Fair is fair.

"Fine," he agrees. "And no more talking about your sex life in front of me. I don't want to know."

"Done," I say. "Make better coffee."

"What does my coffee have to do with anything?" he asks.

"Nothing. But if we're negotiating, I'm going to put it on the table."

"I miss when you were a quiet, studious wallflower."

"I miss when you didn't channel Big Dad Energy."

"Why do you and Alice keep saying that?" he demands.

I open my mouth to inform him exactly why Alice and I have deemed Bradley's behavior since our father died 'Big Dad Energy,' but I'm interrupted by the front door banging open. I jump in surprise, while Bradley only looks mildly annoyed.

"Adler!" a deep voice booms through the brownstone. It sounds vaguely familiar, but I can't place it. "You ready?"

Bradley curses under his breath and I'm about to ask who this person—that seems to feel like they can burst into our house at any hour of the day or night with enough noise to wake the dead—is when I see him, and my words dry up on my tongue.

There, standing in the doorway of our kitchen, is Mr. Beautiful.

Holy.

Shit.

His eyes flicker in recognition before he slides on a casual mask and focuses on Bradley.

"What time is it?" Bradley asks. He pats his pockets for his phone, but it's still on the table from his failed call to Alice for backup.

"Ten o'clock," Mr. Beautiful states. "We have the court reserved in thirty minutes." He gives Bradley a once-over. "You playing pickleball in your PJs?"

"Fuck you." Bradley scowls. "I lost track of time. And fuck your need to be early for everything, too, while we're at it. The courts are ten minutes away."

"On time is late," he quips. "You're a fucking delight this morning, aren't you?"

I snort into my weak coffee because, despite the immense awkwardness, he's not wrong. The sound catches his attention and his eyes flicker to me again. Bradley curses under his breath.

"Kensington, meet my baby sister, Lyla." Bradley motions at me. I roll my eyes at his need to refer to me as his "baby sister." Alice is the *little sister*. I'm the *baby sister*. We both hate it when he refers to us like that, which is probably why he does it. "She just moved here from D.C. Lyla, meet Kage Kensington, my sometimes best friend."

Well, fuck.

"Nice to meet you, Lyla," Kage says, his lips curling into the same smirk that is forever burned into my memories of last night. "Welcome to New York. Best fucking city in the world."

"It's all right," I say, remembering his line from last night as I force myself to remain seated and give nothing away that I might know this man. Which, I don't. Not really. I just know what he feels like inside me. A thought that makes me shift around in my seat to relieve the twinge between my legs. He gives me another smirk before shifting his eyes back to Bradley.

"Sometimes best friend?" he asks. "You wound me."

"You piss me off," Bradley counters as he swipes his phone off the table. "I need to change." He taps at his screen. "Lyla, location, now."

I scowl. "Ask nicely."

He glares right back. "We made a deal."

"No deal was made," I argue. "I extended a courtesy. I can take it back at any point."

"We're sharing our locations."

"When I'm good and ready," I fire back, just because I can.

"Are you trying to stalk your sister?" Mr. Beautiful—Kage, I correct myself—asks Bradley. He has the audacity to look amused when this is all his fault.

I'm not entirely sure how it's his fault, but I'm damn sure going to blame him.

"She didn't come home last night," Bradley starts.

I cannot let this line of conversation continue.

"I came home last night," I interject. "Just much later than *Dad* over there approved of. Where I was and what I was doing is not his business."

Kage appraises me much like he did last night. I'm hyperaware of the fact that I'm sitting at the breakfast table in nothing but a T-shirt that is three sizes too big for me, my hair in a haphazard knot on my head, and remnants of last night's excessive makeup still on my face, even though I've washed it twice now.

"She looks like a capable, consenting adult." Kage shrugs—casual and unaffected by this whole mess that he is thoroughly involved in. "You're just pissed she interrupted your beauty sleep."

I fight back a smirk. He was fun to banter with last night, and it seems that charming personality of his carries over into the daytime. Bradley glares, but Kage just grins and leans against the doorframe. He's dressed in workout clothes and, yeah, he definitely looks just as good in the morning light. He also seems to enjoy getting under my brother's skin.

"She's my sister," Bradley argues. "You know how guys are." He eyes Kage. "Hell, you are *the* guy." If he only knew .. . "She doesn't need to be out at bars by herself, fucking whatever guy comes along."

Every alarm I have goes off. I do not want my brother to know the guy I was fucking—who will probably forevermore be called *Mr. Used-A-Condom-Twice* by my sister—is his "sometimes best friend."

I'm also pissed at what he's implying.

"Are you saying that, because I'm a woman, I shouldn't sleep around if I so choose?" I question. Kage crosses both his arms and his ankles, looking entirely content to watch this unfold.

"Well, yes . . ."

"Wrong answer," Kage mutters.

"You hypocritical asshole!" I seethe, momentarily distracted from my mission of keeping my brother from finding out his best friend had very hot, yet very safe, sex with me last night. Twice. "If he"—I point to Kage—"came home in the wee hours of the morning from a one-night stand, you would high-five him for a job well done."

"Not necessarily," Kage supplies with a look my way.

"Don't help," I fire off at him, and he has the nerve to chuckle. "Before you got serious with Gabe, you were bringing home guys all the time. If I were a man, this wouldn't be a big deal. But because I'm a woman, it is."

"No, it's not because you're a woman, it's because you're my sister," Bradley tries to explain. "Women can do whatever the hell they want, but you're my baby sister and you shouldn't—"

"I dare you to finish that sentence," I cut him off with a glare and he stops, glaring right back.

I get what he's saying. If someone wants to sleep around, that's their prerogative. Unless that someone is one of his sisters, in which case, absolutely not. He would act the same way with Alice—overprotective oaf that he is.

I imagine he'd break Mr. Beautiful—Kage's—jaw if he

knew it was Kage I was getting railed by last night. Although, judging by Kage's size and very obvious attention to his physique, I think he could take Bradley, who isn't exactly small himself, unless standing next to this god-like creature.

Bradley looks like he wants to continue our fight. Instead, he blows out a breath. I recognize it for what it is. Not defeat—never defeat—but retreat.

"You know what? Fine, Lyla. Sleep around as much as you want. Call up Mr. Used-A-Condom-Twice again tonight if you want." Kage raises an eyebrow at that. I would like to die right now, please and thank you. "You're a legal, consenting adult. Do whatever the fuck you want. Just send me a text message and share your location with me."

I consider continuing the fight, but it's not worth it, especially not with Kage standing in the doorway, and the truth so dangerously close. I pick up my phone and accept Bradley's request to share my location.

"Thank you," he says.

"I reserve the right to revoke access at any time," I reply.

"I reserve the right to show up wherever you are if you pull a stunt like you did last night and don't let me know you're not dead."

"Yeah yeah," I grumble and reach for my weak coffee again.

"You done swinging your big brother dick around?" Kage asks as he pushes himself off the doorframe. "I'd like to play pickleball at some point this morning. Will and Theo are waiting on us."

"Be glad you don't have sisters," Bradley informs him even as he types out something on his phone. I watch Kage stride across the kitchen with what I can only call a lethal grace. He's big, imposing, yet moves with a certain finesse.

He opens the cabinet over the coffee maker—he's clearly comfortable here—takes out a mug, and pours a cup of coffee. "Although, knowing your ass, you'd have them locked up in a tower on a remote island somewhere."

Kage takes a sip of his coffee—he drinks it black, I note, which does not surprise me in the slightest—and then looks at Bradley.

"Would it kill you to use like two more scoops of coffee grounds to brew this stuff?" he asks. I chuckle into my own coffee.

"You know what?" Bradley throws his hands up. "Fuck both of you."

He storms out of the room and Kage watches him go, amusement all over his features. He turns back to me once we hear Bradley's bedroom door slam shut.

"Lyla, is it?"

I'm up and out of my chair before I know I'm doing it. He has the foresight to put his coffee on the counter a fraction of a second before I reach him. I fist his T-shirt in both hands and manhandle him across the room, as far away from Bradley's bedroom door as I can get. He goes willingly —he's far too big for me to move this easily otherwise—his hands held up in surrender. I press him against a wall and lean in.

"You absolutely *cannot* let Bradley find out it was you I was with last night," I hiss. "He'll kill us both."

"I'm not exactly afraid of your brother." He lifts a hand and lets his fingertips dance along my wrist. I slap it away, which just fuels his smirk. "Besides, I already wrote all about you in my diary." I shove him, even though he's already against the wall. The asshole only chuckles. "I thought you might be a bit of a fireball when I had you in my lap last night. Looks like I was right."

"Shh!" I clamp a hand over his mouth. "Bradley will hear you!"

He licks my hand and I yelp in surprise, pulling it away. He chuckles again.

"Relax," he says. "I happen to like your brother. I'd rather not have to kick his ass when he tries to come for me to defend your honor."

"Not a word!" I insist.

"Like it never happened," he promises. We can hear Bradley down the hall, but he focuses those beautiful eyes of his on me. "I will, however, remember the night fondly."

I make a face at him, but Bradley is coming down the hall now, so I slip back into my chair at the table. Kage moves back to his spot by the coffee maker, and when Bradley walks in a moment later, there's no evidence that we were just a breath apart.

"I'm ready," he announces, now in athletic wear of his own. I hate men and their ability to be dressed and ready to go in under five minutes. "Do me a favor and don't suck today."

"I'm a hell-of-a-lot-better player than you are," Kage states. He takes one last sip of coffee before he extends his arm to put the mug in the sink, then he pushes off the counter. His eyes fall on me as he follows Bradley out. "Don't stay out too late tonight, Lyla."

I throw what's left of my French toast at him.

I miss.

3

KAGE

I. Fucked. Up.

There is fucked up.

And then there is *fucked up*.

I have, irrevocably, *fucked up*.

I fucked Bradley's little sister. His *baby* sister—he's very clear about that. Alice is his little sister; Lyla is his baby sister. And I fucked her. I might have even told my friends that it was the best sex I've ever had. I should probably confess my sins to them, but the fewer people who know her identity, the more likely Bradley won't find out. Bradley *definitely* cannot find out. He would murder me. Or at least try to.

There's no way in hell he saw her leave the house two nights ago. He plays it fast and loose, until it comes to the people he loves. He wouldn't have let her out the door wearing that tiny thing she called a dress. She knew what she was doing when she put that thing on, and those strappy heels of hers, too. I'm not the only one who noticed her. The whole damn bar looked her way when she walked in.

I was just the only one with enough balls to go up to her.

Well, there was that guy in the back corner—he had his eyes all over her. I saw him about to make his move, so I made mine first. When she was bold enough to outright say what she wanted—to be thoroughly fucked—my fate was sealed. A beautiful woman who knows what she wants might damn well be my kryptonite.

So, of fucking course she's the baby sister of one of my closest friends. In a life full of "fuck yous," that one is right up there near the top of the list. I don't believe in a God of any kind, but if there *is* someone or something up there, they have a shit sense of humor.

I sigh out a breath and run a hand through my hair as I navigate the tight street, searching for parking. The fates smile down on me—write that down—and a spot opens up a block from the coffee shop I'm headed to. I parallel park my entirely impractical but absolutely necessary Bronco with the precision of a surgeon. I absolutely do not look at the passenger seat where Lyla rode me, which also happens to be where her brother sat a handful of hours later, on the way to kick my ass at pickleball. Turns out I'm a shit player when my mind is elsewhere.

I slip on my Ray-Bans and prepare to face my maker. Except, I'm not telling Bradley a damn thing. Cute that Lyla thought she had to threaten me to make me keep my mouth shut. I meant what I said. I don't want to have to kick Bradley's ass when he comes for me to defend her honor. I happen to like the guy, as complicated as our relationship is.

Of course, I'm early. I always am. I order an Americano with a needed extra shot and choose a table, making sure it's good and public. Bradley didn't give me a reason when he asked me to meet him for coffee. He was explicit, too, in asking that I come alone, which is a red flag. Sure, he's probably the closest to me in our group—I'm the one who introduced him to the others, after all. Still, it's weird that he was adamant about this being a one-on-one meeting. Surely he doesn't know I fucked his baby sister.

I take out my phone and scroll while I wait. I check my emails first. I owe a few people replies, and make quick work of paying my phone bill from an app. Then I skim social media—half reading the news, paying more attention to the sports headlines, less because I care and more because my friends do. If I'm going to hear them arguing about quarterbacks and defenses, I'm going to be knowledgeable about it. I *always* know what people are talking about.

Bradley's broad frame lowers to the chair across from me.

"How early were you?" he asks.

He doesn't know about Lyla and me, then. If he did, he would have walked in and took a swing, no questions asked. He'd know his only chance would be to catch me by surprise. "I got here ten minutes early on purpose."

"Been here twenty minutes," I answer, putting my phone down and giving Bradley my full attention. He doesn't look pissed, and he definitely wears his emotions on his sleeve. I'm in the clear. And yet, no clearer on what he wants. "If you're not early . . ."

"You're late," Bradley finishes. "You take that to the extreme, Kensington. Granted, you take just about everything you do to the extreme."

Like convincing his baby sister to stick around, have a couple more drinks, and let me fuck her again because once wasn't enough. Twice wasn't going to be enough either, until I made the whole Bradley connection. Now, she's strictly off-limits. Which sucks because I would very much like to have her again. Maybe even more so now that I've seen her in the morning light.

No, don't think about that. Don't think about how good she smelled while she pressed me against the wall. How pretty she was all riled up. How fucking adorable it was that she thought she could boss me around. How bright the green is in her hazel eyes. I definitely cannot think about any of that. I *don't* think about any of that.

"What do you want, anyway?" I ask, getting right to the point. "You were all cloak and dagger about meeting up and coming alone. Got to admit, Adler, you set off a few alarms."

Bradley sighs, and I note that he looks tired. Weary, even. I know the guy works a lot, but this is a different kind of tired. This is worry. "Everything okay?"

"For now." He gets serious. "I need your help, Kensington."

"You know I'll help you if I can."

That's what I do—I help everyone. If I'm focused on someone else, I don't have to focus on myself. And if I don't have to focus on myself, I don't have to face what an absolute shit show my own life is.

"I need you to keep an eye on my sister."

Shit.

I should have seen this coming. I *cannot believe* I didn't see this coming.

"What do you mean?" I hedge.

"She's not safe, Kensington. You know that as well as I do."

I sigh because he's not wrong. "I thought about that," I admit. Because I have—extensively—since I figured out who she is. Lyla Adler is not remotely safe. Maybe even less so now that she's out from under Senator Adler's thumb. "What does she know?"

"Very little, if anything," he reports. "She believes Dad's death was an accident, and her biggest beef with Mom is that their politics don't align."

"I can get one of the guys . . ." I start, because I see where this is going, and it absolutely cannot go there.

"It has to be you," he cuts me off. "She's my baby sister, Kage. I can't let just anyone watch out for her. I need it to be you. I trust you with her."

Fuck if this didn't just get even more complicated.

"Will can do it," I try, because in no way is me spending more time around Lyla going to end well. There's something about her that I can't shake, but I can't risk everything from friendships to lives over a woman. A beautiful woman, but a woman all the same. "They're around the same age. I'll bring him over, introduce them. He offers to show her around town, he becomes her friend, she's protected and has no idea."

"No." Bradley shakes his head. "I'm not asking you to assign someone to her. I'm asking *you* to be responsible for her safety." He narrows his eyes at me. "You owe me."

Fuck. I do owe him. At least, in a roundabout way. He saved me from myself, after all. And of course he would choose now to draw his trump card. I can't blame him, though. It's exactly what I would do if the tables were turned.

"Tell me about her," I request, drawing out what I know is going to be an agreement because he's cornered me. I'm playing a dangerous game here, but isn't that what my life is? One big, dangerous game?

"She's the best of us," Bradley says with a fond smile. "She's smart. I'm not talking study-for-a-test-and-do-well smart. I'm talking *smart*. Her level of intelligence is scary. She's always reading, asking questions, figuring things out that the rest of us are stumped on. The only thing that seems to trip her up is math, which used to piss her off when she was in school because everything else was easy for her. She still got near-perfect scores because that's who she is."

Beautiful and smart. Things I already know about her.

"What brought her here?" I ask, because there's definitely a reason as to why Lyla is here.

"She broke up with her boyfriend." He pauses. "Deacon Cosse." Everything in me darkens at hearing that last name. "They were best friends growing up—forced proximity, or whatever. It became more in the last few years. Alice and I expressed concerns, but Lyla didn't share them, until they became too hard to ignore."

"Concerns?" I press.

"He was controlling," Bradley tells me. "In subtle ways at first, always trying to tell Lyla what was best for her, holding her back, until he became more vocal about his expectations. The guy wants nothing more than to follow in his father's footsteps, including having the meek little wife at home."

I make a face at the idea. It's not like I actually know Lyla, but meek? I don't think that's an accurate description. Meek doesn't dress like a siren, climb onto a stranger's lap in the passenger seat of a Bronco, or threaten a guy twice her size to keep said Bronco tryst to himself. Meek doesn't throw a shitty, frozen breakfast food at my retreating back. She missed, but that's beside the point.

Also beside the point? The weird feeling in my chest that doesn't like the idea of a Cosse touching her.

"She broke up with him?" I guess.

"She did," Bradley confirms. "Then got back together with him. Broke up with him. Back together with him. This last one seems final. I'm still unclear on what, exactly, went down—she won't give me the details. All she's said to Alice and I is that he 'used information against me.' I have no idea what she means. She and Mom had it out, too. Lyla and Deacon were a whole 'D.C.'s sweethearts' story. Mom thought their breakup would hurt her campaign, never mind the fact that her daughter was immensely unhappy and not being treated well."

Sounds like Veronica Adler. Image over everything.

"Any chance she's in some kind of trouble?" I ask.

"Alice asked her. She swore it was nothing like that."

I'll have to get the actual story, then. Through Lyla, or other means.

"What's her plan now that she's here?" I continue. I tell myself I'm asking so I know what I'm up against if I'm going to agree to protect Lyla Adler. It's absolutely not because I'm curious about her and can't seem to stop thinking about how she looked straddling me in my Bronco, or how she was even more stunning in the morning light, sitting at her brother's kitchen table in a too-big T-shirt with her hair all over the place.

"She's here to start over," Bradley answers. "She's looking for a job, then she'll take it from there."

"What sort of job?" I have so many questions, including why I'm agreeing to this when I know how bad of an idea it is, but I'm dutifully not asking that one. I don't think I'll like the answer, and I'm great at not asking questions I don't want answers to.

"She has three degrees," Bradley tells me, and I raise an eyebrow. Three degrees is impressive. "She double majored in library sciences and linguistics, then got her master's in library sciences. She's always wanted to be a curator of information, in whatever form that might be." Bradley pierces me with a hard look. "Will you do it, Kage? Will you look out for her?"

The answer needs to be no. The answer *should* be no. The right thing to do is say no and convince him to let someone else be on Lyla duty.

"Yes." I nod. "I'll watch out for her."

Bradley's relief is palpable. I shove my anxiety or whatever the hell this feeling is down deep. This is an awful idea, but there was never going to be another answer. I owe Bradley. And no one else can protect Lyla as well as I can.

"Thank you," he breathes. "I don't trust anyone else with her." I rub at my chest, where something that feels an awful lot like guilt is rattling around along with a few other feelings I'm not labeling. "Keep her safe, Kage."

"I will," I promise. That, at least, is a promise I can keep. Lyla is only guilty of being the offspring of the wrong person. I won't let her be a victim of her mother's politics.

"She can't know," he continues. "She will freak out if she knows."

"She can't know," I agree for entirely different reasons. "We'll keep this between us. Let's talk about your security system. Do we need more cameras now that she's living there?"

When I'm back in my Bronco half an hour later, with a laundry list of things to do and figure out regarding my newest project, I drop my head back against the headrest and breathe deeply for the first time in over an hour. I should have said no—I know I should have said no. But I didn't, and now here we are, me, tasked with keeping Lyla safe.

Me, adding Lyla to the too-long list of people I'm trying to keep safe.

Me, trying to tell myself this is just a favor to Bradley,

and maybe because I have a bit of a hero complex, too. It's not because I woke up thinking about her. It's not because I fell asleep thinking about her, too. I've had plenty of one-night stands. Her bartender friend didn't make up my carefully curated reputation, after all.

The others didn't stay in the forefront of my mind after I sent them home, though. They didn't manhandle me against a wall and demand my secrecy. They didn't smell like vanilla, lavender, and a hint of citrus. They didn't look like a fucking goddess sitting at a breakfast table.

Fucking hell.

I definitely should have said no.

4

LYLA

I run my fingers along the spines of the books, comforted by the familiar scent of paper and the quiet of a library. I needed this. I needed the grounding being among books always brings me. So much has changed in the last year, especially in the last few weeks, but books remain a constant—ready to teach me something new or transport me to another world when mine feels too hard.

"Can I help you find something?" A kind-looking woman wearing a nametag that labels her as 'Celeste, Librarian' looks at me expectantly. She looks familiar, but I can't place her.

"Just browsing," I say. "I'm waiting for something to jump out and grab me."

"Take your time." She smiles. "I'm at the front if you need anything."

She walks off as I turn the corner and start down another aisle. I pluck a random book off the shelf. It's a fantasy. I like fantasy, but I'm not in the mood for it right now. I keep going, skipping right over the romance section because I'm definitely not feeling very romantic, and find myself in the historical fiction section. *This* I can work with.

I choose three books set during World War II, all focused on female heroines. I need that—a story in which the female is the hero and not the damsel in distress. I also select a couple of history books, one on Brooklyn and one on New York, and head to the checkout counter.

"What did you find?" this *Celeste* person asks. She picks up one of my historical fictions and observes the cover. "Oh, I loved this one. Have tissues ready."

"Noted," I say with a small smile. She seems kind, and so very familiar. "I need to get a library card first. I just moved here."

"Easy enough." She nods. "Do you have your ID?"

I take out my brand-new New York driver's license I spent the entire morning acquiring. Bradley was shocked I changed it over so fast. I've only been here a week, and I don't even have a car. But this, New York, is my fresh start, and that includes ditching my Washington, D.C. license. I take out my passport, too, for good measure, just in case the temporary paper the DMV gave me isn't a valid enough form of ID, and proof of address.

Celeste smiles. "You really want that library card, don't you?" she asks as she passes me a form to fill out.

"I like libraries," I offer and step aside to fill out my information while she copies my ID and helps someone else. I wait patiently for her to make her way back to me. Then, she hands me my ID and a newly-minted library card. That's when it hits me. "You work at the bar!" I can't remember the name of said bar, but I recognize her. She's the bartender who gave me her number when she realized I was leaving with Kage. Except . . . Wait . . . Didn't she have a different name? Crap, I can't remember.

What I do remember is Kage Kensington . . .

Nope.

No.

Brother's best friend.

Not thinking about that.

"You must have met my sister," Celeste says, her kind smile growing. "Cecily. We're twins."

"Oh!" I shake my head. "Sorry, you looked so familiar, and I only met her briefly . . ."

"She's a great bartender," Celeste says. "She did me a solid this morning by watching my kid. His daycare unexpectedly closed today, and my husband and I both had to work. She texted a few minutes ago to let me know my neighbor is with him now so she can head to the bar for her shift."

I notice a photo of a little boy who looks to be around a year old tacked onto a corkboard behind the desk then. I motion at it. "Is that him?"

"Sure is." Her smile grows. "Levi. He just turned one."

"He's adorable," I offer. He really is, with his scrunched toddler face and wild curls.

"Thank you," she says. "He's the best, but I'm biased." She passes me the receipt with the due date highlighted and then slides the stack of books to me. "Anything else I can help you with?"

I decide to shoot my shot. The old Lyla wouldn't, but the new Lyla is doing things differently. She will be staying out of the front seats of vintage Broncos for the foreseeable future, but she's still going to take a few chances.

"Any chance you're hiring?" I ask, knowing my odds are slim.

"I wish." Celese sighs. "Public libraries—perpetually

underfunded, understaffed, and in my opinion, underutilized." She considers me. "Are you a librarian?"

"I could be." I shrug. "I have a master's in library science. I just finished in the spring."

"Check the listings at the New York Public Library," she recommends. "I heard one of their rare materials people moved on—not sure if they filled the role."

"I'll look into it." It's a brilliant idea; I'm a little annoyed I didn't think about it myself. It's the *New York Public Library*. It should have been the first place I thought to look. "Thank you, Celeste. I'm sure I'll see you soon."

I opt to walk home, since it's nice out—one of those rare late summer days when it's not quite fall, but the promise of it is in the air, if only for a day or two. The sky is crystal clear, and I feel like, maybe, things are going to be okay.

The bar from the other night is up ahead—The Black Dragon. I check the time; it's not quite four o'clock. Too early to have a drink, for me at least. I don't drink much at all, but when I do, I prefer to wait until the sun has gone down. But Celeste said Cecily was headed to work. It was kind of her to give me her info in case things went south with Kage, so I decide to stop in and thank her.

The sunlight falls away as I step through the bar's heavy wooden door. It's an old bar, the walls stone, the wooden tabletops scarred from years of use. It reminds me a bit of a fortress—the name makes a lot more sense now.

Cecily is behind the bar, drying glasses.

"We're closed," she says without looking up from her task as I slide onto a stool.

"I'm not here for a drink," I reply. "I'm here to thank you. We met the other night. You gave me a piece of paper with your contact info."

"You're Lyla," she says, eyes on me now. "The senator's daughter."

I cringe. There's that cover blown.

"That's me." I sigh, already sliding off the stool because I'm not doing this. "I'd appreciate you keeping the fact that I was here to yourself."

"Where are you going?" Cecily asks, confused.

"Home," I say. "I was hoping this could be a place where I didn't have to be the senator's daughter." Here, as in the bar, but here, as in New York, too. I am so tired of being Veronica Adler's daughter. "Thanks for being willing to help me out the other night."

"You think I care that you're the senator's daughter?" Cecily questions. I open my mouth to reply, but she beats me to it. "I'd be more impressed if you were related to, say, Lana del Rey. A politician's daughter? I'm going to need more from you to decide if I like you or not." She pats the bar top. "Sit down. I'll pour you a drink if you want one."

I slide back onto the stool based only on a feeling that Cecily isn't out to sell my whereabouts to a gossip rag. "Seltzer with lime?" I request. "It's too early for me to drink."

"Coming right up." She's quick, placing my drink in front of me within the minute.

"Thank you," I say. "And sorry about just now. I'm a little . . ." I trail off, searching for the right word.

"Paranoid?" Cecily supplies. I cringe, but "paranoid" is the right word for it. "Don't worry, Lyla. No one around here is going to call the press and tell them you were a walking, talking smoke show the first time you were here, and that you went home with none other than Kage Kensington."

"I really want to believe that," I admit. "I'm a little jaded, though." I don't tell her how I was constantly under a microscope in D.C. Every little thing I did got back to my mom, and if she felt I was jeopardizing her chance at re-election? God help us all.

"We'll just have to prove it then," Cecily declares as she goes back to drying glasses. I really want to believe her. I'd love nothing more than to have a place to hang out where my only worry is keeping out of the front seats of Broncos. Cecily nods toward my stack of books. "I see you found the library."

"I met your twin sister," I reveal. "I thought she looked familiar."

"Celeste," she says. "Our parents really leaned into the twin names, didn't they?"

I agree and ask about her nephew, listening as she raves about being his aunt. She introduces me to the other bartender, Sam, and their friend, Oliver, who shows up just before the official opening, brimming with tales from the trenches of his entry-level job in talent management. I learn that Sam is starting his master's in sustainability and Cecily is halfway through an MBA program with ambitions of "running the world." I do what I always do, which is attempt to keep the discussion off me, but they manage to get me to share that I just finished a master's degree after taking a year off post-undergrad, and that I'm looking for a job.

"What brought you to New York?" Sam asks when he returns from pouring a few beers for a group of construction workers ending their day with a cold one.

"I wanted a change of pace." Not a lie, just not the full truth. "My brother lives here and offered to let me stay with him while I figure out my next move."

"Didn't your brother kind of duck out of the whole political thing a while back?" Sam asks. Cecily elbows him, having picked up that I'm trying to distance myself from the political scene, but I shoot her a reassuring smile before I answer.

"He chose to step out of the public spotlight." It's my canned, media-trained answer. "He's focused on his career. He's a doctor."

"You have a sister, too, don't you?"

"Alice." I nod. "She's in the Air Force."

"Hell of a pedigree," he comments.

"How do you know so much about our new friend Lyla?" Ollie asks.

I'm wondering that, too. His questions are innocent enough for now, but I'm always on high alert for someone trying to trick me into saying something I'll regret.

"We studied some of Senator Adler's policies in one of my classes," he admits.

Ah. Got it. "She's not very sustainable," I offer.

"No," he agrees with a small smile, "she's not." He lets the topic drop and I'm thankful. I hate talking politics, but people love to bring them up around me, given who my mother is.

The bar gets busier as people file in for an after-work drink, and I decide it's time to head home. As I slide off the stool and collect my books, I decide to shoot another shot, this time with Cecily.

"Would you want to grab coffee sometime?" I ask her.

"There's a really cool, outdoor, vintage clothing market this weekend," she counters. "It happens twice a month, and I missed the last one. Want to go? We can grab brunch, too."

"That sounds fun." On the outside, I remain casual. On the inside, I'm practically doing somersaults at the idea of maybe making my first New York friend.

"You still have my number?" she continues.

"I do," I confirm. I kept the scrap of paper for no other

reason than to remember the night. Granted, that was before I learned Bradley and Kage were besties. He'll be impossible to forget now.

"Cool. Text me and we'll figure it out." Her eyes twinkle. "Besides, I'm curious to know if Kensington really is as good in bed as he looks like he would be."

I laugh, thank her for my seltzer, and head out.

I'm feeling pretty good about things when I return home.

I swing open the front door and stop in my tracks.

Bradley's house is full of guys. *Familiar* guys. My eyes land on one in particular and—*shit*. It's the softer version of Kage. Is Bradley friends with all of them? I'll never keep the whole Bronco front seat thing away from him at this rate.

"You must be the sister."

I turn and I'm face-to-chest with . . . I look up. It's the guy I deemed the "muscle" from the bar. He has a mop of dark curls, mischievous green eyes, and he's even wider than Kage. His grin matches the mischief in his eyes.

"I'm Lyla," I say. "And you are?"

"I'd say your next boyfriend, but since you're Bradley's little sister . . . Ouch!" He rubs his side and glares at the coifed blond—also from the bar. His eyes are even bluer than I thought, and his smile reveals a dimple. "The fuck, Craven?"

"Don't be an ass," this Craven guy tells the muscle before he turns his attention to me. "I'm Will Craven." He jerks his thumb at the muscle. "That's Luke. He was raised by wolves."

"That's generous." Softer Kage stands from the couch. "More like he was hatched from an egg, then raised by wolves in a barn." He offers me his hand. "I'm Theo."

"Theo," I repeat as I shake his hand. "Nice to meet you." *I have to know.* "You're Kage's brother?"

"Cousin," he corrects with a smile. "Trust me when I say Kage had to be an only child. There's no way Uncle Whit could have survived two of him."

"Facts," Luke mutters as he tries to retaliate with an elbow to Will's gut. But Will is ready for him and simply steps aside. Luke curses. "I'll get you back."

"Best of luck," Will drawls.

I look between the three of them. They are all tall, muscular, and have the same tattoo starting at their left wrists, just like Kage. Luke's takes up his entire forearm before fading into a different design, but both of his arms are equally inked, as are his calves, which are on full display in the gym shorts he's wearing. Theo's trails over his elbow, and Will's ends mid-forearm. Are they in a cult? They might be in a cult. It's fitting that the best sex of my life would be with a cult leader, given the way things are going for me lately.

"At the risk of being rude, what are you all doing here?" I ask. "Where's my brother?"

"It's Fantasy Football Draft Night," my brother's partner, Gabe, answers. He's dressed in scrubs, and judging by his damp hair and soapy smell, he's headed to the hospital. He drops an arm across my shoulders and hugs me to his side. I lean in. I like Gabe. He's good and steady and kind enough to let me crash here with him and Bradley until I figure myself out. He also loves my brother. I'm jealous of their easy relationship, or, well, not easy, exactly, as no relationship is easy, but there's a comfort between them that I envy. I want that for myself. One day. "Bradley is changing out of a rather disgusting pair of scrubs. He'll be out in a minute."

"Opposing shifts again?" I ask.

"Ships passing in the night," he confirms. They are both in their last year of residency at different hospitals, and they work constantly. Gabe is in internal medicine while Bradley is an emergency medicine doctor. Both are brilliant at their jobs and have attending physician offers waiting for them. They know what's ahead, unlike yours truly. I don't even know what I'm having for dinner. "Let's hang out tomorrow, once I get some sleep. I'll take you out for whatever meal it is when I wake up."

"Deal," I agree. We can bitch about Bradley—it's one of our favorite things to do. He tells me goodbye, then tells the three hulks in his living room goodbye as well.

"Want a beer?" Luke offers once Gabe is gone, holding up a can of something domestic from a cooler in the middle of the living room. Did this place become a frat house since I left this morning?

"I'm good," I say. "I'm going to get myself a soda." I turn toward the kitchen, but my manners get the best of me. "Can I get anyone anything?"

"We're good, Lyla," Will says with that same, kind smile.

The quiet of the kitchen is welcome, as I put my bag down and open the fridge for the soda I came in here for.

"Hey! You're home," Bradley greets as he walks in. He looks tired, and judging by his damp hair, he took a quick shower. "I realized while I was cleaning up from work that I should have given you a heads-up that the guys were coming over. Sorry about that."

"It's fine," I say, even though I'm a little annoyed. There goes my peaceful evening. "Fantasy football? Really?"

"It's fun." He shrugs. "Be glad I conned Gabe into being our tenth person. I would have had to beg you if he didn't agree."

"More people are coming?" I might have to go back to the bar to get some peace and quiet.

"No, this is everyone." He opens a cabinet and takes out a few bags of chips. It's then that I notice the mountain of food on the table. I assume the trio I can hear chatting in the living room is responsible for what looks to be the fixings for burgers, more chips, several types of cookies, and various bags of candy. "The rest of the guys are either auto-drafting or drafting from wherever they are. Except Gabe. I'm drafting for him." He flashes a grin. "Doubles our chance at winning."

"You have fun with that," I say. "I'm going to read."

"We're having burgers," Bradley counters. "I'll let you know when they're ready."

I thank him and head to my bedroom. I try to get comfortable on my bed, but the low hum of the guys down-stairs distracts me, so I decide the postage stamp-sized back-yard might be a better bet. May as well enjoy the cooler weather while it lasts.

I head downstairs and out the back door.

Fuck.

Me.

Kage Kensington is there, manning the grill, wearing a fitted, black T-shirt and black jeans. He glances over his shoulder, then does a double take, smirking while I stand there, wondering why my limbs have suddenly stopped responding to my command to turn around and go inside.

"Lyla," he greets.

"Kage," I reply.

"Look at that," he says. "Us, using names." I narrow my eyes in warning and he chuckles. "All that work to keep me from learning your name..."

"Shh!" I look over my shoulder, half expecting Bradley to be standing behind me. Kage chuckles.

"Relax," he says, the picture of composure. "Your brother is busy being the host with the most. He can't grill for shit though, so here we are." He flips a burger and glances at me again. "How do you like your burger?"

"What?" My brain is still recovering from finding him in my backyard.

"How do you like your burger?" he repeats. "Pink? No pink?"

I'm skeptical, but I answer. "No pink."

"Dry and tasteless then, got it."

"Sorry if I don't like my beef still mooing."

"Do what you want." He shrugs. "I'll char a couple of these for you."

I look past him. He has at least a dozen burgers and a few hot dogs on the grill.

When he looks my way again, he lifts an eyebrow. "You looking for something?"

"Peace and quiet," I state. "Clearly something I'm not going to find here." I turn to go back inside and figure out my next move.

"Running away?" he asks.

I huff and turn back to him. I don't know what it is about him, but I can't seem to back down.

"I was going to read out here, but it seems the yard is occupied."

"Only until I finish the burgers—less than ten minutes. Surely you can be in my presence for ten minutes." He smirks again, which may well be his default setting. "Or can you not?"

It's a challenge, and I'm going to rise to it. I make a show of settling down on the patio lounge and opening my book. He chuckles again, and I pointedly ignore him, which is no easy task. He makes it a full two minutes before he speaks again.

"Good book?"

He doesn't look my way, yet I somehow still feel his eyes on me. "What?"

"The book." He motions toward me with his spatula. "Is it good?"

"I just started it," I tell him. "Why?"

"Just making conversation, Lyla."

I go back to ignoring him. Except, I can't get comfortable. I've had a perfectly normal day with a perfectly normal level of activity, but my body is currently in that place where it's trying to decide if it's going to behave or revolt. I shift around, trying to get comfortable, but the new position doesn't work, so I do it again. The third time, Kage speaks up.

"You okay over there?"

"Fine." I nod. "Just trying to get comfortable." He looks like he might say more, but he presses his lips together instead and goes back to his burgers. I definitely don't provide more information. He may have had his cock in me, but he's a still a stranger, and doesn't need to know my medical history. He doesn't need to know that I live with a constant low hum of pain, and that some days, that pain takes over. The new position does relieve some of the pressure building, though, so I try to refocus on my book. That proves to be next to impossible when Kage Kensington is standing *right there*, grilling freaking burgers, his biceps bulging with each flip of the spatula. I drop my book to my lap. "Fantasy football? Really?"

"Not a football fan?" he replies.

"Can't say I spend my Sunday watching sports," I quip. "I

can't believe you actually spend time with imaginary men." I lift an eyebrow at him. "Or maybe that's your thing?"

"You know what my thing is," he fires back with a look that implies "sex in Broncos" might just be his thing. "They aren't imaginary, either. They are actual people playing an actual sport. We're just earning points off them."

"It's lame," I insist.

"It is," he agrees, which surprises me, as he starts moving hot dogs to a platter. "My friends like it, though, so I play. And to be clear, I kick their asses, your brother's included."

"So, you don't like to play?" I clarify.

He sighs like I'm asking him to explain the meaning of life for the fifth time over. "My friends like it," he repeats. "I play with them."

"FOMO." I nod. "Makes sense."

He shakes his head.

I've ruffled his feathers somehow. I don't know how, exactly, but perhaps his male ego can't tolerate me making fun of his hobby. Regardless, I chalk up a point for me and go back to my book. We don't speak again until he's headed inside with a platter.

"Come on," he says without looking back. "Food's ready."

I almost stay where I am, but I'm hungry, and those burgers smell great. I close my book and follow him inside.

It's loud and chaotic; I'm not used to that. My friends in D.C. were like me—quiet, polite, observant. Bradley's friends are the opposite. They rib each other, laugh, eat like endless pits. Bradley, too, is different. Lighter. Happier. I knew his defection from the family was for the best, but seeing him like this makes me wish he had done it sooner. There's familiarity, a sense of chosen family. I think of Cecily and her offer to meet her at the vintage market—the comradery she had with Sam and Ollie. I try not to let the tiny seed of hope in my chest grow at the idea that I might be on the brink of finding this, too.

I'm content to observe the chaos while we eat, but Will and Bradley both try to include me in the conversation. Kage, I notice, is quieter than the others. There's an intentionality about the way he moves, how he handles himself. I have to stop myself from staring, not just because he's gorgeous, but because I'm intrigued. Nothing he does, not even putting toppings on his burger, is done without purpose.

He catches me watching him and winks. I blush and look away.

I make myself scarce when they break out laptops and iPads to start their draft, and spend the next couple of hours sequestered in my room, completely absorbed in the story of a woman running secret missions during World War II. So much so, I manage to drown out the occasional shouts of protest or victory. When my bladder can wait no longer, I put my book aside, go to the restroom, and then head downstairs to the kitchen. It's late in the evening, but I want a cup of coffee and a snack, so I put on a pot to brew and turn my focus on the Oreos I know Bradley has stashed in this kitchen. He's always been a fiend for the cookie and would hide them from Alice and I. Gabe complains that he still does it.

I systematically open drawers and cabinets until I spot the tell-tale blue of the package on a top shelf of a high cabinet. Clever, but not good enough. I grab a chair and climb, but even with the chair, I'm too short. So, I hoist myself up on the counter and reach into the cabinet. My hand closes around the package.

"What the hell are you doing?"

I startle at the deep voice and that's all it takes for me to lose my footing and start falling. I brace myself for an impact that never comes. Instead, I'm snatched midair and fall back into the arms of one Kage Kensington. I gasp in surprise. He's frowning down at me, but I think there might be concern in his features, too. He adjusts his grip on me which only serves to pull me closer. He smells like sandalwood and leather, just like he did the other night.

"You okay?" he asks.

"Fine." I nod. "Perhaps a wounded pride, but no other injuries."

He should put me down, but he doesn't. And I don't ask him to.

"You're sure?" he questions.

"Positive."

We just look at each other. Could this be any more of a cliche? The damsel in distress—*Didn't I just say I was tired of damsels in distress?*—saved by the handsome stranger she had a one-night stand with who just so happens to be one of her brother's best friends. This movie has been made dozens of times, and this book has been written even more. This does not happen in real life. Yet, here we are.

"You can put me down now."

He's quick to set me on my feet and step back, which is probably a good thing because I can feel the pull to explore more of what we did the other night building, no matter how bad of an idea it is. I hardly know him, yet I'm the moth and he's the flame.

"What in the hell were you doing, climbing on the counter?" he demands.

"I was attempting to get those." I point up at the package

of Oreos that's still on the shelf above. "Bradley tries to hide them from me and Gabe. I found them."

He sighs like an aggravated dad and reaches over me for the package. I lean back slightly. He is way too close, given the way I feel flushed all over by his proximity. He plucks them from the shelf without even needing to lift onto his tiptoes, and glances at the package.

"He could have at least gotten Double Stuf." He passes them to me, and I tear into them if for no other reason than to give my hands something to do before they land on Kage. "Don't climb on counters. It's stupid."

He's going to try to tell me what to do? Absolutely not. Too many people have tried to tell me what to do. I'm done with that.

"I'll climb on counters if I want to," I inform him. "Not all of us are six feet tall."

"I'm six-four," he counters. "As far as I know, when someone puts something out of another person's reach, they don't want anyone else finding it." I glare at him. "So maybe you leave the Oreos on the top shelf alone next time and buy yourself your own box of sugar."

"You're an asshole," I inform him.

"So I've been told," he says, unfazed. "An asshole who saved you from breaking your neck just now—even made you dinner."

"Didn't ask you to do either of those things," I fire back.

His eyes smolder. Is he enjoying this banter? God, why does he have to be so hot? And so off-limits? And so irritating that I kind of want to punch him in his smug, pretty face?

"Guess I'm a giver then." He leans in and places his hands on the counter on either side of me, caging me in. It's suddenly very warm and I'm very thankful I have this bag of

Oreos in my hand, otherwise I can't say they wouldn't be on this man. I don't know what it is about him that addles my brain like this, and so quickly, but he takes away a lot of my good sense when he's in my orbit. "Tonight isn't the first time I've given you what you want, is it?"

Forget warm. It's *hot*. So very hot. I look up at him—at his mouth, specifically—and bite my lip. I want to throw this bag of processed sugar aside and mount him, but he's my brother's best friend, and Bradley is just on the other side of the wall.

"Kage!" bellows a voice from the other room. Luke, I think. "You ready to go? I have shit to do!"

The moment is broken.

"Coming!" Kage calls. He holds my eyes as he pulls back, and I find my breath again when there's space between us. He takes in one last look—*is that longing I see?*—at me, and then turns away just as Bradley walks in.

I blow out a breath. That was too close.

"Are those my Oreos?" Bradley demands.

"You can have your stupid Oreos," I declare, tossing them aside, abandoning my pot of freshly brewed coffee, and exit the room, careful not to look at Bradley, and to avoid the gang of Kage's friends piling out of the house. They're too busy arguing over what Luke's "shit to do" is to notice me, which is just fine with me.

I close and lock my bedroom door for good measure, then fling myself onto my bed. I'm flushed and warm and all worked up. I'm not the exercising type, but damn if I don't want to go for a run or something to burn off some of this energy. I pick up my phone instead, opening my texts to my most recent conversation with my friend Heather.

Me: *Hi! Miss you! What's new with you?*

I wait, watching the bubbles that indicate she's typing.

That's one thing I can always count on with her. She replies to texts almost right away—almost always.

Heather: Hi!! Miss you too! Nothing new to report on my end. Same old same old. Let's FaceTime soon?

I read between the lines and sigh. *Nothing new to report.* Dammit. I reply back to the affirmative on FaceTime and toss my phone aside, annoyed the answer isn't different. I can't shake the buzzing in my body though, and I'm still as flushed as I was when I left the kitchen.

I roll over, open the bottom drawer of my nightstand, move a few things around, and find what I'm looking for. I shimmy off my shorts, bend my knees, close my eyes, position the vibrator, and allow myself to fantasize about Kage Kensington.

I have to grab my pillow to muffle the sound I make when I fall apart.

5

KAGE

Lyla Adler.
Age 25.
Birthday: May 27.

Youngest of three.

Born and raised in an exclusive Northern Virginia neighborhood. The best private schools. Top grades. Valedictorian. Double major. Master's degree. A slew of awards for her academic achievements.

Interned at the National Archives.

Spent a semester abroad in Munich. Traveled extensively while there.

Got a speeding ticket two years ago for going fifteen over. Paid the fine and it disappeared.

Had a minor fender bender six months ago—not her fault.

Brother, Bradley, oldest sibling, is in his final year of his residency at Mount Sinai. Sister, Alice, middle sibling, is a Senior Airman in the Air Force, currently stationed in Hawaii. Mother, Veronica Adler, is a Virginia State Senator. Father, Paul Adler, died of a "heart attack."

The quotes are mine.

Everything I could want to know about Lyla Adler is at my fingertips. Except her medical records. That felt like I would be going too far, even though I can easily get my hands on them. People think their information is secure because they have a strong password, or two-factor authentication, or they sign a privacy policy. They have no idea how easy it is to get access to information if you know the right people.

I know *all* the right people.

The problem now is that I have all this information on Lyla Adler. I agreed to protect her because I felt like I had to, but just a few days in, I'm finding it difficult. Something about her makes me throw good sense out the window. Last night is a prime example. She scared the shit out of me, standing on the kitchen counter on her tiptoes for a bag of processed sugar. Then she started to fall, and my heart fucking *stopped*.

I caught her.

Something primal in me took over and wouldn't let her go. She just *fit*. She felt like she belonged there, cradled against me. It's not lost on me that she felt that way that night in my Bronco, too. That's why I was so persistent in having her again that night, not that I recognized it at the time. I wanted to feel that perfect fit again. I wanted to be close to her again.

I cannot be close to her, though. If I'm close to her, I'm going to cross a line. I *cannot* cross a line with her.

"You wanted to see me?"

Will strolls into my office and drops onto one of my armchairs. He is, like always, the picture of calm, cool, and collected. No one would look at him and think, *"Wow, that guy has been through it."* But he has, and he's one of the few people I trust implicitly in this world.

"How was class?" I ask.

"Fine." He shrugs. "Just a standard boxing class."

"Heard from Andie?" I continue.

"She emailed last night. She went ziplining, held a baby monkey, and has plans to go surfing this weekend."

"I think she's missing the point of studying abroad," I muse.

"She's gaining valuable experiences," he says. I have a feeling that's a direct quote from his little sister. Andie is the opposite of Will. He's calm and steady, never quick to anger, happy with a routine, easy to like. Andie is a free spirit with a tendency not to take life too seriously. She has a hard exterior, but if you crack it, she's yours for life. She's currently studying abroad in Costa Rica, although she seems to spend a lot of time anywhere but in a classroom. "You didn't ask me in here to talk about classes or my sister though."

"I didn't," I admit. I jerk my chin at the door. "Close that." He leans back in his chair, rocking it onto two legs, and stretches to shut the door. The chair falls back to the ground, and he gives me an expectant look. "I have an assignment for you."

"I'm listening."

"You will have to be discreet."

"I'm always discreet."

"I mean it, Will." My tone leaves no room for jokes or quips. "You cannot, under any circumstances, be caught."

"You sound like you're about to ask me to pull off an epic heist or knock off some big wig," he says. "What do you need, Kage?"

I hesitate. I've been over and over this in my head. I know I can't do this alone, at least not well—not with all my other responsibilities. I know Will is more than capable. I just . . . know that I would be the best at this. Lyla would be safest with me.

Or something. I'm refusing to dig into why I'm so unsettled about entrusting her safety to someone I would—and do—trust my own safety with.

"Kage?" he prompts.

"I need you to protect Lyla Adler." I force the words out.

"Tell me more," he requests after taking a moment to process.

"Bradley asked me to do it," I tell him. "He was very clear that he wants me to watch out for her. I can't do it alone, though. Not well, at least. Not with everything else I have going on."

"She's not safe." He nods in understanding. "Especially now that she's not living in her mother's shadow."

"Exactly." I nod once. "She has no idea about, well, anything. She's been kept in the dark. Bradley wants to keep it that way. He thinks she's safer."

"Is she?" Will counters. "If she knew . . ."

"I don't know," I admit. "I think, for now, we continue to keep things on the down low. There may come a time when we need to let her in on things, but we'll cross that bridge when we come to it."

I've been debating this very thing. Is it best to keep Lyla in the dark about what her mother is involved in? Or is it better if she knows? I don't have an answer, though, so for now, it's status quo, which means she knows nothing.

"What's the plan?" he asks.

He knows I have a plan. I *always* have a plan. I reach for the dossier I put together on her and pass it to Will.

"This is her file. Memorize it, then get rid of it. Bradley already has a security system, but I had him add a few more cameras and install motion-activated lights outside. She knows he has a security system, and he's shown her how to operate it. He told her the lights were something he's been meaning to install for a while. She took it upon herself to decide he did it because she stayed out too late for his liking and this is his way of keeping tabs on her if she comes or goes late at night."

I watch Will for any kind of realization that Lyla is the woman from the bar. I'm not proud of the fact that I bragged about the woman I took home that night. Before I knew it was Lyla, I was pretty high on just how good the sex was, and sex-induced endorphins make men stupid. The Black Dragon is dimly lit, though, and with all that makeup and her hair falling around her in waves, Lyla didn't look like her usual no-makeup-on, hair-in-a-braid self they have all met. Hell, *I* didn't recognize her that night, and if anyone should have, it was me, given my connection to her mother.

"You'll give me the security system code, app access, all that?" Will asks.

"I will," I confirm. "I've been thinking about how to play this. I think your best option is to befriend her. Make her like you, trust you. Offer to show her around, hang out, whatever it takes. If you're friends, it makes it a hell of a lot easier for you to be around her."

"I can do that," he says. "I only talked to her a few minutes the other night, but she seems cool." He cocks his head as a thought occurs to him. "What about Bradley?"

"What about him?" I counter.

"He asked you to protect her. How are we going to convince him I'm a suitable replacement?"

"First of all, you're more than suitable." He might look like a frat boy and have the temperament of a golden retriever, but Will Craven is not to be crossed. "I'm still overseeing her safety, but day-to-day needs to be you. As for Bradley, I'll handle any objections he might have."

Will is suspicious. He knows me well. He knows I don't go back on my word. It's out of character for me to default responsibility to someone else. I handle my shit. And he's smart enough to sniff out anything that might be amiss. That's how he got involved in my mess in the first place.

"I have a lot on my plate," I remind him. "Never mind that I don't think she likes me very much. I'm not exactly a warm and fuzzy guy."

"Got that right," he quips. I wish it didn't sting, even if just a little, to hear him agree. I also wish I wasn't right about my thoughts on how Lyla feels about me. "You are my favorite asshole, though." I snort. At least I have that. "Why do you think she doesn't like you? You've met her once, twice?"

"Twice." Three times, but I'm purposefully leaving the Bronco thing out of my count. "Briefly the other morning when I picked up Bradley for pickleball, and then again yesterday. I'm not known for making a good first impression." My computer screen switches off, and I instinctively wiggle the mouse to wake it back up. "I'm trusting you, Will. Be smart. Be observant. Don't let anything happen to her."

"She'll be fine," he promises before he checks the time on the smartwatch he wears. "I need to get back downstairs. My next class starts in ten minutes."

"Foundations, right?" He nods in confirmation. "Theo closed his foundations class at one hundred present last night. Think you can match it?"

"I'll match it and sign two of their friends," he says as he gets to his feet. I chuckle. Will and my cousin are nothing if not competitive, which works out well for me when they're trying to beat each other at closing sales of new memberships after their free intro classes. "Make me a deal. I close at one hundred and sign two of their friends, you trade me Mahomes."

"Not a chance in hell." He laughs. I couldn't give two shits about fantasy football, but I know what I've got with Patrick Mahomes. "Hide that file until you can get it home."

"On my way to do just that," he promises, file in hand. "I'll review it tonight, then get rid of it." I nod my agreement, and he opens the door to exit, but his path is blocked by the last person I want to see. "Oh, fuck me. I was having such a good day, too."

"Fuck you?" Brynn Sinclair counters with a perfectly arched eyebrow. "Never." She turns her lethal gaze on me and gives her best sultry smile. "Hi, Kage."

"I don't have time for this," I warn her, but she's unfazed. She tries to slip past Will, but he makes a subtle shift and blocks her path. She glares at him, and he gives it right back. Will tends to see the good in people, but he loathes Brynn—always has. None of my friends like her, but his disdain for her is visceral. "Unless you have an actual business-related need, go back to whatever shopping spree you left to come here."

"Or maybe go troll a bar or something on Wall Street," Will supplies. "Sink your nails into another man that might be willing to float your lifestyle."

"I believe you have a class to teach?" she says to Will. He glowers because she's right.

"Go ahead, Will," I say. "I'll handle her."

He looks at me like he wants to argue, but then he nods once and glares at Brynn all the way out of the room. I brace myself for what will likely be a sharp exchange of even sharper tongues.

"Now that we're all alone . . ." She starts that sultry walk of hers that makes most men fall at her feet. It only furthers my annoyance.

"You can see yourself out," I say. "We're as done today as we were when I ended things six months ago."

"Don't be like that."

I can admit that she's beautiful. Stunning, even. She's tall —her red hair and green eyes a siren's song. Hell, I'll even admit she's decent in bed. But I can't stand her. She's as mean as a snake, and her sole goal is to be powerful. I'll give it to her, she's tenacious.

And I damn near married her.

She rounds my desk and perches too damn close for my liking.

I eye her. "Leave."

"You're being difficult," she says. "You know us together is a good idea."

"Difficult is my default setting," I inform her. "And unlike you, I don't need to marry my way to the top."

I see the wounded look she quickly covers up. I've hit a sore spot, but I don't care.

"You're not all powerful, Kage Kensington," she says. "I have resources that would be beneficial to you."

"Any resource you may have is tied to your uncle, and I sure as fuck can find another way if I can't get what I want from him." The only Sinclair I hate more than Brynn is her smarmy uncle, Alastair.

"I've told you, you can have a mistress." She carries on as though she hasn't heard me. "As long as you're discreet— and extend the same courtesy to me—I don't give a shit who you sleep with. Of course, the Kensington empire does need an heir . . . ."

"You speak as though the Kensington name is attached to a crown," I state. "Any marriage or child I have will not be tied to a power move." That life isn't in the cards for me anyway. "Stop this. You reek of desperation and it's not attractive."

She gazes at me, calculating her counter argument. She never knows when to quit. If she would channel that effort into literally anything besides acquiring my last name, she would be damn successful.

"What are you doing here?" I ask. "It seems like a hell of a waste of time to cross the bridge in the name of trying—again—to get me to renew our sham of a betrothal."

"Engagement," she counters.

"Betrothal," I insist. "I didn't give you a ring." She narrows her eyes, but I'm not wrong. She bought her own damn ring, gaudy thing that it was. "Now, why are you here?"

"I—"

"Dammit, Brynn!"

She's interrupted by the appearance of her older sister, Sydney. There's the answer to why she's here, then. She tagged along in hopes that *this time* would be the time she convinces me to take her back. I sit back and watch as the sisters square off.

"I was just trying to talk some sense into Kage," Brynn tries.

"Personally, I wouldn't waste my time on a man who doesn't want me," Sydney says. "Desperation doesn't look good on you."

"Called desperate twice in as many minutes," I observe. "Really, Brynn, give it up."

Brynn looks like she might argue, but she just slips off my desk, her anger palpable.

"You'll regret this," she informs me, like she always does.

"I highly doubt that," I say, just like I always do.

"Wait for me in the car," Sydney directs. "I won't be long."

"I think I'll stay," Brynn says, determined.

"Wait in the car, Brynn," Sydney repeats with an edge this time. They glare at one another, engaging in a wordless argument. Sydney raises an eyebrow, and Brynn scoffs, but she storms out of the room, making sure not to be quiet about it. I wait, watching. Sydney is perhaps the only person Brynn will take orders from, and if Sydney is showing up here unannounced, there's a reason for it. And I'm probably not going to like it. The Sinclairs don't cross the Brooklyn Bridge unless absolutely necessary.

She shuts my office door and folds herself into the chair Will left. "You have to give it to my sister. She goes after what she wants."

"She's wasting her time," I say. "I hope you aren't here to waste more of mine."

"I have news I thought best delivered personally," she says. "Marshall is on the move again—he's hired Perrin. It will hit the press next week with a lot of pomp and circumstance."

"They must suspect something if they're stacking their deck," I say, acting like this is news to me. But I knew about the contract she's referencing—between Senator Randall Marshall and Doug Perrin, notorious D.C. fixer—before the ink was dry. It has created one hell of a complication on my part.

"Or preparing to make a move of their own," Sydney says. "My intelligence is unclear."

I remain quiet, always extra mindful of what I say in the presence of a Sinclair. I have more information, more resources, more money, more *everything* at my fingertips than she will ever know. I don't need to give her anything, even my curiosity.

She sizes me up. "I hear the youngest Adler moved in with her brother."

Internal alarms go off at the mention of Lyla. Someone has eyes on her besides me if they know she's living with Bradley. That's not all together unsurprising, but I still don't like it. However, I don't let my mask of indifference slip.

"It seems Bradley isn't the only Adler to distance from the family," I say. A vague confirmation of what she already knows.

"She's valuable," Sydney continues. "She would fetch a handsome ransom."

I don't like where she's going with this.

"She's off-limits," I state.

"Oh?" Sydney raises her eyebrow. "Is that so?"

"It is." I nod once. "She's not involved in this, and it will remain that way."

"I'd say she's very involved in this," Sydney says in a pointed way. My eyes narrow. I'm a master at reading people and she knows something I'm not going to like. "Sources tell me she had a very memorable night in the passenger seat of a vintage Bronco." She taps her chin thoughtfully while my insides turn to ice. "Now, who do I know that has a very impractical vintage Bronco in this city?"

"Who knows?" I demand. She only smirks. I lean forward in my chair. "Sydney. Who knows?"

"Have I touched a nerve?" she taunts. "You seem rather protective of the girl."

"I'm not asking again," I warn her. "Who knows?"

"Just me." She's trying to play a game of cat and mouse, but she's going to lose every fucking time when she plays against me. "For now."

Just her and whatever henchmen she has watching the Adlers.

"It will stay that way." Her threat is empty; I'll make sure of it. I will not be manipulated or blackmailed. "Lyla Adler is off-limits. Make sure you pass that message along to your uncle."

"I can't be held responsible for what other people do," she says with a casual shrug of her shoulder.

"If you—or one of your people—touch a single hair on her head, it will be the last thing you do." I'm not threatening, I'm warning. I don't make threats. I only make promises I can keep. "Anything else you think you may know about her stays with you and you alone."

"Think about it, Kage," she tries. "We snatch her off the street—"

"Touch her, you die." I don't mince words. Lyla is under my protection. I tell myself that's where my defensiveness is coming from, that it's because she's my responsibility and Bradley's sister. It has nothing to do with how she felt squeezing around me, her head thrown back in pleasure. Nothing at all to do with the fact that she felt like she was custom made for me. It certainly has nothing to do with how she looked on the lounge chair with her book, biting her lip as she tried to concentrate on what she was reading.

"I'll keep your secret," she says as she stands. "For now." She lets herself out of the office without a goodbye.

I wait until she's gone, then I stand and walk to my window. I stay in the shadows, but peek down at the street. I see a town car, Brynn leaning against it, waiting. I watch Sydney exit my gym. She exchanges words with Brynn before they get into the car. They pull off, but I don't watch them go. Instead, I search the surrounding area. It takes just moments to find the black hybrid that pulls out from a space a few spots down to follow them. It's fitting that the Sinclairs would reduce their carbon footprint while plotting to kidnap a senator's daughter.

I shake my head and go back to work.

I WORK A FEW MORE HOURS, calling it a day around dinnertime. Once I'm behind the wheel of my Bronco, I slip on my Ray-Bans and pull out of the parking lot. A quick glance in my rearview reveals the black hybrid that falls in a few cars behind me. I open the middle console, find the burner phone I stash there, and call Luke.

A few hours later, he's on my couch, drinking a beer and working through a pizza, while I'm perched on a barstool nursing my own beer. We're watching the late local news, listening as the reporter drones on about the fiery explosion of a black hybrid parked near Battery Park.

"Damn faulty batteries," Luke comments. "Imagine. You're just driving along, minding your own business, and then . . ." He mimes an explosion with his hands, complete with sound effects.

I don't reply, focusing instead on the reporter who's prattling on about a defective battery and an as-of-now unidentified man who burned to death inside the car's cockpit. Then the segment cuts to an interview with Sargent Mason who confirms that the battery failed, saying the car maker will be looking into it.

"Look at that handsome fucker," Luke says. "Mason will have the women in the comments throwing their panties at him when the news posts this clip to social media."

"Change the channel," I direct.

I've seen enough.

6

LYLA

I nailed it.

I absolutely nailed. it.

I interviewed for a special collections position at the New York Public Library and I *nailed it*. I left with a verbal job offer and high hopes. The woman I interviewed with said she liked my background, but that my passion for the work shined through and that's exactly the kind of person she wants on her team. She's calling my references today and said to expect a formal offer by close of business tomorrow, aka Friday. Still, there's a niggling part of me that can't quite believe my victory. Too many things have been pulled out from under me over the last few months. I won't truly believe this job is mine until I'm physically sitting at my desk with an official badge.

I'm still going to celebrate this, though. If I've learned anything recently, it's to celebrate the good things, no matter how small they are. I'm just debating on *how* I want to celebrate—massive ice cream sundae? A trip into the heart of Manhattan since I'm already out? Buy myself a new pair of shoes to wear on my first day?—when someone calls my name.

I go on high alert as I stop and turn on the spot, searching. I've let my guard down, let myself get too comfortable without all the eyes and camera lenses that followed the senator's daughter in D.C. I don't think I'm especially noteworthy, but that wouldn't stop the press from running some made-up story about me if they've spotted me. I've been noticeably absent from my mother's recent appearances as she lobbies for reelection, something the press has noted. They know I moved—someone managed to get a photo of the moving truck outside the apartment I shared with Deacon and posted it to a D.C. politico gossip blog—but to my knowledge, they aren't clear on where. It wouldn't be that hard to figure out, given that I have a paper trail, but so far, the news that I'm in New York has stayed out of the public eye. I'd like to keep it that way.

I'm starting to think I imagined it when I hear it again. I spin one-hundred and eighty degrees and spot him—the blond friend of Kage's. Will.

His smile as he weaves through people to get to me is warm and friendly, and I relax immediately. I only spent a few minutes with him when they were at the house for their draft, or whatever they were doing, but he was by far the most approachable one. Luke is big and loud, Theo is, well, not all that bad actually, and definitely softer and quieter than his friends, but he looks too much like Kage. And Kage is *Kage*. Will, though? He seems like someone I could be friends with.

"Will, hi," I greet when he's close enough to hear me.

"Hey," he replies. "Thought that was you." We stand in the middle of the sidewalk for an awkward moment, causing people to step around us. Some of them grumble, most of them don't pay any attention to us. It's New York; they're used to it. "What are you doing in this part of the city? Exploring your new home?"

"Job interview, actually," I tell him. "Just left it."

"Oh yeah? How'd it go?"

I can't stop my smile. "Really well. I got a verbal offer."

"That's awesome!" His excitement is genuine. "Congratulations, Lyla."

"It's not a done deal yet," I say, mostly to mitigate my own hopes. "They're checking my references before they send a formal offer. Hopefully, I'll be gainfully employed by the end of the day tomorrow."

"It's as good as yours," he assures me.

"What about you?" I ask. "What are you doing in this part of the city?" He could live here, I suppose, but I'm under the impression that Bradley's group of friends live in the same Brooklyn neighborhood as him.

"I have a class here on Thursdays." I notice then that he's dressed in workout clothes and has a backpack on his shoulders. He's a student, then. "It's a bit of a pain, but the money is good."

Maybe not a student. "You teach?" I ask. "What subject?"

He gives me a model-worthy smile. "Boxing." I frown in confusion and he chuckles. "I'm a boxing instructor," he explains. "We have this client at the gym who loves my classes. She floated the idea of me teaching her middle schooler once a week. He's homeschooled, so I'm his cohort's Thursday gym class."

There's a lot to unpack here, so I start at the beginning.

"You're a boxing instructor?"

He gestures that we should walk, and I put myself into motion as he falls in step with me.

"Yeah, at Kensington Boxing—"

"Kage or Theo?" I interrupt.

"Kage," he answers. "Theo's last name is Denton. His mom was Kage's dad's sister. Trust me, though. Theo might have Denton as his last name, but he has almost all Kensington characteristics. Except for 'moody asshole.' Whoever decides our genetic makeup poured all of that out on Kage. Theo is only moody when he's hungry."

I snort in amusement, which makes Will's smile grow. I heard no lies told, because from what I can tell, "moody asshole" is Kage's default setting.

"Kage owns a gym?" I clarify, filing away this new piece of information.

"He does." He nods. "Fun fact about Kage? He's one hell of a boxer. Watching him in the ring is like watching a dance."

An image of a sweaty, shirtless Kage comes to mind, and my body reacts the way it always does when I think of him. I shake my head to get rid of the thought of our sweaty bodies tangled together.

"Is this gym in Brooklyn?" I'm dismantling this piece by piece. I don't know why it seems important, but here we are.

"It is." His grin is ever wider, like he knows what I'm up to with my questions. "Kage's gym has a reputation for being the best, and this family I coach for is loaded. It's nothing for them to get in their town car and cross the bridge to Brooklyn for a workout." We stop at a street corner to wait for a light. "Where are you headed?"

"I'm not sure," I admit. "I was debating on if I was going to explore, treat myself to something delicious and unhealthy, or get a coffee when you called my name."

"I know a diner," he says. "It's not far from here—serves breakfast all day, but they specialize in waffles. Any kind of waffle you could dream of, they have. Want to go?"

"Let's do it," I decide.

The diner he takes me to is exactly as described—not far from where we are, and an honest-to-goodness diner with an extensive waffle menu. I order chocolate chip waffles that come doused in whipped cream, sprinkles, chocolate chips, and a drizzle of peanut butter sauce, while he orders an only-slightly healthier blueberry option.

I use the time to pepper him with more questions. He's easy to talk to, charming, even a little funny. I learn that he has a younger sister, Andie, who's doing a studying abroad program in Costa Rica, and that he has a degree in kinesiology, which seems fitting. He goes on a tangent about his belief that a healthy lifestyle can stave off a lot of diseases and keep people out of doctors' offices, then flips the script and asks me about myself. I answer cautiously but honestly, and wonder if my paranoia about people using their knowledge of me against me will ever go away.

"So," I begin, "how do you and Kage know each other?"

It's curiosity, I tell myself, nothing more. Just me, trying to understand the way my brother and Kage and the rest of these guys got tangled up together.

"We were fostered together." My eyebrows shoot up. That is not the answer I expected. "He aged out after a few months, but he looked out for me and Andie. And when he left, he took us with him since he was, technically, a legal adult."

I don't know what to say to that. There is a story, likely tragic, behind why they were in foster care. Their parents could have died or been deemed unsuitable by courts or any myriad of reasons. I want to know, but I'm not going to pry, not into this.

"Anyway," Will says, making it evident he doesn't want to talk about it any further, "tell me about this job."

I take the out and tell him about the job I might have, and he ends up taking the subway home with me. It's a few blocks from the stop to Bradley's, and Will offers to escort me home. I tell him he doesn't have to—I'm more than capable of walking down a sidewalk in broad daylight—but he insists.

"The gym is on the way," he says as we walk. "Mind if we stop? I left my laptop and charger there before I headed over for my private."

"Sure." I shrug, letting my curiosity about Kage's gym win.

The gym is in a nondescript building just a block down from the subway station. Will swipes us in using a key fob and I follow him into a reception area. There's a bored-looking guy behind a plain membership desk who gives him a nod and me a curious glance. I follow Will through another set of double doors and into a massive gym.

I don't know what I was thinking, but it wasn't this. The gym is high end. That's the only way I can describe it. Every-thing is crisp and clean. The space is somehow both a ware-house vibe and light, airy. The ceilings soar and big windows around the top let natural light pour in. A full, well-equipped weight training area is off to one side, and a few people are there, lifting or resting between sets. A line of punching bags hang along a far wall, and there are several mats scattered throughout where people are sparring, and multiple full-fledged boxing rings. All of them are empty right now.

Except for one.

Kage is boxing with Luke. Unlike the others working around them, the only safety equipment they're wearing are their gloves. They are locked into their match, but even to my naked eye, I know that Kage is the superior boxer.

I can't look away.

It's not that he's shirtless, or that his many abs on display are glistening with sweat, although that certainly does not detract from the view. It's that he's graceful. Fast. Calculated. He's mesmerizing to watch as he bobs and weaves, sending a well-placed jab here, an uppercut there, all the while lecturing Luke on his performance.

"You're missing your openings," he says.

"Fuck you," Luke spits back. He fakes a swing, goes for an uppercut, but Kage sees it coming and counters with his own move.

"Told you he was good," Will says from beside me. He's right. Watching Kage box is like watching a dance. Will mutters something about getting his laptop, but I'm too busy ogling what's happening in front of me to acknowledge it.

I don't know if thirty seconds or five minutes pass. I have limited ability to take in anything else, but I do clock the icy-haired girl who was at the bar the night of Bronco Gate. She's watching them move the same way I am. An unwarranted and unwelcome flare of jealousy washes through me at the reality that she has the nerve to look at Kage like that, but I shake it off. I am *not* interested in him, and even if I were, the fact that he's Bradley's best friend makes it next to impossible to pursue him.

Kage shifts his stance, and by consequence, his position, which puts me in his line of sight. He notices me, does a double take, then takes one more definitive swing at Luke who lets out an impressive string of curse words when it lands true.

"We're finished," Kage informs him.

He slips between the ropes, takes a towel someone offers

him, and wipes the sweat from his brow. I do all I can not to openly stare because now that he's not boxing anymore, I'm back to fully appreciating how attractive he is. He accepts a water bottle from someone else, and then he's on the move.

Toward me.

I can't take my eyes off him, even though a small voice in my brain is desperately trying to tell me to stop staring. It should be punishable by law for a man to look this good, especially when he's a sweaty mess. He's like a Greek god with shorts hung low on his hips and his intricate tattoo that travels the distance of his arm and wraps over his shoulder and onto his chest, right over his heart.

"Like what you see?"

That brings me back to reality.

"You put on quite a show," I say.

"That was a normal day of training," he says, then smirks. "Had I known you were watching, I would have given you a show to remember." I blush crimson, a thing he seems well-equipped to bring out in me, and his self-satis-fied grin makes me want to see if I have what it takes to deck him once. How is it that he can disarm and irritate me to no end in the same sentence? "What are you doing here anyway?"

"I'm with Will." I don't explain how I got connected with Will this afternoon. It's petty, but part of me hopes he feels a little jealousy over the fact that I'm in his gym with another man. Even though I think I've friend-zoned Will. He's hand-some and kind, but he's just not doing it for me. Not like *that*, anyway. "He needed to pick up something."

"Got it." He nods. "Thought you might be here to learn self-defense."

"I took a self-defense class in D.C.," I inform him. I hated every minute of it. "I'm good."

"Oh yeah?" He gives my shoulder a gentle but pointed shove. I stumble back a step and narrow my eyes at him.

"Rude."

"Rude?" He does it again, harder. I stumble back two more steps. "Is that what you're going to tell a stranger on the street that decides he wants your bag, your phone, and perhaps, between your legs?"

"You're being crass and paranoid," I inform him. The asshole pushes me again, this time taking a couple of menacing steps forward. I stand my ground this time, and my temperature soars upward at his proximity. "I can take care of myself."

"Prove it," he coaxes. "Show me what you learned in self-defense."

"Dressed like this?" I motion at my very professional and modest skirt-and-blazer combo.

"Your street stalker won't care what you're dressed like."

He lunges for me.

I act without thinking, throwing an arm up to block him as I bend my knee and launch it in an upwards trajectory, like the instructor taught us.

I find myself spun around and pulled flush against Kage, his arm around my neck in a purposeful but not complete chokehold. My breath catches in my chest, but I don't think it's from the adrenaline of a faux attack.

"I could have, at the minimum, broken your arm to subdue you with that move," he says, his lips close to my ear. Yeah, it's *definitely* not the faux attack that has me unable to catch my breath. "Then I could have had my way with you. In whatever way I wanted."

There's no stopping the visions of all the ways I would let him have me if the circumstances were different. I try to find my words to make a worthwhile comeback, but I seem to be incapable of speech at the moment.

"Kage?" Will has reappeared. "You know Lyla isn't here for nefarious reasons, right?"

"I was proving a point," he states as he lets me go. "Self-defense, Lyla. You need it." He holds my gaze as I glare at him. "Will teaches a self-defense class on Wednesday nights at seven. Six weeks and you'll be able to defend yourself from just about anything."

"I do?" Will asks. Kage gives him a quick look. "Oh, right, self-defense. Seven o'clock. Wednesday nights. Sorry, I teach so many classes that it's hard to keep them all straight." I look between them. Something is off.

"Sign up," Kage states before I can question Will's confusion about his schedule. "Next session starts next week."

He walks away.

"Asshole," I mutter under my breath as I watch him disappear through a set of double doors. The icy-haired girl gives me a long, not-friendly look, turns on her heel, and follows him.

"It's not the worst idea to take a self-defense class," Will says. "People are crazy, and you never know who you might cross on a subway."

"You sound like my brother," I grumble. He only grins.

"You ready to go?"

Will and I part once I reach Bradley's. Gabe is home, but Bradley is working the night shift again, so we order an obnoxious amount of Chinese and watch Lindsay Lohan movies well into the night—a perfect way to end what has been one of my better days as of late.

Saturday morning, I'm up and at the vintage market with Cecily before nine o'clock.

"Are you looking for anything particular?" I ask as I sift through a rack of satin blouses, each one uglier than the last. I'll never understand how people find such cute things when thrifting. I don't have the magic touch.

"I'll know it when I see it," Cecily says as she sorts through a table of denim. "Any word on that job you interviewed for?"

"I got it!" I can't keep the excitement out of my voice.

She squeals out a celebratory noise and pulls me in for a hug. We've become fast friends. We've traded a lot of texts, and I've gone back to the bar for past-dinner drinks where I told her about my job interview. I like her friends, Sam and Ollie, too. Sam is quieter, smart, and studious, while Ollie is full of wise cracks and good humor.

"Lyla! That's awesome! Congratulations!"

"I'm really excited," I admit. "I start in two weeks."

"We need to celebrate," she decides. "Me, you, Ollie, and Sam. I'm not working tomorrow, and I bet we can find someone to cover Sam's shift. We'll go out to dinner, then see where the night takes us. How does that sound?"

"Wonderful." She has no idea how wonderful. I had friends in D.C., but there was always an undercurrent of *"I know who your mom is."* Cecily simply wants to be my friend, and it's a welcome change of pace. "Thank you, Cecily."

"Like I'm going to turn down an excuse to have a night out," she teases. "Even on a Sunday. Sunday Funday was created for a reason." She goes back to sorting through the stack of denim. I give the rack another half-hearted sift before deciding there's nothing there for me.

"I'm going to get an iced coffee," I announce. "Want anything?"

"I'm good," she says. "I'm going to try this stuff on." We part ways—her toward a pop-up tent that's been designated as a dressing room, me to a coffee stand I saw earlier. I join the line at the booth and check my phone as we inch forward. There's a text from, of all people, my mother.

Mom: *Lyla, this has gone on long enough. I'm sorry you and Deacon broke up but breakups happen. Moving to another state is an overreaction. Call me as soon as possible to discuss your move home.*

I roll my eyes and delete the message. She acts like it was "just a breakup," and that Deacon Cosse isn't a backstabbing, double-crossing, grade-A asshole. Or that she isn't just as guilty.

I order my coffee and do a quick Google search on my mom while I wait. Unsurprisingly, there are dozens of recent articles about her reelection campaign. There is the usual mudslinging, the promises she swears she will keep that will fall by the wayside once she is guaranteed another term. At least I can say with certainty that she's kept more promises to her constituents than she has her children. That's probably why she's polling so far ahead of her opponent. Honestly, the election itself is just a formality, barring anything crazy.

My order is called and I accept it, thanking the man who handed it to me, before starting to wind my way back through the market in search of Cecily. I'm a little too engrossed in my phone, though, and don't notice the hand that reaches out for me.

"Eyes up, babe."

I look up into a pair of gray eyes. The smile he wears is supposed to be friendly, but I immediately feel uneasy.

"I'd advise against calling random women 'babe,'" I say

as I pull my wrist out of his grip. "I'd also strongly suggest you not grab them against their will."

This only seems to amuse him.

"You're feisty," he says. "I like that." I roll my eyes and resume walking, but he stops me by moving his body into my path. I huff and glare up at him. "What's your name?" I give him nothing. "I'm Clint," he prompts. "Come on, sweet-heart, share with the class. I bet you have a name as beau-tiful as you are."

I am very much not doing this today. I try to step around him. He steps in front of me again. My heartbeat picks up, but I tamp down my fear to portray confidence.

"I'm not interested," I inform him. I try again, to move around him, but he stops me one more time. This time, more aggressively. "Knock it off!"

"Tell me your name," he pushes. "Then we'll get out of here."

"I told you. I'm not interested." I'm firmer this time as I try, yet again, to dodge around him. He stops me with a rough grab of my arm. We're in the middle of a crowded market, yet no one notices I'm in trouble. Everyone is too engrossed in their own phones, their own problems, their own to-do lists, or else too chickenshit to speak up. "Let me go."

He opens his mouth to protest, but before he can, another arm is sliding around me. This one feels familiar. And I know, without needing to look, that the big body that just appeared next to me, seemingly out of thin air, belongs to Kage.

"I've been looking for you." He leans down and presses a ghost of a kiss, so light I'm not sure he actually did it, behind my ear. "Play along," he whispers before he pulls back and turns to this Clint character. "Is there a problem?"

"I was just talking to your . . ." Clint holds Kage's eyes and lifts an eyebrow in question.

"Girlfriend." The lie falls off his lips easily. I lean into him, doing my part to sell this story. He feels like solid ground. "I believe I heard her tell you to leave her alone."

"I was just trying to talk to her," Clint insists.

Kage's grip on me tightens as he draws me even closer. I'm cinched at his side and surprised by the feeling that washes over me at being held against him like this. I feel *safe*.

"You had your hands on her," Kage says. There's a low, dangerous tilt to his voice. They haven't broken eye contact, and something tells me they know each other.

"Hand," Clint corrects with a smirk. Having seen Kage in the ring with Luke, this Clint guy is playing a very dangerous game. "It was a hand."

"You would do well not to touch what's *mine*." Heat rushes through me at the possessive way Kage says *mine*. "Consider that free advice for the day." I let him lead me away. He keeps me tucked into his side, causing people to create a path for us as we walk. "What happened back there?"

"That asshole—he said his name was Clint—came out of nowhere and grabbed my wrist to stop me," I report. "I think he was flirting, but I turned him down and he didn't take it well."

"Stay away from him." It's an order, and just like that, I'm back to being irritated with him. I pull out of his grip. He lets me go.

"Rest assured, Kensington, that I am not about to go chasing after him to get his phone number. I had it handled."

I didn't, but I won't admit that to Kage.

"You didn't," he says, echoing my thoughts. "He was maybe thirty seconds away from hauling you out of here and the idiots around you would have been none the wiser."

"I would have been fine," I say, even if I'm not sure that's the case. I'd like to think I'd be able to get myself out of that mess, but he was huge and I'm not. I'm scrappy, though, and I can think fast on my feet.

"You can thank me for saving you at any point," he states, with a sense of agitation about him. Like he's mad at *me* for what just happened. Absolutely not. He does not get to be irritated at me for minding my own business at an outdoor market only to be harassed by a neanderthal. I stop walking. He takes a few more steps before he realizes I'm no longer with him, then stops and looks back with an annoyed expression. "What?"

"I cannot believe you have the audacity to deem yourself a hero," I inform him. "'Thank you for saving me'? I didn't get into that situation by my own free will. No woman finds herself harassed, or worse, by her own free will. You can fuck right off with your macho posturing and victim blaming. I'm not impressed."

A host of emotions play out in his eyes and I wait, wondering what he's going to unleash. He clenches his jaw, unclenches it, then blows out a breath.

"I know that guy, Lyla," he says, his words calmer than I expect them to be. "I know *of* him, at least. He's not a good guy. You may think you're capable of handling a situation like that, and maybe you are, but he's not some run-of-the-mill creep on the street. Clint Ballard is into some shady shit. I'm not in the business of encouraging you to act like a wilted daisy when you're in danger, and I would *never* victim shame a woman, but I'm damn sure not going to stand by while he overpowers you. Because he was going to, and I don't want to think about what would have happened then."

That little monologue cools my fire a bit. He hasn't apologized, exactly, but he did make his point well enough that I call off my urge to tar and feather him.

"How do you know him?" I ask.

"That's a story for another day." He looks me over, and I try not to squirm under his gaze. "You okay? I should have asked before hauling you off and then pissing you off."

"I'm fine." I nod. Then I flex my wrist. It's a little sore, but doesn't feel broken or dislocated so I'll call it a win. "Didn't even spill my coffee." That gets a little smile out of him—one that's gone almost as fast as it came, like he didn't want me to see it. I don't think it's his first instinct to ask if someone is okay. He's more of a react-now, ask-questions-later guy. "What are you doing here, anyway? I can't say I pegged you for a vintage-market-on-a-Saturday-morning kind of guy."

The T-shirt he's wearing—black again—has a three-figure price tag on it. Kage Kensington doesn't strike me as the kind of guy who goes prowling for vintage anything. His Bronco doesn't count. I actually googled them. The price tag on a refinished Bronco like he has is obscene. He may have a rough, bad boy persona thing going on, but below it is an air of someone who comes from a lot of money. I know the type. I've spent my life around them.

"I check it out from time to time." He shrugs. "Found a great leather jacket once." He jerks his chin at me. "What are you doing here?"

"I'm with my friend, Cecily." I spot her then, and wave to get her attention. She waves back in recognition. "I swear she's not going to drag me off for evil or whatever Clint was going to do."

"Rule number one," he says. "Trust no one."

"That's a sad existence," I say.

"That's lessons learned," he counters.

"Sad," I insist. Cecily is a few paces behind Kage now. She lifts a curious eyebrow.

"Am I interrupting something?" she asks as she draws even with Kage.

"Not a thing," I say.

Kage breaks eye contact with me to turn to her. "I was just telling Lyla that I noticed she hadn't signed up for our self-defense class yet," he tells her. I narrow my eyes at him, catching on to his game.

"Self-defense class?" Cecily asks. "I could be into that."

Kage flashes me a look of triumph before he turns back to Cecily.

"Wednesday nights at Kensington Boxing, seven o'clock. Six-week course. Next session starts this week. You should join us, Cecily." He nods at me. "Bring your friend." I roll my eyes, but Cecily lifts an eyebrow at Kage.

"You know my name?"

"You've been my bartender for the last year," is his answer. No more, no less. Then he gives both of us a polite nod. "I'll see you both on Wednesday. Try not to get into any more trouble, Adler."

With that, he's disappearing through the crowd. I, however, am still standing here, feeling like I ran a marathon, all from another interaction with Kage Kensington.

"Care to tell me why it felt like you and Kensington were on the verge of spontaneous combustion?" Cecily asks.

"What's that supposed to mean?" I counter.

"Girl, the heat between you two was palpable from twenty feet away," she informs me. "I know you went home with him—or went somewhere with him, at least, because you came back to the bar. Is there more going on there than just a one-night stand?"

"No." I shake my head. "Definitely not."

"I feel like there's more to this story ..."

I kind of hate how perceptive she is. I also decide it won't hurt to confide in her. It's been too long since I had a girlfriend to spill my secrets to.

"He's one of my brother's best friends," I admit. "He showed up at our house the morning after, right in the middle of Bradley lecturing me for staying out too late."

Cecily lets out a low whistle. "Does Bradley know ..."

"No." I shake my head. "He knows I had a one-night stand that night—I admitted that. Then Kage walked in, and mortification followed."

"Please tell me he's as good as he looks like he'd be," Cecily prompts.

"So good," I admit. She lets out a wolf whistle. "If he weren't Bradley's best friend, I'd be willing to overlook his endless asshole status and let him do whatever he wanted to me." Cecily pretends to fan herself. "He is, however, very much off-limits."

We start walking again and I fill her in on the Clint character that accosted me.

"We're obviously going to that self-defense thing," she informs me. "I'm off on Wednesdays so it's perfect. I close a lot at the bar, too. May as well know how to defend myself if needed."

I try to protest, but she doesn't let me. She's decided we will both be going to this self-defense course, and that's that. Kage should give her commission.

We finish up at the market, then venture to a nearby hole-in-the-wall restaurant she swears has the best cheese-burgers in the area for an early lunch. Once we place our orders, she turns her expressive brown eyes on me.

"You're sure there's nothing going on between you and Kensington?"

"Positive." I nod, even if I'm not sure if that's the truth. "Why?"

"It's just . . . There are rumors."

She has my attention. "Rumors?"

"I don't know much, but there have always been some low rumblings about the Kensington family. Some are about how they amassed their wealth. Others are about how they protect that wealth." Well, that's my theory of Kage being from a wealthy family confirmed. "He's never caused any trouble in the bar—none of his crew have—but where there's smoke, there's fire, right?"

I nod my agreement, my mind whirling as it sorts through what I know about Kage Kensington. He owns a boxing gym, drives a vintage Bronco, has a cousin named Theo, a friend named Luke, and a foster brother named Will.

Foster brother.

I flag that bit of information to come back to later. A man from a wealthy family, who, by all accounts, still has that wealth, was in foster care for at least a little while, then pulled his foster brother and sister into his own care as soon as he aged out, something I'm assuming he would need money to do, especially at only eighteen.

It's time to do a little digging into who Kage Kensington is.

7

KAGE

"We're teaching *what now*?" Luke asks.

"*We* aren't teaching anything," Will says with a pointed look at Luke.

"Fair." Luke shrugs. "Still. Self-defense? Seriously?"

"Self-defense. Wednesday nights at seven o'clock. Six-week series," I repeat for the millionth time. "I'm not sure why you're questioning this."

"I'm not sure why *you're* suddenly teaching self-defense," Luke counters, forever the one to call me out on my shit.

"Again, *I* am teaching self-defense," Will says. "You'd scare everyone off, completely negating the entire concept of self-defense."

Luke ignores him, his full attention on me. "I suggested adding it to our schedule a year ago and you said, direct quote, 'We coach boxers, not Lululemon-wearing college kids carrying pepper spray,' and walked off."

"I changed my mind," I say. "This isn't open for debate."

"Couldn't help but notice Lyla Adler is signed up," Scarlett says, eyes on me. She doesn't know Bradley asked me to protect Lyla. I'm operating on a need-to-know basis, and so far, she hasn't needed to know. Except, she's too observant for her own good. Her observational skills are what got her into this mess in the first place. She knows something is up.

"Bradley encouraged her to sign up." Not a lie. I'm pretty sure I had her thanks to a purposeful drop of information about the classes to Cecily, but I mentioned it to Bradley, and he pushed her over the edge with Gabe's help. Gabe does know I'm protecting Lyla, thanks to Bradley's commitment to honesty—at least when it comes to his relationship. I think the fewer people who know the better, but I guess it works out if I can use his pull with Lyla to get her to give a fuck about her personal safety.

"Right." Scarlett nods. "*Bradley* encouraged her to sign up for a series of classes we didn't offer a week ago." I can feel her judgment from here, and I let her judge away. If I let other people's opinions about me or my actions get to me, I wouldn't get out of bed in the mornings.

"Does anyone have anything worthwhile to share?" I ask the group assembled in my office. This is supposed to be a team meeting, but it's not exactly going to plan. "Luke, any word on what Doug Perrin is up to?"

"Shaking hands and kissing babies," he reports. "He's working overtime to drum up supporters."

"Supporters for who, though?" Will asks.

"That's the question, isn't it?" Luke counters. "On the surface, he's Senator Marshall's man. We know Marshall is setting himself up for a presidential run and Perrin has a hell of a contact list to ensure the nomination. Below the surface? I'm certain there's more going on. I just haven't cracked it yet."

"Perrin is your top priority," I remind him. He rolls his eyes. I've told him this several times over since Sydney dropped by my office. He doesn't need the reminder that he's supposed to be digging into the D.C. fixer, but I feel better giving it. "What else?" I look at my cousin. "Theo? You've been quiet."

"Not much to report." Liar. "Senator Adler is pretty much guaranteed another term. She's doing a hell of a job of keeping her nose clean. At least, as far as the public knows."

"What about her aid, Mauricio Cosse?" I press him.

"He took a meeting with a lobbyist for a pharmaceutical company two days ago. It appears it was informational, but I'm monitoring the situation." We hold each other's gaze for a moment. There's more he wants to talk about, but not in front of everyone else. "I have eyes on his son, too." I lift a brow at that. "He's moved into a junior role with Adler's campaign. He hasn't set off any alarms yet, but he bears watching."

Cosse Jr., Lyla's ex, is working for Adler? That's news. I need to dig into that.

We run through a few more items, and Luke brings up the self-defense classes again before I dismiss them. Theo gets up and follows them to the door, but instead of passing through it, he shuts it behind them, then returns to sit in one of the chairs across from me.

"Let's hear it," I state.

"The board is pissed at you." He doesn't mince words when he brings up the family business I'm, technically, CEO of, like it or not. "You can't keep fucking around, Kage. They're going to remove you by vote if you don't start at least attempting to do literally anything."

"Let them," I say. "I'd welcome it."

"Kage, it's the family business."

"And?"

"Does that mean nothing to you?"

"I never wanted it," I remind him. "My dad was the real

estate tycoon, not me." I spread my hands out. "If the board has had enough, so be it."

Theo rubs between his eyes. "Our parents worked their asses off for Kensington Enterprises." I hear what he doesn't say. The business that fell to me, whether I wanted it or not, may not mean much to me, but it does mean something to Theo. "Maybe it's not what you wanted, but you can't let it sink into the abyss."

I could—I kind of want to. One could argue it's currently treading water, despite the profit it's turning. A business can be in shambles without the books showing it. But he's right. Our parents worked their asses off to turn the corporate real estate company our grandfather started into what business publications call *an empire* and what I call *a righteous pain in my ass*. My loyalty to my family—specifically to Theo—is the only reason I haven't dumped my controlling shares.

That and the fact that my dad masterminded his will in a way that locks me into running the place. The board can try to vote me out all they want, but it would take more brain power than they have to knock me out of power. Hell, I can't even turn over my shares to Theo, not that he wants the CEO role. He's brilliant with numbers and the "people" of it all. He thrives in it; insists he has no interest in being the "top guy" one day. I'm the one with the strategic mind and the ability to play chess—and win—with powerful players. I just don't want to.

"Give me the rundown," I prompt, and Theo is off, talking about mergers and acquisitions and budgets. I listen, taking in the appropriate details, doing my best to act like the CEO I'm supposed to be, but something he says in passing catches my attention.

"Stop," I say. "Go back. Say that last part again."

Theo furrows a brow. "Frederick wants to hire another assistant—"

"Not that." I shake my head. "About Buzzard."

"You have got to stop calling him that . . ."

"I'll call that son of a bitch whatever I want." I loathe Stanley Carpenter. He's on our board, looks like a buzzard with his pointy nose, and he's always circling around, looking for easy prey. He's a snake in the grass, and I'm going to be the one who catches him. Lucky for him, he's pretty far down my list of people I have a vendetta against. Unlucky for him, I'm working my way through that list at a respectable pace. I'll get to him soon enough. "Tell me again."

"He's interested in partnering with Sinclair Industries on their new solar technology—"

"No." I shake my head before he can finish. "Absolutely not."

"Why not?" Theo challenges. "You've seen their product. It would revolutionize solar-powered energy and make going solar much more affordable for both businesses and homeowners."

"It would also give the Sinclairs access to Kensington Enterprises," I remind him. "I don't trust that family." Especially now that they've threatened Lyla. "It doesn't happen."

"This have anything to do with a hybrid with a faulty battery?" he questions.

"Sydney threatened Lyla Adler," I tell him. "She suggested kidnapping her for ransom. Senator Adler is in direct opposition of almost all of the Sinclair family's sustainable initiatives. Imagine the pull they could have over the senator if they had her youngest daughter as a hostage."

Theo processes that information and I wait, watching

him. I worry about him more than I do the others. He was sheltered from a lot of the shit our family did. His mother made sure he stayed on the straight and narrow, and his father kept him out of rooms, unlike mine who brought me into them, especially after my mother died. I want to keep his hands clean, or at least clean enough, as long as I can.

"I know about you and Lyla."

I stare. "What?"

"I know about you and Lyla." He holds my gaze, so I know he's telling the truth. Theo can lie with the best of them, until he's talking to me. Then it's a shift of his eyes or a rub of the back of his neck if he's not telling the whole truth, both of which are missing right now. "She's the woman you left The Black Dragon with a few weeks ago."

Well, fuck.

"How long have you known?" I demand.

"Since the jump," he reveals. "I recognized her when we were over at Bradley's for that fantasy football draft thing. I kicked your ass this week, by the way."

He did, thanks to an awful defense and a running back that couldn't hold onto a ball to save his life, but I'm not worried about that right now.

"Have you said anything to anyone?" I press.

"Of course not." He's offended that I'd even ask. He keeps my secrets, I keep his. "Even if she weren't Veronica Adler's daughter, I'd have enough sense not to broadcast the fact that you fucked Bradley's sister. The guy is an emergency medicine doctor. He could gut you alive and make it look like an accident. I think he'd do it over either one of his sisters, but he'd make it hurt a little more for his baby sister."

"Who else knows?" I continue.

"No one." He shakes his head.

"You certain?"

"Will doesn't know," he rattles off. "He had his back to her that night, so he wouldn't have gotten a good look at her, and she looked a lot different with all that makeup on. Luke was several beers deep and had his own one-night stand that night so no chance he knows. I can't rule out Scarlett, though. She called you and Luke pigs and left in a huff. Will and I finished our drinks and went back to his place to play video games."

Video games. I was unknowingly complicating my already complicated life with a one-night stand and those two were off playing video games.

God, the sex was worth it though. I think. I don't know. I try not to think about it . . . except, I think about Lyla Adler straddling me in my Bronco way too much.

"Keep it to yourself," I direct. "Sydney already knows—"

"How?" he interrupts, urgent now. He knows how dangerous that bit of information is in the hands of a Sinclair.

"She was having me—and possibly Lyla—followed."

"Hence the hybrid," he understands.

"Hence the hybrid," I confirm.

There's that considering look again.

"Be careful, Kage," he says after several beats of silence. "You're walking an awful lot of razor thin edges right now."

"Aren't I always?" I counter. Theo only looks at me—all he needs to do to show he's worried. "I'll be fine, Theo," I say in an attempt to ease his concern. "I know what I'm doing."

"None of us are invincible," he reminds me as he rises to his feet. "Our parents taught us that."

He opens my office door and takes several quick steps back as a large mass of dog moves into my space. I chuckle and extend a hand to pet Sadie, my pit bull, as she settles on her haunches next to me. Theo just shakes his head and mutters something about "fucking dog" under his breath as he exits. Sadie looks at me expectantly, and I open my top desk drawer, taking out the treat she knows is in there.

"Good girl," I praise. She only cuts me a look that says she's unimpressed with my audacity to treat her like a dog. She certainly doesn't act like one. She found me on the street and attached herself to me two years ago. She's been my shadow ever since. She's a big, beautiful pit bull, so gray she looks blue, all muscle and snarl, and no patience for anyone but me and even then, her patience is thin. Everyone is scared of her, but she won't do a damn thing to them unless I tell her to. Or she thinks I'm in trouble.

The next several hours pass in the controlled chaos I function in. I make some calls and send more emails than I care to count. I get in a workout, coach one of our elite classes, and temper Theo's Kensington Enterprises concerns by scheduling a few meetings. Then, I turn down Luke's invitation to meet him and Theo at some bar to watch football and head to Bradley's.

"You're a scary motherfucker," Bradley determines after I unload most of what I've learned about Lyla's new friends and her job at the New York Public Library on him. In summary, there's no current threat, at least from them.

"I'm resourceful," I counter. "I'm doing the job you paid me to do."

"I'm not paying you," he reminds me.

"Details." I did owe him, but talk about calling in a massive favor. He's going to be in my debt by the time this is over with. "She tell you about the guy at the vintage market yesterday?"

Bradley looks rightfully nervous. "No . . ."

"Clint Ballard cornered her." If the medical board of

New York heard the string of words that Bradley curses in response, they would revoke his license for mental instability. "I handled it," I continue once he's done. "I got Lyla away from him, and I made sure he knew she's under my protection."

"You sure it was smart to let him—and by proxy, his boss —know you're protecting Lyla?" Bradley questions.

"They'll already know." I shrug, casually, like the idea of how much danger Lyla could truly be in doesn't keep me up at night. "It was either intervene or let him pull her out of the market to who knows where."

"You're right." He sits back in his patio chair with a heavy sigh. I actively avoid thinking about how good his sister looked lying across the lounge situated directly across from us while I grilled burgers as he mulls over this new piece of news. He suddenly bolts upright and turns to face me. "If you're here, who's watching out for Lyla right now?"

"Will." I take out my phone and open my texts with Will. "She had dinner with her friends at some shitty Italian place," I report as I read his updates. "They've moved on to drinks at a bar down the street. He's keeping tabs on her from a distance and will make sure she gets home safely. She's none the wiser to his presence."

Bradley isn't satisfied. "I asked you—"

"I can't be everywhere at once," I remind him. "I have other responsibilities besides Lyla." He glowers because he knows I'm right. Too many damn people count on me, and I only have twenty-four hours in a day. "Will is able to be there when I can't. She's safe, Bradley. I'm not going to let anything happen to her."

Not "Will isn't going to let anything happen to her." *I'm* not going to let anything happen to her. He doesn't know half of the strings I've pulled to keep her safe from people who might want to harm her just because her last name is 'Adler.' My grip tightens around my water bottle involuntarily. It's not right, all the shit we have to navigate because of who we're related to and the things they've done. In my case, I've at least rose to the occasion to earn their ire. Lyla is innocent.

"I don't worry about Alice like this," Bradley admits. "She's always been tough as nails and with her being in the Air Force, there's an element of protection there that I can't question. Lyla is different. Lyla is my baby sister."

Not this again. I do not need to be reminded that the best sex I've had to date was with his *baby sister* a second time today.

"I'm not going to let anything happen to her," I say again. "You have my word."

"I know." He nods. "Thank you, Kage. I know what I'm asking of you."

I don't say anything in response. The truth is, even without Bradley asking me to step in, I think I would have done it anyway. I have a bit of a complex when it comes to protecting innocent people, and there's something about Lyla that makes me want to pull her into that safety net and, frankly, reinforce it. I don't pretend to understand it. I just know that it wouldn't take much to put myself in front of Lyla in the name of keeping her safe.

We trade small talk for a few minutes, which is mostly him complaining about his fantasy football team and me pretending to care.

My phone lights up with another text from Will.

Will: *Think they'll head home soon. This bar is dead. Ollie is trying to pick up this woman though.*

He's included a grainy photo of Lyla's friend Ollie and a

woman that is way out of his league. I deem her a non-threat, mostly because Ollie doesn't stand a chance.

Me: *Has she seen you?*

Will: *Nah. I'm tucked away in a corner booth, got a hat on. It's pretty dark in here. We're good.*

Bold of him to go fully into the bar, but if anyone could charm his way out of being caught, it would be Will. Lyla seems to like him, and I'm not too worried that he wouldn't be able to pull off an "I just happened to be in this bar at the same time as you" moment if it came down to it.

A beeping sound emits from Bradley.

"Dammit," he curses as he fishes something out of his pocket.

"Is that a pager?" I question as I take in the device in his hand.

"It is," he says as he reads whatever is on the screen.

"Hospitals still use those things?"

"They're cheap, hard to break, and run on a different wireless network than phones," he says as he stands. "They're more reliable than smartphones. We did a pilot program with a texting app, and it was a disaster between texts not getting delivered and doctors complaining about being interrupted too much." I watch him pocket the pager and take out his phone to send a text, which is in direct contrast to what he just said. "I have to go—multi-car accident. You mind sticking around until Lyla gets home?"

"And tell her what, exactly, when she gets home to find me waiting for her?" I ask. "That her big brother asked me to wait up for her?"

"Yes." He slips his phone into his pocket and looks at me expectantly.

"Got nothing better to do," I agree a little too easily.

He leaves and I'm left to entertain myself. I use an app to

check the security footage around my gym, something I've been doing more of lately given the whole hybrid-following-me-and-then-blowing-up thing, then check on my place. All is well. I close the app and open my dog camera—I can't believe I'm that guy now—and check on Sadie, to find her stretched across my couch. I tap the button that will make this camera thing toss a treat. She only lifts her head and glares directly into said camera, effectively scolding me for interrupting her nap. I snort.

Like that treat won't be gone by the time I get home.

I finish my water and head inside to rummage through Bradley's fridge in search of a snack. I come up empty-handed. The Adlers and Gabe exist on salt, sugar, and takeout.

Settling for a cup of coffee, I find a clean mug, then a K-cup, and load up the Keurig that Bradley said Lyla bought because she's a coffee fiend and wanted to be able to make a single cup. I'm leaning on the counter waiting for it to finish brewing and letting my mind do it's usual gymnastics between my gym, Kensington Enterprises, and *everything else* when the front door bangs open and then slams shut. I remain where I am, eyes on the kitchen doorway, as Lyla rounds the corner. She stops short with a sharp gasp as her hand flies to her chest in surprise.

"Holy fucking shit!" she curses. I can't help but grin in amusement that those beautiful lips can swear like that. "What in the hell are you doing here?"

"Waiting for you," I answer.

Her eyes narrow. "Bradley put you up to that?"

"He did." Look at me, not lying. She rolls her eyes so hard I see the whites of them. Then she reaches past me to swipe my coffee off the Keurig. "Hey!"

"Thanks for the coffee," she states. I watch her open the

fridge, find a sugary hazelnut creamer, and pour a generous amount into the mug. She returns it to the fridge, looks me right in the eye as she takes a sip, and uses her hip to shut the fridge door.

Fuck me, why is that hot?

And why is she in such a bad mood?

"What's got you all rainbows and sunshine tonight?" I ask.

She glares at me like I'm the cause of all the bad things in her life. I've caused quite a few bad things, but I'm pretty sure—to date anyway—that I haven't caused any major disruption in hers. Save for the whole sex-in-my-Bronco thing. But that was consensual and immensely enjoyable.

"Why are all men assholes?" she asks.

I'm back to leaning on the counter, arms crossed over my chest. "That's a sweeping generalization." She opens her mouth to protest. "I'm not saying you're wrong. Just that you're making a blanket statement."

"You're proving my point," she informs me.

"Come on, Lyla," I coax. "What's got your panties in a twist?" I smirk. "Or are you not wearing any?" She all but rips my throat out with the look she gives me. That's also hotter than it should be.

"I hate men," she mutters under her breath as she stomps across the kitchen. She opens a cabinet and starts pawing through it. I watch her, and try not to watch her ass, which her black jeans hug very well. She spots the bag of Oreos, once more on the top shelf, and I wait to see what she's going to do. "Stupid Bradley," she grumbles as she considers the cookies.

"If only you knew someone tall that could reach those for you." She tosses me another dirty look over her shoulder, sets her coffee down, and the stubborn woman goes to climb. I'm across the room and reaching for the cookies in two steps. "Don't climb on shit," I say as I drop them to the counter for her. "You're going to fall and break your neck." She gives me another look but doesn't retort further, instead just opening the bag and digging in. I return for my coffee and make the detrimental mistake of looking back at her just as she darts out her tongue to lick the stuffing off the cookie she's untwisted. The image goes straight to my crotch, and I take a deep breath to center myself. "What's wrong?" I ask one more time. She considers me as she chews that damn cookie. "Come on. Tell me."

"I was having a perfectly good night," she starts after a moment's pause. "I had a great time with my friends, celebrating my new job. Then, on my way home, my ex texted me." I have to control my features at the mention of Deacon Cosse. "He went on and on about how I've made my point and he's willing to try to work things out. He said I should move back to D.C. because that's what's best for me. I am sick and tired of everyone always knowing what's best for me. I'm happy here. I'm starting a job I'm excited about. I'm making friends, and I don't have to spend all my free time pandering to my mother's constituents or trying to make Deacon happy. I don't *want* to move back to D.C."

God, she's beautiful like this, all fire and ice, combative and irritated and emotional. She's dressed in jeans and a sleeveless top with a light jacket thrown over it, her hair in a braid, and very little makeup on. I swear, the only time I can think of seeing a woman more beautiful is when I saw *her*, that morning after, when she was sitting at Bradley's kitchen table and caught me completely off guard in her too-big T-shirt, smudged makeup, her hair messy, thanks in part, to how my hands had been in it . . . I shake my head to stop that line of thought in its tracks.

"Then don't move back."

She looks at me like that's a novel idea. "I'm not . . ."

"Okay then." I nod once. "Block that guy's number and move on. You're the only one that gets to make decisions about your life. Fuck him for trying to get in your way."

She looks perplexed.

"What?"

She shakes her head. "I didn't peg you for the motivational speaker type."

"Trust me, I'm not." I push off the counter, coffee forgotten, and make my way to her. "I'm just a believer in doing whatever the hell you want, so long as you can sleep with your choices at the end of the day."

She gazes at me as I continue my slow approach. "And can you sleep at night?"

"I haven't slept well in ages."

I'm inches from her when I stop. We're two magnets, drawn to each other, no matter how much resistance I try to put in place.

"I was with him for a long time," she says. "Far longer than I should have been."

"He didn't treat you well." It's not a question. I'm positive Deacon Cosse didn't treat Lyla the way she deserves to be treated.

"He wasn't always awful. He used to be my best friend."

I can't seem to look anywhere other than at her. I notice she has a bit of cookie in the corner of her mouth, and my hand moves on its own accord. I use my thumb to brush it away, taking the extra moment to drag my thumb across her lips. Her lips part and the small breath of air that escapes her is enough to harden my cock that much more. I catch myself and take a quick step back.

"I fucking hate that you're Bradley's sister," I admit as my hand falls away.

"Same," she agrees, eyes on mine, tempting me, drawing me closer once more.

"I want to kiss you right now."

"I wouldn't stop you."

There are only inches between us, but it feels like an ocean. The attraction between us is primal. I should turn on my heel and walk out of here, but I can't. This woman has me in a chokehold. I can run recon missions and blow up hybrids, all while running a gym and being a CEO of a real estate empire, but I can't resist this woman.

"Fuck it."

My mouth is on hers, hot and insistent, and she responds in kind. She tastes like Oreos and coffee and *Lyla* and I need more. I use my hips to pin her between me and the counter. I bury one hand in her hair, use the other to cup her cheek and angle her mouth toward mine. Her fingers hook into my belt loops and pull me even closer. She pushes up on her toes to get more leverage, and I don't think twice about looping an arm around her waist and lifting her so she's sitting on the counter. I'm so tall that she's at exactly the right height to be mouth to mouth with me.

Her hands are on me, and they leave trails of heat through my T-shirt. I tangle my hand back into her hair, absolutely wrecking her braid, and use the other to run up her thigh. I pull her to the edge of the counter so she's flush against me and then it's her hands in my hair. *Fuck*, I want her all over me.

I bite down on her lip, gentle, but pointed. She whimpers as her lips part for me and I deepen the kiss, letting her tongue do battle with mine. I'm lost in this woman and that's not me. I don't do this. I don't let a woman have this kind of sway over me. Lyla isn't just any woman, though. She's *Lyla*, and I can't maintain any semblance of control around her.

"Kage," she groans, and I start to think about carrying her up to her bedroom.

The sharp scream of a car alarm crashes through the moment. I rip myself away from Lyla, startled and, for a moment, ready to protect her from whatever threat is lurking, until the alarm ceases as quickly as it started, pitching us back into a loaded quiet. We stare at each other, both breathing hard, the only sounds the soft hum of the fridge and the ticking of an old clock. Her lips are swollen, and her hair is a mess.

What the fuck am I doing?

"We can't do this."

"Kage—" she starts.

"You're Bradley's sister," I continue, talking over her because I'm barely holding on and it won't take much for her to convince me follow through on going upstairs and having her as many ways as I can before morning, or Bradley gets home, whichever happens first. "We can't."

"We can't," she agrees. Fuck if she doesn't sound disappointed. "We shouldn't, at least."

She's leaving the door open, and I clench my fists to keep from moving forward to reattach my lips to hers.

"We can't," I repeat with a shake of my head. I take a few more steps backwards, moving toward the door but never taking my eyes off her, memorizing this moment to come back to when I need it. "Go to bed, Lyla. Don't climb on the counter."

I turn and flee to keep myself from fucking my best friend's sister all over again. I pause just long enough to lock the front door behind me, shutting Lyla safely inside before piling into my Bronco parked down the block.

I exhale a breath, and shift the Bronco into drive, moving quickly because if I don't, there's a real chance I'll go back inside and finish what we started. As I make the drive home, I can't help but think that if things were different, I could be the guy to treat Lyla the way she deserves to be treated. I could be the one to show her how special she is.

Except I'm not that guy.

Not even close.

And she deserves far more than I'll ever be able to give her.

Best friend's sister or not.

8

LYLA

K age Kensington is a phantom.

I'm skilled in the art of sleuthing—most of my education involved research, after all. I'm the person my friends call when they can't find their dating app match on social media. I usually unearth them within a half hour. Yet, I have found next to nothing about Kage Kensington, and I've been searching for an hour. He doesn't have social media—not so much as an inactive account—and his gym's website doesn't mention him or any of his staff. It's a measly few pages of the basics: services offered, class times, how to find it, and a contact form. Nothing else.

The things I *have* found include:

He owns a gym.

His grandfather founded Kensington Enterprises.

His father and aunt took it over when he retired.

His mother died.

So did his father.

The articles about their deaths are a couple of years apart and vague on the details. Their obituaries are even vaguer, although there is mention of a deceased sister in his father's obituary—a woman I assume is Theo's mom. The lack of information on what should be high profile deaths is suspicious.

Kage is listed on Kensington Enterprise's website as the *CEO*, although there's no picture or bio like there is for the other executives.

Who is this man?

Why is he so damn hard to find anything on?

I move on to his friends.

Will is the easiest to dig into. I'm unsurprised to learn he was in a frat in college. He's close with his sister who is pretty in a surly little sister kind of way. He posts on a somewhat regular basis—things like his workout or an artful shot of his food—and his parents are dead. I'm not sure what happened to them, and my research skills so far haven't uncovered much. Like Kage's parents, the details are minimal.

Luke is the most active on social media, which is unsurprising. I've only met him a couple of times, briefly at that, but he's the life of the party and his Instagram shows it. It's all workouts, food, and selfies. I'd bet good money he slides into a lot of DMs.

Theo is the least active, aside from Kage. He's posted exactly five photos to his feed, although he's tagged in quite a few, courtesy of Will and Luke. There is one of him and Kage boxing. Another of a woman that must be his mother that says, "Happy Mother's Day, I miss you," and a similar post of a man I assume is his father. There's a photo of him on a beach somewhere with Will in the background, and the most recent photo, posted a few weeks ago, is a mirror selfie of him in business wear captioned "Work." He's the Director of Finance at Kensington Enterprises, complete with a professional headshot and a short bio that reveals he has an MBA from Wharton.

Who the hell is letting two twenty-something year olds run a massive company like that?

I learn the icy-haired girl is named Scarlett through sleuthing Luke's account. Her feed is all quotes from dead poets and images of street art. She comments on all their posts though, and I find her sarcasm amusing. I'm still not sure if I want to be her friend or steer clear of her.

Every single one of their parents are dead. All of them. Which doesn't make sense. How can an entire group of friends be parentless? Are they some sort of weird support group? Perhaps I wasn't too far off when I thought Kage might be in a cult. And why is there next to no information about their deaths on the internet?

"There she is!"

I startle and slam my laptop shut.

Gabe cackles. "What were you doing?" he asks with a glimmer of amusement in his eye.

"Nothing."

"Liar." His grin grows. "Looking at an X-rated site, perhaps?"

"Gabe!" I gasp. He laughs outright and falls to the couch next to me.

"Dating site?" he guesses. "Don't want the men in the house to give our opinion on who you're dating?"

"Have you seen what the apps have to offer?" I counter. "I'd be safer in the X-rated corner of the internet."

"There's an idea," he says. "Start an OnlyFans as the senator's daughter. Your mother would stroke out."

"I'm not baring it all on the internet," I inform him. "I've had enough of my life documented without doing it on purpose."

"Think of how fun that could be for me though," he says. I laugh again. My mother is not a fan of Gabe, mostly because he and Bradley's relationship flies in the face of some of her party's favorite social issues that they like to trot out when they feel the need to cause a stir. It only makes me love him more. "What about dating? You ready to put yourself out there again?"

"I've browsed a few apps," I admit. "Judging from the sample size I've swiped 'no' on, it's not looking great."

"Bradley and I know some single guys," he ventures. "Of course, Bradley refuses to think of either of his sisters dating. He seems to think 'Air Force' equals 'convent' for Alice and believes you to still be an innocent seven-year-old."

"I can assure you that Alice is not having a convent experience in the Air Force." He laughs again, and I smile. Gabe is one of the good ones. He makes my heart happy. "As for me, Bradley will just have to get over himself."

"One of the biggest regrets of my entire life is not being present when he realized you had a one-night stand a few weeks ago," he says. "He was so upset that you had sex with a stranger, *twice*. Meanwhile, I was like 'well, was it good?' He did not have those details, nor did he appreciate my inquiry." He looks at me. "*Was* it good?" I'm certain my cheeks are crimson because he looks delighted. "Oh, it was *so* good, wasn't it?" He claps his hands together. "You hussy! I love it!"

"It was phenomenal," I admit, because why not tell at least some of the truth? As long as he doesn't know it was Kage, there's no problem.

"What was his name?" Gabe probes. "I bet he had a hot name. Something like 'Malachi' or 'Dexter.'"

"We didn't exchange names." Not a lie. I didn't know

Kage's name until he showed up in the kitchen the morning after. Gabe wolf whistles.

"Mysterious," he says. "I approve." It was mysterious—until the morning after. "Seriously, we could set you up with someone," he continues, reverting back to his earlier comment. "Bradley's group of bros are all single to my knowledge."

"Isn't that a red flag in and of itself?" I ask. "Not a single one of them in a committed relationship?"

"Possibly," he agrees, unbothered. "Let's see. That oaf Luke is out. Nice guy. Great sarcasm. Excellent taste in liquor. But he has a rolodex of women, and you will not be one in it." It seems my interpretation of Luke is correct. "How about Will? You've been hanging out with him. Any sparks there?"

"None." I shake my head. "He's a good friend, but he's not boyfriend material. Not for me anyway."

"Shame," Gabe muses. "He's so pretty to look at."

"I entirely agree." I may have friend-zoned him, but that doesn't mean I don't appreciate his good looks.

Gabe purses his lips, thinking. Then his eyes light up and he excitedly turns his entire body to me, tucking a leg under him like we're two gal pals about to have a gossip session. "I've got it! I'm a genius, Lyla. An absolute genius. Go ahead, tell me I'm a genius."

"Not until you tell me why you're a genius," I counter. "I'm not committing to anything when you're over there trying to set me up on a date. Which, I haven't agreed to, by the way."

Especially when he's sifting through a pool of Kage's friends as candidates.

"I'm a genius," he says again. "I have the perfect guy for

you." He pauses for dramatic effect, then makes a show of spreading out his hands in a grand reveal. "Theo!"

I choke on the water I just took a sip of. "Theo?" I squeak out.

"Theo." He nods. "It's perfect. He's got the same good looks as that cousin of his—we're not touching that one with a ten-foot pole—but without all the surliness. He's an absolute gentleman, has a great job. Literally the only complaint I have about him is that his fantasy football team is stacked and crushing all of us."

"Theo?" I repeat.

"Brilliant, right?" He nods excitedly.

I have no idea what to say. Not out loud, anyway, because the first thought I had was Kage would kill me and Theo both, and probably Gabe, too. Which is a weird thought to have as Kage has no right to tell me I can't date Theo if I wanted to, and Theo is a catch by all accounts.

"I don't think that's a good idea." I shake my head.

"Why not?" Gabe demands. "You got something against hot men with good jobs? You said it yourself, Lyla. The dating apps are a cesspool of questionable DNA. Theo is a nice guy, has some fancy director job at the family business, and is loaded. Also? That. Body."

"He's Bradley's friend and Kage's cousin," I say. "It could get complicated."

"Bradley likes him," Gabe muses. "He would come around. As for the cousin? Who cares?"

I do, and I really don't want to. "What do you have against Kage? Why the ten-foot pole?"

"He's got a lot of baggage," Gabe tells me. "I don't know much about him, but any guy who's that moody all the time has issues. He's fantastic to look at, of course, and I'd bet he'd even be a good fuck." I can confirm. "But he's not a relationship guy, and we're not going there with you."

I don't need a relationship with him. Just maybe one more night to get him out of my system. That stunt he pulled last night, kissing me on the kitchen counter, was . . . Well, I needed my vibrator to get me through the aftermath of that, and I'm still sexually frustrated.

"Think about Theo," Gabe says. "Now, what are we doing today while my only-slightly better half—aka, your brother—is at work saving lives?"

"I should probably go shopping for work clothes," I say. "I start my new job next week."

Gabe lights up. "Yes!" He springs to his feet; I wish I had his energy. "We shall shop! Give me a half hour to groom myself properly and then we'll venture out. It's my duty as your sort-of brother-in-law to make you the hottest woman in the office."

"I'm going for professional, not hot," I say. "I'm going to be working with rare books, after all."

"All I hear is 'sexy librarian vibes,'" Gabe says with a wave of his hand. He gives me a once-over. I'm in shorts and a long-sleeved, oversized Georgetown shirt, my hair piled on top of my head. "Change. You're not going into public, on my arm, looking like that."

I glare at his back as he retreats to his and Bradley's room for what I guarantee will be at least forty-five minutes of primping. I consider his suggestion of dating Theo as I stand, laptop in tow, and make my way to my own room to change into something Gabe might find respectable.

If I had met Theo first, I might consider it. But it was Kage's Bronco I climbed into. And whether I want to admit to it or not, it's Kage I thought about when Gabe was suggesting guys to set me up with.

And naturally, it's Kage that I can't have.

9

LYLA

"This is going to be epic."

Cecily cuts an eye at Ollie.

"Why are you here again?" she asks.

"I'm learning to defend myself." Both of us give him a pointed look. He spreads his arms. "Look around, ladies. I'm in my Mecca."

I do look around. There are a dozen women—plus Ollie and Sam—mulling around Kensington Boxing, waiting for this stupid self-defense class to begin. A few of them look like they might be from an office or something, based on their oversized T-shirts, workday makeup, and how they're hovering together. A few others are definitely not here to learn self-defense but to show off for the boxers working out around them. I've already seen Luke fall at the feet of a blonde in hot pink spandex. Ollie seems to think he's going to meet a similar fate.

"Why are you here?" I ask Sam. He's tall and in shape, although he doesn't carry around the kind of muscles Kage and his crew do. He's got the build of a runner who occasionally lifts weights. I'd bet he could handle himself in most situations, though. Never mind that he's a man and doesn't have to worry about these things like women do.

"I want to see how this works out for him." Sam nods at Ollie.

"Fair," I agree. I, too, want to see if Ollie is successful in his quest to pick up a—his words—*damsel in faux distress.* Will asked them why they're here, too, and Ollie's answer was to point out that there was nothing that said this was a women-only class. An argument Will didn't have anything to counter with because what measly advertising I saw— one post on the gym's Instagram—only gave the date, time, place, and duration.

"Okay, everyone!" Will calls out. "Let's get started."

We gather around him, on one of the larger mat-covered areas. I half-listen as he introduces himself and gives an overview of how class will work.

I know Kage is here before I see him, thanks to the goosebumps that erupt on my skin. I glance over my shoulder and there he is, leaning against the far wall, watching.

Watching *me.*

I do everything I can not to look his way again as Will leads us through a warm-up, all the while lecturing us on the fact that the best line of self-defense is running away. Face your threat, if you can do so safely, make sure they know you see them, and then run as fast as you can in the opposite direction. Don't look back. Try to run toward people. All common sense, really, but apparently, when it's time to decide between flight or fight, people tend to choose fight.

"Flight doesn't make you weak," he tells us while bending his arm overhead and instructing us to bring our hand between our shoulder blades and grasp our elbow with the other hand. I focus on not overextending said shoulder—it's been sore today for no reason other than the fact that it's Wednesday. "Flight keeps you alive."

I still feel Kage's eyes on me as I stretch. I don't understand the attraction between us—I know next to nothing about him. I don't even know if he's a decent guy. I just know that I spend five minutes around him, and I lose most of my good sense. I shake my head and refocus. Theo has been nominated to play the part of poor, defenseless woman. I watch as Will demonstrates how an attacker might seize their opportunity and coaches us on how to get out of a chokehold. Then, we pair off to practice.

"I feel wrong attacking you," Cecily says.

"We should leave and get drinks," I suggest. She chuckles, her eyes flickering over my shoulder. I know exactly what she sees.

"The owner of this place is staring at you."

"I'm aware." I told her about the kiss and his wish that I weren't Bradley's sister. I've thought about that declaration and fantasized about what it could be like if I weren't Bradley's sister a little too much.

"What if you just said 'fuck it' and went for it?" she suggests as we get into position. "Your brother would get over it, right?"

"Bradley holds a grudge like no other," I say as I try to remember where Will said my hands should go once Cecily has me in a hold from behind. "He hasn't spoken to our mother in three years. He came to D.C. for our father's funeral and still managed not to say a word to her. It was an admirable battle of wills, and she lost."

I try to maneuver out of her hold.

I'm on the floor with a cry of pain within moments.

"Lyla!" Cecily drops next to me. "What happened? I'm so sorry . . ."

"My shoulder," I lament, working to hold back tears as I awkwardly push myself upright with my good arm. "I dislocated it. It's fine."

"It's fine?" Cecily shrieks. "Lyla! Oh my God . . . I'll call . . ."

"Lyla."

Kage is there, kneeling next to me. Not Will, not Ollie or Sam, not even Cecily.

Kage.

"What happened?" he demands. He sees my shoulder then, and his eyes darken. He turns his glare on Cecily. "What did you do to her?"

"Nothing," she stammers. "I mean, I don't think . . ."

"She didn't do anything," I manage to tell Kage through my pain. "It's my joints—this happens. I need to relocate it . . ."

I try to stand.

"Lyla, don't try to move . . ." Cecily reaches for me. Kage, however, loops an arm around me and helps me to my feet.

"Lyla?" Will trots up. "What happened?"

"I've got her," Kage answers for me. "Continue the class."

"But—"

"Continue the class." His tone leaves no room for argument. "I'll take Adler to the ER."

"You don't need to," I try. "I'll call a cab or something . . ." No one hears me. Cecily is gathering my stuff, others are whispering.

"I'm taking you to the ER," Kage informs me in that same "no arguments" tone. Cecily joins us with my bag. He reaches for it, but she pulls it back.

"I'm going with you."

"I've got it," he states.

"No, I did this—"

"You'll stay here—"

"You didn't do this," I cut Cecily off. My shoulder hurts and I don't have time or patience for them to argue. "This happens sometimes—it's just how I'm made. I swear, you aren't responsible. I just need to have it reset. I'll be fine."

"I'm going with—"

"I'm taking care of it," Kage cuts her off again. They glare at each other. Meanwhile, I feel woozy from the pain.

"You don't—"

"You two carry on." I take a single staggering step. "I'm going to take myself to a doctor before I pass out from the pain."

That gets both of their attention. Kage still has his arm around my waist, and he tightens his hold as though I might actually fall. Which, honestly, I might. The longer I stand here, the worse it hurts. Never mind the fact that the longer it's left out of socket, the worse it's going to hurt when it's maneuvered back into place.

"Hospital," Kage determines. "Now." He tugs me toward the door, as abrupt as ever, but there's still a gentleness there. I remain where I am despite my desire to get this over with and focus on Cecily. She's still braced like she intends to come with me. Her guilt is palpable.

"Lyla?" she questions.

"It's okay," I tell her. "You stay—finish class. I'll call you later."

"Are you sure?" Her eyes flicker to Kage and back to me.

"I'm sure." I nod. It takes her a moment, but she relents and turns her gaze to Kage.

"Get her to the ER," she directs him. "If you don't, or if she ends up worse off than when she leaves here, I'll figure out how to hide a body."

He has the audacity to roll his eyes. "Come on, Lyla."

I manage a small wave at Will, who is watching with all the concern in the world, and notice Theo watching us with a curious expression I'm in too much pain to think about. Luke and the icy-haired girl—Scarlett, I remember—are by the door. Kage and Luke exchange a look that says a thousand words only they can decipher because damn if I know what that loaded gaze means, nor am I in any condition to dissect it. Meanwhile, Scarlett scrutinizes me like I'm gum on the bottom of her shoe. I have no idea what I did to her, but she does not like me. If I have to make an educated guess, I'd bet it has something to do with the way Kage has me cradled to his side.

He leads me through the gym, out a set of doors that open into a small parking lot behind the building, and right to his Bronco. He opens the door for me, and I can't help but stare, remembering the first time I was in this Bronco.

"You going to ask me if I want you to drive us somewhere again?" he asks.

And there he goes, ruining the nostalgia by speaking. I scoff and try to be the hero I think I am and get into the vehicle without assistance. I'm unsuccessful. He has the damn thing lifted—*Was it this high that night? Is this even legal in the state of New York? Why the hell does he drive a Bronco in the city?*—and I need the arm attached to my shoulder to haul myself into the thing. He sees my dilemma and easily lifts me into the vehicle, leaving my dignity in the parking lot.

"You doing okay?" he asks as he buckles my seatbelt for

me. He's close and he smells good. Like sandalwood and leather, of course.

"Fantastic," I quip. A fresh wave of pain chooses then to roll through my body. I close my eyes and try to breathe through it.

"Lyla?" I open my eyes and meet his. They're soft and full of concern. "I'll have you at the ER in a few minutes. Hang in there." I nod as another wave of pain washes over me. I'm only vaguely aware of him taking his phone out to make a call as he shuts my door. He's already hanging up when he slides behind the wheel.

We don't talk as he makes the short drive to the hospital. I sit back, keep my eyes closed, and try to stay as still as I can to avoid jarring the joint any more than necessary. An impossible task, given that the Bronco isn't the smoothest riding vehicle I've ever been in. He parks, and then he's helping me out of the Bronco and into the ER.

"How can I help you?" asks the nurse behind the triage desk.

"She's here to see Bradley Adler," Kage informs the woman.

"Wait, what?" I ask.

The woman lifts an eyebrow at Kage. "Does she have an emergency?" I look around for signage and then zero in on the hospital's logo on a nearby wall. Of course he brought me to Bradley's hospital.

"I didn't bring her to the ER for the hell of it," he counters.

"What's the emergency?" she asks, surveying me like she's looking for a bullet hole or a missing appendage.

"Her fucking arm—"

"I dislocated my shoulder during a self-defense class," I jump in, giving Kage a filthy look. He's being rude, I'm in pain, and I have no time for the equivalent of a pissing match between him and this triage nurse. "I have Ehlers-Danlos syndrome—I'm hypermobile. Bradley Adler is my brother. He's fixed me more times than I can count, but I'll see whoever is available."

"She'll see her brother," Kage insists. I give an exasperated sigh. I see sympathy in her features as she reaches for a clipboard so I can start the intake process, but I can also see she's ready to go to the mat with Kage. The pain is revving up again, going from a constant thump of hurt to a shout, and try as I may, I can't hide the little gasp that escapes me when it cranks up another level. I don't look at Kage, but I feel his hand land on my lower back. It's oddly comforting. "Let's get you triaged, then someone will see you as soon as—"

"She'll see Dr. Adler," Kage cuts in again. "I've already called him."

This woman is not having it. "Sir, I understand you're worried about your—"

"It's fine, Sheila." Bradley walks up to the desk, looking the part of ER doctor in his hospital-issued scrubs, stethoscope around his neck, front pocket crammed full of pens, a mini notepad, and who knows what else. His name badge swings from where it's clipped to said pocket. "I'm expecting her. Room three is open. I'll see her there."

"But . . ." Sheila does not go against hospital protocol it seems.

"I've already put her in the system," Bradley soothes her. "It's fine, Sheila, I promise." He jerks his head toward a set of double doors. "This way." I don't know why I expect Kage to remain in the waiting room because he certainly doesn't as he follows Bradley and I through the double doors. "Did you have to be an asshole to Sheila?" Bradley asks him.

"She's my favorite triage nurse. She runs a tight ship, and makes sure I get out of here on time if she can help it."

"Not my fault she chose not to hear what I very clearly said," he states.

"Tell me what happened, Lyla," Bradley requests, shifting his attention back to me. I quickly relay the story of how I dislocated my shoulder.

"Pop it back into place and I'll be on my way," I finish.

"You're getting X-rays first," he informs me.

"No, I'm not."

"You are," he insists. "I already put in the order, and lucky for you, it's oddly slow in the ER today, which means we're likely in for a rush of traumas around midnight. It won't take long."

"I don't need an X-ray," I say stubbornly.

"You do. I need to see how much damage you did before I reset it."

I argue, but it's a lost cause; I'm getting an X-ray. I sit on the bed in my designated room in a huff while I wait to be fetched for said X-ray. Kage has been uncharacteristically quiet since his showdown with Sheila, and I take advantage of the moment to observe him. He's sitting on the room's lone chair, aimlessly scrolling his phone, head bowed, but there's an anxiousness to him that isn't usually there. It's present in the way his knee bounces, and how his thumb is flicking across his screen far too fast for him to actually be reading whatever he's looking at.

"You okay?" I ask.

He startles—minutely, but I still notice—and looks at me. There's a haunted expression around his eyes that vanishes with a single blink.

"What?" he asks.

"Are you okay?" I ask again.

"I'm fine." His answer is too quick to be true, and he's already back to flicking his thumb across the screen.

"Kage."

"Lyla." He doesn't look up.

"Are you okay?" I repeat one more time. "You seem twitchy." It's the best word I can come up with for how he's acting. He sighs one of those heavy sighs of his—the one that sounds like I've asked him to explain the meaning of life yet again—and leans forward, elbows on his knees, eyes still on his phone.

"I don't like hospitals."

"You don't have to stay," I tell him. "Bradley will take care of me, and I'll be out of here in no time. I can call an Uber to get home."

"I'm not leaving."

He offers no more, and I don't push. I let him sit in his stony silence while I send one-handed text messages letting my friends know I'm okay. Heather has texted a *"FaceTime me when you can—want to catch up!"* that catches my eye. I desperately want to call on the spot, but I can't, not with an audience. I let her know it'll either be late tonight or tomorrow before I can follow through, and she responds with a *"Can't wait to talk! Miss you!"*

I get my X-ray and, thankfully, there's no additional damage. Kage remains on the quieter side and doesn't protest when Bradley asks him to leave the room before he relocates my shoulder.

"Who knew all it took to shut him up was a hospital visit?" I say as I prepare for my brother to snap me back together.

"He doesn't like hospitals," Bradley says, just as Kage had. I wonder again what kind of history the two share. He knows Kage, trusts him to hang out at his house and wait for me while he's not there. Kage is comfortable enough to let himself into our house without knocking, grill in the backyard, and make himself a cup of coffee.

Comfortable enough to avoid having any sort of physical anything with Bradley's sister. Which, one could argue, we're not doing an altogether great job of given that kitchen kiss.

"How did you meet Kage?" I ask, hoping I sound casual.

"We crossed paths not too long after I moved here for my residency," he says as he moves me into position. It's a vague answer—there's more at play here. I can't explain it, I can't even prove it, but I can sense it. "You ready?"

"You know I don't like to—Fuck!" He snaps my shoulder into place before I can remind him that I don't like to know when the move is coming. It's well-played, I'll give him that.

"How's that?" he asks.

"I hate you," I mutter. He chuckles and turns away to retrieve the sling he brought in with him. Kage appears in the doorway, and maybe it's the fluorescent light of the hospital, but I think he looks a little pale.

"You good?" he asks, worry in his features.

"Peachy," I reply as I try my shoulder. "You?"

He grunts in reply.

"Stop trying your shoulder," Bradley chides. "You know it needs to be stabilized for a while." Kage moves back into the room just enough to lean against the wall next to the door as Bradley adjusts my sling. "You'll need to wear this for at least a couple of weeks, maybe longer."

"You really are a doctor," Kage comments as he watches Bradley work. "All this time I thought the scrubs and pager were just for show."

"Stitched you up, didn't I?" Bradley retorts. Kage scoffs

but says no more as Bradley finishes tightening the straps of my sling. "All set. How's the pain?"

"It's been better," I admit. Bradley reaches into his pocket and I shake my head. "No."

"I know you hate how they make you feel," he says in what I call his "big brother" voice. "I only prescribed two. One for now, one for in the morning. Let them take the edge off and help with swelling. You can go back to your usual pain control methods after."

I consider his proposal, but I hate taking the stronger pain meds. They make me loopy, slow, and groggy. He has a point, though. My shoulder is still throbbing, and sleep will be hard to come by otherwise. I hold out my hand in agreement. He keeps a close eye on me as I toss the first dose back and take a swig of the water bottle he offers. Satisfied, he turns to Kage.

"You mind giving her a ride home?"

"I didn't stick around for my health," Kage replies.

"She probably shouldn't be alone on those meds," Bradley continues with a quick glance my way. "I'm on overnight, and so is Gabe . . ."

"I'll stick around," Kage says without hesitation.

"That's not necessary," I say, because me on these pills with Kage around is not a good idea. "I can take an Uber home."

"Just until she falls asleep," Bradley says, ignoring me. "I'll be there around sunrise tomorrow. So will Gabe."

"I'll be fine . . ." I try again.

"I've got it handled," Kage says. It's like I'm a kid again, except, instead of it being my brother and sister pretending they don't hear me, it's my brother and his best friend—who I am very attracted to. And this time, there's an undercurrent of a challenge there that I can't quite figure out. Like

Kage is daring Bradley to question him. "You ready to go, Lyla?"

"I have a choice now?" I counter, even as I awkwardly slide off the bed. Both Bradley and Kage reach out to steady me as I lose my balance. I don't need either of them—I have plenty of experience with being down a joint or limb—but I do catch the look that passes between them. Bradley's is questioning. Kage's dares him to ask. We say our goodbyes and Kage shepherds me to the Bronco yet again. I don't protest this time when he helps me in. He's gentler, I note. Not that he was rough the first time, but there's less sharpness to him now. This might be the most mellow I've ever seen him. I wonder what it is that makes him live so on edge.

He remains quiet as we drive back to Bradley's, and I can't stop glancing at him. He's deep in thought, his mouth set in a grim line, a slight crease in his forehead. There's an open spot on the street right in front of Bradley's. He parallel parks with enviable ease, then I go to let myself out of the Bronco, but he's already there, opening my door and offering me an arm.

"Who knew you're a gentleman?" I ask as I allow him to help me out of the Bronco.

"You did." I lift an eyebrow at that, but before I can ask, he's reaching back into the Bronco for my bag. "Where are your keys?"

"Front pocket," I instruct. He finds them, shoulders my bag, and there's that hand again, gentle but firm on my back as he guides me inside. "I'm going upstairs to change. I'll be back down in a few."

"Do you need . . ." He stops, starts again. "I mean, can you? With the sling and all?"

"This isn't my first time in a sling by a long shot," I tell him.

"You're sure?" he questions. "I've seen you naked. It's not like I would see anything I haven't already seen."

"Have you seen me naked though?" I ask him pointedly. He's seen my breasts—or maybe not since his mouth was attached to them most of the time we were together. And the second time he took me, I was bent over, my dress hiked up to my hips.

"A fair point," he concedes. "Might be my only regret from that night."

Desire blooms within me in an instant. He does nothing to quell it with the way he's looking at me. I know he's remembering it, too—the way we fit together, the tight quarters of his Bronco, the risk of him taking me in the women's bathroom at The Black Dragon with just the flimsy lock to keep people out. I pull myself out of his gaze and head for the stairs before I do something stupid.

"Ten minutes," he calls after me. "If you're not back down here, I'm coming up there."

I strongly consider staying upstairs just to lure him to my bedroom, but the meds are starting to have their woozy effect, and I think it wise to navigate down the stairs while I still can. How I'll get up them to go to bed later is something future Lyla will have to figure out.

When I'm done, I find Kage in the living room with food.

"Figured you haven't eaten yet," he says. "Might be good to get something in your stomach with that pain pill you took."

"Oreos?" I ask as I join him on the couch, leaving a respectable amount of space between us, admittedly touched by the gesture.

"Seems to be the only food you eat." He motions to the coffee table. "I also got two kinds of chips." He, however, is slicing chunks off an apple with a paring knife and dipping them into a smear of peanut butter on a plate.

"Pass the peanut butter?" I request as I reach for an Oreo. I realize quickly that my plan is not going to work, and not only because I don't have a butter knife handy, but because I only have one available hand. "Crap."

Kage looks at me for a moment, gets up, and walks out of the room. I forgo the peanut butter and bite down on the Oreo. I have another one in hand when he returns with the jar of peanut butter and a butter knife. He says nothing as he sits down and takes the Oreo out of my hand. He smears it with peanut butter and offers it to me. It makes me swoon a little; I blame the drugs.

"Thank you," I say as I take it. He nods, considers the Oreos, then reaches for one like it might bite him. He skips the peanut butter and bites right into it.

We continue like that, me eating chips and the peanut butter-covered Oreos Kage makes for me, him cutting into a second apple. It's peaceful and kind of . . . nice.

"You really don't have to stay," I tell him. "I'm going to fall asleep any minute now."

"I told Bradley I'd stay. I keep my word." I only nod and reach for the remote, wincing as my shoulder feels the movement. I settle on a chick flick I've seen a hundred times and try to get comfortable on the couch. I have every intention of lying down, knees pulled up to give Kage room, but then I realize that will mean laying on my injured arm if I want to see the TV, and that's a no-go. Kage stands again. "Trade places with me."

"What?" I question.

"Trade places," he prompts again. "You want to lie down, and you can't on that side of the couch." The next thing I know, he's guiding me upright and directing me toward the other side of the couch. I go willingly, and I can't say I hate the outcome as I settle far more comfortably onto the couch. Kage cuts the lights before he takes the spot I just left, the TV casting us in a soft glow. "Better?"

"Better." I nod. "Thank you."

I try to focus on the movie as a woman denies that she's falling for the guy whose parents hired her to get him to move out of their house, except I'm hyperaware of Kage at the other end of the couch. It's hard not to be with his big body keeping watch over me. I fight to keep my eyes open as the medicine does its best to drag me under.

Kage pulls my feet into his lap.

I lift my head in question.

"You didn't look comfortable all balled up like that." He doesn't take his eyes off the movie. I wonder what I would see in them if he looked my way.

Then he starts to massage my ankles.

I lift my head again to question him. He's still looking at the TV, though I doubt he's actually watching it.

"Do you hurt all the time?" he asks—careful, curious. He learned about my condition tonight, and I know if I don't want to tell him, I don't have to. He won't be offended or get upset. Except, I want to. Some innate part of me trusts Kage Kensington, even though I barely know him.

"Pretty much." My head feels light, my eyelids heavy. I won't be able to resist sleep much longer. "Some days are worse than others. It could be because I overdid it the day before or, like today, my shoulder was extra sore just because it's Wednesday. I've learned to live with it."

I've learned to manage it, but I can't remember my joints not hurting or moving a little too freely. I've lost count of how many dislocations I've had. I bruise easily and my wounds take time to heal. Some days, I'm so dizzy I can't function. It's not uncommon for me to feel nauseous, and on the worst days, the fatigue is so deep I can't get out of bed. I used to think of my body as a prison. I know now that had a lot to do with the kid gloves my mother and all the aides and helpers around her treated me with. Even my dad was careful with me.

I'm so tired of being careful.

Maybe that's what propelled me to The Black Dragon that night and then into Kage's Bronco. Not the idea of revenge sex, but freedom.

He doesn't ask anything further, just continues to rub my ankles with his calloused hands. It feels like a wall has temporarily been lowered between us, so I decide to try my luck.

"Why don't you like hospitals?"

He doesn't answer right away, and I'm starting to think he won't when he finally speaks.

"My mom died in a hospital."

My heart aches for him with that simple but significant admission. "I'm sorry," I offer.

"No need to be. Not like there's anything to be done about it."

If I wasn't so heavily weighed down by the pill Bradley gave me, I'd push myself upright and hug him. I wonder when the last time someone hugged him—really, truly hugged him—was. He doesn't strike me as the kind of guy that gives or receives a lot of affection.

Yet, he's massaging my ankles.

And fetching me peanut butter for my Oreos.

I do the next best thing I can think of in my addled state and offer him something I hold close to my chest. A hurt for hurt.

"My dad died," I tell him as my eyes flutter closed. On

the TV, a group of friends watch over closed-circuit cameras as the couple reunites.

"I know," he says softly.

"They say it was an accident." My words are slurring. "That he had a heart attack while driving and crashed his car."

"I know," he says again.

"I don't think it was an accident."

It's the last thing I say before I fall into a deep sleep. When I wake up hours later, I'm alone, in my bed, with no idea how I got there.

And I swear my sheets smell faintly like sandalwood and leather.

10

KAGE

My head swims as I take in still more information.

Ehlers-Danlos syndrome is complicated. From what I've gathered, it's a group of inherited disorders affecting connective tissue. People with the diagnosis usually have overly flexible joints and stretchy, fragile skin. There's a more severe form of it that involves the vascular system and is, in sum, fucking terrifying. I don't think Lyla has that form of EDS, but I'm not sure. I'm not going to ask, and I'm not going to snoop through her medical records, even though I could have that information within a half hour if I wanted to. I might have Will tailing her, a top tier security system monitoring her house, and her location shared to my phone thanks to Bradley, but going through her medical records feels wrong, even for me.

That fact that I'm researching EDS "for the good of the job" is the lie I'm currently telling myself. If she's susceptible to dislocations, tears, aches, and pains, I need to know—in case I need to extract her from a situation, or if another incident like last night's self-defense class happens on my watch. My research has nothing to do with the desperate need I had to take away her pain last night.

I can lie with the best of them, especially to myself.

"Yo!" Luke bursts through my condo's door with his usual lack of knocking. I, once again, regret giving him the code to my keypad lock. I should change it, but someone needs to be able to access this place besides me. Just in case. "Where have you been today?"

"Working," I answer as I click on another link to another medical journal. I've been googling EDS on and off for hours now, starting last night in the hospital.

"You weren't at the gym." He's in my fridge now, going through it like he lives here.

"I had to go to the Manhattan office—do my part to keep the peace."

"Who did you piss off?" he asks. He opens the lid on a Tupperware container, sees it's full of leftover roasted Brussels sprouts, grimaces, and puts it back.

"Would you like that list in alphabetical or chronological order?" I counter. It suffices to say my presence was felt at Kensington Enterprises today. Buzzard is most definitely not my biggest fan, and he's moved himself up on my list of people to deal with for purely existing.

"Good day at the office, then," Luke says. He takes out a container of strawberries, looks at it like it offended him, and puts it back.

"Why are you here?" I question.

"You have food," he answers, as I watch him shove aside a head of lettuce to see what's behind it. "Make any noteworthy deals?"

"Stopped one with the Sinclairs," I answer as I skim the article. "They're throwing that solar solution of theirs at anything with money."

"Brynn throw herself at you?" He closes the fridge, sans food, and leans on the counter across from where I'm perched on a stool. He has his phone out and his fingers fly across the screen.

"You know she did." I type in my next search phrase. "She showed up at my office in next to no clothes. I threatened to file a sexual harassment complaint."

"She's not your employee though," Luke says, trying to work out the details on that threat.

"She's not," I admit. "But it did the trick."

"For now," he accurately states. "Whatever you do, don't fuck her again. With your luck, the condom would break."

"The only fucking of Brynn Sinclair I'll be doing is in her fantasies." Luke snorts his amusement. "Where's the food you came here for?"

"I DoorDashed McDonald's," he answers. "You only have healthy shit." He looks at me like he just remembered I'm here. "Did you want something?"

"You and the Adlers keep fast food chains in business," I state. Lyla DoorDashed herself a greasy McDonald's breakfast just this morning while Gabe and Bradley slept off their night shifts. I might have checked the security footage when I got an alert to movement on the property, and got to witness her stepping outside in nothing but an oversized T-shirt to pick up her bag of grease. Not the worst start to my day.

"The economy needs all levels and manners of contribution," he says. I slide off the stool and cross the room to the fridge to retrieve a bottle of water. Luke wolf whistles. "Looking sharp. Ish."

"I had to look the part," I offer.

"You couldn't have added a pop of color?" he asks.

"Maybe get a little crazy and select a navy button down instead of all black?"

"Fuck off," I say as I settle back on the stool. I'm wearing uncomfortable black dress pants and a black button-down that I untucked the moment I walked through my door. I unbuttoned the top three buttons before I ever walked out of Kensington Enterprises. The suit jacket I wore is tossed over the back of my couch. Still wore my boots, though. I can only bend so much.

Sadie meanders out of my bedroom. She side-eyes Luke on her way to the water bowl and outright ignores me. I pick up my phone, tap into the dog camera app, and use it to dispense a treat. It lands right in front of her. She looks at it, looks at me, and then walks back the way she came, the treat untouched. If she could slam my bedroom door, she would.

"What did you do to piss her off?" Luke asks.

"I didn't come home last night," I say without much thought. "Then I was only home long enough to change clothes, and I wouldn't let her go with me today."

"Where were you last night?" he asks, eyes glittering.

No point in lying to him. "The Adlers."

He lifts a thick eyebrow. "The Adlers, huh?"

I know what he's implying, but I refuse to admit he's right—to myself or him. "You know I told Bradley I'd look out for her."

"Yeah, with security cameras, keeping tabs on any potential threats, that sort of thing," he says. "But making up self-defense classes, hauling her off to the ER, spending the night . . ."

"She needs to be able to protect herself," I argue. "She needed to go to the ER, and as the owner of the gym she was in when she was injured, it was my responsibility to take her. Then Bradley gave her some pain meds and asked me to keep an eye on her until he or Gabe got home from their night shifts."

"Right." He nods, skeptical. "I'll give you the self-defense thing. I'll even give you the ER thing, because I'm generous." I snort. "But spending the night? Was that necessary once she was inside and asleep?"

No, it was not.

I don't know what happened last night. I saw Lyla go down and nothing else mattered to me but getting to her. And absolutely no one else, not even Will or Cecily, was going to take her to the ER. The feeling that overtook me was deep and primal and it rocked me. I don't react like that. I don't go full protective asshole. I contain the situation, do what I need to do to make sure everyone is okay, and let everyone involved play their part to get us to the other side. I just move the chess pieces. Not last night, though. Not with Lyla.

Once the adrenaline of getting Lyla to the ER ebbed, it hit me that I was in a fucking *hospital*. I avoid hospitals at all costs. Yet there I was, sitting in a room with Lyla, convinced if I left something would happen to her, all the while trying not to think about losing my mom in another hospital across town. Somehow, Lyla saw that fear. Somehow, she knew I wasn't okay. My mask didn't work on her. My mask *always* works.

I was always going to take her home. I could tell myself I was going to leave once she was settled on the couch, but that would have been yet another lie. I was never going to leave her alone, even if Bradley hadn't asked me to stay— not while she was hurt and woozy on pain meds. The next thing I knew, I was putting peanut butter on Oreos, trading places on the couch so she would be more comfortable, and massaging her ankles in a feeble attempt to relieve some of her pain while reeling at her admission that she's *always* in some degree of pain.

What I didn't need to do was carry her upstairs to her bed; she was perfectly fine on the couch. Still, I carried her upstairs, tucked her in, and then I just kind of—stayed. I lay next to her, on top of the covers, watching the clock and waiting for Bradley or Gabe to come home. Gabe got there first and found me on the couch like a good friend to Bradley thanks to the security cameras that alerted me he was coming.

"She was on pain meds." The best argument I have for last night is the pharmaceuticals. "She was groggy. She could have fallen, gotten hurt." Luke only hums in response and checks his phone. I see a flash of the DoorDash app and know he's checking the status of his food. I seize my opportunity to change the subject. "Anything noteworthy happen at the gym today?"

"Standard day of operation," he reports. "Although, if Will is going to be babysitting Adler, we need to discuss his coaching schedule."

"I need him both places," I admit, already thinking through how to problem-solve the need to have him on Lyla but also coaching classes.

"He can't be everywhere at once," Luke reminds me. "You know that better than anyone."

"I'll figure it out," I say, just like I always do.

"Maybe Theo can pick up a few of the morning classes . . ."

"Theo is already stretched too thin." I shake my head. "I need him at Kensington Enterprises. I think he prefers that over the gym anyway." My cousin and I have a lot of similarities in both mannerism and looks, but we are on exact opposite ends on the spectrum when it comes to our career interests. He likes the wheeling and dealing of the family business—thrives in it. I'm happier coaching and programming workouts at my gym. Not that I get to do much coaching these days. "Scarlett can pick up a few classes if needed."

Luke purses his lips but doesn't argue. "I placed a cleaning supplies order," he says, moving on. "I also met with a rep from an apparel company that wants us to stock their gear in the pro shop. He's supposed to send some samples to try out. Scarlett has the marketing calendar for next month planned out; she's working on some community outreach opportunities for you to sign off on, too."

"Productive day," I comment. *Community outreach.* God, I wish I had more time for that.

"I didn't have your ass there to distract me," he quips, and I chuckle. He does seem to end up in my office when I'm at the gym. I know people look at him and see muscle, brawn, and a good time, but he's the Director of Operations at Kensington Boxing for a reason, and he does one hell of a job. Never mind the other stuff he does for me.

"Anything on the other front?" I ask.

"Nothing." He shakes his head. "Another quiet day."

"That's concerning," I comment.

"Most people would say that no news is good news."

"I don't know if it is in this case," I muse.

"It's not," Luke says with certainty. "Shit is going to hit the fan at some point. I'd like to be as prepared as possible."

"Agreed."

We fall quiet, pondering over what could be ahead.

Luke lets out heavy sigh. "How long are we going to do this, Kage? You've been burning the candle at both ends for a long time. The rest of us are living on tightropes. One wrong move and we're either dead or in prison for the rest of our lives. This, straddling worlds, can't go on forever."

And just like that, the weight I carry on my shoulders feels oppressive.

"You can exit at any time," I remind him. I didn't ask any of them to follow me into this mess. I even tried to insist they didn't get involved. No one listened to me.

"You know I'm not leaving you on your own," he says. "I go where you go. We made that deal a long time ago." He taps his tattoo that looks like mine. I avert my eyes to cover up the swirl of emotions the gesture conjures. I didn't ask them to get tattoos either—another thing they did all on their own. Another thing I don't deserve. "I'm just trying to be realistic. And to maybe remind you that you can have a life outside of all of this."

I don't dare let myself conjure up what any other version of my life could look like. I've walked this tight rope for too long to allow the dream of something else to throw me off balance. "There's still work to do," I say. "I don't quit."

"You don't quit," Luke agrees. "I'll say two more things, then I'll drop this whole uncharacteristically introspective bit." I nod for him to continue. "First of all, do you have a thing for Lyla Adler?"

It's hard to surprise me, but Luke manages it. "Lyla is a job," I state with as much conviction as I can, which isn't much. "Bradley is a friend, and I owe him."

"You sure?" he presses. "I've never seen you like you were last night. You were feral after Lyla went down—total tunnel vision. No one else was going to touch her."

"She's a job," I say again. He has to be exaggerating. I was not *feral*. Concerned, maybe, but not feral.

I expect him to push the subject, but he shakes his head

and moves on. "Second thing: Is everything okay with Theo?"

I frown. "What do you mean?"

"I don't know," he admits. "It just feels like something is off with him."

"I had lunch with him today," I say. "He seems fine."

"Yeah, he does." Luke sighs. "I don't know, Kage. It's just a vibe I get. Like he's got something going on that he's not talking about."

"He's the one that wants to be involved in this the least," I remind him. "He does it because of our family."

Because of me.

If I'm not careful, the guilt I feel for Theo being dragged into this mess has the power to pull me under. He never wanted any of this—neither of us did. He wanted a career in finance, a quiet family life. At least he has the career part, even if he risks his life each day he steps into Kensington Enterprises. It's my job to protect him as much as I can from getting in over his head.

"I'll keep an eye on him," Luke determines, and I make a mental note to do the same. His phone chimes and his eyes light up like a kid on Christmas. "Food's here!" He practically bolts for the door. No one is more motivated by food than Luke Cross. He opens my door and startles backward. "Fuck, Craven!"

Will chuckles from where he stands on the other side, poised to knock. I can tell he's going out based on how he's dressed—clean jeans, a well-fitting button-down, freshly shaven, hair combed into submission.

"What happened, Cross?" he asks. "Worried I was one of your one-night stands come home to roost?"

"Fuck off," he says, which only makes Will chuckle

again. Even I let a corner of my lips turn up. Luke does love the ladies.

"I'm on my way out," Will says to me. "Just wanted to drop this off." He holds up a flash drive, then discards it on a table by the door.

"Thanks, Will." I nod.

"Where are you going?" Luke asks as he looks Will over. "This is like the third time in all the years I've known you that I've seen you not in athletic clothes." He leans in and sniffs. "Is that an entire bottle of cologne?"

"I'm going to dinner with Lyla," he says as he bats Luke away. I sit up straighter.

"Dinner with Lyla," Luke repeats. He leans against the doorframe, arms crossed, his food forgotten as he stands there looking between me and Will with an amused grin that makes me hate him. "Interesting."

"And her friends," Will clarifies. "Got an invite and everything. No hiding in corners this time."

"Keep an eye on her," I say as I try to ignore the foreign feeling trying to claw its way out of my chest. "Bradley only gave her two doses of that pain medicine, but she could still be groggy."

"She's fine," Will says. "We got coffee earlier. She's pissed about the sling, but otherwise fine."

That foreign feeling—I think people call it jealousy— breaks through. I *hate* the idea of Will getting coffee with Lyla.

"Coffee, huh?" Luke asks, egging things on. I have half a mind to cancel his food. I could do it. I once hacked into my building's security system just in case I ever needed to lock this place up tight. Getting rid of a food delivery driver would take seconds. "Really taking your assignment seriously, aren't you, Craven?"

"It's easier if we're friends," he says, oblivious to what he's walked into.

"And harder if and when this comes crashing down," I remind him. Because I'm certain of that. This thing will crash down around us eventually. The only question is who will be left standing in the rubble.

"I'll worry about that if and when it comes," he says as he checks the time on his smartwatch. "I should get going. I'm meeting Lyla so we can go together to meet up with the others."

"What are you doing for dinner, Kage?" Luke asks me with a shit-eating grin.

Forget it. I'm not going to bother canceling his food. I'm going to break his jaw so he'll have to take all of his meals through a straw for the foreseeable future.

"I'll figure it out. But a homeless person on the street is about to have McDonald's," I warn. He laughs and leaves without another word. Will looks amused. I motion at the flash drive. "Thanks for that."

"No problem," he says as he reaches for the knob to close the door on his way out. "It was easier to get than I thought. I'm no Luke at hacking into things, but I'm not half bad." He gives me a nod. "I'll text later, report in tomorrow."

The door is almost closed behind him when I speak. "Will." He stops, opens the door enough to look back at me with a questioning raise of his eyebrow. I shouldn't say it, but I'm going to. I *have* to. "You can't date her."

"I know," he says with a single nod. "Don't worry, Kage." He gives me a knowing smile.

"She's all yours."

"That's not—"

The door clicks shut behind him. I huff out an annoyed breath and decide I've had enough of screens, button-downs, and people. I change into something comfortable, attempt to make up with Sadie who wants no part of it, and cook myself dinner—my usual chicken breast and vegetables. I try to turn my mind off, to be normal and veg out on my couch with some shitty TV show or other, but I can't. I'm not wired that way. I huff out an annoyed breath and get my laptop. Sadie, who has at least come out of the bedroom now but still refuses to join me on the couch, watches me with a look that may as well say "told you so."

It takes less than five minutes for me to break the encryption on the files Will downloaded and find what I'm looking for. Or rather, to confirm what I suspected.

Lyla has a friend at the National Archives helping her look into her father's death.

And her mother's involvement in it.

11

KAGE

I don't see Lyla for a week. I have no need to. Will is doing his job, and I'm doing mine. I check the cameras a few times, just to make sure all is well at Bradley's, and I confirmed that she got to and from work on her first day with no issue, but that's it. Now it's Wednesday, self-defense night, and even though she's still in a sling, she's here, sitting on a bench to observe. I make myself busy for the first half hour doing shit that Luke normally does and that he'll bitch at me for doing later because I've messed up his system or something, but whatever. I own this place, and I can order more cleaning supplies if I want to.

Now, here I am, taking a seat next to her, unable to resist her draw. She's wearing leggings and a sweatshirt, and her hair falls over her shoulder in her usual braid. She looks bored.

"Adler," I greet.

"Kensington," she replies, never looking away from the demonstration Will is in the middle of. "Haven't seen you around this week."

"Miss me?" I ask.

"Not in the slightest."

I let that slight go.

"How's the shoulder?"

"Fine, if you ask me. As delicate as a tissue paper, if you ask Bradley."

"It's somewhere in the middle then," I muse. "Good. Come with me." I stand and don't give her any choice but to follow. She, of course, does not follow. I stop and turn to face her expectantly.

"Where are we going?" she questions.

"On an adventure." Her eyes narrow in defiance. God, *why* do I find that so attractive? "My office," I relent. "I want to show you something."

"Something you can't bring down here?" she questions.

"Are you being difficult for a reason, or just because you like to piss me off?" I ask.

"If I'm pissing you off by asking perfectly reasonable questions, then the second one," she states. I sigh out a long breath.

"Just come with me, Lyla."

She hesitates, but she stands. Little does she know, she's been my biggest source of stress this week, and not just because I'm trying to tamp down an absolute need to press her up against the nearest surface and have my way with her. That need is hormonal and I'm a grown-ass man—I can control my hormones. This is about the fact that she's digging into her father's death on the sly. Except, she's not nearly as stealthy as she thinks she is. Her friend is downright reckless. The thing I'm unclear on is if she remembers telling me she doesn't think her father's death was an accident the night she dislocated her shoulder.

I lead her out of the gym and to my office. I open the

door and hold it for her, getting a whiff of her perfume—lavender, I think—as she passes, and it does nothing to stave off the physical want I have for her. I move to shut the door.

"Leave that open," she states, and I lift an eyebrow.

"Why?"

"You and I can't be trusted alone in small spaces."

Well, fuck me. She delivers the line with absolute seriousness. So, I do what I do best and cover up how it affects me with sarcasm. "Worried you can't keep your hands off me?"

"Evidence shows I have more self-control than you," she volleys back.

I scoff at the idea. I am nothing if not controlled, though she has a point. It was me who walked over to her at the bar. Me who touched her first. Me who got her into my Bronco. Me who took a few beats too long to put her down when I caught her falling off the counter. Me who claimed her as mine at the vintage market.

It was definitely me who kissed her in Bradley's kitchen.

It was absolutely me who massaged her ankles, carried her upstairs, and laid next to her while she slept last week.

I leave the door open.

Then, I go behind my desk and jiggle the mouse to wake my computer up.

"Who is this?" Lyla asks.

I glance around the monitor to find that Sadie has decided to make her presence known. I don't even know where she was. She wanders around the gym, doing whatever she pleases, and returns to my side periodically like she's checking up on me. I suspect she uses me for lodging and food and nothing more.

"That's Sadie," I tell Lyla. "She hates everyone but me."

Sadie approaches Lyla and I watch, not sure what's

about to happen. She doesn't approach people, ever. To my surprise, she sniffs Lyla and then damn if she doesn't allow Lyla exactly one pat to the head before she turns and meanders out the door. That's a glowing approval from Sadie.

"So," Lyla says, eyes on me, "what's this whole office visit for?"

"I found something you might be interested in." I turn my computer monitor so she can see the screen. I watch as those hazel eyes of hers narrow in interest.

"That's an article about my dad."

I nod, careful as I watch her features for any clue as to what she's thinking.

"Why do you have it?"

The logical next question and one I anticipated.

"Bradley was bitching about one of your mom's policies." A half-truth. Bradley is always bitching about his mother's policies. He might be the only one of us that actually cares about politics, despite our involvement in them. "I googled it to learn more. One click led to another, and I found this." Again, not entirely untrue. I google Veronica Adler—and cover my digital tracks—on a regular basis. "You mentioned him the other night—sounded like you missed him. I wasn't sure if you'd seen this article, so I saved it to show you."

Lyla leans in to read the first few sentences. "I've read this one," she confirms. I figured she had, I just needed a means to an end. "His college alumni magazine wrote it about his work in the National Archives. He was a brilliant archivist. He believed in preserving history accurately so we can learn from it and not repeat it." Her eyes shift to me. "I mentioned him?"

"You mentioned that he died." Again, not a lie, I just don't add what she said afterward. She shakes her head dismissively.

"Pain killers make me so loopy," she says.

She doesn't remember.

She could be lying, of course, but I don't think she's that good of a liar. Meanwhile, I have something else up my sleeve.

"Next thing." I stand up and indicate she should follow me. I'm shocked when she does. "No protests this time?"

"Probably best we get out of this small space," she says. I grind my jaw to keep from saying something that gives away exactly where my thoughts have gone.

We step back into the gym, and I make my way over to the weight area, Lyla trailing behind me. Scarlett glares daggers at me as I approach. I give her a warning look that only minutely softens her features. "Lyla, this is Scarlett," I introduce. "Scarlett, meet Bradley's sister. Scarlett will be training you."

"Training me?" Lyla asks. "In what?"

"Strength training," Scarlett clarifies. I note the absolute lack of pleasantries. I expected that from Scarlett. She's been pissed at me all day for assigning her Lyla as a client. "You need to get stronger."

"I don't *need* to do anything," she informs us—mostly me. "Thank you for the offer, Scarlett, but it won't be necessary."

"I didn't offer, and sounds good to me," Scarlett snips.

"I talked to Bradley," I explain. "Strengthening your muscles will have a positive impact on your joints. He agrees it's a good idea."

Lyla is not happy. I see it in the way her eyes flash.

"So, you and my brother have been making decisions for me?" she demands. "You two put your heads together and determined what I'll be doing in my now-limited free time?

It's because of you two that I'm even taking this stupid self-defense class!"

"Which you're not even attending at the moment," Scarlett supplies, unhelpful as ever. I focus on Lyla, and I see the error of my way with sudden clarity. Of course she's pissed at me.

"Scarlett, give us a minute?" I ask. She rolls her eyes and stomps off. I give Lyla my full attention. "I'm sorry. I realize it sounds like Bradley and I are telling you what to do." She only looks at me, waiting for me to say more. "I suppose, in a way, we are."

"You absolutely are," she interjects. I purse my lips to remain patient.

"You don't like being told what to do, or having your choices taken," I continue. "I've deduced that based on a few things you've said." She nods. "I was curious, so I did some research. I saw a few things that said strength training could help with EDS symptoms. I asked Bradley and he confirmed it would be a good idea. I apologize for telling you what to do, but my intentions were good. As someone who doesn't apologize, this is a pretty big moment, so please, accept it."

She studies me, and while I wait for the verdict, I consider the fact that I just apologized. And meant it. I don't apologize for my actions. I make decisions and I stand by them. Yet here I am, apologizing. To Lyla.

"You googled Ehlers-Danlos syndrome?" she asks.

"Like I said, I was curious. You said you hurt in some way most of the time and, I don't know, I thought strength training would help."

"That's . . ." She pauses, searching for the right word. "Sweet."

"I'm not sweet, Lyla." It's a warning as much as a fact.

"Don't get confused about who I am just because I googled something."

Her gaze stays steady. I can see the gears turning in that mind of hers and I wonder what she's thinking—if she'll even tell me, because I'm certainly not the only one with secrets now.

"I'll consider the weight training," she relents. "Once my sling is off."

"Deal," I agree. "The one thing I'll insist on is that you let me or Will give you private self-defense lessons once you're cleared. You're going to miss at least a few weeks."

"Fine," she agrees. "But only because Cecily has been demonstrating her new skills on Ollie and Sam all week and it looks like fun." My lips threaten to twitch into a smile. "Anything else? Or am I free to return to observing?"

"One more thing." I take out my wallet and find the card I slipped in there earlier. I offer it to her, and she takes it with the care of someone trying not to detonate a bomb. She reads the front. It's the gym's general business card with the main phone number and email on it. "Turn it over." She does. My messy scrawl greets her. "That's my personal cell. Hang on to that. Call or text if you need anything."

She does that *studying thing* again and it unnerves me. It's like she's calculating something, putting pieces together I'm not privy to. Then she gives me a single nod and slips the card into the sleeve of her sling. She leaves me standing among the free weights to cross the gym and settle back on her bench.

I spend the next half hour doing absolutely anything I can think of to stay busy and not think about things like how my dog let Lyla pet her, or how good Lyla's ass looks in her leggings.

Will dismisses the group, and they disperse. He locks

eyes with me across the gym, and I give him a subtle nod that he returns. Then he disappears into the locker room, while I head to the parking lot.

I hang in the shadows as I watch Lyla tell her friends goodbye. They go their separate ways, Cecily right toward where she lives a few blocks away, Sam and Ollie across the street to take the subway to their own shared apartment two stops away. Lyla goes left, toward Bradley and Gabe's brown-stone. I hate that she walks all over Park Slope, but here I am, making sure she gets home okay because Will has a FaceTime call scheduled with his sister and I won't make him miss that.

I let her get a decent head start before I step out to follow her. Except, I'm not the only one that comes of hiding. Three men emerge from behind vehicles and start in the same direction.

I don't let them get far.

I stoop down and pick up a small pebble. I take aim, and throw, hitting the middle one square on the neck. He stops, turns, and doesn't look all that surprised to find me.

"Kensington," he greets.

"I believe I've told you you're not allowed on my proper-ty." I gesture at the two men that flank him. "That extends to the company you keep."

"You'll have to forgive my trespassing," Clint Ballard replies. "The company *you* keep is too valuable to ignore."

"I told you not to touch what's mine," I remind him.

"Lyla Adler is yours?" Clint taunts. "Interesting."

"You have about ten seconds to get the fuck out here," I warn. "Then all bets are off."

"You're rather bold for someone who is all on his own out here," the one on the left says—Jonathan something or other. His last name isn't worth remembering.

"It's three against one," the other one, I think his name is Tyler, echoes. "Your odds aren't good."

"Three against three." Luke appears on my left from out of nowhere.

"I'm not surprised you can't count," Theo says, stepping up on my right. "Never struck me as the intelligent type."

"You know her worth, Kensington," Ballard says in a shit effort to negotiate with me. He's nothing if not an absolute pushover when the stakes heighten. Even if our numbers are even, he knows he's outmatched. "Our boss wants her for leverage. Don't worry, we'll keep her alive." He smirks. "She's worth less if she's dead."

Everything in me wants to rip him limb from limb. Instead, I keep my head about me.

"Theo, make sure she gets home okay."

He hesitates. I don't take my eyes off Ballard, but I turn my head enough that Theo knows I'm talking to him. I give him a single nod that tells him I've got this. He blows out a breath, but he returns that nod and sets off at a jog.

"Last chance," I tell them once he's out of sight. "Get the fuck out of here, or risk not living to see sunrise."

"You think people are afraid of you," Ballard taunts. "You may have half the NYPD in your pocket and more money than God, but actions have a way of catching up with you all the same."

He doesn't have time to register what I'm doing before my throwing knife is out of my boot and sailing through the air. It lands exactly where I want it to—in Jonathan's shoulder. He howls in pain. Next to me, Luke has his own knives out. Both of us are excellent shots, but we prefer a knife. It's more personal, and if I'm forced to use a weapon, I want them to know me personally before all is said and done.

"The fuck, Kensington?" Clint bellows as Tyler lunges to help Jonathan.

"That's your warning shot." I casually toss a second knife end over end, catching it by the handle with practiced ease. "My next will be a kill shot. And this knife has your name all over it."

"I say we take care of them," Luke says. "Been nothing but a pain in our asses for years."

"What will it be?" I ask Clint. "You going to head home, or are you going to bleed out in my parking lot?"

"I fucking love using the power washer," Luke comments. "So cathartic, watching all that dirt and grime and blood wash away. Come on, Clinty Boy. Give me a reason to use it."

"Might be doing you a favor," I say. "Your boss won't be happy when you come home empty-handed."

Jonathan whimpers next to him.

"He needs a doctor," Tyler says, a note of panic in his tone. "It's close to an artery. If he tries to pull it out himself . . ."

He'll die. That's the point. He currently has a choice.

"You're going to meet your maker," Clint promises me as he signals for his two goons to follow him. "I hope like hell I'm there to see it when it happens."

"Tell Perrin to keep his hands off of Lyla Adler," I reply. "Otherwise, I'll draw his last breath myself. And I won't even attempt to make it look like an accident."

Clint glares at me for a long moment before he backs out of the parking lot while Jonathan stumbles along with Tyler's assistance. He doesn't turn his back on me until he's safely around the corner of the building.

"That was anticlimactic," Luke complains as he tucks his knives into hidden sheaths on his person.

"Perrin is going to be a fucking problem," I reply, mind racing.

"Just how many people want Lyla Adler for ransom or revenge?" Luke asks.

"Perrin and Senator Marshall. The Sinclairs. Potentially Mauricio Cosse, depending on what he's up to." The list is too fucking long. "Can't rule out her own mother."

"And she has no idea?" Luke asks with disbelief.

"None." Something that might be a close cousin of fear clenches in my gut. I don't know if we're doing the right thing by keeping Lyla in the dark about the tangled web she's intricately caught up in. But telling her will wreck her, and I don't want to do that, either. There's something to be said for letting her carry on with her normal life—going to work, hanging out with her friends, exploring her new city. She's happy and I don't want to ruin that if I can help it. "Let's keep it that way. For now."

"For now," he echoes as he tilts his head toward the direction Clint went. "Leave him alive?"

"Stay out of sight." I nod. "Make sure he gets wherever he's going, then double down on the surveillance around him. Tonight was bold. I don't put it past them to get even bolder."

He's gone as quickly and as quietly he appeared.

I stand there for a full minute and focus on centering myself now that the danger has passed. When I feel grounded again, I head back inside and get to work digging even deeper into Doug Perrin. The man has a laundry list of accusations against him from his time in the service. Surely, I can find something strong enough to bring him down, or at least deliver a crippling blow to whatever he's up to with Senator Marshall until I can get rid of him once and for all.

My phone chimes.

I take it out of my pocket little too fast. It's Theo.

Theo: *She's home. Looks like Bradley and Gabe are, too.*

He's included a grainy photo of Lyla letting herself inside. Relief floods my chest. I text him back a thank you and then I open the app that's tied to Bradley's security system. I can control the locks thanks to his keypad situation. All the doors are already locked, but I click the button again to make sure. Just in case.

12

LYLA

"I can't find the files he had in his custody when he died."

I purse my lips as I process Heather's latest update. It's a risk, FaceTiming her on my lunch break while cowering in the corner of an unused conference room, but it's the best option I have between coordinating our schedules and making sure I'm somewhere I won't be overheard by Bradley or Gabe.

"I'm certain it was classified," I say. "Maybe national security reports?"

She shakes her head. "The trail has gone cold."

I sigh and thank her. She promises to keep looking, and we chat for a few more minutes, catching up on one another's lives, before we both need to return to our respective duties. She's taking substantial risks by digging around highly classified and protected material, but I need to know, and she's been my friend since undergrad. She's both the only person I trust to help me find answers, and the only person I know that has access to the kind of documents I'm looking for.

I believe my father was murdered.

The public story is that he was driving home from work on a cold, rainy night after staying late at the office. He was crossing the Potomac River when he had a "Widow Maker" heart attack. According to the autopsy report, he was dead before his car ever veered off the bridge and into the water. I believed that for a while—it's hard not to believe it in the moment. When you go to bed with two parents and wake up with one, you grab onto anything that might make it make sense. But, over time, the pieces didn't add up. There was no reason for him to be at the office so late. He said it all the time: *The good part about working with history is that it isn't going anywhere.*

I mentioned the oddity of the late hours to Deacon who had the gall to suggest my dad was having an affair. I admit there were cracks in my parents' marriage. My mom called Dad the love of her life—she still does—and he adored her. He was always her biggest supporter, the first to make her excuses when she missed yet another school function or recital, and to remind us of how lucky we were to witness a woman do such big things firsthand, but they couldn't hide that they were arguing a lot more. There were a lot of cold shoulders, and evenings spent apart. I had moved in with Deacon by then, but it was hard to miss, given how much time I spent with my dad.

And he was healthy. I know things happen, but he'd just had a physical a few weeks earlier. He bragged about how everything was "A-OK." I have since confirmed it by getting my hands on his medical records to ease the fear that there had been something very wrong with him that he had kept from us. The only thing remotely wrong with my father was his terrible eyesight.

Mom tasked me with cleaning out his office. There were

a dozen photos of us, including one of him and Mom on their wedding day, another of me on my graduation from Georgetown, Alice's from the Air Force Academy, and Bradley's white coat ceremony. I shoved those into a box to avoid the reminder that he was no longer here to celebrate our milestones. He had a lot of notebooks full of his personal notes and observations. There were lots of reminders penciled in, too. "Coffee with Bradley" was in a notebook dated six years ago. "Lyla's immunologist consult" was in one from two years ago, and "FaceTime with Alice" was just a few days before he died.

Then there were the stacks and stacks of papers. My dad was brilliant, but he was messy. I started sorting. Some of it went into a personal pile, things like bills or an article on using Artificial Intelligence in preservation methods. Most if it was work-related—I left those for someone at the Archives to figure out what to do with. But when I opened his desk drawers for one last pass to make sure I didn't miss anything, that's when I saw it, a corner of a piece of paper sticking out from under the bottom drawer. It took me a moment to figure out it was a false bottom and when I did, I had to sit down.

A few dozen copied pages of classified documents were wedged into the three-inch space. They detailed under-the-table foreign trades and dealings, specifically in the energy sector, that would rock alliances and potentially even threaten national security. The more I read, the more convinced I became that my dad had uncovered something dangerous. Something that involved my mom and some of her fellow senators. Their names were right there in black and white.

I didn't know what else to do, so I crammed them in my bag and managed to exit without drawing suspicion. That's a perk of visiting your dad at the National Archives often and interning there—most of the security team knows you, and they only quickly peek into the boxes you're carrying out to make sure you aren't taking anything classified, never bothering with a look into my tote. They don't think, even for a moment, that sweet little Lyla Adler may have damning evidence of wrongdoing by several of our nation's leaders on her person.

That was the beginning of my unraveling. The more I dug into what I found, the clearer it became that my dad was trying to piece together the truth and expose it. I've managed to unearth a few more pieces to the puzzle, but I can't get the full picture, and without the full picture, I have no way of proving anything. What I need right now are the original documents. The photocopied ones are redacted. I need the source of truth before I can go any further, or at least before I can confront my mother.

I finish the day out and leave the office on a high note. It's Friday, the end of my second week, but I feel like I'm finding my feet. I'm getting good feedback and developing good working relationships. I like this whole going-to-work thing so far.

I manage to snag a seat on the subway and pop my earbuds in to zone out to a podcast. It's a short commute by New York standards; I can usually make it door-to-door in forty-five minutes. I meet up with Will after he finishes teaching his classes some days. He waits for me, and we make the trek together. Not today, though. He's at Kensington Boxing all day on Fridays.

I get off at my stop and climb the stairs to the sidewalk. It's unseasonably chilly out, though, and the sun is already setting as the early October days grow shorter and fall makes itself known. I pull my jacket tighter around me as I start to walk the few blocks home. Bradley is on nights this week and Gabe swapped shifts with someone who will owe him at a later date. It's so rare that I have the whole house to myself and I can't wait to put on pajamas and crack open a book to start my weekend.

Something isn't right.

The feeling is sudden and swift. I'm adept at knowing when someone has eyes on me thanks to paparazzi and reporters always trying to catch Senator Adler's daughter out and about. I use my wits, keep my gait steady, and act normal so I don't draw attention to the fact that I know someone is watching me. I scan with my eyes, searching.

Then, I see it.

A black hybrid sedan is a block away, moving too slowly for it to be up to anything good. I maintain my casual pace, but my heartbeat quickens. I know in my very gut that whoever is in that car is up to no good.

I slip my phone out of my bag—a little hard to do one-armed, thanks to the sling I'm still wearing—and pause my podcast. I keep the phone in hand and fumble to open the keypad. I type in *9-1-1* and keep it at the ready, just in case. I glance over my shoulder to see the car has crept closer. I quicken my pace. I just need to make it to the corner, turn right, go two more blocks, and then . . .

Kensington Boxing stands like a beacon on the corner ahead. I know, as much as I know that this hybrid is bad news, that I'll be safe inside. Still, I walk faster. The car picks up more speed.

I break into a half-assed run, my bag heavy and the arm strapped to my chest throwing me off balance. I slip my arm out of the sling and feel the difference having the limb free makes right away.

The hybrid speeds up.

My heartbeat pounds in my ears. I don't pause at the corner to look right or left, just scan as I run for any oncoming traffic. I cross the street. The gym is *right there*— no more than twenty feet away. Tires screech to a halt, doors open, and footsteps pound on the sidewalk. They're coming. Fast.

But I'm faster.

I reach the door, grasp the handle, pull, and—nothing. It doesn't open. I remember then that there's a key fob to get in. They gave all of us one at the first self-defense class. I fumble for my bag, no hope in finding it in time, when the door flies open, and I stumble in.

"The fuck, Adler . . ." Scarlett's eyes blow big. "Shit!" She grabs my good arm, pulls me inside, and slams the door shut just as the two goons reach us. She shouts at someone behind the desk to lock down the gym while shoving me through the reception area and into the gym. It's quiet, save for two people boxing in a ring. Kage and Will.

"Kensington!" Scarlett barks, snagging his attention. He looks our way and his eyes land on me. Even from across the gym, I see confusion fill his features. Scarlett shoves me toward one of the benches around the perimeter. "Stay here," she orders. "Don't move."

I'm too busy trying to catch my breath and figure out what the hell just happened to protest. Scarlett marches up to the ring, speaks to Kage who has already climbed out of the ring, then everyone moves at once. Will catapults over the ropes and takes off for a side door at a sprint. Scarlett does the same, moving toward the door Kage led me through when he took me to his office. Kage comes straight for me.

"What happened?" he demands. "Tell me. Now."

"Someone followed me from the subway stop," I babble.

"A black hybrid. I broke into a run. They sped up and then two people got out. They chased me. Your gym was closer than home, so I did what Will said and ran for safety." I'm too worked up to see the quick flicker of emotion in Kage's eyes at the mention of his gym being safe. "I'm lucky Scarlett was in the lobby because I don't think I would have found my fob to get inside in time. I don't know what they wanted."

He's enraged. Anger fills every pore of his body and his eyes flash dangerously. Yet, when he puts a hand on my injured arm, he's gentle. So gentle it disarms me.

"Are you okay?" His tone, too, is in direct contrast with the anger pulsing from him.

"I am." I nod. "Just shaken up."

"Come on." I follow him without hesitation. I'm safe here. I'm safe with *him*. He leads me to his office. "Sit," he directs. I do so and it's only then that I realize he's shirtless. And sweaty. This is *not* the time for me to notice such things. He bends over his computer, hits a few keys, and turns the screen to me. Several views of security footage from around the gym greet me. "Is this them?" He enlarges one of the screens and I see the hybrid. I'm there, too, the video paused as I remove my arm from my sling.

"That's them," I confirm. He hits play, and we watch together as I run towards the gym. Seeing it makes my stomach churn. The men who get out of the hybrid are large, dressed in black, and while not wearing masks, take measures to obscure their faces. I let out a gasp when I realize just how close they got before Scarlett snatched me inside.

If I thought Kage was angry before, I was wrong. Whatever he is now is rooted far deeper than anger. A muscle in his jaw twitches as he watches the men sprint back to the hybrid. They pour into it, and it takes off out of the frame, but movement in another frame, half hidden behind the enlarged one, catches my attention. It's Will, erupting from a side door. He disappears from the frame in a flat-out run. Kage notices me watching and turns the monitor away. A dozen questions spring to mind, but I don't voice a single one. Not yet.

"You're sure you're okay?" he questions.

"I'm fine," I confirm again.

"Is your brother home?" he continues.

"He's back on nights."

"How about Gabe?"

"He's covering for someone—also working overnight." I can practically see him sorting through information in his brain, but I think we're missing the obvious next step here. "Shouldn't we call the police?"

"It's being taken care of." He pushes off the desk. "Stay here. I'll be right back."

"What do you mean *it's being taken care of*?" I question.

"Just what I said." He motions at my sling hanging around my neck. "Put that back on."

Then he's gone. I scoff at his attitude, but I do maneuver back into my sling.

Something is off, obviously. I was followed and nearly kidnapped and that's not normal, but Kage's reaction—Scarlett and Will's reaction—is not normal. Scarlett seemed to recognize the two guys who were after me. Then she shoved me toward a bench and said "stay here" while she told the other two. To my knowledge, none of them have actually called the police. Will running out the backdoor doesn't track either. Most of all, Kage's anger doesn't add up. I can give him being ticked off that someone would try to kidnap me, but he was ready to burn the world down.

My eyes fall on the computer. I shouldn't . . . but he left me alone . . . I move behind the desk and startle. His dog is there, curled under the desk. She eyes me like she's daring me to follow through.

"Don't tell," I direct her as I wiggle the mouse to wake up the screen which is, of course, locked. I'm not a cybersecurity expert, but I try to break his password anyway. I type in things like his name and "123." I even try his dog's name. It takes longer than I'd like given that I'm typing with one hand, but I bite my lip in concentration and start spelling out "Kensington" to try again.

"Good luck." I jump and find Kage in the doorway. He's wearing a shirt now and that hard edge is there still, but there's a faint glint of amusement in his eyes. "I have the kind of password that makes IT security geeks salivate. You'll never guess it." I glower at him as he moves into the office, picks up my bag, and shoulders it. "Let's go."

"Go where?" I'm getting tired of him ordering me around.

"My place."

His place? Interesting. "Why?"

"I don't want you home alone."

"I'll be fine at my place." I'll lock every door and double check every window, set the alarm system I'm suddenly very grateful for, and not go back out until morning, once Gabe and Bradley are home.

"No." He shakes his head.

"What about the police?" I ask.

"What about them?" he counters.

My God, why is this so hard?

"They'll want to talk to me, seeing as I'm the victim."

He considers me and I'm more convinced than ever that I'm missing something.

"There are no police," he admits after a beat. "I'll explain more when we get to my place."

I make no moves to stand up, and he huffs out one of those exasperated sighs of his. "You'll explain now," I inform him. "What's going on, Kage?"

"You're not going to leave this office until I tell you, are you?" he asks.

"Nope." I pop the "p" and stare him down. "Someone followed and tried to kidnap me. And instead of calling the police you're—I have no idea what you're doing. Now you're trying to drag me to your place. You're hiding something and I'm not moving until you tell me what it is." A stretch of tense silence passes between us. He doesn't move from the doorway; I don't move from the desk chair. Sadie walks to Kage and sits next to him, making it clear whose side she's on. "Well?"

Another exasperated sigh, but I know I've won.

"You may have left D.C., but you're still the senator's daughter," he says. "Bradley noticed a black hybrid hanging around the neighborhood and alerted appropriate authorities. They've been on the lookout. Things escalated today."

I digest that information. It should scare me, and I suppose it does, but my mom has always been in politics, and I've always been a target in some way shape or form because of it. I'm not sold that this is all there is to it.

"And?" I push.

"And what?" he counters.

"Bradley couldn't tell me any of this? And how, exactly, are you involved in it?"

"Bradley didn't want you to worry. And he told me when he found out about the self-defense classes. There's a reason he pushed you into them, Lyla."

I'm not buying this story, but I don't see any cracks to pick at. "Why your place? Why can't I go home?"

"Someone tried to kidnap you off the street today," he reminds me. "You home alone isn't a recipe for safety. You can stay here and wait for your place to be deemed secure—which could be a while—or you can go to my place where there's a television and a fridge full of food."

Curiosity over where he lives gets the better of me. "Fine," I determine as I stand. "I'll go with you to your place. But I want to see the security footage again."

"Fine," he agrees, but he doesn't sound like he likes it or even means it. "I'll pull it for you later." He jerks his head. "Let's go."

I find myself back at the passenger side door of his Bronco. He opens the door for me—I don't know why that surprises me, but it does—and while he lets me climb in under my own power this time, he stays close, a hand hovering in case I need help. He rounds the Bronco, opens his door, then pulls the seat forward to let Sadie into the back. He has to negotiate with her to get in the vehicle, and I deduce that I've taken her usual seat and she's not happy about it. He puts my bag on the back floorboard before he slides behind the wheel and slips on a pair of Ray-Bans. As impractical as the Bronco is in this city, he looks good driving it.

"Why a vintage Bronco?" I ask him as he backs out of his parking spot. "No one really needs a car in this city, but if you had to have one, why not get something practical?"

"I wanted a vintage Bronco," is his answer. It's a half-assed answer and yet it's perfectly Kage. He wanted a vintage Bronco, so he bought a vintage Bronco. End of discussion.

We don't talk as we make the drive to his place. He's lost

in thought and I'm reeling from what just happened. I
expected his place to be nearby, but it's not. We cross the
Brooklyn Bridge, inch through traffic, and finally turn into a
sleek high-rise in the Financial District.

"What?" he asks.

"What?" I counter, turning away from cataloging one
luxury vehicle after another as he winds through the
parking garage to look at him.

"You have that look on your face."

"What look?"

"The 'I'm thinking too hard' look."

"I thought you lived in Brooklyn."

"My gym is in Brooklyn."

"Hence why I thought you lived in Brooklyn."

Why is it so hard for him to have a conversation?

"I live here."

I blow out an exasperated breath.

He pulls into a numbered parking spot, cuts the Bronco's
engine, and turns to me. "What's wrong now?"

"Your tone could use an adjustment, for starters," I
inform him. "In case you've forgotten, I've had a rather shitty
afternoon, what with being nearly kidnapped and all. I'd
planned to go home, put on pajamas, and spend my evening
reading in a quiet house, but nope, can't do that because
apparently, my mom's political ties are still haunting me. I'm
pretty sure you're not telling me the whole story, and I've
just been hauled across the Brooklyn Bridge to a condo
building that belongs to someone who can't answer a simple
question. The literal least you could do is try to be one-
fourth of the asshole you usually are."

Stunned is the only word that can describe Kage's
features. I'm riled up and restless now, though, and the
adrenaline from today is rebounding to once again course

through my veins. I throw open the door, half stumble out of the Bronco, and set off toward what I think is the exit, no idea where I'm going, just determined to move before I completely boil over. I hear Kage utter a curse and get out of the Bronco.

"Lyla, wait." His hand catches my elbow, gentle but firm. I turn to him with a raised, challenging eyebrow. "I'm sorry." He runs his other hand through his already messy hair. "I'm not used to this."

"Not used to what?" I question. "Being a human?"

"Kind of." He shrugs, and there's a sadness there, one that's deep and well-hidden. It softens me some. "I'm used to telling people what to do and they do it. Being personable isn't my strong suit."

"Clearly," I mutter, and I think a corner of his lips twitch in a threat of a smile.

"You've probably figured out I'm, technically, the CEO of Kensington Enterprises." I nod. Good on him for knowing I'd google him. "Headquarters is nearby, which is why I live here. When I was looking for a place to open Kensington Boxing, I couldn't find what I wanted in this part of town, so I opened in Brooklyn. Frankly, I prefer Brooklyn, but here we are."

"Was telling me that so hard?" I ask him.

"You have no idea," he says which makes me chuckle. And just like that, the tension between us dissolves. "Now, are you going to continue your trek to parts unknown, or are you going to go upstairs with me? Please note the choice I'm giving you."

I quirk another smile. He *is* giving me a choice, all things considered. "Fine," I agree.

I'm surprised when he puts a gentle hand on my lower back and steers me back toward the Bronco. He gets my bag and lets Sadie out, then he's back by my side. He touches between my shoulders with his fingertips to point me in the direction of the elevators, and I swear I feel electricity course through me.

We take the elevator to a floor near the top, and step out onto a sleek, modern hallway. He leads me to a door halfway down the hall and types in a code on a keypad to unlock it. He holds it for me, and I enter, but not before Sadie, who keeps moving straight through the condo and disappears into what I assume is a bedroom.

The condo looks like him and entirely not like him at the same time. It has the same ultra-modern look as the hallway—all blacks, greys, and metal accents. It's not espe- cially big—this is New York after all—but the floor-to- ceiling windows along one side and the open floor plan make it look bigger. His view is crap, just more buildings, and the furniture is all black. I wonder if he owns anything that's *not* black. There are no personal effects, nothing that says, "I live here."

It's also impossibly neat. Utilitarian, even.

"Want something to drink?" he asks from the kitchen.

I glance over my shoulder at him. He's scooping protein powder into a plastic shaker bottle. "No, thanks." I shake my head as I watch him. "Why am I not surprised you're one of those guys?"

"One of those guys?" I motion at the protein powder. "I didn't get these muscles by being pretty, Lyla."

I pull myself away from the view of his biceps flexing as he works and continue my exploration. There is one pop of color, and even that is in shades of blue. It's a painting hung on the wall near his massive television. It's abstract, all swirls and whorls, and it's mesmerizing. Beautiful.

Familiar.

I look over my shoulder again. He's watching me as he sips his protein shake.

I point to the painting. "It's your tattoo."

He nods once, his expression hard to read. "My mom painted that." He doesn't give me a chance to ask a follow up question. He picks up a set of keys. "Make yourself at home. There's plenty of food in the fridge, glasses are here"—he points to a cabinet—"and there's coffee in the cabinet over the coffeemaker, since you seem to drink the stuff like water. I'll be back later."

"You're leaving?" I frown.

"Got work to do."

"But . . ." Is he serious right now?

"I'm a small business owner, Lyla," he says. "Work never stops."

"You drove all the way here just to drop me off and drive back?" I clarify.

"I did." He tosses his keys in the air, and the jingle serves to summon Sadie who trots out of the bedroom with an expectant look. He catches them, then picks up his phone. "Bathroom is there." He nods toward a door as his thumb taps across his screen. I hear my phone chime as he pockets his. "I just texted you my number since I doubt you saved it when I gave you my card the other day."

I didn't save it, but I did keep the card. Just in case.

"How did you get my number?" I ask.

"Bradley." He starts towards the door. "Call or text if you need anything."

"I'm going to go through your stuff," I warn him, arms crossed over my chest.

"Go ahead," he says as he pulls the door open. He holds my eyes. "I've got nothing to hide." He's a liar and we both know it. "Be back later."

Then he's gone, Sadie with him. I hear the door lock in his wake.

"Asshole," I mutter under my breath.

Speaking of assholes.

I find my bag where Kage dropped it on the counter, dig out my phone, and rip my brother a new one via text. He calls me between patients, and we have it out. He's worried about me and doesn't understand why I'm pissed at him. I'm mad that he hasn't bothered to tell me anything about a potential threat and I get even madder when he says he didn't tell me to keep me safe. He has to hang up to take care of a trauma patient, but I make sure he knows we will be finishing this argument later.

Then, I go through Kage's things.

His kitchen is spotless. There isn't a single dirty dish in the gleaming sink—not even a fork or glass. His drawers are organized with the precision of a surgical tray and there's even order to his dry goods, which are confined to a single cabinet.

I open the cabinets of the console under where the TV hangs and am unsurprised to find his cable box, Blu-Ray player, and some gaming system that looks like it hasn't been touched in a while neatly organized, their cords corralled. His Blu-Rays and video games are lined up in a row.

I close the cabinet and move on, judging him a little for still owning Blu-Rays, but it seems so *Kage* of him to own physical media.

There's a built-in bookshelf along one wall, but the shelves have knickknacks and trinkets that look like they probably came with the place—all chromatic and coordinating. There's a photo, though. One single picture in a chrome frame. I lean in for a closer look. The woman in it is beautiful. Her long dark hair falls over a shoulder, and she's beaming at the camera. It's an older photo, taken up close, but I think it may be her wedding day. She looks happy.

I'm certain this is Kage's mother.

It tears at my heart that the only personal effects I've found so far are related to her.

I head to the bathroom next. It's small and simple, with a decent-sized glass shower stall. A bottle of two-in-one shampoo, and a bar of soap are the only items on the built-in shelf. Of course, he uses a single, cheap drugstore product and still manages to look like he does. His electric toothbrush is on the small vanity, and his medicine cabinet is practical, just his toothpaste, deodorant, a bottle of ibuprofen, a balm for muscle soreness, and a bottle of Tums. Looks like Kage Kensington has heartburn on occasion. Guess he's not flawless after all. The cabinet underneath is where he stores his extra toilet paper and a small first aid kit. The linen closet is narrow and only contains said linens—uniformly folded white linens.

I hesitate at his bedroom door. I might be taking it too far, but he's seen my bedroom, so I can see his. I push open the door and the contrast between the living room and here is striking. It's still obnoxiously tidy, but there are signs of life here. The large bed is made—unsurprising—but the bedding is a deep blue. A T-shirt is tossed over the end of the bed, and a dog bed is in the corner. There's a book—a biography on some military leader—on his nightstand, and an empty water glass. I almost open the drawers, but I draw the line there. This room feels lived in, and opening his drawers is a step too far.

I return to the living room, settle on the couch, figure out how the TV works, and stop my channel surfing on re-runs of *Married at First Sight*. I'm sinking into the cushions and wondering if Kage has a spare blanket when the door flies open. I spring from the couch and throw the first thing I find toward the intruder. The remote hits Luke Cross square in his broad chest.

"Fuck, Adler!" He rubs his chest. "Glad that wasn't a knife. Would have been a kill shot."

"The hell!" I breathe out. My shoulder twinges in protest of my sudden movement. "You don't just burst into someone's place!"

"I burst into Kage's place all the time." He closes the door, picks up the remote, and returns his attention to me. "What are you doing here? Where's Kage?"

"It's a long story, but in sum, I almost got kidnapped, Kage brought me here, then left under the guise of having work to do."

Luke goes rigid. "You almost got kidnapped?"

"Some guys in a hybrid," I answer. "Something to do with my mom—I don't know. It's all being handled by Kage and my brother and/or the authorities they've had watching Bradley's house. The details are sketchy."

And my annoyance is clear.

"Kage left you here alone?" he clarifies.

"Do you see him around?" I counter.

He continues gazing at me. "Fascinating." I lift an eyebrow at that. He provides no further details, which must be a prerequisite to being friends with Kage. Even Will can be a little vague sometimes and he normally comes across as an open book.

"Did he send you here to babysit me?" I ask, because I wouldn't put it past him.

"He didn't." Luke shakes his head. "Surprisingly." He motions at the fridge. "You hungry? I came over here to raid his fridge."

My stomach reminds me at exactly that moment that it's dinnertime and I haven't eaten.

"I could eat," I decide.

"Let's see what we can forage—because trust me, Adler, we will be foraging. Kage's photo is in the dictionary next to 'health nut.'"

I can't help but grin at that. Luke throws open the double fridge doors and starts listing his findings. "We have three kinds of lettuce. Or something . . . I don't know, it's all green and leafy. There's a bag of raw Brussels sprouts, a crown of broccoli—basically, just assume if it's green, it's in this fridge. Let's see . . . Tomatoes—three sizes. So, big, medium, small. Carrots. Hummus. He has celery. Who eats celery?" I chuckle. "There's eggs, turkey bacon— God forbid he get the good stuff—two chicken breasts, probably what he intends to eat tonight, three flavors of seltzer water . . . Fuck it, there's nothing in here." He closes the doors and opens the freezer drawer below it. "Nothing but frozen bags of vegetables, chicken, and steak." He closes the drawer and turns to me. "How do you feel about takeout?"

"I love takeout," I say. "Takeout is how I feed myself."

"What'll it be?" he asks as he takes out his phone. "Cheeseburgers? Tacos? Chinese? Lady's choice. I'll eat anything Kage doesn't have in his fridge."

Forty-five minutes later, we're on the couch with a large pepperoni pizza, chicken poppers, garlic knots, and cheesy bread, because we couldn't pick. Luke went back to his place, which I now know is across the hall from Kage's, and returned several minutes later with a couple of beers.

"Kage really left you here alone?" he asks as he shovels poppers onto a flimsy paper plate that came with the food delivery.

"He did," I confirm as I load my own paper plate with pizza. "I told him I was going to go through his things."

"Did you?" Luke's eyes are lit up in amusement.

"I'm a woman of my word." Luke almost chokes on a piece of chicken, thanks to the laugh he can't hold back. "I kind of want to pour this beer in a glass, drink it down, and leave it in the sink to give this place some character."

Luke laughs harder. "I like you, Adler," he decides. "He'd shit a brick if he finds out we ate dinner on the couch. He only ever eats at the counter or table. 'Food stays in the kitchen' he says."

"I'm not using a coaster."

Luke howls.

I use dinner to pepper him with questions. I learn he's the Director of Operations at Kensington Boxing, and that he only went to college for a year before deciding it wasn't for him. He's won a few titles as an amateur boxer and was a star wrestler in high school. He was recruited by a few universities, did that one year of college on a wrestling scholarship, and the dislike of the rigors of being a student athlete was one of the reasons he dropped out.

"How did you meet Kage?" I ask, bringing the conversation around to the details I want to know.

"I've known him my whole life," Luke reveals. "Our dads were best friends. It's a good thing Kage and I get along so well, because I don't think we ever had a choice in the matter. He's my best friend. Me, him, and Theo."

"And Will?" I ask.

"He came along later. Brought his little sister along."

"Scarlett?" I continue.

"What's with all the questions, Adler?" he counters.

"I'm just trying to figure out how you're all connected," I say. "I mean, you all have semi-matching tattoos."

"Our parents worked together at Kensington Enterprises," he shares. "They all died in a small plane crash on their way to Nassau. Whit Kensington did this thing where he took his employees on a yearly retreat that doubled as a vacation. Leadership would go down a few days early to do whatever the hell executives do, then their families joined for the vacation part. The plane went down and there were no survivors."

I almost wish I hadn't asked.

"I'm so sorry," I say. "I shouldn't have pried."

"It's fine." He shakes his head. "Shitty things happen to all of us. Some are just more tragic than others." I want to reach over and squeeze his hand or even hug him, but he doesn't strike me as the affectionate type. "Kage got his tattoo a few years before that. Pissed his dad off because he was underage when he did it. After they died, we all got tattoos. They don't match exactly, but are similar. A show of solidarity. We've been our own dysfunctional family ever since."

My smile is small and sad. It's tragic, but there's something beautiful about the way they chose one another.

"Kage told me his tattoo is his mom's painting." I gesture toward it, figuring Luke knows the origin story of Kage's tattoo. Luke gives me a long, curious look.

"He told you that?" I nod. He gives a little shake of his head. "Fascinating."

"That's the second time you've said that tonight," I observe.

"Second time it's warranted being said." He motions to the TV. "Hit rewind. I need the backstory on whatever the hell is going on with these people." It's an end to this particular line of questioning and I don't press any further. He's told me enough.

We fall down the rabbit hole of *Married at First Sight*. I've seen these episodes before, but it's brand new for Luke and he's all in. I didn't think there could be a better partner for watching trash reality shows with than Gabe, but I was wrong. Luke is snarky and judgmental and it's incredible. We're debating whether or not one particular couple stands a change at making it long term when the condo door creaks open. Sadie enters first, followed by Kage. My eyes don't leave Kage.

Something is wrong. He's moving slower, the way one does when their body is sore and tender, a feeling I'm intimately familiar with. We watch him as he makes his way to us. He stops, observes our chaos, and when he tilts his head to consider the food, the TV glow casts light on the damage.

"Kage!" I sit forward and take in his split lip and bruising jaw.

"Damn, man," Luke comments. He's far less concerned than I am—doesn't even sit up from where he has his feet kicked up on Kage's coffee table. "Hope you gave better than you took."

"What happened?" I demand.

"I own a boxing gym," he says. "Busted lips are common."

He's lying. Or at least, not telling the whole truth.

He looks at the garlic knots like they might bite him, but then he reaches for one. I see Luke raise an eyebrow. He's more interested in his friend eating carbs than he is why said friend is beaten and bruised. Kage bites into it and winces when the garlic hits his bloodied lip.

"That needs to be cleaned," I determine.

"It's fine, Lyla."

"It's not, Kage," I counter as I start towards his bathroom.

"Where are you going?" he calls after me.

"To get your first aid kit. Don't worry, I know where it is. I told you I was going to go through your stuff." I can hear the low hum of him and Luke talking as I retrieve the kit and a clean cloth. The TV has been turned off, and Luke is preparing to leave when I return.

"I'll check in tomorrow," he tells Kage. Then he gestures toward me. "Let her clean that up." Kage says nothing, just tenses his jaw. "Lyla, it was a pleasure." Luke gives me a jaunty little bow. "Don't watch another episode without me."

I laugh a little and thank him for the pizza he insisted on paying for. Then he's gone and I'm pulling out a stool for Kage. "Sit."

"I'm fine," he insists. "Not the first time I've busted my lip, won't be the last."

"Sit," I say again, this time with a purposeful point at the stool. It takes him a moment, but he finally moves to sit on the stool, his gaze never leaving mine. I turn the overhead light on to get a better look. His lip is split on the lower left corner, and a bruise is forming on his left jaw. "What happened, Kage?"

"Boxing match," he tries again.

"Kage."

"It was a boxing match," he insists. "I won."

"I don't believe you."

"Your choice." I just shake my head and open the first aid kit. "You and Luke looked cozy."

"We ate pizza and watched trash TV." Is he *jealous*? Ridiculous. I dampen the cloth and step between his legs for better access. I try to ignore the way my heart beats faster at his proximity. "He proved to be good company."

"I had things to do," he says, like he's defending himself for leaving.

"Where did you actually go, Kage?" I try.

"I told you. Work."

I sigh. He's not going to tell me what he was really doing and I'm not going to waste my breath trying to pry it out of him. "Stay still." I place my hand on his uninjured jaw to hold him steady, then lift the cool cloth to the mess that is his bottom lip. He winces. "Sorry," I whisper. "It's dried; I'll try to be gentle."

"You don't have to do this," he says, twitching like it's costing him everything to sit and allow someone else to do something for him. "I can clean up—"

"I'm already doing it."

His eyes meet mine as I work to lift the dried blood. He doesn't look away and neither do I. I swear I could see into his soul if it weren't for how stormy his emotions are. I can't pick apart what I see reflecting back at me, but I try. There is curiosity. Desire. The hum of a spinning mind.

Vulnerability.

I'm learning Kage has tall, reinforced walls around him. He keeps everyone at arm's distance, even those he's closest to. I don't know his story, but I know he's been through a lot. I also know he's cracked a window to show me the man beneath his hard exterior a couple of times, perhaps without meaning to, and there's a chance he's on the verge of doing so again tonight.

"Ow," he says so softly I barely hear it.

"I'm sorry," I say reflexively. "I'm almost done." I finish cleaning the dried blood away and survey the damage. It's not as bad as I initially thought now that it's clean, but it's going to be swollen in the morning. "You need ice." He watches as I navigate his kitchen to cobble together a cold compress. Then, I resume my position between his legs. "This will help with the swelling. You should ice your jaw, too."

The intention was for him to take over and hold the compress to his lip, but neither of us make a move to trade responsibility for it. His hand lifts and settles on my waist with a touch so light I hardly feel it, yet it sets my skin on fire all the same.

"Luke told me about their tattoos," I say in a quiet voice because I feel like I should confess to knowing such an intimate detail about him.

"I didn't ask them to do that," he says with another hint of defensiveness I don't understand.

"I know." My free hand moves on its own accord to brush my fingertips along his sharp, unblemished jaw. My touch makes the muscles tense. "He told me about the plane crash, too."

"He was full of information tonight," he says in that same strained tone.

"I'm sorry," I offer. "I know it's probably meaningless to say, but I am all the same."

He swallows hard and his fingers on my waist go into motion, a gentle brush back and forth, just above my hip. It shouldn't send a wall of heat through me, but it does.

"My mom and Theo's mom didn't die on that plane," he tells me, his voice low and gravel-like. "They died a few years earlier, a block or so from Kensington Enterprises. They were on their way back from lunch and a car jumped the curb—plowed into them on the sidewalk. Theo's mom died on impact. My mom died in the hospital a few days later. I was fifteen."

I don't let the dampness that wants to flow into my eyes come forward. He will take my heartbreak as pity which will make him push me away, and that's not what I want.

"That's horrible," I offer.

"Just as well she died," he says in a detached way. "With her injuries, her quality of life would have been shit."

Like with most things Kage, I think there's something more that he's not sharing. I wisely don't push on this particular bruise.

"Thank you for sharing that with me." His brow furrows in confusion as I move the cold compress from his lip to his jaw. "I know that's not something you usually talk about."

"You seem to have the infuriating ability to make me talk." That makes one corner of my lip turn up. He purses his lips but immediately releases them with a cringe that tells me it didn't feel all that great. "I'm not used to this, either."

"What's 'this'?" I question, just like I had in the parking garage.

"Being taken care of." My heart shatters for him. I don't have the full picture, but I know he's lost both parents and spent some time in foster care before turning around and becoming a foster parent. "Being bossed around—talking."

Talking about hard things, he means.

I know I shouldn't do it, but I can't stop myself. I lean in and press my lips against his—careful, gentle, mindful of where it's split. This kiss isn't passion-filled and fire-fueled like the others we've shared. This is tender. Caring. His hand fists into my shirt at my side and he returns my kiss in the same way. Cautious, maybe even a little hesitant. His hand slides around to my lower back and he pulls me closer. He doesn't deepen the kiss physically—he can't with his lip in its current condition—but it grows deeper all the same. He pulls away, just enough to meet my eyes.

"We can't," he says without conviction.

"I know." I'm still holding the ice to his jaw. "I'm not entirely sure why." I run my opposite hand through his hair and he leans into it. His guard isn't entirely down, but it's down enough that he's letting himself give in to whatever this attraction is between us, at least to a point. "Bradley would get over it. Eventually."

"I'm not good for you." It comes out like a warning. "You shouldn't fall for me."

It's too late for that. I'm not sure exactly when it happened or even how, given the way he antagonizes me and is clearly hiding things, but here we are.

"I think you're better than you think you are." I don't list my reasons, but I've put enough pieces together to know Kage has not only suffered loss but been handed, or else taken, a lot of responsibility for other people. He's holding down jobs as owner of Kensington Boxing and CEO of Kensington Enterprises and his friends love him enough to get tattooed for him. I don't know where this self-deprecation comes from, not when his ego barely fits through the door, but it stems from *somewhere,* and I want to find that place and free him from it.

My hand dances along his jaw again. He leans into this touch as well—practically chases it. He places a messy kiss to my palm as I try to pull away. It's like he's touch-starved and that breaks my heart, too.

"You wouldn't like me if you really knew me," he promises. Still, he leans in and repeats that same soft kiss. "Give me a minute and I'll drive you home."

"It's late," I chance, testing the waters. "You don't want to drive me back to Brooklyn after already making several trips back and forth today . . . and whatever else you did." I can't resist at least a small dig at him for the way he's keeping things from me.

"You'd stay?" he asks, his tone that of someone trying not to hope.

"Could I borrow a shirt to sleep in?" I counter. "I'm still in my work clothes and they're a far cry from the pajamas I planned to spend my evening in."

"I can do that."

I take his hand and guide it to the compress. "Hold this on your lip a little longer and then ice both your lip and your jaw in the morning." He nods and we both pretend like he's going to listen.

"I'll get you a shirt."

He stands and disappears into his bedroom. I repack the first aid kit I didn't actually use and rinse out the washcloth. He returns with a shirt that is, of course, black. I thank him and take it into the bathroom to change. It's a Kensington Boxing T-shirt that falls to mid-thigh and smells like Kage. I decide I'll be keeping it.

I use my finger to half-ass brush my teeth and splash water on my face to wash away some of the light makeup I wore today. When I return to the living room, he's cleaning up the pizza.

"Let me." I collect the empty chicken popper box and the garlic knots while he carries what's left of the pizza and cheesy bread to the kitchen and pretend like I don't notice the way he's doing his damnedest to not stare at me wearing his shirt. He's failing epically. I look at Kage as I start condensing the leftovers into one box while he tosses the trash. "Have you eaten?"

"No . . ." He drums his fingers against the counter, then makes up his mind and reaches for a slice of pizza. "Don't tell Luke I'm eating pizza; he'll never let me live it down."

I reach out and catch his wrist before he can take a bite. "That tomato sauce is going to sting your lip," I warn.

"I'll be careful," he says dryly. He tries to free himself, but I hold on tighter, and he stops fighting. He's fooling no one. He could pull away if he wanted to, he just . . . doesn't want to.

"Let me heat it up for you?"

He relinquishes the pizza but resumes watching me as I go to the cabinet where I found his plates earlier. "Why are you doing this?"

"Doing what?" I ask as I plate a few pieces of pizza for him and throw in a couple of garlic knots and cheesy bread for good measure.

"This." He motions between us. "Cleaning up. Heating up my dinner."

"Because that's what people do," I say and offer no more. It will just make it awkward if I tell him it's because I think it's been a while since he's had someone take care of him.

He eats slowly, mindful of his lip, and I use the time to question him about whatever the hell happened earlier. I get no new information, other than "it's been taken care of" and "the house is secured, but Bradley will be adding additional security tomorrow." I know something more is at play, but I'm not going to figure out what that is tonight.

There's no question about where I'll be sleeping, so I slip into bed on the opposite side of the nightstand with the book and water glass, picking up on context clues that he prefers one side over the other. I hear him come back from taking Sadie out, and he goes into the bathroom, but Sadie trots into the bedroom. She stops short when she sees me.

"Hey girl," I greet. I'm not sure if dogs can roll their eyes or not, but I'm also very sure Sadie does. She goes to her bed and lays down with her back to me. Okay then.

Kage appears in the doorway. He stops in a very similar manner to Sadie, his eyes reflecting the same desire he must see in mine. He's *delicious*, standing there in nothing but a pair of sleep pants slung low on his hips. It's impossible not to notice the "V" that disappears into his waistband.

He clears his throat.

"Need anything?" he asks.

"I'm okay," I reply. "Come to bed."

His steps are slow and measured as he makes his way to his side of the bed, his gaze never leaving mine. He's even deliberate in the way he pulls the blankets back, like everything he has is going into controlling himself. He can't hide the sigh of relief that escapes him when he lays down, though. It's a crack in his armor, one that tells me he's had a really long day. Once he's under the covers, I roll to my side to face him, my sling abandoned, even though my shoulder is sore.

"Sadie doesn't sleep in your bed?"

"Never has," he answers. "She's always preferred her own space." He turns the lamp off to pitch us into darkness, then settles in to mirror me. The bed is more than big enough for both of us to be solidly on our own sides, but there's less than a foot of space between us. Even in the dark, I can feel the hungry way he's looking at me. "You're making this hard, Lyla. Literally."

"You could do something about it," I suggest. "I wouldn't stop you." I really wouldn't. I'd give just about anything to be pinned under him right now.

"We can't." He shakes his head.

"Because I'm Bradley's sister?" The hint of annoyance is undeniable.

"It's on the list," he says as his hand finds my hip. He pushes me gently so I'm on my back and then he's moving closer.

"What else is on the list?" I question as I let him continue to manipulate my position so I'm now on my other, non-injured side, and he's right behind me. His warmth seeps through my shirt as he pulls me against him—big spoon, little spoon. I close my eyes and breathe deeply because this feels so good. So *right*.

"You deserve better," he says. "I won't bring you down with me." I don't know how to reply to that, so I don't. I snuggle closer and his arm around my waist tightens. His actions are a direct contrast to his words. "Sleep, Lyla." His face burrows into my hair as his leg slips between mine. We're a tangle of limbs, and I don't want him to ever let me out of this bed. "I'll take you home tomorrow."

I hear what he's saying. Tonight, he'll let himself tangle around me. Tomorrow, he'll pull away and we'll go back to business as usual. This time, with even more left unsaid between us.

13

KAGE

I study the board, working out my grandfather's next move. By my calculations, he has two options. I think ahead, strategizing what *my* next move will be depending on which move he makes, and then I'm projecting his next move after mine in an effort to remain two steps ahead of him. He picks up one of his white pieces and dots it around the board. It's a third move I didn't see coming.

"Fuck," I mutter under my breath.

A sharp sting lands on my shoulder.

"Language!" my grandmother chides me as she tops off Grandpa's tea glass. He chuckles while I glare at her and rub my shoulder. "More tea?"

"Please." I hold my glass out for her.

"He developed that mouth from your saint of a son," Grandpa tells her.

"Whit didn't talk like a sailor on leave," she says. She has no idea what her precious only son was capable of. And if she does, she chooses to stick her head in the sand about it.

Just like she does with me. "I'm going to see about lunch. You two wrap this up."

She floats out of the room with the kind of refinement that screams "money." Looking at her now, you'd never know she was raised by a single mother and shared a shitty one-bedroom apartment in Queens with three siblings. Or that she met my grandfather at what she calls a "Gentleman's Club" but was really a seedy strip joint, and convinced him to fall madly in love with her. Now, she's the one of the wealthiest women in upstate New York. Good thing for Grandpa, she loves him just as fiercely as he loves her.

"You were thinking several moves ahead, weren't you?" Grandpa asks. My silence is his answer. "That's your problem, Kage. You're always too busy thinking two, three steps ahead to stop and appreciate what's right in front of you."

"I have to be ahead of everyone else," I argue. "If I'm not, lives are on the line."

"When was the last time you were in the moment?" he questions as he watches me consider the board now that he's thrown my plan out the window. "When was the last time you stopped worrying about what comes tomorrow and focused on today?"

Two nights ago, when Lyla was in my condo and then in my bed.

Yesterday morning, when I woke up before her and we were still tangled together, her wrapped in my arms where I knew she was safe. Unlike right now, when I don't have eyes on her and can't quite let myself trust that she's safe with Bradley and Gabe on whatever family day excursion Gabe has dragged them off on. All I know is it's out of the city and if she's out of the city, she's safer than if she's in it. Still, I don't have eyes on her, and unease sits heavy in my stomach. I don't admit any of that to my grandpa, though. I don't even admit it to myself.

"There's too much at stake for me to be in the moment," I say instead. His heavy sigh tells me he disagrees.

"Give me an update," he requests, just as Grandma returns to the room.

"A quick one," she directs. "Lunch will be ready in ten minutes." I vaguely wonder when the last time either of them cooked for themselves was. They've had staff at their beck and call for the last twenty years. I'm not sure Grandma even knows how to wash a dish at this point.

"Theo mentioned the Adler girl was almost kidnapped?" Grandpa prompts.

"When did you talk to Theo?" I question.

"Yesterday," Grandma supplies. "He calls more than you do."

Another point of contention. Theo seems to have forgotten that our grandparents were off on one of their grand adventures when that plane went down. Forgotten that while we were being divided up and sent off to foster care, the one set of living relatives we had couldn't be reached on their African safari or Mediterranean cruise or rainforest excursion or whatever the hell they were doing. By the time they came back on the grid and found out their son's plane went down in the Caribbean, I'd already aged out of foster care, taken in Theo, Will, and Andie, and held the reins to Kensington Enterprises. I haven't forgotten, though. They're lucky I come around at all.

"Let's not get him started on that particular topic," Grandpa says. "The Adler girl?"

"The Sinclairs seemed to think holding her for ransom would make her mother back off of some of her less sustainable policies," I answer. "It was taken care of."

"What did you do?" Grandma asks with more than a little trepidation.

"There were no bodies to hide if that's what you're asking." Her relief is palpable.

"You sent them a message, I presume?" Grandpa asks.

"I did. They got in a few swings, but I sent them back to their boss, worse for the wear."

"That explains the split lip, then," Grandma frets. I ignore her.

"Senator Marshall and Doug Perrin seem to be focused on their campaign," I continue. "Senator Adler is pretty much guaranteed another term. We know the Sinclairs are solely focused on pushing their solar solution through. The wildcard is Adler's aide, Cosse. He's up to something and fuck if I can figure it out."

"Language!" Grandma chastises again. Again, I ignore her.

"He's still Veronica's right-hand man?" Grandpa asks.

"In theory," I confirm. "He's been taking meetings with an awful lot of pharmaceutical lobbyists lately. Best we've been able to find out is that he's either working on something for Veronica to roll out once she's officially re-elected, or he's cooking up his own scheme. I have eyes on his son, too, but so far, all I've found out about him is that he's a privileged former frat star whose daddy got him a job he didn't earn."

And that he treated Lyla like shit, but I don't offer up that piece of info.

"Don't be so judgmental," Grandma says. "You're rather privileged yourself."

"We have a very different definition of privileged," I tell her. "I'd give up the money, and I'd sure as hell walk away from Kensington Enterprises tomorrow if I could."

"You don't mean that," she says.

I just sigh. I can't get upset with her. Her intentions are good. She really thinks that this lifestyle, the money, the big job title, the family name, is what is best for me and Theo. If I had a choice, though, I'd have my boxing gym, a quiet place in Brooklyn, and a lot less stress. Hell, I might even ask Lyla on a—No. There's no use thinking about what could have been.

"How does the Adler girl fit into all of this?" Grandpa asks.

"Bradley asked me to look out for her. Clearly, he was right to do so, given that she was damn near kidnapped."

On the outside, I look unbothered. On the inside, I'm still seething. Only Will's presence kept me from killing the men who tried to take her. I also had to stew on the fact that my first inclination was not to go after them myself, it was to go to *her*. Make sure *she* was okay. Get *her* to safety. I made sure Will and Scarlett were on their tasks, loaded Lyla into my Bronco, and drove her to my place where I knew she was secure before I lit out of there to meet Will who had single-handedly apprehended the assholes sent by Brynn and Sydney's uncle to take her and, with Scarlett's help, was holding them at the gym for me to deal with.

And then I raced back to my condo, desperate to see with my own eyes that Lyla was still safe, even though Luke had texted that he was with her.

"Is she the bargaining piece everyone seems to think she is?" Grandpa wonders. "Veronica has never seemed to care much about her youngest."

"That's the thing," I say. "I'm not sure."

On the surface, Veronica is an absent parent. But I have a feeling that, deep down, she has maternal instincts to rival any mama bear in the wild. If nothing else, someone taking

Lyla for political gain would up Veronica's profile. There would be a whole media circus as she worked to get her daughter back and inevitably pressed charges against whichever of her many rivals ended up being the responsible party. She would use it to her advantage—pad her polling numbers even more.

Or she would say *fuck it* and let them keep Lyla. I'm not willing to risk Lyla to find out what Veronica would do.

"Focus your attention where it's most needed, Kage," Grandpa advises. "The girl isn't your priority."

I purse my lips even though it pulls at my healing split. He's not wrong. If I were to sit with my list of priorities, protecting Lyla shouldn't be at the top of them. I have people for that. Hell, I've made it Will's main objective. Except, I'm the one that's constantly stepping in. I don't trust anyone else with her, and I can't stand the idea of anyone even thinking about hurting her—another thing I don't let myself wonder about. The list of things I'm ignoring is getting longer and longer and they all seem to tie back to Lyla.

Their latest house manager calls us to lunch, saving me from a response, and I start counting down to when I can make my excuses to get the hell out of here as I sit down. It's going to be at least another hour, probably longer. Grandma makes every meal a production and I hate it.

"We're leaving for our winter home on Wednesday," Grandma says as she pours a stream of dressing over her salad. "You'll check in on the place from time to time?"

"I always do." One more thing pawned off on me. "You're leaving early this year."

They are as cliché as they come, leaving upstate New York every winter for the warmth of Florida. They have a sprawling estate in a quaint beach town, set up in a way that ensures everyone knows the Kensingtons have money. I've been there twice. I hated it both times.

"There's a hurricane predicted to hit the coast," Grandpa says. "We're going to get out ahead of it."

I've heard mention of this so-called super storm on the news. It's following almost the exact same path as Hurricane Sandy did years earlier. I'm not worried about it yet—it's still several days out and things change—but the city is starting to pulse with a low sense of nervousness.

"You recognize the irony that you're fleeing to Florida to avoid a hurricane," I say.

"It's not lost on us," Grandpa agrees. "You and Theo should take precautions as well."

"We'll be fine," I tell them. We always are, no thanks to them.

I'm hovering, waiting for the house manager to finish packing up leftovers for me to take back to the city at my grandma's insistence, when Grandma corners me. She does it with all the stealth disguised as grace in the world, using the guise of preparing a tray of her and Grandpa's afternoon coffee and cookies to make sure she has me to herself.

"Tell me, Kage, are you seeing anyone?" she asks as she works.

Fucking hell. I was so close to getting out of here without this coming up. "No, Grandma, I'm not." The same answer I always give in the same uninterested tone I always use.

"It's been a while since you ended your engagement," she continues. "Is Brynn still trying to get you back?"

"Trying. Failing."

"Don't fall for it," she advises. "I never liked that girl. Snake in the grass, that one." She pours the coffee someone else brewed into a tankard of a mug for Grandpa and a dainty cup for herself. "You sure you aren't seeing anyone?"

"If you're looking for a wedding to plan or great grand-children to spoil, Theo is your better bet," I inform her.

"Are you interested in the Adler girl?"

"Fucking Theo," I mutter under my breath, certain he said something to them.

"I knew it!" She lights up. "No need to blame your cousin, although I certainly asked him about his love life and yours. You would both like me to believe you're monks, wouldn't you?" I glare at her. "Theo didn't need to tell me a thing. It was all over your face when your grandfather told you the girl isn't your priority."

"I'm doing her brother a favor," I say. "That's it."

"What would you owe Bradley Adler a favor for?" she asks.

"That's not important," I say a little too quickly. "Also, he's my friend. Friends help each other out."

"So, the girl—"

"Lyla," I correct automatically, which is my mistake because it only fuels her fire.

"Lyla," she repeats. "That's a lovely name. What's she like?"

"She's a pain in my ass," I state.

"Oh good, you need that." Grandma nods in approval. "You need a woman who will call you out on your stuff, because you have plenty of it." I give her a dirty look she ignores. "I assume Theo has met her? You should bring her around for dinner. Of course, we'll be in Florida until spring, but you could bring her up before we leave later this week. Oh! Bring her down to Florida! It's been so long since you were at the Florida compound . . ."

At the word "compound," I decide I've heard enough.

"I need to get going," I say just as the house manager puts a bag on the counter for me to take. I nod my thanks.

It's not her fault I'm in a bad mood now. "I have work to do."

"It's Sunday," Grandma tries. "Stay for dinner! We're having surf and turf—"

"Can't." I shake my head. Or rather, I won't. "Too much to do." I've already told Grandpa goodbye, so I gather my leftovers and head for the door, Grandma on my heels.

"Really, Kage, come visit us in Florida. You and Theo. Bring Lyla, too."

"Grandma, I don't have time for a vacation." There's no point in telling her there's nothing between Lyla and me. "Running the gym and being CEO of the family business doesn't leave me a lot of time for anything, let alone jetting off to Florida for a weekend visit."

She stops next to my Bronco and considers me. I wait for her to reprimand me for parking in the front of the house rather than around back or in the garage where cars are meant to go. Instead, she lets out a sigh that makes her seem older than she is.

"You don't have to live like this, Kage." The way she says it grabs at my chest. She antagonizes me, gets under my skin, and I'm mad as hell at her for letting Theo and I down, but I know she cares. "You can walk away from this vigilante justice thing you're involved in. All of you can."

"I can't." I shake my head. "I have to see this through."

"Then at least stop pushing this Lyla away," she continues, like she has any idea as to what I'm navigating when it comes to Lyla Adler. "If you think she can make you happy, it's worth leaning into what could be."

"I couldn't even if I wanted to," I tell her. "She's Bradley's sister." I open my driver's side door. Sadie sits up from where she's been perched in my passenger seat, ready to go, since I let her outside an hour ago. The look she gives me says "finally." I feel that to my very bone. I drop my leftovers in the back and slide behind the wheel. Grandma, of course, moves in so I can't shut the door and drive off.

"There is never a good time to fall in love," she tells me wisely. I frown. Maybe I can sort of admit that there's something between Lyla and I, but it sure as hell isn't love. "I was a barely legal kid dancing for tips, and your grandfather was a twenty-year-old college dropout a month behind on rent when we met. Your mom was the granddaughter of the CEO of a company who tried to steal Kensington Enterprises out from under us when your dad saw her across the lobby and fell head over heels. Grandpa was furious when he found out the two had been seeing each other, but they got married, had you"—she pats my knee fondly—"and built a beautiful life together. So much so her grandfather left her the controlling shares of their company and his blessing to fold it into Kensington Enterprises when he died. She was the love of your father's life. You could have that, too, Kage, if you'd allow yourself to."

I don't say anything; I don't know what to say. She's not wrong about our family history. I'll do a lot of things, but I won't argue with her on the fact that my mom was the love of my dad's life. He never recovered from losing her.

"Be careful, okay?" Her concern is genuine. "I worry about you and Theo." She shakes her head. "I couldn't stand to bury another one of my babies."

It's a knife to the gut. The threat to life is very, very real given what we're doing. We've been lucky so far, but our luck is bound to run out. Losing either of us would destroy her. She barely made it through losing my dad so soon after my mom and aunt died.

"Send us a text when you get home," she directs, shifting the subject in that graceful way of hers that tells me she doesn't want to dwell on the thought of me or Theo coming home in a body bag. "Tell Luke to enjoy the leftovers because I'm certain he'll be the one that eats them. Tell him to come see me soon, too. It's been too long. We're Facebook friends, though. Did you know that? I send him messages, and he replies."

I smile at that. Luke has always been a third grandson to her. I give her a one-armed hug, and then she's strolling back to the house and I'm taking my phone out of the inside pocket of my jacket to queue up the podcast I was listening to on the way up here. I have several texts, and I skim them before I shift into drive. The group chat I have with Theo, Luke, Will, and Scarlett is as unhinged as ever, so much so that I don't bother to read through it. It's all trash talk about fantasy football, Scarlett calling everyone a pig, and the occasional rib at me for being MIA like I usually am when they go off like this. Luke texted to inform me I'm now out of milk, peanut butter, and the "tasteless-but-okay-if-you-add-enough-sugar" cereal. Theo wants me to check my Kensington Enterprises email for some report and a meeting request to talk about fourth quarter hiring. Andie has sent me and Will yet another photo of her surfing.

I also have a text from Lyla.

Her texting is a new thing. She started yesterday afternoon, not finished being pissed off at me for being vague about the kidnapping attempt as I drove her back to Brooklyn. She then lit into both Bradley and I for keeping her in the dark about the black hybrid lurking in the neighborhood the moment she walked through the door of their brownstone, demanding answers, all fierce and beautiful. She can really dig in when she's mad, and while Bradley had to stay there and take her wrath, I didn't. I left and she let me know her thoughts about that via text. She'd be even more pissed off if she knew how amusing I found her temper.

Lyla: I'm still pissed at you.

I grin at that.

Me: Unsurprised. How's family day?

Lyla: Gabe took us hiking. Bradley hates it so best day ever.

I chuckle at that. Before I can reply, she sends a photo. It's of her, Gabe, and Bradley at some scenic overlook, the backdrop a picturesque fall landscape. Gabe looks like he has never had a better day, Bradley has only managed a half-grimace—not a nature lover, that one—and Lyla is beautiful. She's wearing leggings and a fitted jacket, hiking boots on her feet, that hair of hers in a braid. She's not wearing a stitch of makeup and she's absolutely beaming.

Fuck, I want her.

And I can't have her.

Me: Bradley looks miserable.

Lyla: Like I said, best day ever.

Me: You really are the annoying little sister, aren't you?

Lyla: I'm very good at it.

I chuckle again. I should put this Bronco in drive and point it back toward the city, but I stare at my screen instead, debating on what to say back. She spares me again with another text.

Lyla: Gabe said strength training might be beneficial. I'll think about working with Scarlett.

I scowl and my fingers fly across the keyboard.

Me: So Gabe says exactly what your brother and I both said, and suddenly it's a good idea?

Lyla: Look at you, catching on.

Me: Next week, Monday, six o'clock. Be there or don't. Your choice.

Lyla: I'll think about it.

I make myself put my phone away and finally get on the road. I head to Theo's building a few blocks from mine once I'm back in the city. I park in the garage—perks of Kensington Enterprises owning the building—and head up to Theo's floor. I tap out the rhythm we used to knock out on each other's doors when we were kids to let the other know who was there out of habit, then key in his code to open his door. He's camped out on the couch with a bag of chips and a family-sized bag of peanut M&Ms, football on the TV.

"Hey," he greets, one eye on the TV.

"Hey," I reply as my eyes sweep his space. His condo practically vibrates with him. Where mine is surgically clean, his is borderline messy. There are dishes in the sink and an empty takeout carton from the Chinese place down the street on the counter even though his trash can is *right there*. A jacket is tossed over the back of one barstool, a sweatshirt draped over another. His gym bag is by the door, open, clothes and wraps spilling out, and the messenger bag he carries back and forth to Kensington Enterprises is on the floor next to the couch, his laptop on the coffee table, his iPad on top of it. "Did you fire your housekeeper?"

"She came two days ago," he says. "You're about to break out in hives, aren't you?" I roll my eyes. I've always been obsessively neat. It helps me think. I move yet another sweatshirt out of the way before I sit on an armchair.

"Have you left that couch this weekend?"

"Went out last night." His cheeky little grin tells me he did not finish the night alone. He's far more discreet than Luke about his hookups, but he's not a lonely guy overall. "I've only left this couch to meet the saint who delivered a hangover breakfast today." He motions to the TV. "I'm kicking Luke's ass all over fantasy this week, by the way."

I haven't checked my team. I'm not even sure who I'm

playing. I've been a little busy these last few days. "I visited the grandparents today."

"You drove up to Kensington Manor?"

"Took one for the team," I quip. "Heard you chatted with them yesterday."

"I try to call them once a week," Theo says. "They're getting older."

"You told Grandpa about the kidnapping attempt."

"He asked for an update on the Sinclairs." He picks up his remote and mutes the football game. "Was I not supposed to mention that?"

"He doesn't agree that protecting Lyla should be a priority." Understanding dawns on Theo's features.

"You disagree."

"What else did you tell them?" I ask, plowing right past what he's implying.

"If you're asking if I told them about you declaring that Lyla Adler was the best sex you've ever had, no, I didn't. I haven't breathed a word about that to anyone." He looks at me. "Although I do think you'd do just about anything to have her again." The look I level on him is murderous. He grins. "You're into her, Kage. Don't deny it."

"There's nothing between us," I say with no conviction whatsoever. "I'm doing Bradley a favor."

"A favor that involves enlisting half the people we know." I open my mouth to explain my reasoning, but he holds up his hand to stop me. "I get it. She's the bargaining piece an awful lot of people want and she's innocent in all of this. I'm not questioning your decision to protect her—I even agree with it. What I am questioning is why you never tap me in."

Leave it to Theo to catch me off guard. I was hoping he hadn't realized I'm asking him to do the bare minimum when it comes to Lyla—and most everything else I'm involved in, too.

"You have a lot going on. Let's not pretend you aren't the one holding Kensington Enterprises together."

"You're trying to protect me," Theo accurately calls me out. "I don't need you to protect me, Kage. I'm aware of what I'm involved in, and I'm more than capable of taking care of myself." He holds my eyes. "You made sure of that."

He's right, on all accounts. He's only a year younger than me and is entirely capable of taking care of himself, thanks to years of training with me, but he's *Theo,* and I don't want him to have any part in the worst of this if I can help it. Yet here he is, pissed that I'm leaving him out, which might explain what Luke was worried about. My best shot with him is honesty.

"I don't want you involved in this." He opens his mouth to argue and it's me holding my hand up to silence him this time. "I realize you are involved. It's just . . ." I sigh out my defeat. "You're the only family I have, Theo. It's one thing to have you doing recon. It's another to send you out to take care of a threat. The only thing worse than you ending up in prison because of something I asked you to do is you ending up dead."

"Again, I can handle myself," he says. "You're basically my brother, Kage. I want to help you." He holds up his tattooed arm. "I got this for you."

It's suddenly hard to swallow. Theo was the first to get a tattoo. Luke saw it and was off to get his own, then Will, Scarlett, and even Andie followed. But it was *Theo* who did it first. *Theo* who declared he was with me, no matter what. I search for something to say, but he fills the space.

"You don't have to protect everyone all the time, Kage."

"Is this some kind of intervention?" I ask. "Because Grandma had a similar narrative."

"She did?" I only look at him. "It's just a coincidence," he promises. "Although, I suppose if we're both telling you to calm the fuck down, there is some merit to it."

"I'm doing what has to be done," I say, like I always do.

"Then I'll remind you that you don't have to do it alone."

We're at an impasse. He's not going to back down, and I'm not known for being agreeable.

"I won't have you kill for me," I tell him.

"I will if I have to," he counters, utterly serious.

"I'll take it under advisement."

He rolls his eyes and digs into his M&Ms.

"Tell me about this report you want me to look at." I change the subject.

And he's off, talking about balance sheets, profit margins, cash flow. I understand it, so I can follow him well enough. But he loves this stuff while I have to tolerate it. This is what he should be doing—running numbers, controlling budgets, making smart investments. He shouldn't be trying to avenge our family's name. He shouldn't be trying to keep Lyla safe. Lyla shouldn't *need* to be kept safe. We're all in a situation none of us deserve to be in.

I'm at home a few hours later, in my bed, ready for another shitty night of sleep, when my phone lights up with another text from Lyla.

Lyla: *Slightly less mad at you but still not happy.*

I full on smile.

Me: *An improvement, then.*

Lyla: *I'll do that training thing. Bradley cleared my shoulder after I sought a second opinion.*

My smile grows. What she means is Gabe cleared her shoulder.

Me: Tomorrow, 6pm?

Lyla: Is that a question mark? You're actually asking?

Me: I'm confirming, I counter.

Lyla: Make it 6:30?

Me: Are you being difficult because you can be?

Lyla: Possibly. It seems to annoy you.

I chuckle again.

Me: People generally do what I say.

I send another text right after it.

Me: Then there's you.

I wait, watching my screen, and wonder what the fuck I'm doing. I'm not the guy that texts women. I don't even text my friends back half the time. One of the many issues between Brynn and me was my inability to be responsive to her incessant texts. Yet here I am, watching my phone to see if Lyla texts back. The gray dots that say she's typing appear. Disappear. Appear again. I'm so irritated with myself for watching the screen like this that I want to throw my phone across the room. Five full minutes go by before she finally graces me with a response.

Lyla: So, 6:30?

All this waiting and watching fucking *bubbles,* and this is what she sends back?

Me: 6:30.

❧

THE NEXT DAY, I'm in my office at the gym when Luke appears.

"Can I get your company credit card?" he asks. "I need to order stock for the pro shop, and I left my card at home." I take my wallet out of my back pocket, find the card, and pass it to him. "Thanks." He slips it into his own pocket. "You're not getting this back."

"You can't take my card," I point out.

"Just did," he quips as he lowers himself onto one of my chairs. "You're cut off from ordering cleaning supplies. We can build a fort with all the boxes of disinfectant wipes alone." I have no doubt that if I go into the back room where supplies are kept, there is already a fort.

"You realize I'm the account holder, right? I can cancel that card and request a new one with a couple taps of a button."

"At least it'll slow down this new, anxious cleaning-supply-ordering tick you've developed." He leans back in the chair, apparently intending to stay awhile, which tracks. He only ever sticks around my office when I have shit to do. "So, are we going to talk about it?"

"Talk about what?"

"The fact that Lyla spent the night at your place."

My mistake for thinking he wouldn't bring that up given that he and Lyla are apparently best friends now. I was just dumb enough to hope he was going to let it go since that was Friday night and now it's Monday afternoon and he hadn't mentioned it.

"It was late." That's all I offer. No need to fuel his fire.

"Okay, since we're not talking about that, how about we talk about the fact that you didn't call me when shit was going down on Friday?"

I swear there must be something in the water around here. Grandma and Theo with their "you don't have to live like this," Theo and Luke with their "you didn't call me." At least Scarlett won't come in here dispensing advice and whining about not getting called into action more often.

That's not her style. I wouldn't put it past her to key my Bronco, however.

"A lot of shit happened in a short amount of time. Will and Scarlett were here—they chased down the Sinclair goons. I got Lyla to safety, then I dealt with them."

"Imagine my surprise when I opened your door and found Lyla Adler on your couch," he says.

"You took it upon yourself to hang out with her." There's more bite in my tone than I mean for there to be, but Luke has commented on Lyla's looks, and he loves women. I don't think he's made a move on her, but, well, if he has, there's not a damn thing I can do about it.

"You're jealous," he calls me out, grinning. "This is fantastic."

"I'm not jealous." I pretend to read my email so he can't see how just saying that makes me grind my jaw.

"You are so fucking jealous," Luke continues, absolute delight in his tone. "Rest assured, bestie, I didn't make a move on her. I happen to value my life."

"Did you just call me bestie?" I ask.

"I did." He nods. "Don't tell Lyla, but I started watching another season of that show she and I were into. A loophole, you see. I told her not to watch another episode without me, but it doesn't count if I watch episodes from a different season without her."

"Your logic is faulty," I tell him.

"My logic is sound," he insists. "Anyway, some of the language seems to have infiltrated my vocabulary. I told Theo I liked his *drip* this morning." I don't bother asking what that is.

"When, exactly, do you plan to watch another episode of trash TV with Lyla?" I ask.

"When are you bringing her over to your place again?"

he counters. I don't answer. "Cool, we're not talking about it, we're not jealous, and we're pretending like Lyla Adler isn't going to be back at your condo anytime soon. Got it. Moving on." He leans forward now, resting his elbows on his knees. "What the hell happened on Friday? The Sinclairs were bold, trying to snatch her in broad daylight like that."

"I've had words with Sydney," I tell him. That was how I spent most of Saturday—involved in a showdown with the Sinclair family's second in command. "Their uncle ordered the attempt. Veronica and her supporters blocked another piece of legislation that would have benefited the Sinclairs and their solar solution. He was pissed and his kneejerk reaction was to try to grab Lyla and hold her for ransom. He didn't have much of a plan, just gave the order. To her credit, Sydney didn't agree with his choices."

"It's just stupid," Luke says. "It was broad daylight."

"They were almost successful," I remind him. "If Scarlett hadn't been in the lobby to let her in, we'd be in a different situation right now."

"You're beating yourself up about that," Luke guesses. I don't confirm which is an answer in and of itself. "She's safe, Kage." We just look at each other.

I know she's safe. I also know I'm going to do everything in my power to make sure she stays that way.

"You have to tell her what's going on," Luke continues. "Fuck what Bradley wants her to know or not know. She's safer if she knows. *You* know that."

I do know that. I've argued with Bradley about it as recently as this morning. Lyla needs to know *something* at this point. I don't want to cause problems with Bradley, but I want Lyla walking around clueless even less, especially when she's digging into her father's death and already dangerously close to finding out at least some of the truth.

"I'll work it out," I say, then decide to confide in Luke. "Lyla knows her dad's death wasn't an accident." His surprise is clear. "At least, she suspects it wasn't an accident. She's got a friend at the D.C. National Archives doing some digging on her behalf. They aren't as stealthy as they think."

"Mirroring her phone?" Luke guesses. I shake my head.

"Didn't need to. She offered up that she didn't think his death was an accident when she was high on pain meds—she doesn't remember telling me. I did my own digging, made a few calls, and figured out what she was doing pretty damn fast."

I'm also not mirroring her phone. I've come close several times over, but I haven't crossed that line. I'm already invading so much of her privacy, and I'm lying to her about so much, at least by omission. Every conversation I have with her is full of selective truths. Letting her have her phone to herself is a risk, but I just don't want to take things that far. I will if I have to, I just desperately don't want to.

"I'm going to guess you haven't told Bradley she's looking into their dad's death?" he asks.

"I haven't," I confirm. "He's a wildcard. He cares almost too much about his sisters. He's overprotective to a fault."

"Pot, meet kettle," Luke mutters under his breath. I ignore that.

"If he finds out, he's going to go nuclear and could fuck up a whole lot," I continue. "We have to play it just right."

"Like everything else we do." He nods.

Will appears in my doorway then, looking nervous.

"What?" I demand. Luke shifts so he can give his full attention to Will.

"I need to tell you something," Will says, eyes on me. "And I really, *really* don't want to."

"Is Lyla okay?" I demand. I shelve wondering why that

was the first and only concern that popped into my head at Will's appearance. My heart is suddenly pounding and dread fills my chest.

"She's fine." Will nods. "Swear it. It's just . . ." He looks like he'd give just about anything for the earth to open up and swallow him whole right then and there.

"Spit it out, Craven," I demand.

Will takes a deep breath.

"Lyla has a date."

14

LYLA

I have a date.

His name is Harrison, and I met him on a dating app. He's the co-founder of a tech start-up, was born and raised in New York, went to college at UCLA, and found his way back to the east coast recently—says he missed the seasons. He's supposedly over six feet tall—Ollie tells me men lie about their height on dating apps—with blond hair and blue eyes. Judging by his photos, he actually is as tall as advertised, towering over everyone in the photos he's posted, and he looks like freaking Prince Charming. It can't hurt to have a drink with him.

I am also absolutely *not* telling Bradley, or Gabe, but only because Gabe would tell Bradley. I'll tell Gabe after, so we can either commiserate about how terrible it was, or enjoy the hell out of looking at his photos and talking about how handsome he is.

I put a little extra effort into my appearance. It's a casual drink at The Black Dragon, chosen because Cecily and Sam are both working and Ollie has sworn he will remain across the bar and not interfere while also promising to assess the situation from afar and be my emergency phone call. We've even worked out a hand signal if it comes to that. I'm wearing jeans, a black sleeveless top—the weather has turned unseasonably warm for mid-October, something about the hurricane tracking up the coast—and I've curled my hair into waves. I'm wearing a little more makeup than usual, too. I'm not nearly as over the top as I was the first night I went to The Black Dragon, but I'm not my usual simple makeup, quick-braid self, either. I'm even wearing heels.

Harrison waits for me outside. He's better looking than advertised and I find myself wondering what, exactly, is in the water around here that produces so many attractive men. One of which I am actively *not* thinking about as I return Harrison's smile and accept the arm he offers to lead me inside once he confirms I am, in fact, "Lyla from the app."

We choose a high table in the back where it's quieter and the lights are dimmer. Harrison pulls out my stool and steadies it as I lift myself onto it. I scope out the scene while he goes to the bar to get us drinks. Ollie is at his usual spot at the far end of the bar, and my usual seat next to him is empty. He catches my eye and gives me an enthusiastic two thumbs up that makes me chuckle. Sam is helping a group near him, and even though he's busy serving shots, he throws me an approving nod. It is, of course, Cecily pouring our drinks. She's less subtle in her approval, fanning herself to indicate Harrison is hot as he's walking away from her.

Harrison is attractive, but he's also kind. He's polite and easy to talk to. He tells me about his job and asks a lot of smart questions about mine. He has two brothers, both younger, although the middle brother died in a sailing accident a few years ago. His youngest brother is my age and is in his final year of Harvard law. They seem close. Their dad is a big shot divorce attorney in Manhattan and thinks Harrison is wasting his talent in tech instead of going into the family business. I get that. My mom is devastated that none of us followed her into politics.

I know within the hour that I want to go out with him again. I see no red flags yet, and I think he's worth getting to know—

I feel Kage before I see him.

I don't know how I know it's him. It's an intuitive kind of knowing that makes my heart quicken and my breath at least feel short even though I'm perfectly normal on the outside.

What in the hell is he doing here?

I casually shift around in my seat like I'm trying to get more comfortable, but I'm really positioning myself so I can confirm it's him.

It is, and he's not alone; Theo and Luke are with him. I watch him go straight for the bar, Theo and Luke following a few steps behind him. Theo glances my way, then does a double take. Luke lights up like the Rockefeller Christmas tree and full-on waves when he spots me. I lift my drink to my lips to hide my amusement before I dutifully turn my back to them.

It's easy to ignore them for a while. Harrison holds my attention, and I don't give Kage the satisfaction of looking his way, even when Harrison leaves me alone at the table to get us a second round. It becomes harder to ignore him as the night goes on, however. He's across the room, but his presence manages to fill the entire bar. I'm not looking at him, but I feel him all around me until I can't ignore him anymore.

I'm aware of what I'm inviting in when I offer to get our third round.

I signal my order to Cecily, then slip onto a stool to wait. Kage does exactly what I thought he would. He's on his feet and next to me within moments.

"Where'd you find the Ken doll?" he asks as he leans on the bar, his forearms folded, his stupid biceps straining at the sleeves of his T-shirt. I'll give him that—he's the brawn to Harrison's bronze. Harrison is built like a runner, tall and lean. Kage is built like a fighter.

"He's not a Ken doll," I say. "What are you doing here?"

"He is a Ken doll," Kage insists. "Stick him in a box and he's fucking Ryan Gosling."

"What are you doing here?" I repeat, my annoyance clear.

"I wanted a beer after work. That's a thing people do. It's called Happy Hour."

"You never come here," I call him out.

"I come here all the time," he counters.

"No, *I* come here all the time. You haven't been here since . . ."

"Since you found yourself in my Bronco," he finishes with an obnoxious half smirk, his eyes on me. "I've been a little busy lately—haven't had time for drinks with the guys."

"And the night I have a date you magically have free time to go to a bar for a beer?" It can't be a coincidence that he's here, and by my calculations, the only common factor we have who knows about my date is Will. Will, who is suspiciously *not* here. "I've seen the inside of your fridge, Kage. You eat celery and carrots. Beer doesn't fit your macros, or whatever the hell you count."

"I don't count macros, and it's all things in moderation," he states.

"What's up, Lyla?" Luke appears on my other side, wearing an absolute shit-eating grin.

"Hi, Luke," I say, cautious. He's too damn happy.

"How's your date going?" he asks. "Attractive guy. Good job." He offers me a fist to bump. I lift a pointed eyebrow, and he lowers it. "Rude. Where'd you meet him? Can I guess?" He glances over his shoulder at Harrison. "Looks like a grocery store meet-cute—in the produce section, both of you searching for the perfect melon."

My lips twitch as I fight the urge to grin. Luke is such an idiot and yet he's so damn likable. "An app, actually. I had to message first."

"Making the first move." He nods. "Bold. I like it." He looks past me at Kage, and I turn back to look at him too. He looks murderous. Luke chuckles, as carefree as ever. "Good talking to you, Lyla," he says as he pushes off the bar. "I'm going to go catch up with my dear friend Theo. Haven't talked to him in the last two minutes ago, could have a big life update to share."

He's gone as quickly as he appeared. I swear, I think he did that just to mess with Kage.

"What are you up to, Kage?" I demand once we're alone again.

"I'm just getting another beer," he says. "If the bartenders ever make their way over here."

"They're busy," I tell him, my patience with him, and him alone, thin. "You can be patient."

I wait for him to volley back. He doesn't. He just looks at me, contemplative and calculating.

"What do you know about this guy, Lyla?" he questions, softer than I expected, like he might actually be concerned.

"I know enough to know he's not going to kidnap me off the street," I quip. His features darken at my making light of the fact that I was almost kidnapped. Bradley said the authorities confirmed the men who tried to take me have been captured and that it was a ransom thing in hopes of my mom voting on some bill or other in their favor. They wouldn't give him names—said it was classified—but I let it go. It's not the first time I've been the target of one of my mom's rivals, although it's the first time one has been that brazen. I'm fine, and the people who tried to take me are no longer a threat. Let's all move on.

"I'm being serious," he says. "Have you checked this guy's story? How do you know he's not some sadist off the street?"

"I've confirmed he is who he says he is," I state, because I have. I googled him within an inch of his life. So did Cecily and Heather. He is, in fact, exactly who he says he is. It would be impossible for him not to be based on how very on the internet he is, unlike the gym owner brooding next to me. "Why do you care so much?"

"I don't." His casual shrug of a shoulder does nothing to hide his tense jaw or the way his right hand is balled into a tight fist.

"You're jealous," I realize.

"I don't get jealous," he informs me, which only further proves I'm right. "Jealousy is for insecure frat bros. I'm neither insecure nor a frat bro."

"Jealousy is the manifestation of wanting something someone else has," I counter. "You were jealous the night I hung out with Luke, too."

"Slept in my bed that night though, didn't you?" he fires back.

"You're the one who said we can't," I remind him. "You don't get to have it both ways. You want me or you don't."

"You know we can't," he states. "Bradley . . ."

"Would be pissed for a while and then get over it," I cut him off. "You had your chance, Kage, you chose not to take it. I'm not going to sit around and wait for you to change your mind. That's not fair to me. I've spent enough of my life catering to the wants and needs of a man. I'm not doing it again."

He opens his mouth to reply, but Cecily shows up with my drinks. "Everything okay?" she asks, looking between us.

"Everything is fine," I assure her. We exchange a "we'll talk later" look before she drifts away to greet another customer. It's busy tonight, especially for a Tuesday, which is good for their tip drawer. I wrap my hands around our glasses, slip off my stool, and turn to walk away. My muscles protest, though, and I can't stop the wince or the quiet hiss that has Kage reaching for me.

"You're in pain," he observes, his touch light and hot on my elbow.

"No, I'm sore," I correct. "I'm always in pain. There's a difference. This is purely related to your evil friend Scarlett." I try to pull my elbow out of his grip without spilling my drinks. He lets me go and looks vaguely amused, even through the concern etched in his features. "I'm fine."

I walk away, but my muscles protest every step. I'm a whole different kind of sore thanks to my first workout with Scarlett last night. I thought I was going to go in, curl a few light dumbbells, maybe walk on the treadmill, but no. She had me doing squats and deadlifts and lunges and every other tortuous lower body exercise she could think of with more weight than I thought I was capable of lifting. I tried to reason with her, but being reasonable is not one of her personality traits.

I also didn't see Kage. And yet, I knew he was there. I could feel him, much like I can tonight. He was hovering in the shadows—an omnipresence. I'd seen Luke, Theo, and of course, Will. Will and Theo were each coaching a class and Luke was, I assume, working. I didn't ask, but Luke offered up a "Kage is having a shit day" with too much of a grin for it to truly be a bad day. Will had elbowed him, and Theo had looked confused. Their group dynamic is perplexing, and I keep finding myself wanting to lean into it, wanting to know more.

I focus on Harrison.

Tall, handsome, kind, not-an-asshole-that-I-know-of Harrison.

"Tell me more about what it's like to spend your days among historical documents," he prompts, genuinely interested.

I can talk about my job all day, so I dive in, telling him about my job in the special collections department at the New York Public Library. I realize as we talk that Deacon didn't really listen to me. He made appeasing noises and often did something else while I talked, like check his phone or work on his laptop. Harrison maintains eye contact, doesn't touch his phone, asks good questions. It's nice to have someone's full attention.

But I can feel Kage's stare burning into my back. He's stopped being subtle, and while I refuse to do it, I know if I look over my shoulder, I'll find him across the room, at the same corner table he was at *that* night, staring at me. It's *why* he's staring that I can't figure out. He's the one that says we can't do this—whatever *this* is. I know he feels the pull between us. And I know that it's not just Bradley that's stopping him from exploring it. I spent a good part of my weekend stewing on the fact that he says one thing and does another when it comes to me. I even hashed it out with Cecily who is very certain he's into me, but also not willing to commit and therefore not worth my time. Evidence says she's right. He's all "We can't do this," yet he's leaning into my touch and spooning me in bed. Old Lyla might have kept pursuing him, kept trying to chip away at his hard exterior. New Lyla knows her worth, and she deserves more than a man who doesn't want her. If he's not going to make a move, I'm not going to wait around.

Harrison notices Kage—I know he does. His eyes keep flickering past me, and I see his irritation growing. Finally, he sighs and puts down his nearly-empty beer.

"Lyla, I'm sorry, I have to ask, do you know that guy?" He gives a subtle tilt of his head. I finally give in and glance over my shoulder. Sure enough, Kage is eyeing us. He lifts a beer bottle to his lips and quirks an eyebrow at me like he's daring me to say something. I give him the dirtiest look I can muster and pointedly turn back to Harrison.

"He's one of my brother's friends," I tell Harrison. "My brother is overprotective, and apparently, his friends know it."

A half-truth. No need to tell him we had nameless sex in the front seat of his Bronco, I found out he's my brother's friend, and we've been playing a half-assed game of cat and mouse for the last two months.

"He looks like he's going to rip me in half," Harrison observes.

"He won't," I assure him. "Trust me, he's all talk."

It's a burn I wish Kage had heard. Because I actually *do* think Kage would take a swing at Harrison. It's just *me* he's all talk with. Or maybe not talk, since it's gentle touches, soft kisses, aggressive make out sessions in kitchens, and fucking in Bronco front seats with me. God, he's confusing.

We finish our drinks and call it a night. Harrison offers to walk me home and I agree, even though both Bradley and Gabe are home. We part ways on the sidewalk with a hug, a sweet kiss to my cheek, and the promise of a second date. Then he walks off into the night as I climb the steps to the door. I'm admittedly a little paranoid despite the assurances that the guys who tried to nab me are no longer a threat. I glance around, taking in my surroundings as I work to dig my keys out of my bag and reprimand myself for not having them in hand already. Yet another thing women have to think about that men don't.

Movement out of the corner of my eye snags my attention. I look over my shoulder, searching, heart rate increasing.

Kage is standing across the street.

I blink and look again.

There's no one there.

15

LYLA

It's lunchtime the next day when things take a turn. The hurricane that everyone has been watching is headed straight for the Jersey Shore, taking a near-identical path as Hurricane Sandy. It's a few days out, due to make landfall sometime on Saturday, and is bigger and stronger than Sandy, but here we are, on a Wednesday afternoon, with the notice that, as of close of business today, the New York Public Library is closed through at least Monday.

My boss sent us home a little early, but today is one of the days I usually meet up with Will for the commute, so I send him a text that I'm out early, and browse a nearby independent bookstore while I wait for him to finish up his class. I buy four new books—may as well have something to read if I'm stuck inside for the foreseeable future—and he meets me on the sidewalk outside the store. I use the opportunity to confront him.

"Good day at work?" he asks like he always does.

"Did you tell Kage I had a date?" I counter.

"Um . . ." He has the good sense to look guilty.

"Dammit, Will!"

"How was it?" he asks in an effort to keep the peace. "Was it okay?"

"It was great," I answer. "Harrison is wonderful. He walked me home and has already texted me today. I plan to see him again. You can tell Kage that, too."

"I'm sorry." Will sighs. "Luke was giving me a hard time about how much time we spend together. I told him you're just a friend and that you had a date with another guy. Kage overhead, and I'm assuming if you're pissed, he did something last night."

"He showed up at the bar and made his presence known," I inform him. I'm not sure I believe his story, but he also has no reason to lie, and Luke would absolutely give him a hard time about being *just friends* with a woman.

"I guess he wanted to make sure the guy was decent," Will says. "He and Bradley are tight, and Kage has this protective thing going on. He probably thought he was helping out a friend."

His story has holes in it, but I decide to let it go. Will doesn't know Kage and I have a history, and I'm not going to tell him. "In the future, keep that kind of stuff to yourself. Otherwise, I'm going to stop telling you things."

"Deal." Will nods, relieved I'm letting him off the hook.

We talk about the hurricane the rest of the way home, like pretty much everyone else is doing. Will reports that grocery stores are chaotic and that things like bottled water and batteries are hard to find. I wonder if Bradley and Gabe have supplies, or if I should do a food run. Will promises to go with me if I decide to brave the grocery store. I don't. Instead, Bradley and I go out to dinner, and I confess I went on a date, one he already knew about thanks to his stupid cameras. Gabe convinced him not to give me a hard time about it and, I'm told, deemed Harrison a "total hottie."

Thursday starts off great. I sleep in, then wander downstairs for a breakfast of Pop-Tarts and coffee which I have on the back patio while reading my book. I find Bradley and Gabe in the kitchen, both dressed in scrubs, when I return inside for another cup of coffee.

"I was just about to come out and get you," Bradley greets.

"Good morning to you, too, Dad," I say as I pour another cup. The coffee is freshly brewed, and I can tell by the boldness of it that Gabe made it.

"There's a hurricane coming," Bradley starts.

"Is there?" I lean against the counter. "I had no idea." He glares at me, and Gabe chuckles. He doesn't have siblings of his own, and he's endlessly amused by Bradley and my constant bickering. Throw in Alice and Gabe lives his best life.

"Don't be a smartass," Bradley corrects, right on cue. "This is serious."

"Is this Big Dad Energy?" Gabe pipes up with a gesture at Bradley. Bradley shifts his glare to Gabe who only gives him his most dashing smile in return.

"Classic example of it," I confirm. Bradley shakes his head and mutters something that sounds like "fucking sisters" under his breath before he continues.

"I have good news and bad news. The bad news is that Gabe and I are leaving for our respective hospitals soon, and we plan to stay there for the duration of the storm. All-hands-on-deck."

"I'm going to be home alone for a few days?" I ask, all the possibilities of how I'm going to take advantage of that already forming. I'm not too worried about the storm, all things considered. It's going to be bad, but as long I'm inside, I should be fine. "I fail to see how this is bad news."

"Wait for it," Gabe says in a singsong voice.

"The good news," Bradley continues with one of those "not another word from you" looks that could be meant for either me or Gabe, "is that I've arranged for someone to stay with you."

No, he did not.

"Who?" I demand, certain I know the *who* in question, just as the front door opens without so much as a warning knock.

It's like I conjured him up.

In strolls Kage, dressed in his usual uniform of black jeans and a black T-shirt. He looks completely unbothered, and I am very much bothered. The look I give Bradley should be enough to kill a man, but of course he continues to stand tall.

"No." I shake my head. "Absolutely not."

"You shouldn't be alone, Lyla," Bradley says as Kage helps himself to the coffee pot. Gabe looks like Christmas has come early. It's his own reality TV show playing out in front of him. He doesn't know that Kage and I slept together, but he's well-informed on the fact that I spent the night at Kage's. Of course, he thinks Kage slept on the couch. "This storm is going to be bad. We're most likely going to lose power all over the city, and New York without power can be a wild place. There's going to be flooding, wind damage. Kage is going to stay here with you."

"Actually, I'm taking her upstate."

Every head in the room looks at Kage as he casually leans against the counter with his mug.

"Excuse me, what?" I demand.

"You're doing what?" Bradley asks at the same time. Gabe merely leans on the table and props his head up with his hand to take it all in.

"I'm taking her upstate," Kage says again. "To Kensington Manor. It will be safer out of the city. If we lose power, there are generators." He jerks his chin at me. "Pack a bag. We'll leave when you're ready."

I cross my arms and prepare for a fight. "No."

He sighs that dramatic sigh of his and looks to Bradley for help.

"Lyla, he has a point," Bradley tries. "People are trying to get out of the city. You may as well go with him."

"I'm not . . ."

"Your buddy Will is going," Kage pipes up. "So is Theo, Scarlett, and your new BFF Luke. We won't be up there alone if that's what you're worried about."

I consider throwing my coffee at him.

"Why would she be worried about that?" Bradley asks.

Kage shrugs. "She hardly knows me."

"Stop talking about me like I'm not here," I demand as I glare daggers at Kage for all that he's implying right under Bradley's nose. "Where's my phone?"

"Who are you going to call?" Bradley asks as I exit the room in a growing temper. I find my phone in the living room and call Will.

"Hey, Lyla," he answers. "What's up?"

"Are you going to this *Kensington Manor* place?" I demand.

"I am," he confirms. "Waiting for Kage to pick me up. He was going to fetch you first."

"And Theo, Luke, Scarlett—they're all going, too?" I continue.

"They are. You don't sound too excited to be joining us."

"It was sprung on me five minutes ago," I complain. "Bradley called Kage to stay with me and Kage just informed us he's planning to take me upstate."

"Bradley is just looking out for you," Will reasons. "I promise it'll be fun. Think hurricane party but make it a sprawling mansion. Kensington Manor is beautiful. There's plenty of space, a media room, a whole game room in the pool house. If nothing else, there's always a well-stocked bar. Do you really want to be alone in the city during a storm like this?" I don't answer; he has a point. Despite my talk, I'm not positive I *actually* want to be alone during a major hurricane. "Come hang out with us, Lyla. Treat it like a mini vacation."

I stay on the phone with Will for a few more minutes, listening as he continues to talk me into joining them upstate before I hang up and return to the kitchen. It then occurs to me that I'm only wearing my preferred sleeping situation of an oversized T-shirt, but fuck it. It's my brother, his partner, and Kage who has certainly seen less of me. Kage is still leaning on the counter, Bradley is hovering by the toaster waiting on whatever is in it, and Gabe is topping off his travel mug with creamer when I walk back into the kitchen.

"Do we have a verdict?" Gabe asks. Kage and Bradley look at me.

"Will convinced me to go," I inform the group. "I'll go pack a bag, but I won't be rushed while doing it."

"Take your time," Kage says. I give him another dirty look before I leave the room.

I do take my time packing, and I do it out of spite. It's immature and petty, but I don't care. I call Cecily and update her on what's transpired as I pack. She's holing up with her sister, brother-in-law, and nephew, and reports that Sam and Ollie plan to ride it out in their apartment. I contemplate calling to ask if I can crash with them, but she encourages me to go to Kensington Manor—says she's heard rumors that the place is stunning, and someone should see it for themselves.

"Ready?" Kage asks when I come back downstairs half an hour later.

"Sure."

He gives me a look I can't read as he takes my overnight bag and tote and heads out the door.

"Kage Kensington is carrying your bags to his Bronco," Gabe comments, watching him go. "Have mercy, the ass on that man..."

"Gabe," Bradley warns.

"Did I say ass?" Gabe says. "I meant biceps." I grin at him, and he winks at me in response.

"I kind of hate you for this," I say to Bradley. "I'm not a kid who needs to be babysat."

"I know." He sighs. "I do, Lyla. But this storm is going to be bad and after everything that happened on Friday, I need to know you're safe while I'm stuck at the hospital."

I soften a little. He was pretty shaken up by the whole almost-kidnapping thing. He hugged me long and hard when Kage brought me home, even while I was yelling at him, and spent the rest of the day hovering. He even watched *13 Going on 30* with me without complaining. He means well, even if he's going about it all wrong.

"Besides, we are woefully under prepared for this thing," Gabe says. "We have one water bottle in the fridge, Lyla. *One.*"

"I was going to attempt to go to the grocery store today," I offer.

"Now you don't have to." Bradley reaches to hug me. "I didn't know he was going to evacuate up to Kensington Manor, but he's right, it's going to be safer up there, and a hell of a lot more fun than if you were stuck here, especially if the whole group is going."

"Steal a fork," Gabe advises as he joins in on our hug. "The Kensingtons are loaded. One fork will pay off our mortgage."

"You two stay safe too," I say, ignoring Gabe. "Check in when you can?"

"You do the same," Gabe agrees.

"I love you, Lyla," Bradley says, giving me one last squeeze. "Even if you drive me insane."

"I love you, too," I tell him. "Even if you're an overprotective ass."

"Hear, hear!" Gabe chimes in.

Kage is leaning against his Bronco, arms folded over his chest, Ray-Bans on even though it's cloudy out when I step outside. It's so unfair that he's so damn attractive.

"I thought the storm was going to hit before you got out of there," he says.

"In a hurry?" I counter.

"I've got all day." He reaches for the handle and opens the door for me. I give him a cold look but lift myself into his Bronco—Sadie is in the backseat in her usual good mood. Kage closes the door, and then he's rounding the Bronco and sliding behind the steering wheel.

"Why upstate?" I ask. "We'd be perfectly fine in Brooklyn."

"You're the one that said you and I in small spaces isn't a good idea," he says, casting a sideways glance at me as he pulls off the curb. "Your brownstone and my condo? Small spaces."

"Don't worry," I shoot back. "I have no plans to seduce you."

Just like that, the tension between us is so thick I'm surprised I can't see it.

"Trust me, Lyla," he says as he brakes at a stop sign, glances both ways, and continues on, "you don't have to try."

"You can't do that," I inform him. "You can't say stuff like that while also insisting we can't go there. It's an asshole move, and it's not fair to me."

"Fine." He blows out a quiet breath like he's trying to calm himself. I scooch closer to the window to try to put more space between us because damn if I don't want to reach across the console and sooth away his furrowed brow. "How was your date the other night?"

I look at him in disbelief.

"Good?" he prompts when I don't answer. "Terrible? Seeing the Ken doll again? Delete him from your app?"

"Why do you care so much?" I question.

He doesn't answer.

We don't speak again during the ten-minute drive to Will's, who's waiting on the curb, backpack over his shoulder, duffel at his feet. He lives in the same building as Sam and Ollie, a fact we figured out at dinner a couple of weeks ago. I'm tempted to get out and follow through on my idea of crashing with them.

"Hey Lyla, Kage," Will greets as Kage gets out so he can move the driver's seat forward and let him climb into the back with Sadie.

"Hi," I reply. Kage barely manages a slight nod of his head in greeting.

"Glad to see we're all getting along," Will comments.

I snort.

Kage simmers.

Will catches us up on the latest storm updates and I fact-check him as we go with the help of Google. He's right—this storm is going to be rough. I haven't been paying all that much attention to it, relying on secondhand knowledge while I focused my interests elsewhere, but now I'm glad to be getting out of the city. Not that I'll admit that to Kage or Bradley.

The roads out of the city are a parking lot. We sit in place for minutes at a time before inching forward. Will does most of the talking, and Kage remains quiet—contemplative, even. Sadie dutifully looks out the window and ignores us all.

My phone lights up with a text from Will.

Will: Adding you to a group chat. It's me, Luke, Theo, and Scarlett. Kage isn't in it because he's no fun.

I'm added to "Hurricane Crew" a moment later.

Will: Added Lyla.

555-431-1667: Lyla! MAFS! Me and You!

I chuckle and save that contact as Luke.

555-431-2211: No TV until you help me cover the pool.

I can't decide if that's Theo or Scarlett.

Luke: We'll do it later.

555-431-2211: No, now. I sent the staff home. It's on us. Let's go.

Theo, then.

555-205-2564: Cover the pool, then we go to the store. Food supply is lacking.

Scarlett.

It's a flurry of activity with everyone chiming in on what junk food to get and how many pizzas to order for dinner. Scarlett makes a quip about ordering a salad for Kage, and Theo decides we *will* order a family-sized salad—says we need to still have *something* healthy. Luke calls him "Kage Jr.," and Theo replies with a vulgar gif. There's a trading of

Venmos, a flurry of activity as we all Venmo Scarlett, then I send Will a separate text.

Me: Should we ask Kage what he wants?

Will: You can try.

Me: It feels wrong to not include him.

Will: We do it all the time. He probably has his own agenda for this weekend anyway.

I frown at that but decide to do what I think is the only fair thing. "We're ordering pizza for dinner, and the others are making a grocery store run," I tell Kage. "What do you want?"

He doesn't answer.

I take a good look at him. He's in his own world, one hand on the wheel, the other propped on the window, Ray-Bans hiding his eyes.

"Kage?" I prompt. "What do you want?"

He rebounds back to the present. "What?" he asks with a quick glance at me. I repeat my question, curious about where he just disappeared to. "Tell them to make sure we have coffee. Creamer. Stuff for burgers. Some seltzers—doesn't matter what flavor, just get a couple of cases. Some fruit—berries, apples, maybe some oranges." He glances at me again. "And Oreos."

I can't describe the feeling that burns through me at the mention of Oreos. Those are for me. I've already directed them to get a package, and Luke said make it two, plus milk, but Kage is making a point. Or something. Yet again, his actions and his words don't match.

"Got it." I nod, keeping my expression neutral. "Pizza okay? Theo is ordering a salad, too."

"Pizza's fine. Tell Scarlett I'll Venmo her when I stop driving."

"How do you know—"

"It's always Scarlett," he cuts me off. "Luke is too irresponsible with money that isn't directly related to Kensington Boxing, Theo is too responsible with money in all shapes and forms, and Will hates math."

"It's true," Will supplies as I text the group Kage's list, leaving off the Oreos.

We finally make it out of the city and drive for a while until Kage pulls into a travel center for gas. I'm unbuckling my seatbelt before the Bronco is at a complete stop. I have to pee, for one thing, but I secretly love these places—where it feels like you can get every kind of drink or snack your heart desires along with a gas station hot dog or a slice of greasy pizza, never mind all the tacky souvenirs, car fresheners, and cheeky bumper stickers. I round the Bronco and lean against the front fender as Kage inserts his card into the reader. "I'm going to get snacks. Want anything?"

He does that thing where he glances my way again but doesn't let his gaze linger. "I'll be in after I fill the tank," he replies. I huff out my annoyance and pivot on my heel without another word. I catch up with Will who is waiting for me a few paces away.

"What's wrong with him?" I ask.

"You don't know?" he counters.

"Know what?"

Will smiles and shakes his head.

"Know what?" I repeat.

"You unmoor him." He holds the door open for me, and I mutter a "thank you." "It's probably frustrating as hell for you, but it's entertaining to watch for the rest of us."

I try to make sense of what Will means as I go through the motions of using the restroom and washing my hands but come up as empty as I always do about all things Kage.

I'm browsing the candy aisle when Kage joins me.

"You going to eat anything besides sugar this weekend?" he asks.

"I'm going to make a candy salad," I inform him as I add another bag of gummy candy to my basket of junk food. "Perfect hurricane food."

"That's not a thing," he says.

"It's very much a thing." I toss a bag of Twizzlers Nibs in my basket. "My dad used to make it for us—pour all the candy into a bowl, mix with a rubber spatula, enjoy."

"Do you ever eat a vegetable?" he wonders.

"One of tonight's pizzas will have peppers and onions," I quip. He rolls his eyes, but there's the faintest hint of a smile on his lips.

"May as well add these." He takes a bag of sour Skittles from the rack, tosses them in my basket, and walks off. I chuckle, convinced he has a secret sweet tooth he tries to hide. I add two more bags of candy to my eclectic assortment and head for the coffee. I'm trying to figure out how the touchscreen works when a freshly brewed cup appears in front of me, accompanied by the scent of sandalwood and leather.

"I made you a cup," Kage says. "You drink even more coffee than I do—it's paid for. I'll let you add copious amounts of sugar to it."

He walks off before I can say thank you, and I'm more confused than ever.

I add my "copious amount of sugar" to the coffee—he has a point, not that I'll ever admit it—and pay for my candy and snacks. Will walks out with me, and we find Kage leaning against the Bronco's front bumper, sipping his coffee. He pushes off the vehicle when he sees us and opens the passenger door for me.

"See?" Will says just loud enough for me to hear. "Unmoored."

I still have no idea what he means.

The landscape becomes greener as we drive, although the leaves are tipped with the colors of fall. Will and I trade small talk, but Kage continues to remain largely quiet. As we get closer to our destination, the houses grow bigger and further apart. I'm starting to wonder how much longer we're going to drive when Kage slows and turns off the main road onto a secondary road that is even more well-groomed and grand. He drives another couple of miles before turning into a drive.

It's like something out of a movie. The gates are towering and wrought iron. Kage taps in a code on a small box, and they groan open. He passes through and we wind down a long, tree-lined drive before the house comes into view. I barely hold back an audible gasp. It's imposing and beautiful.

The Kensington family's pockets are far deeper than I realized.

A lifted Jeep and a sleek Mercedes coup are parked outside. I guess the Jeep is Luke's and the Benz belongs to Theo.

"Theo might want to move that shiny toy of his into the garage before this storm hits," Will comments as Kage reaches across me to open the glove compartment. His proximity makes me hold my breath. He finds a small remote, hits a button, and then tosses it back in before closing the glove compartment again. I exhale as he drives us into a spacious garage.

"I have the spare garage opener," he tells Will. "Trust me, Theo made sure I brought it with me. He'd park that car in the house if he could." He shuts off the Bronco and opens his door. "Lyla, let Sadie out of the back."

I follow instructions, fumbling for a moment to figure out how the seat folds forward, while Will climbs out of the other side. Sadie jumps out and wanders away without a backward glance, as Kage removes bags from the back. I reach for mine, but he picks it up and heads inside without a word. I have no choice but to follow.

There's chaos upon entry. The others have just returned from the grocery store, and the counters are covered in food waiting to be put away. Theo immediately asks Kage for the garage opener, Luke gives me a bear hug that lifts me off my feet, and Scarlett is demanding help with the groceries. Sadie adds to the noise by barking for the hell of it.

"I'll show you where you're sleeping, Lyla," Kage says. Then he's walking and I'm once more left to follow. He directs Will to fill a water bowl for Sadie, tells Theo the remote is in his Bronco, and to put it back when he's finished, and orders Luke to help Scarlett all before we're out of the kitchen. Even here, he's the one in charge.

The interior of the house is even more stunning. It's all high ceilings and rich fabrics, textures, and colors. It's somehow both over the top and welcoming. The antique sconces that line the hallway Kage leads me down are unnecessary, for example, but I spot a large sofa in a room off said hall that invites me to come in and sit down. It's not the kind of house where things are to be looked at but not used. It's a home. It even *feels* like a home.

"Is this place yours?" I ask, confused about who it belongs to.

"It belongs to my grandparents," he corrects as we climb the stairs. "They left for the Florida version of this place yesterday. They spend winters down there."

I frown. Grandparents? But he was fostered . . .

I don't ask.

The winding staircase dumps us into a wide hallway that stretches away from the landing on both sides. Kage turns right and stops halfway down the hall. "You'll be in here." He opens the door and holds it for me. I glance at him as I slip past. He's as tense and stoic as ever. "I'm across the hall," he continues as he puts my things down just inside the door. "Theo is all the way at the other end of the hall—last door on the left. You have an en suite bathroom." He motions toward a door across the room. "We'll be here for a few days, so get comfortable. Let me or Theo know if you need anything."

Then, he's gone.

I shake my head at his abruptness, freshen up, and return downstairs. Theo offers to give me a tour, and I take him up on it. The house is a maze of rooms, each one well-appointed yet inviting. He takes me outside and shows me the pool house, where I learn Luke, Scarlett, and Will are staying. Then Theo tells me their grandparents remodeled the house for him and Kage when they were teenagers and it shows with all of its navy and leather decor, the pool table, the built-in bar.

We return to the main house and find the others in the media room. Kage is settled on an armchair, his feet propped up, laptop open, working away. His brow is furrowed in concentration, but it's still the most relaxed he's been all day. Will is messing with the TV remote, and Luke and Scarlett are bickering over something—it sounds like fighting just to fight. Kage glances my way, but says nothing as I settle on the couch. Will declares his victory over whatever he was doing, then he and Theo are playing old school Mario Kart and Luke is challenging me to a game of darts.

I put him to shame.

"How?" he demands after I beat him for a third time.

"She's better than you," Scarlett supplies. Luke flips her off.

I chance a smile at Scarlett. She doesn't return it, but she doesn't glare at me either, so I suppose that's progress.

"My turn," Will declares. I beat him, too, then Theo. Scarlett passes on her chance to take me on, and she and Luke dissolve into another argument over whether she's afraid of losing. I'm personally wondering about the ETA of the pizza we're supposed to be having.

"I'll play you."

The room goes silent. Kage, who has been largely quiet and glued to his screen, closes his laptop, puts it aside, and stands, eyes on me. The room charges with challenge as he goes to the board, plucks out all six darts, and comes back to me. He offers me the blue-tipped ones I've been playing with.

"Ladies first."

I stare him down as I take my position, then break eye contact to focus on my throw. My dart sticks less than an inch from the bullseye—not terrible. But then Kage throws and his dart lands a centimeter closer. He turns back to me with that smirk of his.

"Your turn, Lyla."

Game on.

We go back and forth until we reach our final turns. I'm winning, but barely. We've been trading the lead the entire game. The others have placed bets and provided commentary, but they may as well not exist. All I can focus on is the dart in my hand and Kage. He's playing dirty—watching me while I throw, standing a little too close, brushing against me when he goes to retrieve the darts.

I take a deep breath, preparing my final throw, and Kage is suddenly right behind me, so close I can feel his breath on my ear.

"I've already won," he says in a low voice.

"How do you figure?" I ask, all my focus on the board.

"Trust me." His hand subtly wraps around my hip—hidden from view of the others by the position of our bodies—squeezes once, and then he lets it falls away. "I won."

He steps back, and I have to take a breath to steady myself from the dazzling feeling of his existence. Then, I throw my dart.

It lands just shy of the bullseye.

"That'll be hard to beat," I tell him, sure I've got this in the bag. His eyes burn into me as we switch spots.

"I told you. I already won."

He throws the dart without hardly any preparation.

It sticks dead center.

He wins.

Turning to me, he winks.

I want to throw something at him and throw myself at him at the same time.

"Rematch," I state before I do either of those things. "Best of three.

"Maybe tomorrow," he says as he takes his phone out of his pocket and glances at the screen. I see the briefest glimpse of security footage before he puts it back. "Pizza's here."

It's only then that I remember the rest of the crew is still there as their voices infiltrate the space I'd carved out that was just Kage and I. They all move at once to greet the pizza delivery one of them must have scheduled. I intend to follow them, but Kage stops me by grabbing the back of my sweatshirt and pulling me flush against him. His chest is hard against my back.

"You're killing me," he says in my ear.

"How so?" I dare ask.

"Your ass in those leggings." His fingertips brush along the sliver of bare skin my cropped sweatshirt reveals. "I want to peel them off you and learn what it's like to hear you scream my name."

I lean into him and I can feel the outline of him through his jeans. He's hard and he wants me. "But you won't," I challenge him.

"Fuck if I don't want to," he admits before he lets me go. "Let's get dinner."

I have to remind myself to breathe as I follow him to the kitchen for dinner.

I choose a seat between Theo and Will at the table and keep my distance from Kage the rest of the night. He makes it easy though, disappearing to who knows where as soon as he eats a large serving of salad and a couple of slices of pizza. We watch a movie afterward, and while everyone else decides to watch another, I head upstairs to my assigned bedroom to read for a while. I pause outside Kage's door, but the light is off.

He's somewhere in this house, but it's not in his room.

The books take over. I finish my hardback, then start another. I eventually turn off the lights, but I can't fall asleep. I toss and turn for a while before I give up and go downstairs in search of tea.

I round the corner into the kitchen, quickly finding I'm not alone.

"Shit!"

"Fuck!" someone exclaims at the same time. Theo.

"You scared me." I breathe.

"Same," he replies. "I was making a cup of tea. Want one?"

"I came down for something to help me sleep," I admit. "I always have trouble sleeping when I'm somewhere new. It takes me a day or two to settle in."

"The storm is still a day and a half or so out," he tells me. "You'll be sleeping soundly by the time it hits." He opens a drawer. "Grandma is a tea snob. Name it, she probably has it or something close to it."

"Chamomile?" I ask.

"Front and center." He plucks out a bag. "That's what I'm having, too."

I decide to do some digging, if for no other reason than I haven't spent as much time with Theo as I have the others. "Kage said your grandparents are in Florida?"

"They have a house down there," he confirms. "They spend winters there—it's as cliché as it sounds. I usually go down around the holidays, maybe one more time if winter in New York gets to be too much." He puts a mug in front of where I've leaned on the kitchen island and mimics my stance across from me. "Kage talked to you about our grandparents?"

"Just mentioned them in passing."

"Figured as much." There's a hint of sadness to his tone. "His relationship with them is complicated." He purses his lips, just like Kage does, and makes up his mind about something. "Lyla, I think it's only fair that I tell you the truth."

"The truth about what?" I ask cautiously, suddenly on high alert.

"I know about you and Kage."

I'm glad I'm not drinking my tea yet, because I would have spit it all over this counter.

"I saw him leave with you at the bar that night, and the next morning he said something about the best sex he's ever had. When I saw you at Bradley's for our fantasy football draft, I recognized you and put the pieces together."

Best sex he's ever had? I mean, same, but way to stroke my ego. I don't question Theo about exactly what was said though—I don't want to talk details about his cousin fucking me. "You can't—" I start.

"Tell anyone, I know." He nods. "I promise, I'm a vault. No one else knows."

"We don't want Bradley to know," I offer. It's the least complicated of the reasons we're not mentioning our passenger seat romp. Although, if I'm honest, I'm not even clear on what the reasons we aren't mentioning it are at this point.

"He likes you, you know," he tells me.

"He's got a terrible way of showing it," I state, thinking again of how he continuously says one thing and does another. His little display in the media room alone was enough to mess with any woman's head.

"Not surprising." Theo shakes his head. "It's hard for him to let people get close. I think it's even harder for him to get close to people. He's hard to know, but he's worth the effort . . . if you're interested, of course."

I study Theo as I take a sip of my tea. He looks so much like Kage, but he has a softness Kage doesn't. The edges aren't as sharp, the corners not as jagged. His life hasn't been easy either, a fact that probably plays into his buttoned-up maturity, but he hasn't let circumstances pull him apart.

"You two are close," I observe.

"Kage is all I have in a lot of ways," Theo confesses. "He's been the one constant in my life. I owe him everything." He smiles at me. "Including talking him up to the woman he likes since he's so bad at actually showing it."

"He's not bad at showing it," I correct Theo. "He sucks at doing anything about it."

I change the subject by asking Theo about his work and listen as he tells me about what he does at Kensington Enterprises, and how he helps out at the gym when he can. When my tea is gone, I leave him in the kitchen to make himself a late-night snack before he turns in. I return to my room, check the time—it's one-thirty in the morning—and think I'm finally ready to fall asleep.

I'm just getting into bed when there's a knock at my door. I huff, toss the blanket I just pulled over me back, and cross the room to the door, pulling it open.

Kage.

Irritation rises in me, swift and fast. He's screwing with my head, and I'm fucking tired of it. "What do you want?"

His eyes burn into mine.

"You."

16

KAGE

It's reckless, showing up at Lyla's door like this, but my control is shredded. I fucking *need* her. I've done everything I can think of all day and into the evening to fight off the attraction, the desire. I even locked myself in my bathroom and jerked off in the shower like a teenager going through puberty to try and sate my want. It worked for all of ten minutes. Then she walked into the media room and started throwing around darts, and all I could think about was how hot it would be to teach her how to throw knives with that accuracy, and how devastating her ass looked in those leggings. I made myself scarce after dinner and sat in Grandpa's study, attempting to get some work done just as much out of necessity as it was to put space between Lyla and I, but only capable of wondering what kinds of sounds Lyla makes when she has a man's head between her legs.

Fuck, I want to be between her legs.

"What do you want?" she demands, all fierce and beautiful.

"You," I tell her without hesitation. I'm playing with

white hot fire, and I no longer care about getting burned. "I want you."

"What happened to the whole 'we can't'' line?" she questions.

"I came to my senses." A lie. I've lost my goddamn mind. "Tell me I can lay you down and fuck you until you're hoarse from calling my name and your legs no longer work." She just looks at me. "I don't have to lay you down," I babble. Something wild and unbound has taken over and the only thing that will ground me again is losing myself in her. "I can take you against the wall." I nod toward the nearest wall. "I can bend you over that desk." I motion at the desk pushed into a corner. "I can take you to the ground, if that's what you want. I just need to be with you again."

"You're exhausting," she informs me, crossing her arms over her chest which only makes her breasts more pronounced. "All this back-and-forth bullshit—telling me you want me and doing the exact opposite—and now you're here, begging to be let into my bed?"

"I've tried to resist you," I tell her. "You're Bradley's sister, and that's just one of many reasons why we shouldn't do this. But I don't fucking *care* anymore, Lyla. Bradley will get over it and all the other reasons I have just don't seem to matter anymore."

At least they don't at the moment. They will be a problem later, but right now, I'm not thinking straight.

I chance a step toward her. She doesn't back down.

"Theo knows about our night in the Bronco."

"He does. He'll keep it quiet." I brush a few pieces of hair that have escaped her messy braid away from her face. My god, she's beautiful. "Once wasn't enough, Lyla. Fuck, twice in one night wasn't enough. You've flipped some kind of switch in me, and I fucking *need* you." She still says nothing.

I put a hand on her hip and cup her cheek with the other, tilting her head up so I can look into her gorgeous eyes. "I'm right here, Lyla. Next move is yours."

"Define 'here,'" she demands. "Are you here to fuck me? Or are you here for more than an orgasm?"

"I don't know," I admit. My thumb brushes over her cheek as my bravado threatens to waver. "All I know for sure is that I can't stay away from you."

"You showed up at the bar when I was on my date."

I huff out a breath. If she would just say the word, I could give that mind of hers something else to think about besides my previous actions.

"I know Will told you I had a date. How did you know it was at the bar?"

"A lucky guess." A lie. I made Will find out where they were going, and then he refused to come out with us when I decided to oversee the date myself. Luke enthusiastically joined me because he's a dick, and Theo thought he was getting a beer with his friends until we got there. He wasn't happy with me when he realized what I was up to. I pull her closer. "It made sense that you would go somewhere familiar, with your friends nearby, for a first date."

"You admit that you showed up on purpose."

I don't deny it, and her eyes narrow.

"Why, Kage?"

I don't answer.

"Why?" she demands again, this time with less patience.

I slide my arm around her waist to hold her to me. "Because I hate the idea of anyone else's hands on you."

There. The truth. I swore to Theo and Luke that it was to make sure she was safe and the mystery man in question wasn't a threat to her—not a single one of us believed me. I was so worked up by the time she went inside after letting that Ken doll kiss her cheek after he walked her home that I went to the gym and beat the hell out of a punching bag until my arms were too heavy with fatigue to keep going. I've been stewing on the fact that there's another guy who wants my woman ever since. I don't know when she became *my woman*, but she is, dammit.

"And yet, you won't put your hands on me?" she asks.

"I'm trying to put my hands all over you right now," I say. "You're the one keeping our clothes on."

"Because you're the asshole who keeps saying one thing and doing another!"

It dawns on me that this is not going well.

"You don't get to have me when you want me, but *only* when you want me, and you don't get to keep anyone else from having me, either."

"I'm not the good choice, Lyla." I pull the tie holding her braid in place out and unravel the strands with the hand that isn't wrapped around her. She's tense in my arms, but both of her hands are resting on my chest and she's not attempting to get out of my embrace. "I have a storage locker worth of baggage. I'm not the safe choice, but staying away from you is exhausting and I've been absolute shit at it anyway. Let me into your bed tonight. We'll figure out the rest after."

She considers me again, that brilliant mind of hers analyzing my every word. A small, quiet voice that tells me to walk away now and put both my bedroom door and hers between us. Never mind Bradley, if she's involved with me, that makes the target on her back even larger. But if she's with me . . . She's with *me*. And I'd rather die than let anything happen to her. I can't figure out when that particular change in my existence took place, but it did, and I don't see it going anywhere any time soon.

"Next move is yours," I repeat. Everything in me wants to toss her onto the bed and make every single one of the many fantasies I've had about her come to life, but I won't. Not until she gives me the green light. Still, I lean forward in anticipation, ready for her lips to be on mine, just like that first night at The Black Dragon when I put the ball in her court, and she surged forward on her barstool to kiss me.

She pulls back.

"Go to bed, Kage."

Wait . . . What?

"Lyla—"

"Go to bed," she says again, stronger this time, as she steps out of my embrace, and it feels like she took a piece of me with her. "We're not doing this."

"But—"

"No."

Her tone is final, and no is a complete sentence—one I use a lot, but don't especially like when it's directed at me.

"You're serious," I realize.

"I am." She nods. "You don't get to come to my door to scratch an itch. Not after weeks of telling me we can't while you do shit like making sure I have Oreos for the hurricane and holding me while I sleep. You could have acted on whatever this thing is between us at any point, but you chose not to. At least, not until I decided to go on a date. Now that there's a threat of me not being there for you and you're suddenly asking to be let into my bed? *No*, Kage. I deserve more than that. Go to bed."

The flaming desire I felt when I knocked on her door seeps out of me like air from a busted tire, and for, perhaps the first time in my life, I want to turn tail and run out of—

Is this embarrassment I'm feeling?

"Fine," I say, a little edgier than I mean to. "I'll leave. Good night, Lyla."

I all but flee the room.

But my room across the hall is still too damn close to Lyla, so I go downstairs and find myself by the covered pool. I'm tempted to uncover it and take a plunge—anything to take this edge off. Instead, I sink onto a nearby chair and stew on what in the hell just happened.

Lyla rejected me.

I don't like it. It—though I hate admitting it—*hurts.* More than I think it should. So she didn't want to sleep with me. Big deal. So what, I don't get to have sex tonight? It's not the first time I've been shot down. I've made a move, been cockblocked by a best friend or even my own friends, if they think I'm making a mistake. I kind of wish that one of them would have stopped me from walking up to Lyla that night. If I hadn't had her then, maybe we wouldn't be in this mess now.

Except . . .

I think we would be.

I don't know when it happened. I can't pinpoint it, and God knows I've tried. I can't point to the moment where Lyla went from "one night stand in my Bronco" to "woman that I can't stop thinking about" but it happened, and it happened without my knowledge or even my consent. I had no choice in the matter. She's beautiful, sure, but she's so damn smart. Stubborn. Sharp with her tongue, yet soft with her touch. She's kind and caring, fierce and brave. I want to be where she is all of the time.

All of the time.

Fuck, I hate this.

I run my hand through my hair and try to make sense out of all the up, down, and sideways feelings coursing through me. It only serves to agitate me more, so I do the only thing I know to do, which is go to the home gym my grandparents never use and run on the treadmill until my legs are Jell-O. Then, I do what I *never* do—I take a melatonin. I sleep like shit on a good night, and I never take sleep aids, despite probably needing them because what if something goes down and I'm too groggy to respond? I'm banking on the fact that a pending hurricane is going to keep everyone who might stir up shit at bay as I lie down on the couch in my grandpa's office and finally fall into a fitful, Lyla-filled sleep.

17

KAGE

I t's Sadie that wakes me up the next morning. She paws at my face, letting me know her breakfast is late. I push her paw away with a groan, close my eyes again, and give into the sleep that's trying to pull me back under. Or at least try to.

"There you are."

Fucking Luke.

"Go away," I grumble.

"We thought you were dead," he says, ignoring my request to be left alone. "Your bed hadn't been slept in, you weren't in the gym, and your Bronco is in the garage. Figured if you weren't in here, you might actually be dead."

"Considering killing *you* if you don't stop talking," I say, now with my arm over my eyes. He smacks my foot, and I try to kick him and miss. This is why I don't take sleep aids. It's too damn hard for me to wake up. "Get out."

"You're cheerful this morning." He smacks my foot again. "Theo and Lyla are cooking breakfast. We know Theo can cook; jury is out on Adler, but I'm willing to give her a chance."

"She eats Oreos by the sleeve and thinks candy makes a salad," I state. "She can't cook." It's an asinine judgment, but I make it anyway.

Wait.

Lyla.

Last night.

Fuck me.

"Probably not," Luke continues, oblivious to my dilemma. "But our options are limited. Scarlett refuses to cook, which is a cover for the fact that she can't but won't admit it. Will exists on those pre-made meals that get shipped to his door, and we know I keep the New York area DoorDash drivers in business. You and Theo are the only two that for sure know your way around a kitchen. But you're apparently dying on a leather couch that smells like cigar smoke, so here's to hoping Lyla can come through."

Right now, in this moment, I have no idea why I'm friends with him. He's right, though. This couch does smell like Grandpa's cigars.

Sadie bats at me again just as the smoke alarm goes off, followed by a lot of noise as whoever is in the kitchen tries to shut it off. Every breathing being in this house seems to be hell bent on not letting me go back to sleep.

"Want to put money on if it's Lyla or Theo that set that off?" Luke asks. He's across the room now—judging by the clinking of glass, he's at the bar. "My money's on Lyla, but if you want to take a chance on your cousin, I'll give you good odds."

I suck it up, open my eyes, and lift my head to see he's poured a finger of whiskey.

"It's"—I check the time on the ornate grandfather clock—"ten o'clock in the morning." I can't remember the last time I slept past seven. Melatonin and rejection are one hell of a combo.

"On a Friday on the eve of a hurricane," he finishes as the smoke alarm ceases its blaring. "Want a pour?"

I debate the offer. I'm going to have to face Lyla at some point today, and a hit of liquid courage is probably a terrible idea. "Fuck it," I decide as I push myself upright. "May as well."

Luke lifts an eyebrow as I stagger to my feet and make my way to the bar. "You okay, man? The pleasant mood isn't entirely out of character, but you look like shit, and we can almost never get you to join us for a drink after work, let alone before lunch."

"Didn't sleep well," I grumble as I pour a shot of Grandpa's best whiskey. I knock it back and the burn helps jar me out of my stupor. I put the bottle back before I can be tempted by another. I know who I am. I'm an extremist. Everything is controlled, purposeful. Given the mood I'm in right now, if I don't put this bottle back, I'll let that control break and have the breakdown I probably deserve to have, which will involve this bottle of liquor and what's left of my pride.

Sadie barks at me, short and sharp. "I hear you," I tell her. "I'll get your breakfast in a minute." Two sharp barks inform me she wants it right now. I ignore her.

"Why'd you sleep down here?" Luke asks.

"Just did." I offer no more. "Go make sure there's still a kitchen. I'm going upstairs to change. Feed Sadie for me."

I leave him in Grandpa's office, telling Sadie to stop side-eyeing him or he's withholding her breakfast, and go to my room. I can't help but notice Lyla's door is open, her bed made, her books neatly stacked on the nightstand, and an unsettling pang rattles around in my chest. We could have been in that bed together. I could have slept with her in my arms. Maybe then, I would have actually slept.

It's not lost on me how much better I slept the night she stayed at my place.

I do absolutely everything I can think of to avoid going downstairs. Seeing Lyla in the morning light . . . I don't know what's going to happen. With me. With her. And *fuck,* I don't know how to handle it. Once I've showered, tidied my room, checked my email, and even fluffed the stupid throw pillows Grandma insists on keeping on all the beds, I have no choice but to face the masses.

The kitchen is controlled chaos. There's a spread of pancakes, bacon, eggs, and fruit on the counter, and they're already having mimosas judging by the bottle of cheap champagne next to Scarlett. Every eye looks my way when I walk in, but Lyla's quickly dart back to her plate.

"Morning," Will offers.

"Morning," I mutter back, going for the coffee.

"Excellent breakfast," Luke says, watching my every move. He's far more perceptive than the others give him credit for, especially when it comes to calling me out. "Adler didn't disappoint with the pancakes."

"Whose idea was the mimosas?" I ask.

"Mine," Scarlett answers, like she's daring me to contradict her. I don't. I figured as much. I make a plate and, of course, the only seat available is next to Lyla. I sit next to her, careful not to so much as brush against her. She stiffens enough for me to notice but otherwise acts unbothered.

"Did you actually sleep in?" Theo asks as he spears a bite of egg.

"I was up late," I offer. "I couldn't sleep so I sat by the pool for a while and then fell asleep on Grandpa's couch."

"You slept on that thing?" Theo continues. "It reeks of cigars."

"I've had better nights," I say, careful not to look at Lyla who's doing an impressive job of devoting her full attention to her food. I look around the table for the syrup, and where else would it be but on the other side of Lyla? I lean toward her just enough to get a nose full of her lavender and vanilla scent like the masochist I am. "Pass the syrup?"

She doesn't so much as glance my way as she moves the bottle from one side of her plate to the other.

"Thank you."

Nothing.

Lyla doesn't say one word to me all of breakfast. She talks to the others—laughs with Luke, debates with Will, asks Theo questions about the house that I try to answer, but she acts like she doesn't hear me. She even talks to Scarlett about training sessions. I offer to refill her coffee, and she holds out her mug without ever looking at me. Luke catches that moment and chokes on his juice, which serves him right. It's then that I notice the time.

"Theo, we have that call with the insurance company in ten minutes," I say.

"I know." He nods as he wipes his mouth. The shift in him from a guy having breakfast to polished professional happens before my eyes. "We have our leadership meeting right after that."

I open my mouth to beg off.

"Nope, don't try it. They know we're together and you've missed the last two. The agenda is attached to the meeting invite and you're perfectly capable of running a PowerPoint over Zoom."

Looks like my day is going to continue to go down the shitter.

"You're working?" Luke asks. "There's a storm coming. Didn't you close your offices?"

"The offices are closed, but we need this call with our insurance agent ahead of the storm, and leadership wanted to keep our weekly meeting to plan for any storm response that may be needed for our properties," Theo explains.

"I sign your paycheck," I remind Luke. "I bet you could find something to do."

"It would be cleaning supply ordering day if someone hadn't already ordered the entirety of the Clorox brand," he fires back. "Will, Lyla and I are going to introduce you to the absolute trash that is *Married at First Sight*. You're going to love it."

"I can't wait," Will says wryly.

"Want to join us, Scarlett?" Lyla asks, and I purse my lips to stay quiet. Scarlett is an absolute bitch to her most of the time and yet, here she is, extending an olive branch. I can't even get her to look at me.

"Got nothing better to do." Scarlett shrugs.

Theo directs Luke, Will, and Scarlett to clean the kitchen since he and Lyla cooked, and then he and I take over Grandpa's office to work. The insurance call is boring but necessary—Kensington Enterprises is a real estate empire and hurricanes damage real estate. Plus, this call was at my insistence. I want to make sure we're covered, and since our guy covers my gym, too, it's two birds, one stone. I let Theo handle the numbers, and by the time the call ends, we're not only assured we're covered in the event of damage, Theo has saved us a good chunk of change moving forward. He's so damn good at this stuff. I feel my usual twinge of guilt that he has to split his attention between this and everything our family name got him involved in.

The leadership call is painful. I play the part of CEO,

realizing as I navigate the slides about emergency responses, more insurance bullshit, and updates on several projects, that Theo has saved my ass yet again by putting together this deck, complete with notes. He even DMs me answers to questions a couple of times.

"You need a raise," I declare when we hang up.

"My performance review is in December," Theo deadpans, and I chuckle. Theo sits back on the couch, and just as quickly as it came, the professionalism fades away and he's just my cousin again. "Enough work. Let's get to the good stuff. What's going on with you and Lyla?"

The automatic response on the tip of my tongue is "nothing." It wouldn't be wrong. Nothing is going on between us. She sent me out of her room last night and that was that. Except, it's also one of the bigger lies I've been trying to convince myself is true. And at least Theo knows she and I had our night together. Hell, maybe talking to someone might be helpful.

"Fight club?" I ask him, falling back on the movie reference we always used as kids when we had a secret to share or mischief to get into. His small grin tells me he remembers, too.

"Fight club." He nods—a promise that this is between us.

"I went to Lyla's room last night," I admit. "She kicked me out."

"You went to her room . . ." He keeps his gaze on me as he puzzles out my words. "Tell me you didn't show up and solicit sex."

"Of course not! I . . ." I stop. Isn't that exactly what I did? I showed up at her door like a sex-starved lunatic and any woman in their right mind would have turned me away. "Dammit."

I drop my head in my hands and dive into the deep end of the "I don't deserve her" pool I carry around in the pit of my gut. Of course she turned me away. From her point of view, I only wanted her body. I did want her body—I think I always want her body at this point—but I also want . . . her.

I want *her*.

"Walk me through it," Theo prompts.

"You're suddenly a relationship expert?" I ask.

"No, but I am the only one who knows you and Lyla had wild sex in the passenger seat of your Bronco, and I happened to have had a conversation with her last night in which I talked you up. I assume that was before you showed up at her door, so way to dock any points I may have gotten you."

"What did you say?" I half ask, half demand.

"The truth—that you like her, that you're shit at showing it, and that you're hard to know, but worth it if she's willing to put in the effort."

That sits me back on my heels. A dozen thoughts pass through my mind, one right after another. From being humbled that Theo would say that about me to wondering if, maybe, Lyla doesn't *want* to know me. He's right; I'm difficult to know—maybe she doesn't want to put in that kind of effort. Maybe she doesn't think I'm worth it. I certainly don't think I am, not with everything that comes with me.

"Worth noting?" he continues. "She said you're not shit at showing you care, but that you suck at doing anything about it."

"I tried to do something about it last night," I say, still wrestling with all the thoughts and feelings related to whether Lyla even wants to know me.

Theo lets out a sigh so dramatic it's like looking in a mirror.

"Kage, yes or no. Do you like Lyla?"

"She's perfectly likable—"

"Kage."

He's not going to let me out of this.

"Fuck." I sigh as I run a hand through my hair. "Yeah, I do." I'm not sure if admitting it out loud makes it better or worse. "I shouldn't, but I do."

"Glad you were honest about that." Theo nods. "Saves me some time from having to call your bluff, because it's immensely obvious to literally all of us that you're in deep."

"Do you have a point here?" I ask, annoyed.

"Look at it from her perspective," Theo prompts. "She knows you're into her, yet you've told her you can't do anything about it. You've sworn to us that she's 'just a job,' so I'm not even going to touch the fact that she is, in fact, in the loosest terms, a job for us."

"I think she stopped being a job a long time ago," I admit. Not just for me, either. She and Will are genuine friends. Luke, too, considers her a friend. She and Theo are apparently having late night chats. Hell, even Scarlett, notorious for her cold exterior, is thawing toward her. She's infiltrated not just my life, but my friends' lives as well. Time will now be marked as "before Lyla" and "after Lyla" for all of us.

"Doesn't change the fact that there's a lot she doesn't know. But, like I said, I'm not going to touch that," Theo says. "You showing up at her door last night, to her, looks like you wanted a quick fuck and nothing more. Lyla might have had a one-night stand with you, but at the end of the day, she's looking for the real thing. That's why she went on a date with that blond guy. She wants what she thinks you're not willing to give her."

He's right. Hell, Lyla has told me all of this herself, and

I'm the one that's been hot and cold. Yesterday alone I made sure there would be Oreos and coffee creamer for her at Kensington Manor, bought her coffee when we stopped for gas, and opened her door for her, but then, I was abrupt with dropping her bags off and leaving her in a strange place. I hardly spoke to her as we drove, still licking my wounds because she went on a date with someone else and maybe because I was all knotted up about having her in my Bronco and taking her to my family home.

I was so knotted up that Theo had to give her a tour.

I should have been the one to do that. I should have taken her around the property, showed her all my favorite places, pointed out things I think she'd like because God knows I cataloged a list of things about this place I want to share with her when I made the decision to head upstate to ride this storm out and bring Lyla with me.

"The physical is easy," I confess. "The rest of it . . ." I shake my head. Because that's what this comes down to. I can do the physical. I can bring her body pleasure, make her fall apart. I can use my body to show her how I feel. It's the rest of it—being vulnerable and allowing myself to not just feel things but show her those feelings that scares me shitless.

"Then you have to decide if you want her enough to allow her in," Theo says as he stands. "Otherwise, you need to let her go. You can't keep her at arm's distance, but not let anyone else have her, either." He squeezes my shoulder as he passes. "Fight club," he says again, a promise.

"Fight club." I nod as I watch him walk towards the door. "Where are you going?"

"To see what this trash reality TV show Luke and Lyla are watching is all about," he answers. "You coming?"

I consider it, but I need a minute, so I shake my head.

Theo gives me an understanding nod and leaves me alone. I spend most of the next few hours trying to work but mostly stewing on what to do about Lyla. It doesn't take me long to conclude that letting her go isn't an option. I probably should, given everything I'm hiding from her, but I just can't. I have no idea how to take the next step, or what that step even is, though. I'm so far out of my league it's laughable.

I'm working up the nerve to rejoin the group and face Lyla's icy silence when I find her browsing my grandmother's bookshelves. I stay in the doorway and take advantage of the opportunity to silently watch her. She runs a finger along the spines as she reads the titles, catching her bottom lip between her teeth as she plucks one from the shelf.

"Find something you like?"

She startles and looks up. "Sorry," she apologizes, closing the book and slipping it back on the shelf. "The door was open . . . I saw books . . ."

"This isn't an off-limits kind of house, Lyla. If there's a door open, you're allowed in." I cross the room, drawn to her like a magnet to its opposite. "Grandma calls this her tearoom. I have never, not once, seen her have tea in here." An awkward silence settles between us, and I start scanning the shelves. I find what I want and remove it from its place. "Ever read this one?" I hold the book out to her. She takes it and spares me a curious glance before she gives her attention to the book.

"*As I Lay Dying*?" she asks.

"It's my favorite book." That gets her attention. "It reminds me of my family." I cross my arms over my chest to keep myself from reaching for her and watch as she flips it over.

"*The death and burial of Addie Bundren is taken by members of her family, as they cart the coffin to Jefferson, Mississippi, to bury her among her people,"* she reads. *"But the task is much more difficult than anticipated. And as the intense desires, fears and rivalries of the family are revealed in the vernacular of the Deep South, Faulkner presents a portrait of extraordinary power —as epic as the Old Testament, as American as Huckleberry Finn."'*

She lifts her gaze back to mine. "This reminds you of your family?"

"It hits close to home," I tell her. "Guessing you haven't read it?"

"I haven't." She opens the cover, skims the first page, then the second. Apparently, I'd be okay standing here and watching her read all day, because I can't look away. "Could I?" she asks, eyes still on the pages. "While I'm here?"

"Of course." She closes the book, gives me a little nod, and turns to leave. I reach out and touch her elbow, purposeful in keeping my hold light, grateful that she pauses and looks back at me.

"I'm sorry, Lyla." The words tumble out of me, and I absolutely mean them.

"Sorry for what, exactly?" she asks.

A fair question. I could be apologizing for more than she knows.

"I handled myself all wrong last night. I meant what I said about having a lot of baggage. I'm not the good guy. I'm no knight in shining armor. I'm certainly no Prince Charming. I keep my circle small and the innermost part of it smaller. The fact that you're here, at my family's home, should tell you where you fall." Her eyes grow imperceptibly bigger—so minute that no one else would notice. I notice, though. I notice everything about her. "I'm not an easy person to know, and while my cousin might think I'm worth the effort, I have my doubts."

"Kage—"

"Please, Lyla," I cut her off gently. "Let me get this out?"

She nods.

"I have a laundry list of reasons I should stay away from you, the least of which is the fact that you're Bradley's sister. But I can't seem to stay away, and I'm tired of fighting it. That's what drove me to your room last night. I don't want to fight it anymore."

"I'm going to need you to be clearer," she says. "I'm not interested in a friends-with-benefits situation, Kage."

"I'm not either."

She's surprised as I catch her fingers in my hand, keeping my hold light. Touching her immediately settles something in me. "I realize it looks like I was only there for sex last night. And I'll admit I did come to your door with the intention of burying myself in you for the foreseeable future."

"You can't exactly deny that," she says, keeping me honest.

"That's what I'm trying to explain, Lyla. I can do the physical—I'm confident in that. I don't know how to do . . . this." I sigh out a frustrated breath, wishing I was more eloquent. "I can't even explain what *this* is. I just know that I want to be wherever you are, all of the time."

"You hardly spoke to me yesterday," she says, absolutely refusing to let me off the hook for my actions. I think I like that. I think I like that there's finally someone in my life who holds me accountable. Luke, Theo, Will, they all try—Theo is probably the most successful at it—but even they bow out after a point. Not Lyla. She holds her ground, and I didn't know until right now that I've craved that.

Someone to challenge me.

Someone to make me better.

Someone to make me *want* to be better.

"I was unfairly mad at you," I admit. The look she gives me tells me she's ready to light into me, and I rush ahead before she can. "I hated seeing you with someone else, especially when that someone probably deserves you a hell of a lot more than I do. I had no right to be mad, but I was."

"For someone with such an ego, your self-confidence is in the tank," she observes.

"Only with you," I tell her. "You're messing up everything, Lyla." She has no idea how true that statement is. "But fuck if I'm not willing to let you." She doesn't respond, just looks at me, thinking. I keep going, if for no other reason than if I'm talking, she can't reject me again. "I'm willing to try. I can't make you any promises, and I can guarantee I'm going to fuck up, but I want to try." I swallow my pride. "If you'll let me."

I can't read her. I have no idea where her head is, what she's thinking. A big part of me wants to press her against this bookshelf and kiss her until she agrees to try. But that didn't work out well last night, so I keep my mouth shut and let her put her words together.

"You want more than sex?" she clarifies.

"I do." It makes my stomach churn to admit it, but I want this. I want her. I want *us*. I give her a lopsided smile. "It's your move, Lyla."

A myriad of emotions flash through those expressive eyes of hers before her lips settle into a small smile. "Okay."

Then, she turns to walk away.

What the hell?

"Wait, Lyla . . ." I catch her by the wrist, and she looks over her shoulder. "Please . . ."

"You said the next move is mine," she reminds me. "I'm

going to consider what that will be"—she holds up *As I Lay Dying*—"while I read my book."

I let her go.

I swear it takes a few minutes for the air to return to my lungs.

I can't figure out if that went well or not.

I poured my heart out as much as I ever have and she just walked out. She didn't seem upset, though. Maybe it went well? Fuck, I'm going to talk myself in circles.

I get to work distracting myself which turns out to be pretty damn easy because the grandparents call. I screen them, so they call Theo and, of course, he answers. Once they figure out where we are, they give us a list of chores to do ahead of the hurricane, which is hours away at this point.

"They didn't think to have any of this done before they left?" Theo complains as we secure the outdoor furniture.

"Of course they didn't," I state. "Notice Will and Luke have made themselves scarce."

"They piled into the car with Scarlett for one last grocery store run like their pants were on fire," Theo says as he stacks patio chairs. "Lyla, however, wasn't with them."

"She's reading." I spotted her in the enclosed part of the patio while I cleaned out the firepit a few yards away. She was curled up on a wicker loveseat, lost to Faulkner, and so beautiful I had to remind myself to behave.

"You two talk?" he asks.

"We did." He looks at me expectantly. "I'll let you know how it went when I know how it went." He chuckles and gets back to work.

I grill burgers for dinner and make sure I cook Lyla's just the way she likes them—no pink—and purposefully sit next to her. She's not nearly as cool toward me, and I take that as a good sign. I also don't push it, even though I do reach under the table to squeeze her knee and definitely leave my hand there for a while. I deem it another good sign when she doesn't make me move it.

The group decides to head to the pool house for a game night once dinner is cleaned up.

"You coming, Kage?" Will asks.

I want to. I have no interest in playing board games, but I want to hang out with my friends, with Lyla. But I have a mountain of emails that require a response, and a number of items that need my approval. It's my own fault my Kensington Enterprises to-dos have piled up like this and now I have to face the consequences. Luke gives me a hard time about being no fun, but if I can get most of the backlog done this evening, I won't have to worry about it once the storm blows in.

I'm typing out a borderline professional email that essentially says "hell no" when Lyla appears a couple of hours into my work session. She's changed into sleep shorts and a sweatshirt and has fuzzy socks on her feet. I didn't know I could be attracted to someone wearing fuzzy socks, but I definitely am.

"I saw this couch when we got here yesterday," she says, motioning to the cigar-stained couch I'm sitting on. "It looks comfortable. I was hoping I could read on it."

A slow smile spreads across my features. This is her move. "I told you, this isn't an off-limits kind of house." She smiles and starts to walk across the room, and I swear it's the longest it's ever taken someone to cross a room. She goes to settle on the opposite end of the couch, but since I'm taking chances with her today, I take another. I lean over and block her from sitting down. "There is a condition with this couch, though."

"Oh?" she questions.

I smirk and sit back. "You have to use me as a cushion."

She rolls her eyes, but there's a smile there. "You're working."

"I can work while you read," I promise. She settles next to me, then moves so she can stretch her legs across the couch as she leans into me. I wrap an arm around her and bring her closer. "Perfect."

She opens her book, and I note she's more than halfway through it. I balance my laptop on the sofa arm and continue to work with one hand. We stay like that for a while, her lost in the pages, me wading through my inbox.

It's when she starts to shift around that I glance at her, noting the goosebumps on her bare legs. "Cold?"

"A little chilly," she replies. "But I'm fine." I don't want to move, but I'm invested in this whole show-her-I-care thing, and I read that her EDS makes it harder for her to regulate her temperature. I gently sit her up and put my laptop aside. "Where..."

I go to an ottoman opposite the sofa meant more for looks than actual use if you ask my grandma, meant for propping up your feet on after a long day if you ask my grandpa, and open it. I take out one of the throws Grandma stores there and return to Lyla, spreading it over her legs.

"Better?" I ask.

"Thank you." She nods. I resume my position and she scoots a little closer. I certainly hold her a little closer, trying to focus, but I can't. She's right here, willingly, and everything about this moment is just so domestic. This is what I imagine normal people who aren't trying to run their own business, keep the family business afloat, and exact revenge while keeping everyone they care about safe experience.

Now that I've gotten a taste of it, I think it might be addictive.

I want more.

The memory surfaces out of nowhere.

My dad sat with my mom like this on the couch in our place in the city. He would work most evenings, after we had dinner as a family, and she would lean on him much like Lyla is doing to me, sometimes with a book, often with her own laptop. They were a unit, two parts to a whole that needed the other to function. My dad once said he looked forward to those evenings every day—when I'd come from school and do my homework at the kitchen table once it was cleared of dinner, and they would relax on the couch. I used to be embarrassed by how openly affectionate they were with one another. Now, I know how lucky I was to have parents that loved one another that much. Maybe that's why I've been so closed off to the idea of any sort of relationship. I saw what it did to my dad to lose my mom. That kind of pain . . . I never want to experience that.

Yet here I am, dangerously close to being just as wrapped up in a woman as my dad was.

I drop a kiss to the top of Lyla's head, and she glances up at me. She must see something in my eyes because she lifts her head so she can see me better.

"Everything okay?"

I fight off the instinct to say something like "everything is fine" and make myself be honest with her because she's *her*.

"My mom and dad used to sit like this most evenings," I share. "I'd forgotten about it until now." I play with the end of her braid. "I forget about the good stuff, but there was a lot of it. A lot more of it than the bad stuff, but it seems like the bad stuff is what I remember the most."

"You have a photo of your mom in your condo," she says, carefully.

"I do." I rest my head against hers. "I miss her."

It's more than I've ever admitted to anyone, but it's true. I miss my mom. I miss her more as I get older. I'd give just about anything to tell her about Lyla, but the best I'll ever be able to do is visit her grave and I damn sure don't do that. I tried once, but seeing her name etched in stone, her life reduced to two dates separated by a dash . . . I couldn't handle it.

"I miss my dad," she echoes. "He was the best." The mood is noticeably heavier now. She lifts the book. "Tell me how this book reminds me of your family?"

"It's about how a family navigates the death of their matriarch, right?" She nods. "Each of the Bundrens deal with Addie's death in their own way. Cash builds her coffin outside her window while she's dying so she knows how nice it is. Vardaman drills holes in her coffin so she can breathe, and Darl thinks the sounds her body makes while its decaying is her speaking. Jewel is her favorite son, but he only saves her in death, and Dewey Dell barely mourns her mother at all. That's how I see my family in the wake of all the loss we've had. We all handled it differently, some more healthy than others."

She's quiet, contemplative.

I wait.

"My dad used to say death and weddings bring out the worst in people," she finally says. "The more of both I experience, the more I think he was right."

"I've never been to a wedding, but I think he's on to something about death."

"Which character do you relate to the most?" she asks.

"Darl."

I feel exposed under her steady gaze. I just told her I see myself in the character that everyone was wary of because he had a knack for knowing all their secrets. He was ultimately committed to an insane asylum.

"I know everyone thinks he's crazy," she says, "but I think he might be the sanest of them all."

Later, I'll look back and know this is the moment I go from being deeply attracted to her to completely and wholly in love with her. For now, I focus on the feeling of something heavy being lifted off my chest. It's something that's been there for so long it has to be pried loose and wrenched away. I feel lighter. I feel *seen*.

"Not many people think that," I say, not talking about Darl anymore.

"Well, I do," she says, and I don't think she's talking about Darl anymore either. She returns to her position, and I go back to attempting to work, though, I can't concentrate now. I close my laptop.

"Want a snack?" I ask.

"Sure," she decides. "I'm on the last chapter. Can I finish . . . ?"

"You read that whole book this afternoon?"

"I have a high capacity for literature," she quips, and I chuckle.

"You finish that book," I agree. "Then meet me on the patio."

I go to the kitchen, gather what I need, then head out to the enclosed part of the patio where there's still furniture. Lyla is already there, perched on the same wicker loveseat she was reading on earlier, and she beams when she sees me.

"Oreos?" she asks.

"With peanut butter and milk," I confirm as I take in the

way she lights up. "Put it on a tray and everything." I settle next to her and position the tray between us. She reaches for an Oreo with one hand, the jar of peanut butter with the other.

"Not a vegetable or fruit in sight," she notes. "You feeling okay, Kensington?"

"All things in moderation," I state, using my old standby.

"I think you have a secret sweet tooth," she teases, and I smile at her.

"Don't tell Luke." Her laugh is worth everything.

"It looks like they're still going strong in the pool house," she observes, gesturing across the property to where every light is on and the faintest pulse of music can be heard.

"You didn't want to hang out with them?" I ask. "I'd bet Luke is playing bartender, which means Scarlett is loose enough to be less of a bitch, Theo has stopped thinking about budgets and investments, and Will . . . Well, Will tends to be steady no matter what you throw at him."

"I played a few games," she says, eyes on me. "But I wanted to read." She doesn't look away. "And maybe be around you."

My heart stutters, or at least it feels like it. She's choosing *me*. I reach out and tuck a loose strand of hair behind her ear.

"I told you, Lyla. I want to be wherever you are, all the time."

I lean in and she does, too until our lips meet, and it's like an unspoken promise is sealed. The tray teeters precariously and she pulls away, but only long enough to move it to the ground. Then, she's climbing into my lap, straddling me, her hands on my face as she brings her lips back to mine. My hands go to her hips.

"I'm starting to think you like being in my lap," I say.

"It's nostalgic."

I laugh and find that place on her neck that I recall, with clarity, just how much she likes to have sucked and nipped. Sure enough, she gasps in pleasure, and I pull her closer.

We make out like teenagers as the wind starts to pick up, the first hints of the incoming hurricane making itself known. By lunch tomorrow, it should be perfect weather for spending the day in bed. With Lyla.

It's the promise of having at least another two or three days tucked away here at Kensington Manor with her that has me pulling back enough to rest my forehead against hers.

"We're going to do this right," I tell her. "I plan to fuck you thoroughly, but not tonight. Tonight, we're going to go upstairs, sleep next to one another, and cement the fact that we're doing this whole relationship thing and that it's not based entirely on sex." I smirk. "Even though it certainly started with sex."

"The best sex you've ever had, if Theo is to be believed," she says.

"Until the next time I have you naked, which will likely be sometime in the next twenty-four hours," I say, unashamed of my declaration. She full-on blushes. God, she's *perfect*. "Can I convince you to turn in?"

"It's getting late." She nods. "Let's go to bed."

We clean up our snack and I turn off lights downstairs, leaving on the strategic one here and there for whenever Theo decides to make it back up here, if he does at all. The lights are still blazing in the pool house, and Luke isn't known for pouring weak drinks.

I take Lyla's hand and lead her upstairs. We pause in the hallway between our rooms and despite every other decision I've made today that supports it, it's the one I make next that cements that she and I are together now. I tug her hand to indicate I want her to sleep in my room.

I have never, not once, had a woman in my bedroom—not here, not even at my condo. I was supposed to marry Brynn and even she didn't get to spend the night at my place. She didn't come to my place much—said it was too small, too clinical. And she certainly never got to sleep in the room I grew up in, even when I was forced to bring her here. I purposefully put her in a room on the opposite hall, near Theo. One of many, many signs that it was never going to work between us.

Lyla, though?

Across the hall wasn't close enough to me from the jump.

"I need to wash my face and brush my teeth," she tells me. "Meet you in bed?"

"Keep saying things like that and you're going to ruin my plan to be a gentleman tonight and tonight only," I tell her, even as I lean in to kiss her cheek.

"Maybe I should keep insinuating things then," she says, eyes sparkling, as I turn her toward her bedroom.

"Go, now, before I do something indecent."

"By all means, think of all the indecent things you can do to me," she says as she steps into her room.

"Trust me, I'm making a list and I'm going to mark off every single item on it." Her cheeks heat and her eyes flash with desire. "We're sleeping tonight, though," I say, just as much for her benefit as mine. "We need rest for all the ways I plan to pass the time waiting for this hurricane to blow through."

Then, I'm moving into my room to brush my teeth because if I stay in that hall one moment longer, clothes are coming off and condoms are getting rolled on.

Shit.

Condoms.

I have a couple—I keep them in my wallet. But if things progress the way I hope they will, I'm going to need more than two. I hope like hell one of the others in this house has condoms on them, or maybe the grocery store will be open in the morning, in final preparation for the full force of the storm. Because two condoms will not be enough.

Lyla is still in her bathroom when I come out of mine, so I make myself busy collecting her phone charger from her room to plug it into the outlet on what will now be her side of the bed. I notice her Kindle, see the charger laying on the bed, and plug it in so it's charged for her in case the power goes out. I've just gotten into bed when she finally joins me, looking like an absolute goddess with her hair down, her face glowing from whatever the hell took her so long. I flip the blankets back and feel my entire being relax when she slips in next to me.

"This is a very big, very comfortable bed," she declares once she's settled.

"I'm a big guy," I remind her. She smirks at me.

"I remember."

I think *I* blush this time. Then, I roll over, turn off the lamp, and pitch us into darkness.

"Come here." I pull her into my arms, and she settles with her head on my chest. "Comfortable?"

"Very," she says. A particularly strong gust of wind rattles the windows. "It's going to be gross tomorrow."

"It's not going to be great," I agree, kissing her shoulder. "But I'll keep you safe."

From the hurricane. From everything and everyone.

"I'm pretty good at looking out for myself," she says. "But I'll let you stand in as needed."

I only hold her tighter.

The urge to tell her something, to be honest with her about something, is sudden and demanding. I was never going to be able to keep her in the dark, but now that we're here, giving whatever is between us the chance to actually be something, I can only keep things to myself for so long. I kiss her hair and prepare myself.

"The night you dislocated your shoulder and were falling asleep on the sofa, you said something," I venture.

"What did I say?" she asks carefully.

"You said you didn't think your dad's death was an accident."

Dense silence fills the room. I wait, letting her decide how to respond.

"They said he had a massive heart attack while driving," she speaks into the darkness nearly a full minute later. "I believed it at first, but the more I've thought about it, it just doesn't make sense. I can't prove it, even though I've tried, but I think he was involved in something he shouldn't have been, or at least found out about something he wasn't supposed to know about."

"If you think there's more to it, then there's more to it," I say, because I have that much faith in her, and because I know there *is* more to it.

"My ex didn't think so," she says.

"Screw your ex," I state. "If you want to find out what really happened to your dad, we will."

"How?" she asks. "I've made a few inquiries around D.C., but there's nothing . . ."

"There's always a way," I say. "We'll figure it out." I bring her even closer. "In the meantime, sleep. Like I said, I have plans for you."

"Don't tell Bradley," she says.

"About us?" I ask. "We're going to have to—"

"Not us, although I suppose we should figure out how to break it to him gently." I can't say I'm especially looking forward to Bradley finding out I'm with his sister, but that's something to worry about when we're back in the city. "I mean about Dad. I don't know how he'll take it."

"I'll keep it to myself," I promise, even though he's already well-aware that his father's death was no accident.

"Thank you," she says.

"Anything for you, Lyla." And I mean that to my very marrow.

Outside, the wind increases to a steady gale.

Inside, Lyla drifts off to sleep, wrapped in my arms, safe and protected and cared for. I lie awake a while longer, my mind humming the way it always does at night. Tonight, I dare to think about what could be—the possibilities. The chance to spend evenings on the couch with Lyla like we did tonight, like my mom and dad did before it all fell apart. I'm selfish enough to want that. To want to find out what a life with her could be like.

The hope is there, brewing just below the surface.

If only it wasn't so dangerous to hope.

18

LYLA

I wake up slowly.
I'm warm, comfortable.
Weighted down.

It takes me a moment to remember I'm in Kage's bed at Kensington Manor. He's curled around me, an arm around my waist, his leg thrown over mine like he's afraid I might bolt if given the chance. His other arm is under the pillow I'm using, and his face is buried in the crook of my neck. I smile to myself and marvel at how we ended up here. We went through the entire spectrum of emotions yesterday, from me kicking him out of my room in the wee hours of the morning to him doing his best to try to convey his feelings in fumbling words. Part of me wanted to make him wait around, suffer a little longer. But the part of me that saw how hard it was for him to articulate his feelings had to give in.

I stay put for a few more minutes, until my bladder demands I get out of bed. I don't want to wake him—I don't think he sleeps well—so I try to extricate myself from his embrace the way one would defuse a bomb.

"No." He mutters the word as his arm tightens around me.

"I need to use the bathroom," I tell him. "I'll come back."

"Hmmm," he groans, but his arm slackens around me. I slip out of his embrace, cross the hall to my bathroom so I can also brush my teeth, and I'm on my way back to him a few minutes later. A cup of coffee sounds good, however, so I veer right and head downstairs. The house is quiet. It's not super early, but I'd guess the others are worse for the wear and sleeping it off. I put on a pot and gaze out the window while I wait.

Kensington Manor is stunning, with its sweeping, manicured lawn, flowerbeds full of seasonal plants, and the trees in the distance changing colors. The sky is a heavy gray, and the wind has picked up to a steady blow. The promised storm feels imminent, and I'm grateful that we're here, out of the city, safe.

A long beep tells me the coffee is ready. I find two mugs, pour a generous splash of my preferred hazelnut creamer in one and then pour coffee into both. Kage is just waking up when I walk back into his room.

"You were supposed to come right back," he says into the pillow he's now hugging in place of me. It's kind of sweet.

"I had to make a pit stop," I say as I move to my side of the bed. "I brought you coffee."

He lifts his head, hair messy, eyes half-lidded with sleep. "Coffee?" he repeats.

"Black, like you like it." I hold his mug out. He's quiet as he pushes himself upright and takes it from me. I take a sip of mine while he gazes thoughtfully at his. I'm starting to think I was wrong about the black coffee when he lifts his eyes to mine.

"I've never had someone bring me coffee," he admits, and I vow right then and there to bring him coffee whenever I can.

"Now you have." He sends me a half smile as he lifts his mug to his lips. "Hopefully it's okay. I like strong coffee."

"Best cup of coffee I've ever had," he says as he looks past me, out the window. "It's not raining yet?"

"No." I shake my head. "The sky is heavy, though, and it's windy. No one else is awake. Or at least, if they are, they aren't downstairs."

"They're all passed out in the pool house," Kage predicts as he takes another sip of coffee, all while gazing at me. We're both leaning against the headboard, the blanket bunched around our waists. It feels very domestic. And awkward.

"Everything okay?" I ask after another long moment of him gazing at me.

"Just taking it all in," he says. "I've never . . ." He trails off.

"You've never what?" I prompt.

"Done this." He gestures between us. "Woken up with a woman like this. Had someone bring me coffee." He pauses. "Cared this much."

The world skids to a stop. He transitions before my eyes from the too-handsome-for-his-own-good, smooth-talking, egotistical ass he can be to a vulnerable, unsure man who's a little lost and more afraid to find himself in a relationship than he will ever admit. I'm learning he's like a piece of mica —hard at first glance, but as the thin layers start to peel away, you see how fragile it really is. He's not fragile in the physical sense, not remotely. But as each thin layer that makes up Kage Kensington flakes away, I see a little more of the wounds he tries to mask.

Instinct tells me talking isn't what he needs. He shows

he cares through his actions, not just with me, but with everyone he cares about. But I think, maybe, he receives care through physical touch. It was in the way he leaned into my touch the night I cleaned up his busted lip and how he wraps himself around me when we sleep—the way he always finds excuses to touch me. His apparent lack of romantic relationships and the loss of his parents explain why I thought he might be touch-starved that night at his condo.

I steady my coffee and move to his side. I lift his arm, drape it around my shoulders, and lean into him. I feel him relax and I know my guess on touch is right. That's going to take some getting used to. Deacon wasn't much on displays of affection, especially in public.

I like how it feels to be close to Kage, though. I feel cared for. Safe.

"Did you sleep okay?" he asks as his fingertips brush up and down my arm.

"I did," I confirm. "What about you?"

"Better than I have in a while," he says. "You're better than any melatonin, Lyla."

"Glad to know I put you to sleep," I quip.

"That's not what I mean." He shakes his head. "I don't sleep well, and I hate taking sleep aids. I was so groggy yesterday morning that I barely knew my own name. When I've slept next to you—last night, at my condo—I've slept better." He pauses. "A lot better."

I feel oddly warm inside over the simple admission. "Play your cards right, and maybe you'll get a decent night's sleep more often."

"Like I'm going to let you sleep," he replies, those beautiful brown eyes of his burning into mine. He puts his coffee on the nightstand, then reaches for mine. "I haven't kissed you good morning yet."

"You haven't," I agree. Then he's kissing me, hungry and scalding, one of his big hands on my cheek, the other arm still wrapped around me and pulling me closer even as I lean in for more. Kissing him is like what I imagine it's like to freefall from an airplane. It feels so good, so right, so exhilarating. In the back of my mind, something warns me to pull the cord on my parachute, but I don't. I keep falling, keep kissing him, trusting that the landing won't break me.

"Mmm," he hums as he presses me into the pillows, careful as he slots his body over mine to deepen the kiss. I hitch a leg up around his hip and thread my fingers in his hair to hold him to me.

This is easily the best good morning kiss I have ever been a part of.

It's already ending too soon with a few short pecks on the lips. He rests his forehead against mine, breathless, like me. I run my hands down his bare back. The skin is rough in places, soft in others. He lets out a content sigh.

"That was one hell of a good morning kiss," I say.

"Wait until I kiss you good night," he counters. And just like that, the faint ache between my legs becomes a much more demanding throb. He kisses me again, then starts to pull away. "Let's get breakfast."

"Or," I counter, "we could stay right here."

For a moment, I think I have him, then, he shakes his head and pushes himself up and away, tossing the blankets off him as he goes. I let out an indignant sound at the loss of his warmth that draws a chuckle out of him.

"Soon," he promises, his gaze squarely on me. "I'm not planning to keep my hands to myself much longer." He rounds the bed to my side and I'm foolish enough to think he's going to kiss me again, but instead, he reaches for the comforter and pulls it back, letting the cool air wash over me. I glare at him, but he just chuckles again and leans down to kiss me before catching my hand and tugging me out of bed. "Let's have a hot meal and make sure there's no last-minute hurricane prep before we find a way to spend the rest of the day."

We make no moves to leave his room, however. He pulls me into his chest, and I wrap my arms around him and lean into his embrace. It only lasts a few moments, but it feels like reassurance that last night really happened. He passes me my coffee, picks up his, catches my free hand in his, and leads me out of the bedroom.

I see his back then.

My gasp is audible. He looks over his shoulder.

"Everything okay?"

"Your back," I say. "What happened?"

A large, jagged scar cuts diagonally across his upper back, from his left shoulder to just below the right one.

"Fell through a window a few years ago," he offers. "Didn't feel great."

There's more to it than that. That scar looks intentional. "How did that happen?" I ask as we start down the stairs.

"I was out, there was a confrontation, things got out of hand."

That's all he's going to tell me. That's all he *wants* to tell me.

"When did it happen?" I press.

"I told you, a few years ago." He glances at me. "You've seen my shirtless before, Lyla."

"I can't say I've paid attention to your back." It's not like I could see his back when we were in the Bronco, and the couple of times I've seen him shirtless at the gym, I've been either salivating over the sight of all those abs or shaking from being nearly kidnapped. The night I spent at his condo, what little time he was shirtless, was spent with my back to his front while we spooned. "I only just noticed it. I'm sorry for asking."

There's enough of a bite in my tone to make him sigh heavily as we reach the bottom of the stairs. He turns to me, leaving me standing on the bottom step. He still has me in height by several inches.

"It happened on a pretty shitty night," he tells me. "I don't like to remember it."

"Thank you for telling me," I say. He nods and I see it again, that hint of the vulnerable man he tries to keep tucked away. He's like a wild animal, trying to decide if the person in front of him is friend or foe. I brush my hand through his hair to let him know he's safe with me, and he leans in, like he did that night in his condo. "Breakfast?"

"Breakfast," he echoes. "Waffles, I think."

"There are a couple of boxes of frozen—"

"No way," he cuts me off. "We're having real waffles." He looks over his shoulder at me as we enter the kitchen. "You missed that morning, by the way."

I furrow my brow. "What?"

"The morning after we . . ." He gestures between us to indicate the whole Bronco experience. "You threw a waffle at me when Bradley and I left."

"It was French toast," I correct him. "I only missed because I wasn't trying to hit you."

He laughs. "Speaking of throwing things, how did you get so good at darts anyway?" he asks as he starts gathering supplies from the pantry.

"Summer camp. Mom used to ship us off every summer.

I sprained my ankle one year and couldn't do a lot of the activities, so I stayed inside, read a lot, did so many arts and crafts. There was a dart board in the mess hall, and I would throw darts to pass the time. I had to work a little harder at it because I was on crutches and off balance, but now I can beat almost anyone."

"Didn't beat me though, did you?" he asks, eyes shining.

"There will be a rematch," I inform him.

"I'll take you on anytime, Lyla."

His tone promises so much more than a game of darts. By all means, sign me up.

I top off my coffee and his for good measure. That look of wonder is there again, and it only serves as further evidence that he's been taking care of himself so long that he's knocked off balance by something as simple as a refill. "Can I help?"

"Wash and cut some fruit?" he requests as he removes mixing bowls from a cabinet. "Strawberries, blueberries, whatever's in there."

We work in a comfortable rhythm. He knows his way around the kitchen—isn't using a recipe but working from memory. He brings out a waffle iron from the pantry and directs me to get the air fryer out as well. I'm put in charge of loading it with bacon.

"Where did you learn to cook?" I ask.

"Taught myself, mostly," he says as he pours waffle batter onto the iron. "And my mom was a good cook." That's all he offers. I hold onto it all the same. We've done this thing backwards, after all. We've had sex, now we're getting to know each other. I drift toward him, drawn to him in a way I've never been pulled to another human. I put a hand on his lower back and lean into him while he monitors the waffle's progress. The smile he sends over his shoulder at me is almost shy.

The moment is interrupted as the sound of voices in the distance float to us.

"It's like they somehow know there's food being prepared in the main house," he says as my hand drops away. The back door opens and the voices get louder.

"Are we telling—"

He kisses me. Full out, no holds-barred kisses me. He has a hand in my hair, the other splayed across my back to hold me close. He's making a statement and I'm not going to stop him. I put a hand on his hard chest, letting the other wrap around his shoulder. I desperately need this man to take me upstairs and have his way with me.

"Oh . . ."

I try to pull back at the sound of Will's voice, but Kage holds me in place for one last lingering kiss before he lets me go. My cheeks are red when I turn to face the group gathered in the kitchen entrance. Will looks mildly embarrassed, Scarlett has her usual bored expression, and Theo looks relieved.

Luke is delighted. "Excellent!" He claps his hands together. "Waffles!"

The tension breaks. I laugh and even Kage chuckles.

It's coordinated chaos. Will makes a fresh pot of coffee while Theo decides we also need hash browns. He takes a bag of the frozen kind out of the freezer and goes to work "elevating the experience" by chopping up peppers and onions to stir in. Scarlett and Luke set the table, which takes twice as long as it should with their bickering, and I wonder if I'm imagining the spark between them.

The full force of the storm unleashes as we finish our

meal. We're far enough inland that the worst of the storm will stay east, but it's still massive and strong. It's the kind of weather meant for lounging in oversized sweatshirts with books. Instead, I end up on the couch with Will watching a movie. Kage, Luke, and Theo are in the home gym, and Scarlett left us to FaceTime her sister. I half watch the movie as I text Cecily a detailed recap of the last twenty-four hours.

"So, you and Kage," Will says, drawing me out of my screen.

"Yes?" I ask, unclear on if he's asking a question or making a statement.

"What's the deal there?"

"We're giving things a try," I answer. "As of last night."

"Trying is more than I've ever seen him do," Will observes.

"I like him," I admit because it's Will and I can. "I have no idea what's going to happen, but there's something there and I think we owe it to ourselves to explore it."

"He cares about you, Lyla," Will tells me. "When Kage cares about someone, he will do anything for them. Remember that."

I register that it's an odd statement to make, but I also realize Will is an available resource on Kage Kensington. I choose to pursue that path while I can.

"You mentioned that Kage fostered you," I say, choosing my question carefully.

"He did," Will confirms. "We were fostered by the same family at first. He was seventeen, so he aged out within a few months. I don't know how he did it, but he had custody of me and my sister a few weeks later." He smiles. "He was a shockingly good 'dad.'" He makes air quotes around "dad." "Unless you ask Andie, then she'll tell you he was an absolute dictator. She gave him a run for his money." The way his eyes ghost over tells me he's remembering the past. "We all deal with loss in different ways. She tried to run from it." He gives a sad half shrug. "She's still running from it, but at least she's learning something while she's at it."

"When does she come home?" I ask.

"Just before Christmas." He smiles again. "I can't wait for you to meet her."

"I'm looking forward to it." I feel like I already know her, considering how much he talks about her. I choose my next question carefully. "What about Luke and Theo?" I don't ask about Scarlett. I feel like I know Luke and Theo well enough now to ask about them, but Scarlett is still warming up to me. She needs to remain a mystery for now.

"Luke's grandmother was still alive back then—she took him in. Theo was sent to a family in Pennsylvania. It took Kage a little longer to get legal custody of him."

"I ran away."

I jump at the sound of Theo's voice. Embarrassment flames through me at him overhearing my questioning, but he just gives a soft smile that says he's not upset and sits down on a nearby armchair.

"Kage handled his grief by doing what he's always done which is, for better or worse, figure out what the problem is and solve it," he continues. "I acted out. I took off from my foster family twice. They weren't bad people or anything, but I'd lost my mom and aunt already, then I lost my dad and my uncle. I had a hard time being apart from Kage—I tried to get back to him. But by then, the courts were concerned about my behavior and dragged their feet granting Kage custody."

"It was the three of you and Andie?" I question.

"Three men and a baby." Will nods. I roll my eyes and Theo snorts back a chuckle which makes Will laugh. He has a deep love of '80s movies and he's constantly referencing them. "We made it work."

"I would be remiss not to call out the fact that we had access to resources most kids in our situation don't have," Theo says. "I, personally, have a lot of guilt around that."

I search for the right thing to say, but nothing comes to mind. It's obvious that Theo has a lot of complicated feelings about his past. They all do, I suppose. Still, a dozen more questions come to mind, namely where Theo and Kage's grandparents were in all of this. I don't ask though, because I think this conversation has come to an end. "Anyway," he says, confirming it has, "what are we watching?"

"Let's find something," Will says, reaching for the remote.

"Where are Kage and Luke?" I ask Theo.

"Still working out," he says. "They're maniacs. *I* am not."

"Debatable," Will quips, and Theo throws a pillow at him. He bats it away. "Let's watch *Top Gun*."

I leave them to argue over movies, deciding my time will be best spent in the very large tub I saw in Kage's bathroom. I text him as I climb the stairs.

Me: Taking a bath. Using your tub.

His response comes as I'm waiting for the water to heat up.

Kage: Two doors down from mine there's a linen closet. Should have bubble bath in there.

I smile and follow his directions. I find a couple of options for bubble bath, choose a lilac scent, snag my Kindle from my nightstand, and return to Kage's bathroom. I'm submerged in hot water and deeply invested in my book when the door creaks open.

"Hey," Kage greets from the doorway.

"Hey," I reply, smiling at the sight of him. He's sweaty

from his workout, still shirtless. He hasn't had a shirt on so far today and I'm not complaining. "Good workout?"

"Good enough." He shrugs a shoulder. "There's only so much we can do in their home gym." He doesn't move from the doorway. "You find everything you need?"

"I did." I nod, still watching him. "You can come in, you know."

He pushes the door wider but doesn't step inside. "I need a shower."

"You can use mine," I offer, a challenge to see if he stays or goes.

"Why walk across the hall when there's a perfectly good shower right here?" He crosses the bathroom, leans into the shower stall, and turns on the water. Then, he's moving toward me. "I could get used to walking in on you in this tub."

"Have you seen the tub at Bradley's?" I ask. "It's basically a kiddie pool. That fantasy of yours could be arranged."

"I have immense regrets about not having a tub in my condo," he says as his fingers dip into the water. His fingertips trail from my elbow, up my arm, and then along my collarbone.

This water may be steaming hot, but I have goosebumps all over.

"I'd have you over to take a bath all the time." He cups my chin and tilts my head back as he bends over to lower his lips to mine. It's a long, lingering kiss, the kind that promises more. He bites my lip before he pulls back. "Be right back."

He saunters toward the shower stall, and I'm not sure which one of us is more blatant—him in the way he drops his gym shorts, or me as I take in the view. It's useless to try to focus on my book with him naked and showering *right there*, but I certainly try. Anything to distract myself from the remerging ache between my legs. He steps out of the shower a few minutes later and keeps his eyes on me as he wraps a towel around his waist. I can't look away.

"Want to join me?" I ask. "The water is still hot."

"I want you to get out of the tub," he counters. He reaches for the towel I set out, unfolds it, and holds it open. "Come on."

I hate being told what to do and he knows it, but there's something in his tone that makes me willingly comply. I hold his gaze as I stand, the room charging around us. Soap suds cling to me and rivulets of water trail along my curves. I step out of the water and right into Kage's waiting towel. He wraps it around me, tucks the end in, and pulls me to him. He releases the claw holding my hair in a knot, letting it tumble down around my shoulders, and looks at me like I'm the answer to every prayer he's ever prayed.

"Are you going to just stand there?" I ask. "Or are you going to take me to bed?"

It's a bold ask. The girl I was in D.C. would have dropped some hints about what she wanted, but she wouldn't have asked. The woman I'm becoming in New York wants to see if Kage Kensington is as good in a bed as he is in a Bronco.

"That's the thing, Lyla," he says as his finger trails along the curve of my shoulder. "I am going to take you to bed. And I'm not going to let you out of it for the foreseeable future."

I hold his eyes. "Promise?"

That one word pushes him over the edge. He seals his lips to mine and we're moving, him steering us, me letting him. We're in the bedroom, at the edge of the bed, when he stops our progress.

"This comes off." He plucks the corner of the towel from where he just folded it and it falls away, leaving me naked.

He kisses me as he lowers me to the bed. "Something of note? The others braved the weather to go back to the pool house for a video game marathon or something. You're free to scream as loud as you want."

"You think you're going to make me scream?" I ask.

"Repeatedly." One of his big hands lands on my stomach, and his fingers turn downward as his hand drifts south. "Let me help out with that ache between your legs."

"How do you—Oh!" My question is cut off by him taking my nipple into his mouth as his fingers reach my folds. I'm already keyed up and he's masterful as he works his mouth and tongue at my chest while casually stroking between my legs. I part my knees and lose my breath in an instant. I whine out his name, and he pulls off my nipple to press a kiss to my jaw.

"Relax," he whispers. "I vividly remember how tight you are. I'm going to take my time, make sure you're ready for me." I draw him to me and kiss him as thoroughly as I can manage. We're both breathless when we break apart. "I've daydreamed about being with you again." He brushes my hair back, the gesture sweet, gentle, a direct contrast to the way he is in every other area of his life, including the way he's hovering over me. "It feels too good to be true."

"Same," I say, thinking of the times I've used thoughts of him to get me off with my vibrator, often after times he left me hot and bothered in the first place. I run my hands down his chest as I look into his eyes. "I want you, Kage."

He leans in for another kiss, then rests his forehead against mine.

"You're everything I didn't know I wanted, Lyla."

He starts moving down my body then, before I can react to his admission, his lips and hands tracing my every line and curve. I keep my hands on him, letting them drag along his back, up to his shoulders as he descends my body. He settles in between my legs, and my heart picks up its pace. He kisses the inside of my thigh and my breath stutters. He does it again, closer to my core this time, then he flicks his tongue over my clit. I gasp as my body involuntarily clenches, and Kage lifts his head.

"Lyla?"

"I'm fine," I say automatically.

His brow furrows as he considers me. "You're not."

"I am," I insist as he moves his way back up my body.

"Tell me what's wrong," he pushes, "so I can fix it." He's gentle as he brushes my hair back again. The sweet gesture makes me nearly cry. "You don't have to do anything you don't want to do. I just need to know what that is."

"I want to," I tell him. "I do. I just . . . I've never really . . ." I struggle to get the words out. Kage's expression shifts to one of understanding.

"You've never had someone go down on you, have you?"

"My ex . . ." I take a moment to swallow down my embarrassment. "Didn't like to, and I've only slept with two other guys, neither of which took the time to do much foreplay."

I watch as Kage's features cloud over. "You're embarrassed about that."

I would very much like to disappear into the ground right now. I try to pull a pillow over my face to hide my embarrassment, but Kage won't let me.

"No, don't do that." He tugs it away from me and tosses it to the floor, then cradles my cheek so I have to look at him. "That asshole didn't understand what he had. You're fucking perfect, Lyla. You deserve to be worshiped."

"I'm not perfect—"

"You are," he insists. "To me, anyway." He strokes his thumb across my cheekbone. "Do you want me to go down on you?" I just look at him, this beautiful man who insists he's not the knight in shining armor. Maybe he's not—I certainly don't need him to be. I can save myself. He's something though, at least with me. A dark knight, perhaps, or the antihero. "I want to taste you more than I want most things in life," he continues, "but I'm not going to do anything that's going to make you uncomfortable. Do you want me to go down on you?"

God, I do. I want him between my legs in any way he'll be there. I've always wanted to experience a man down there, to experience what I've heard about, read about. Deacon refused me, but Kage . . . Kage wants it. Wants *me*. I nod my confirmation.

He shakes his head. "I need words. I'm a lot of things, but I'm not the guy that makes a woman do something they don't want to do. Do you want me to go down on you?"

"Yes," I say. "Just—go slow?"

"Whatever you want," he promises. He kisses me, gentle, careful. "You deserve to be worshiped, Lyla, and I'm about to put you on a fucking pedestal."

He takes my breath away. Then, he's on the move, going slow as he works back down my body, letting me get used to the feel of both his hands and his lips on me. He places a kiss on my hipbone, then slides off the bed and I lift my head.

"Kage?" He's kneeling at the foot of the bed, then he hooks his arms around my knees and pulls me to him, looking at me to check in. "I'm okay." He nods once before lowering his head to press open-mouth kisses along the inside of my thigh. It feels anticipatory. I fist the sheets, eager for him to be where I want him. My breath quickens and I close my eyes as he reaches the crease of my thigh again, and just when I think he's going to bring his mouth to my core, he pivots and starts the same ministration along my other thigh. "Kage!"

He chuckles against my skin but doesn't let up. Again, he has me worked up in anticipation when he pulls back. This time, though, he lifts himself up to kiss my lips, reassuring me, before he settles back on his knees.

And licks the length of my seam.

I cry out, clutching the sheets. He drapes my legs over his shoulders, uses two fingers to spread me open, and dips his tongue into me. I buck my hips in reaction, but he drapes an arm across my hips to hold me in place. He licks and sucks and even nibbles, but he stays away from where I need him the most.

"Kage!" I beg. "Please! I need . . ."

"I know what you need," he says. "I'll give you everything you want, everything you need, and more. In due time."

He goes back to his ministrations, and I'm absolutely panting. The coil within me winds tighter and tighter. I try to move against him to create the friction I need, but he holds me in place with his arm over my hip until *finally* he brings his mouth to my clit.

One touch, and I fall apart.

I've never felt an orgasm like this. It fills me and erupts from me in the same instant. I cry out, grabbing at my own hair to have something to hold onto. Kage keeps working me through it, and the moment my orgasm ebbs, he slips a finger in me.

"Kage," I groan.

"I know," he soothes. "You're doing so well." I make a sound I can't believe I'm capable of and let my legs fall open. They slide off his shoulders and remain wide for him. "Good girl." A second finger enters me, and my muscles spasm around him. I remember my theory from that night in the Bronco, that he was *that guy*—a little dominant, a lot dirty. I was into it then, and I'm very into it now. He tongues my clit again as he pumps his fingers in and out of me. I scramble my hands around, looking for something, anything, to hold onto. "My hair."

"What?" I ask, aware that he said something, but no idea what. All I can think about is the way I'm already on the cusp of coming again.

"Grab my hair," he directs. "I like it."

He resumes his task as my hands tangle in his hair and yes, I like this, too. His fingers hit an especially sensitive spot that makes me cry out and tug his hair. He groans and the vibration does delightful things to me.

"Kage!" I breathe.

"Mmm," he replies. Then, he crooks his fingers just so and I'm falling apart a second time. Just like last time, he keeps going until I start to come down. This time, he removes his fingers from me and moves back up my body, trailing kisses up my torso, chest, and neck as he goes. "You're a fucking drug, Lyla Adler. I'll never get enough of you."

"You . . . are way too good at that." I breathe.

"You liked that?" I see the self-doubt in him, the need for me to confirm that I enjoyed what he just did to me.

"It was incredible." I pull him to me so I can kiss him. I taste myself on his tongue and that only turns me on more. I trail my hand down his body and find the towel he's somehow managed to keep around his waist. I tug and it falls away. He's thick and hard against my thigh. I take him in my hand and pump once, twice. He jerks and I enjoy the heady rush of power I have. I move, intending to take him in my mouth, but he stops me.

"Where are you going?"

"To return the favor," I say.

"You can return it later," he counters. His pupils are fully blown, and I can feel his heart pounding against my hand that's resting over it. "I fucking need you, Lyla. Please."

The *please* does me in.

Kage Kensington is begging for my body. He can absolutely have it.

"I'm all yours," I promise him. "Take me, Kage."

He pulls away.

"Where are you—"

"Condom," he answers. I'm glad one of us is thinking straight. "Give me thirty seconds."

"I hope you're going to last longer than thirty seconds," I say as I watch him fumble with his wallet. "I've daydreamed about this, too."

"I'm going to make you come as many times as I can before I lose myself in you," he promises as he rolls the condom on. "I've been too damn eager to be with you again to let it end prematurely." He positions himself between my legs, and I wonder what I look like right now, sweaty and breathing heavy, my legs parted, my core a dripping mess of need. He apparently likes what he sees because a low, primal growl emits from deep in his chest. "You're perfect," he tells me again as he starts to push in. "You're mine." I close my eyes, relishing the stretch of him. He meets some resistance and rather than push through it, he uses his thumb to rub small circles on my clit. "Relax," he coaxes. "I've got you."

My muscles let go like they're breathing a sigh of relief and let him slip further in. He repeats the gesture one more time until he's fully sheathed in me and he hinges forward, finally giving me the weight of his body. He doesn't move, though, giving me time to adjust.

"You've daydreamed about this?" he asks. I open my eyes and find him looking at me with all the wonder in the world. I run a hand through his hair.

"You have no idea how many times you've left me wet and wanting after an encounter with you," I confess. I rock my hips a little, teasing him, finding power in the stutter of his breath. "I've come around my vibrator daydreaming that it was you more times than you know."

"Fuck, that's hotter than it should be," he breathes, and his hips buck involuntarily. That first slide of him in me is so good and so not enough. "I'm going to make sure your reality is far better than any fantasy you've had." He kisses me and I chase his lips for another kiss when he pulls away. "I'm guilty of fantasies about you, too." He gives me another subtle rock of his hips. "You've done a number on me, Lyla." Another kiss. He rests his forehead against mine. "Ready?"

"Ready." I nod. "Please, Kage, fuck me." I smirk and harken back that first night. "Thoroughly."

"Fuck," he curses under his breath as he presses himself up on his forearms. "Bend your knees for me." I do, opening myself up more, letting him slip in a little deeper "Remember, you don't have to be quiet."

He pulls out, snaps his hips to plow back into me, and with just one thrust, I'm certain I'm ruined for any other man because surely it will not get better than this. He sets a steady pace, pulling almost all the way out before slamming back into me. His lips are everywhere, and my hands and lips explore whatever I can reach of his body as that coil inside me begins to tighten again. And yet, even though it feels so good, I need more.

"Kage," I try. "I need . . . Different . . ." I can't form words.

"Different position?" he asks. I manage to nod as his balls slap against me with his next thrust. He stills. "How do you want it? Say it, and it's yours."

"From behind?"

It comes out as a question. And even though I'm so locked in on being with Kage, I find myself realizing just how physically unsatisfied I was in my last relationship. Deacon wasn't interested in my pleasure. If I came while he was getting his, great. If I didn't, he might rub my clit to get me there while he lay next to me, or he might not, depending on how spent he was. Kage wants nothing more than to bring me pleasure.

"That's a question," he calls me out. "Tell me what you want, Lyla."

If anyone were to overhear, they'd think he was being demanding, that I might be in a position I didn't want to be in. Except he's pouring confidence into me, unleashing a dormant part of me that has always wanted to emerge in the bedroom but never had the chance to.

"Take me from behind," I direct. He goes to move, but I stop him. I cradle his face so he has to look at me. "Hard."

"Fuck me," he groans as he pulls out.

"No," I say as he flips me over and I willingly prop up on my knees, putting my ass in the air for him. "Fuck *me*."

He goes feral.

He slams into me so hard I cry out. It's all pleasure, though, and I want more. I try to thrust back into him, but he's holding my hips and moving them in time with his own. All I can do is hang on to the bed sheets I'm once again clawing at.

"You feel so good," he says, breathless. Another thrust that makes me wail in the best way. "You're fucking incredible."

One of his hands moves. He starts to rub my clit and the way I fall apart, fast, sudden, and intense, is a holy experience. I pulse around him, begging him to keep going. It's never been like this. I've never come this hard, this rapidly, and yet still not sated. I can't get enough of him.

He pulls out but artfully flips us over so I'm straddling his hips. I don't need direction, I'm sliding onto him within the moment, desperate to have him back inside me.

"Take what you need," he directs as his hands settle on my hips, his eyes on mine, his hair mussed from my hands. "I'm all yours, Lyla. Take it."

There he goes again, making me feel confident. Beautiful. Desired.

Seen.

I take him hard and deep. I'm in complete control and it does something to me, to see this big, strong man fighting his own need to come undone as I ride him. His fingers dig into my hips so hard I'll probably have bruises there tomorrow, and he struggles to keep his eyes open and on me as bliss takes over his angular features. I'm doing this to him. *Me.*

"You feel so good in me," I breathe as I take the length of him again.

"You take me so well," he replies as one of his hands moves up to my breast and squeezes. "You were fucking made for me, Lyla."

I come apart without extra stimulation. When I come down this time, I know I'm done. I collapse on top of him, and he wraps his arms around me, kisses my shoulder, then my neck.

"You're doing so well," he tells me, and damn if the praise doesn't make me want to preen. I had a hunch I had a bit of a praise kink. It tracks, given my need to be the best in the classroom, the best at my job. He's confirming it in spades tonight—the perfect complement to his dominate nature. "Can you give me a little more? Or are you done?"

I know he needs to come. He's rock hard inside of me.

"I want to see you fall apart," I tell him. "I want you to come inside me. I can take more."

"You're sure?" he asks as he moves my hair over one shoulder. "I haven't been gentle."

"You've been perfect." I lift my head and kiss him. "Now, let go." He takes a moment to look at me. I guess he sees what he needs to see, because he's flipping us over and I'm parting my legs once more. "Your turn," I coax as he slides into me. "Take what you want."

His strokes are long, hard, and thorough. He hitches one of my knees up so he can drive deeper, and then his rhythm begins to falter. His breaths grow shorter. I throw my hands back, bracing them against his headboard, and give him every ounce of me.

Watching Kage Kensington fall apart is a thing to behold. He's pure pleasure, his guard down, bliss all over his features. His shout of my name reverberates in my bones. He releases one final shudder before he collapses his full weight on top of me, and I'm quick to wrap him in my arms. I soak in both the weight of him and the way his heart thunders against mine.

"Lyla," he breathes. "That . . . Incredible."

"Even better than the Bronco?" I ask.

"Infinitely better," he confirms. "You wrecked me."

I think he did the wrecking, but I'm going to take the compliment.

We stay like that for several minutes. I run my fingers through his hair, and he sighs in contentment. He's more relaxed than I've ever seen him, and I don't think it's just from the sex.

Eventually, he moves off me, but he pulls me to him in the same movement, so I'm the one resting on his chest now. We lie there together, listening to the rain lashing at the windows, the wind howling around the corners of the house. It's late afternoon, but as dark as dusk outside. I'm in no hurry to get out of bed, and Kage doesn't appear to be, either.

"We're doing that again," I tell him once I have enough energy to speak again.

"Again and again," he agrees as he kisses the top of my hair. "Except . . ." I lift my head to look at him. He looks pained.

"Except?" I prompt.

"We have to be judicial about a round two. I only had two condoms on me. I sucked up my pride, but the others in this house are ill-prepared in that department. I checked the grocery store, drug store, and even the gas station down the road, but everything was already closed for the storm. So, unless you have condoms on you, we're only fucking one more time until we're back in the city." He manages a smirk. "We can do other things, though."

I cross my arms over his chest and prop my chin on them to look at him, making what turns out to be an easy decision.

"I'm on the pill," I reveal. "I've never missed one, and I had my annual appointment right before I moved here. I'm clean. I trust you, and I'm comfortable forgoing the condom, but only if you are. If you feel more at ease being covered, that's what we'll do."

He looks at me with that same awe-struck expression as earlier. It's like he can't believe I'm real—that I'm here and I chose him. I let him come to whatever conclusion he decides on.

He plays with my hair while he thinks.

"I've had my share of one-night stands," he admits. "Not frequently, by any means, but at the risk of sounding like a jerk, if I decided I wanted sex, it wasn't hard to get. Most of the time, it was to distract myself, or maybe I needed to feel something." He's rambling, and I let him, learning more about him as he goes. "I haven't been with anyone else since you."

"No one?" I ask in disbelief. He's the kind of guy women will drop their panties for.

"Wasn't much use, seeing as the woman I picked up in a bar and took to my Bronco ruined me for all other women," he says

Touché.

"I haven't been with anyone else either," I say. "It's your call, Kage. I just wanted you to have all your options."

"I've never fucked without a condom," he admits. "That's one of the things my dad drilled into my head. Sleep around if I must, but do it responsibility." He stops playing with my hair and holds my eye. "You trust me?"

"You haven't given me a reason not to," I reply.

Something dark crosses his features. It's gone so quickly I wonder if I imagined it.

"I'm clean," he says. "I got tested not all that long ago. I did it on a whim, when I'd been thinking about you and how much I wanted to be with you again. I figured I should check on things, just to make sure." I smile and peck his lips. He gives me a kiss in return. "I'm happy to let you take my no-condom virginity."

"Hell of a way to put it," I say which makes him chuckle.

"Next time we do this, it'll be latex-free?" he clarifies.

"If you want it to be." I nod, and his answer is to kiss me.

I settle back into his embrace. His fingers trail up and down my back, a sweet gesture that makes me fall for him a little more. Soon though, his hand stills.

He's fallen asleep. I smile and cuddle into him, closing my eyes, and doze as well.

He wakes me up a couple of hours later as he tries to slip out of bed to use the bathroom. I cross the hall to use mine and find him waiting for me when I come out. We have every intention of going downstairs to figure out dinner, but the next thing I know, I'm spread out on my bed, and he's buried inside me. It doesn't last long this time—the feeling of skin on skin is overwhelming for both of us and he's spilling into me far quicker than I think he intended to.

We eventually make our way downstairs for dinner. I have my heart set on boxed macaroni and cheese while he tries to feed me grilled chicken and a salad. I make the macaroni out of sheer stubbornness, and he makes his healthy dinner for the same reason, but then he's eating my macaroni, making quips about carb loading, and I suck it up and eat a piece of chicken and some salad because he did go through the trouble of cooking it. We clean up together, he forces Sadie to go outside during a brief break in the rain—it's only kind of pouring—then we head to the media room to watch *Fight Club* because I've never seen it, and Kage has taken that as a personal offense. He's settled in the corner of the comfortable sectional couch and I'm curled up next to him, my head on his shoulder, his arm around me, one of his legs thrown over mine, when Luke and Theo show up.

"Is this what we have to look forward to?" Luke asks by way of greeting. "The two of you all over each other all the time?"

"Yes," Kage answers without looking at them.

"You two ventured out in that mess?" I ask. It's raining harder than it has all day now, and the wind is absolutely howling. I checked the weather forecast not that long ago, and it sounds like the worst of this massive storm is only just moving in.

"We need supplies," Luke says. "Namely, junk food."

"*He* needed supplies," Theo corrects. "I'm sleeping in my own bed tonight. The pool house couch is for a younger man."

"You're twenty-seven," Kage points out.

"My point still stands." He grins. "Don't worry, I'll wear ear plugs." Kage flips him off, making him laugh, and I fight off the blush that wants to color my cheeks.

"Scarlett and Will refused to come, so they don't get the fruits of my labor," Luke reports. "I'm about to make the biggest ice cream sundae this house has ever seen."

I perk up. "I could be into that . . ."

"Sundae-making party it is," Luke decides. "Even if it's just us because anyone with Kensington DNA is lame."

"I'm lactose intolerant," Theo protests.

"Lies," Luke states. "To the kitchen!"

I laugh and try to unwind myself from Kage to follow. He pulls me back to him. "Stay," he says as he nuzzles my neck. "I'm comfortable."

"I'll be back," I tell him. "Pause the movie?"

He grumbles but lets me get up before pausing the movie and following us to the kitchen. Luke is already rifling through the pantry for sundae toppings. He emerges with chocolate syrup, sprinkles, and chopped nuts, all of which I'm reasonably certain he bought while they were on their grocery run the day we arrived. It occurs to me that I haven't made my candy salad yet, so I find a bowl and start pouring in candy. Luke is over the moon, Theo is amused, and Kage is resigned.

We sit around the kitchen island eating ice cream and candy. Kage refuses his own bowl of ice cream, but he gets a spoon and helps himself to mine. So much so he ends up adding another scoop of ice cream with a guilty grin. Will and Scarlett eventually join us after Luke FaceTimes them to show them what they're missing. They arrive soaking wet, and I'm more certain than ever that there's something between Scarlett and Luke. Something they ignore, but something all the same.

It takes a while for everyone to go their separate ways. There's some debate about everyone sleeping in the main house, but Scarlett didn't bring her phone, Will wants to brush his teeth, and Luke states he can't let them brave the elements alone, so they make a run for it. I chat with Theo for a few minutes while Kage forces Sadie to go out one more time, and then I'm left alone when Theo decides to go to bed.

I find Kage in his grandfather's office, and I stand in the doorway for a minute, watching him. He's seated behind the desk, frowning at something on his computer.

"Everything okay?"

He looks at me and even though he tries to hide it, I can tell I've caught him off guard. "Everything's fine," he says. "Just checking in on the gym."

"Security cameras?" I guess as I push off the door and start toward him. He taps his keyboard a few times before turning in his chair so he's facing me when I step behind the desk. Instinct tells me there was something on the screen he didn't want me to see.

"Turns out it's pouring in the city, too," he reports. "The gym looks lonely." He sits forward and spreads his legs so I can stand between them and loops his arms around my waist while I drape mine around his neck. He peers up at me, serious. "I want you to train with me when we get back."

"Train with you?" I question. "I train with Scarlett—"

"You'll still workout with her. I told you I wanted you to get caught up on the self-defense lessons you missed while you were hurt. I'm going to train you myself."

"I thought Will was going to—"

"I'm going to do it," he says, a note of finality. "Will is perfectly capable, but I'm going to personally make sure you can protect yourself."

I've always trusted my instincts and right now, they are saying to ask questions. "Protect myself from what?"

"Every woman should know—"

"Kage." I cut him off, lifting an eyebrow that tells him I'm on to him. He sighs and starts rubbing circles on my hips with his thumbs.

"Someone already tried to kidnap you, Lyla," he reminds me.

"As long as my mother is in politics, there's always going to be some sort of threat against me," I tell him. "I was pulled out of my fourth-grade classroom and put on lock-down for some anonymous threat or another. I got the mail after school once when I was in seventh grade and there was a white powder in one of the envelopes. It was harmless, but we didn't know that at the time. In high school, I had my own bodyguard for six weeks because someone threatened my mother's life. There have been paparazzi and overzealous political fanatics who can't separate me from my mother. It's been like this my whole life, Kage. I'm used to it."

"Your lack of care for your personal safety is concerning."

"I'm fine—"

"You're a target," he counters with more of an edge than I think the situation warrants. "Not only because you're Veronica Adler's daughter, but because you're with me." My confusion at that statement must show on my face because he sighs and runs a hand through his hair. "I'm the CEO of Kensington Enterprises, Lyla."

"I know that . . ."

Well, I know it in theory, but I kind of forget. He takes a half-assed approach to it. He spends most of his time at his gym, in his office, on the computer. What does he actually *do*? Especially at a gym when logic says he should be out on the floor instead of glued to a screen.

"I'm the CEO," he says again. "I fucking hate it, but I am. And Kensington Enterprises has enemies. My dad didn't grow the company into what it is by being a nice guy. You're now a target simply because you're with me, and I'll do whatever it takes to keep you safe without compromising your agency. It's not up for debate."

I take a moment to figure out how I feel. I don't need protecting—I'm not a glass doll. I'm stronger than anyone has ever given me credit for, except, maybe, this man in front of me, and even he seems hell bent on being the protector. I remember what Will said about Kage doing anything for the people he cares about. Apparently, *anything* includes teaching me how to defend myself.

"I don't need you to protect me," I tell him firmly. "I don't think being with you puts me at risk." He opens his mouth to argue the point, but I put a finger on his lip to silence him. He simmers, but he shuts up. "However, if you think there's a need for me to be able to protect myself, fine. I'll allow you to teach me self-defense."

"This is important to me," he says as he brings me closer. "I have a history of losing the people I care about. Maybe I'm being overly cautious. Maybe there's a hell of a lot wrong with my psyche. I don't know. All I know is that I will theoretically sleep better at night if I know you can fight off someone who wants to take you from me."

My lingering annoyance with him ebbs away. "Theoretically sleep?"

"Sleep is a commodity I don't get a lot of. Although, having you next to me seems to help." He smirks. "Not that I intend to let either of us sleep when I take you upstairs in a few minutes."

I kiss him in response, and when I pull away, I catch a glimpse of the computer. An intricate spreadsheet is visible. "What, exactly, do you do all day? You're always in your office at the gym."

"Whatever needs to be done," he answers. "I try to teach a few classes when I can. I'd rather be doing that, honestly. But otherwise, it's a lot of spreadsheets and meetings." He looks at me. "I wanted the gym, Lyla. I didn't want Kensington Enterprises."

"Then why do you have it?" I ask.

"Because my dad is an asshole." He reaches around me, saves the spreadsheet, and closes out of it before giving me his full attention. "Can I interest you in letting me take you upstairs?"

"As long as you promise to do indecent things to me."

Later, when we're in bed sated and wrapped around one another, he drops a kiss to my shoulder.

"Lyla?"

"Hmm?"

"Tell me about your dad."

The request catches me off guard. "What do you want to know?"

"You said you don't think his death was an accident. Tell me why you think that."

"It just doesn't add up," I say. "He had a clean bill of health from the doctor just a couple of weeks before his accident. I know things happen, but there are other things, like the fact that he was out so late—that wasn't like him. He didn't stay at the office late, either. He was big on being home for us, even though we had all moved out by then. Something was going on with him and Mom, too. Lots of hushed arguments, things like that." I purse my lips, debating on what to tell him about what I found in his office. I decide to be vague. "Mom had me clean out his office, and I found a few things that I don't think he should have had in his possession."

I expect Kage to push, and he does. "Such as?"

"Classified documents on trade agreements, things like that. They were potentially damning evidence against some very important people." Including my mother. "That wasn't the type of document he usually handled."

Kage is quiet longer than I expect him to be. "Do you have those documents?" he eventually asks.

"Copies," I admit. "They weren't originals." I don't reveal that they were hidden in a false bottom, nor the sheer volume of them.

"I'll see what I can do," he says, and I furrow my brow.

"You'll see what you can do?" I repeat. "We're talking about classified documents, Kage."

"I have a lot of resources at my disposal, Lyla, and I'm not afraid to use them. If your dad's death wasn't an accident, we'll figure out what really happened to him."

This will be the moment I revisit over and over again down the road—the first inkling that I was falling for a dangerous man. For now, though, I nod and trust that me and my secrets are safe with him. He rolls over, turns off the light, then comes back to me, pulling me into his arms. I cuddle into him, naked, satisfied, cared for.

My last thought as I drift off to sleep is how I barely know this man—even if I think I know him better than most.

19

KAGE

For the first time since before my mom died, I'm reluctant to leave Kensington Manor. I usually can't wait to get out of here—I keep my visits short and infrequent. Today, though, as I brake to watch the gates close in my rearview mirror, every part of me wants to stay one more day.

Lyla's sitting in my passenger seat. It's been three days since I gave in. Three days of having her as mine. Three days of giving all the reasons I should stay away from her a massive middle finger. Three days of having her all to myself. I want one more day. One more day of, at most, having to wrestle her away from TV marathons with Luke or board games with Theo and Will. One more day of knowing she's safe. One more day of peace.

Instead, I press the gas and point my Bronco toward the city.

It's just us this time. Will is with Theo, which was their original plan anyway, but then I asked him to ride with me because I didn't trust myself to be alone with Lyla after seeing her on a date with someone else, never mind that I don't think she would have agreed to come if it hadn't been for him. I rest a hand on her thigh as I drive, and she covers my hand with hers and smiles my way. I feel like the luckiest man in the world.

We talk as we drive. She's easy to talk to, which is dangerous, because I keep telling her things I don't normally talk about before I realize I'm doing it. There's so much she doesn't know—so much I'll have to tell her, eventually. Maybe if I'm honest, if I come clean sooner rather than later, it won't be so bad. Maybe she won't hate me.

Maybe she won't leave me.

My chest clutches at the thought, and by proxy, so does my hand on her thigh. Her hand squeezes mine and I realize she's taken it for affection. I'll take that. It's better than having to explain my tendency to catastrophize all the ways the good things in my life can go wrong.

We stop at the same gas station we stopped at on the way up for fuel, coffee, and snacks. I try to keep an eye on her, just in case, but I lose her in the aisles a couple of times and only breathe easier when she's in my sight. The rational part of me knows she's fine, that there's most likely nothing or no one out here that's going to try to harm her. The less rational part of me—the part she seems to be the main trigger for— is convinced someone is going to grab her right out from underneath me.

I hold her hand as we roll into the city. Everything is still largely shut down as flooded streets dry up and wind damage is assessed, but it's time to come back. I have a business to run, things to take care of, and Lyla has work—her friends. We have to return to the real world and leave the Kensington Manor bubble. Except . . . Maybe . . . Not tonight.

"Did you tell Bradley or Gabe we were coming back today?" I ask.

"No." She shakes her head. "They were both due home early this morning after one last overnight. I decided not to risk waking them with a text. They probably need the sleep."

"Stay with me tonight," I propose. "Your office is still closed tomorrow, right?"

"We go back the day after tomorrow," she confirms.

"Stay with me," I say again. "One more night before I have to let you go back to sleeping in a less-comfortable bed."

"How do you know my bed isn't comfortable?" she asks, and I flash a grin at her as I switch lanes.

"I might have stayed the night you dislocated your shoulder."

"I knew it!" she exclaims. "I knew my sheets smelled like you."

"You know how I smell?" I ask, amused.

"Like sandalwood and leather," she confirms. "And a giant ego." I laugh and squeeze her hand. I laugh a lot more with her. She makes things *better*.

"Stay with me," I say one more time. "You'll make me happy, give Bradley and Gabe some much-needed alone time, and I'll even let you order whatever disgusting takeout you want for dinner."

"You're fooling no one," she says. "You like takeout just as much as the rest of us."

"All things—" I start.

"In moderation," she cuts me off with an eye roll and a grin. "You really want me to stay?"

"I want you to stay." I nod. "I'm not ready to share you with the real world."

Or navigate her pissed-off big brother. Or figure out how to mitigate all the ways in which my decision to be with her has increased her value as a target. All of that can wait until tomorrow. I'm taking one more day.

"Okay," she agrees. I smile to myself and squeeze her hand again, letting myself think about which of the many ways I've daydreamed about having her in my condo I want to do first. But I'm also happy. It's a foreign feeling, but I'm surprisingly hopeful it will be a regular thing.

Despite my good mood, I feel the low hum of anxiety that never quite goes away growing louder the closer we get to my building. There's a new level to it now, though, and while I resist the therapist Theo swears I need, I know enough to know it has everything to do with Lyla. It's not just the increased danger I'm putting her in or the added complications being a part of one another's lives will bring. It's that I don't know how to do this. I don't know how to be in a relationship.

What I had with Brynn wasn't a relationship. It was an arrangement that worked until it didn't. I didn't care about her wants, her needs. I was respectful enough of her in the bedroom and I can admit we had decent sex, but I just didn't care. Not like I was supposed to. Yet here I am, making a mental list of things I need to pick up at the bodega down the block from my place so Lyla will be comfortable in my condo—her favorite coffee creamer and the brand of chips she likes, some of that boxed macaroni. Things that have never come through my door before.

I swear that I'm going to do this right as I turn into my garage. I'm going to make sure Lyla knows she's cared for. I'm going to take her on dates, hold her hand, tell her how incredible she is. Deacon Cosse didn't treat her well. His loss is my substantial gain. She will not tell her next partner that she wasn't worshiped, wasn't treated well, wasn't told daily how special she is—if she even has a next partner. I'm not exactly thinking about forever, but, well, the idea of her with anyone that isn't me makes me nauseous.

I park, then let a disgruntled Sadie out of the backseat. Lyla meets me behind the Bronco to retrieve our bags.

"I'm perfectly capable of carrying my own bags," she says as I haul my well-worn duffel bag and hers, plus her tote, over my shoulder. She stands there, arms crossed, giving me a pointed look.

"I know you are," I say. "But you don't have to." I lean down and peck her lips. "My mom never carried her own bags. You won't either." I jerk my head for her to follow me. Sadie is already sitting next to the elevator lobby's door, annoyed we're taking too long. "For the record?" I ask Lyla as we walk. "She always told my dad she could carry her own bags, too. He told her the same thing."

She smiles at me in that way of hers that says I got to her. I like it when she smiles at me like that, like I just gave her a piece of treasure by sharing something about myself. Maybe one day she'll truly know all of me. Maybe one day I won't be afraid to let her.

"Key in the code for me?" I request. She positions her fingers over the keypad and looks at me expectantly. I rattle off the eight-digit number, and the lobby door opens. She pushes the elevator call button and then I have her key in the same code again to take us to my floor. This building is nothing if not secure, and I want Lyla to be able to let herself in whenever she wants or needs to. "One more time," I say when we reach my door. She types it in without any prompting from me and I grin. She's already memorized it. "That code is unique to me, and will get you in the building, up the elevator, and into my condo. Use it whenever."

"You're inviting me over whenever?" she clarifies. I try to appear casual, like my heart isn't thundering in my ears at the idea of essentially giving her a key to my place, as I make my way across my condo which suddenly feels too small now that I've spent several days upstate.

"I'm not far from your office." I drop our things just inside my bedroom door and turn back to her. "And I like waking up with you."

"Depends on how comfortable your bed is," she says. "You implied mine wasn't all that comfortable."

"I'll need a true night spent in your bed to form an informed opinion on the matter," I counter. "I stayed on top of the blankets and kept my distance, so it doesn't count."

"We'll have a sleepover the next time Bradley and Gabe both work an overnight."

We stand there for a few beats, several feet between us, her unsure of what to do now, me marveling at the fact that I have a girlfriend, and she's standing in my condo. At least . . . I'm pretty sure she's my girlfriend.

"Want to walk to the bodega down the block?" I ask. "I need to pick up a few things."

"Okay," she agrees. "I could stand to stretch my legs after being in the Bronco."

I make sure Sadie has water and then take Lyla's hand. When we step out onto the sidewalk, I realize this is it. This is me, making a statement. This woman is *mine*. Every soul in this city who wants my blood will soon know the quickest way to take me down will be through her. I pull her into my side and kiss her hair to send a message to anyone who's watching because someone is *always* watching.

Lyla is mine.

And I will do anything to protect her.

I get the few items I need until I can make a grocery

order tomorrow, then I take her to a coffee shop a little further down for an afternoon coffee and pastry. I get her to key in the code on our return to make sure it's still fresh, and then I collapse on the couch, bringing her with me.

"Are you sure you don't need to go check on the gym?" she asks. I'm stretched out on the couch and she's lying on top of me. She's lost her mind if she thinks I'm moving from right here for the foreseeable future.

"Luke headed over there. He'll let me know if there's anything that needs my attention." My hands start to explore her curves. "I'd rather give you my attention."

"I do like being the center of your attention," she says as she shifts so she can see me better.

"You're quickly becoming the center of my entire world." I pull her in to kiss her before she has time to process my overt admission of how I feel about her.

I start to debate how I want her as my pants tighten. There is some merit to having her right here on the couch. I've thought about taking her in the shower and have quite the fantasy about her on my kitchen counter. God knows I'm going to absolutely ravage her in my bed at some point. I'm about to move this to the floor when there's a knock on my door, and she starts to pull away.

"Ignore it," I say, my hands working under the waistband of the leggings she's wearing. I'm convinced she wears these things just to torment me. Whoever it is knocks again, a little less patient this time.

"What if it's important?" she asks as she tries again to pull away.

"It's not," I say even though I have no idea. "Let's go to the floor—"

More knocking. "Kage!"

Fucking Luke.

"It's Luke," Lyla says as she moves away.

"He'll go away." I try to keep her close, but she's insistent.

"What if it's important?" she asks again.

He calls my name and knocks again and that's the thing —he knows Lyla is here. He wouldn't be beating down my door if it weren't important. I sigh and stand, before leaning down and kissing Lyla because I can't *not* kiss Lyla, then start toward the door with the decision that if someone isn't dead or dying, Luke himself is dead. I check over my shoulder to make sure Lyla is decent—debatable, given how her cheeks are flushed and her hair is mussed as she sits on my couch, but she's at least covered up—and swing open the door to find Luke about to knock again. He looks apologetic.

"Sorry to interrupt," he says, eyes darting past me to Lyla. "I figured it was safer for me to knock than to burst in like I usually would."

I glare at him, but Lyla greets him. "Hi, Luke."

"Hey, Lyla." He gives her a little wave and then turns to me, who I can guess looks a lot less friendly. "My bathroom sink is spewing water. I can't get the damn thing to shut off."

I frown. "Call building maintenance—"

"I did, but they're on call, need to drive in. Meanwhile, my bathroom is flooding. I can fix it myself, just need some extra muscle."

I open my mouth to argue, but he subtly widens his eyes, and I realize this is *Luke*. He wouldn't be banging down my door about a plumbing emergency. He'd handle the damn thing and move on. Something else is going on and it is, in fact, important.

"Fine." I turn to Lyla. "I'm going to see if I can help him. I won't be long."

"Take your time," she replies with a smile that has a hint of amusement around the edges. "I need to call Cecily anyway."

"I'll be right back," I promise.

"Take your time," she says again, already reaching for her phone, and I grin at her.

"Say good things about me?"

She rolls her eyes, and I chuckle as I close the door. I cross the hall to Luke's condo, my mood shifting back to annoyed at being interrupted, and push through the door he left partially open for me. I stop in my tracks. Theo and Will are also here. My brain shakes the lust-addled fog off fast.

"What happened?" I demand.

"I went to the gym," Luke says. "Everything was fine, no damage from the storm, nothing out of place, etcetera." I lift a warning eyebrow. I have no time for his theatrics. "I got home, got a notification of movement on the gym's security cameras, which, normal, right?" I pat my pockets for my phone but remember it's on the counter across the hall. "People on the sidewalk set that fucking thing off all the time. I checked it out of habit though, and . . ."

I snatch Luke's phone out of his hand. "Which camera?" I demand as I hold up his phone to his face so it unlocks. I turn it back to me and start tapping through screens.

"Front door," he answers. "They aren't subtle, are they?"

I don't answer. I find the feed for the front door camera and use my thumb and forefinger to zoom in. A large black SUV is parallel parked directly across the street from my gym.

"Burner phone?" I request.

Luke pulls out an unsuspecting gray canvas basket from

a shelf of his entertainment console. It's full of new burner phones. He tosses me one and I power it on.

"What are you two doing here?" I ask Theo and Will while I wait for it to turn on.

"Will saw the car on his phone, and we headed here," Theo answers.

"We intercepted Luke in the hall," Will adds. "You didn't see this on your own phone? You get all the security camera alerts."

"Lyla is at my place," I remind them. "I was occupied."

"Hence why I knocked," Luke tells them. They nod in understanding. If I weren't so wrapped up in what's happening right now, I'd knock their heads together. The phone finally boots up, and I bang out a number I memorized a long time ago. That's a personal rule of mine—memorize important codes and phone numbers in case you're caught without your own phone. They answer after a single ring.

"I need a word with you."

"Look at you, knowing who's on the other end of the call," I quip.

"An educated guess," they counter. "Now, send one of your minions to unlock the door."

"Can't, gym's closed," I say. "Hurricane, remember?"

"Then open it."

"We'll be open during regular business hours tomorrow." I think through what needs to happen before this meeting takes place tomorrow. "I'll be in my office after three o'clock."

"You'll meet me before then."

"I'll be in my office after three o'clock," I repeat. "Take it or leave it. I'm sure you know which I prefer."

"Which office?" Their annoyance is thick, but they know

me well enough to know I'd split hairs and go to my office at Kensington Enterprises just to piss them off.

"You'll have to make an educated guess," I state.

I hang up, and Luke, Theo, and Will stare at me.

"You sure that was wise?" Theo asks.

"I can occupy Lyla if you need . . ." Will offers.

"I don't bend to other people's wills," I remind them.

"Except Lyla's," Luke says. I glare at him, but he only grins.

"Three o'clock tomorrow, and not a moment sooner." I quickly think through tomorrow again. Three o'clock gives me time to have a slow morning with Lyla. But then I need to make sure she's occupied and far, far away from Kensington Boxing. And Kensington Enterprises, too, for good measure. I look to Will. "I may need your help with Lyla tomorrow."

"Say the word," he agrees and I shift to Theo.

"Can you be at the gym around three tomorrow?"

"I think so," he replies. "I need to move a meeting, but it shouldn't be a big deal."

"Luke . . ."

"I'll call in backup," he finishes.

"Thank you." I stand there for a moment, thinking, debating, before I determine my next step. "Let's keep an eye on the cameras, but they won't do anything tonight. Tomorrow? They wait. We don't see them a moment before three o'clock."

"Not a word to Lyla?" Luke guesses.

"None," I confirm. "I'll be with her all morning and into the afternoon, but she's to have eyes on her at all times." I look at Luke. "Let Bradley know what's going on." He nods his affirmation. I take another beat before deciding I've done all I can for now. "I'm going back across the hall. If anything happens, handle it. Only get me if it's absolutely necessary." They exchange a look. "What?"

"It's good to see you putting something else—*someone* else—first," Theo says.

I purse my lips but don't say anything. Lyla is an unexpected kink in the plan, yet . . . I don't care. Let her mess it all up, so long as she's safe.

"You can't keep her in the dark about this forever, Kage," Luke says. "She's going to find out eventually and it's going to be a hell of a lot better if it comes from you."

"I know," I say. "I'll tell her. I just . . ." Don't want to. Because I know when I do, she's going to walk away. "I need more time."

More time with her. More time to convince her to stay with me.

"Speaking of Lyla." Theo stands and crosses the room to where he left his messenger bag on Luke's kitchen counter. He takes a folder out of a side pocket and holds it out to me. "As requested."

"Thank you." I reach for it, but he pulls it back, lifting an eyebrow. "You're sure about this?"

"I'm sure." I nod. "She already knows. She just doesn't *know*."

Theo hands me the folder. He's reluctant and I can't blame him. Despite my "I'm sure," I'm reluctant, too. I give them a parting nod of my head and step out into the hall. Will follows me.

"You can't keep lying to her, Kage," he says in a low voice so as not to alert Lyla to his presence. "*I* can't keep lying to her. She's my friend. If you don't tell her soon, I'm going to."

"I don't like lying to her either," I say. "I fucking hate it. But how do you drop something like this on her? It's going to crush her, Will."

"So will knowing we all knew and didn't say a word." He holds my eye—doesn't so much as blink. "I mean it, Kage. Tell her soon, or I'm going to. You're my brother and I love you, but I care about her, too. She deserves to know the truth."

"I'll tell her," I promise. "What are you doing on this side of the bridge anyway? Theo didn't drop you off at your place?"

"He was going to, but then we decided pizza and video games at his place sounded more fun and we saw the camera alert in the process of getting there."

I just shake my head. It was like this when they were in my care, too. I'd be in the kitchen fighting with Andie over homework and wondering how in the hell I got myself in this mess while those two were off playing video games or hanging out wherever people who had half a shot at having an actual teenage experience hung out. I'm glad they're still close.

"Tell her," he says again before he lets himself back into Luke's condo. I take a moment to collect myself and appear normal before I key in the code to re-enter mine. I find Lyla in the kitchen, waiting on another cup of coffee. She looks like she belongs here.

"Everything okay over there?" she asks as she watches her mug fill.

I slip the folder onto the console by my door while she has her back to me. "Everything is fine. He needs a new seal." I start toward her. "More coffee? It's a wonder you ever sleep."

"I'm pretty sure I'm immune to caffeine," she says. "Want a cup?"

"I want you."

The words tumble out of me. She stops mid-reach for

the cabinet where my mugs are, like she was going to make me a cup despite my denial. Her cheeks flush and that seals the deal. I'm taking her to bed.

"I assume we're picking up where we left off?" she asks as I reach her.

"That would imply returning to the couch, and I need room to move around. We're going to the bedroom." I take her hand. "Come."

She follows me into the bedroom and every thought I have about the SUV outside of my gym and what waits for me tomorrow falls away. She goes to lie on the bed, but I stop her. She looks at me in question, and I hold her eyes as I move around her, breaking eye contact only long enough to take my shirt off and toss it. I drop my shorts and my boxer briefs and then sit on the edge of the bed. Lyla watches me expectantly.

"Undress."

I see the moment she slides into a place of, not submission exactly, because my woman is not submissive, but of being willing to play this game. I'm figuring out what she likes, what turns her on, what she doesn't like. I know she likes it when I praise her. She doesn't hate missionary, but she doesn't love it either and I suspect that has a lot to do with her previous relationship. Her ass is fine for me to hold onto, to squeeze while I'm thrusting, but anal is off the table. She loves my mouth and tongue on her, and she generally needs her clit rubbed to come. She makes these breathy little noises before her orgasm hits, and she needs something to hold onto when she's falling apart. She likes being taken from behind but doesn't like reverse cowgirl—said it felt awkward. I immediately struck it from the list, right along with anal.

She fucking *loves* when I tell her what to do in the bedroom and *only* in the bedroom.

She smirks and begins a slow, sensual strip out of her clothes. Her leggings go first. She peels them down her perfect legs, revealing inch by perfect inch of flesh that I'm about to have wrapped around me. She steps out of them and kicks them aside. She holds my eyes as she pulls her sweater overhead, leaving her in a bra and panties. I'm shameless as I stroke myself, letting my eyes burn into her. She reaches behind her to unclasp her bra, and it falls away. I need my hands on her right now.

"Come here," I order.

"One second . . ." She drops her panties and it's suddenly hard to breathe. She saunters to me, and I part my legs for her as she drops her hands on my shoulders. "Is this what you want?"

"Not quite." I continue to stroke myself as I put the fingertips of my other hand on the inside of her knee. "I want *you*, Lyla. I want you across this bed, writhing and begging for me." My fingers drag along her inner thigh. "I want you screaming my name so loud the neighbors file a noise complaint." Her grip tightens on my shoulders. "I want you to wake up tomorrow morning and know exactly who you belong to." My fingers creep between her legs. "Let's see if you want me." I slide my fingers through her folds and groan at how slick she is. She whimpers in response. "All that for me, sweet girl?"

"All of it," she pants as my fingers make another pass, intentionally avoiding that bundle of nerves she's trying to guide toward my fingers with how she rocks her hips. "You make me insatiable, Kage."

"Glad I'm not suffering that affliction alone." I dip a

finger into her, and her fingernails dig into me. "Want me to fuck you with my fingers?"

"Please." She nods.

"How about my tongue?"

"God, yes," she moans as I push another finger into her.

"What about my cock?"

"Inside me," she manages, already being carried off by waves of pressure.

I remove my fingers, and she squawks in protest. I hold her eyes. "Take me first, then."

She fucking *drops* to her knees, like she can't wait to have me. I remove my hand and let her replace it with her own. Then she's suckling my tip, and I know I'm going to blow my load before I ever get inside her. Just as well, I can use the time it takes me to recover to make sure she's panting for my cock by the time I'm ready to take her.

Her mouth feels like heaven as it slides over me, taking a decent amount of me down her throat. She works the rest of me with her hand and I'm humming in pleasure.

"That's it," I say as she moves. "Just like that." I let her work, let her adjust to things for a few minutes before I pull her off me.

"I wasn't done . . ." she starts.

"I know," I say as I stand. "I want a better angle." I might come just like this, looking down at this beautiful angel on her knees for me.

"Bet I can take all of you."

I lift an eyebrow. "That's a bold declaration."

"I have excellent control of my gag reflex."

What little hold on sanity I have snaps as I reach for her face. She lifts, opens her mouth, and then I'm sliding down her throat. I might be the six-foot-four man in the room, and Lyla might be on her knees for me, but she has every ounce of power right now. She bobs her head, swirls her tongue, and I fist her hair, thrusting into her mouth, careful to let her set the depth. When her lips touch my balls, I'm jolted out of a state of pure bliss to reality. A fucking glorious reality in which my woman has all of me down her throat. She looks up at me with those big, beautiful eyes, tears trickling from them, and this is easily one of the most intense things that has ever happened to me.

"God, Lyla," I pant. "You . . . I can't . . ."

She pulls back slowly, dragging her tongue along the length of me, eyes never leaving mine. I can't decide if I want to chase her mouth and reclaim it or let her do whatever she's doing right now. My indecisiveness leads her to sitting back on her heels and beaming up at me.

"Told you I could take all of you."

My knees buckle.

They actually buckle.

She has taken me down.

I collapse on the bed, dragging her with me, kissing her hard.

"Finish me off?" I ask. "Please?"

"Happily."

She kisses her way down my body, and I've never been this much of a mess over a woman. It's not even just how good this is, how incredible her mouth feels as she takes me again. It's that this is happening with *Lyla*, and I can't believe my good luck that she's mine.

"God, that feels good," I groan as she swirls her tongue the way I like. "That's it," I encourage again as her head bobs and my hips thrust outside of my control. "Fuck, Lyla, your mouth . . ." She grazes her teeth along my length, and I shudder. "More," I beg. *Beg*. Me. Begging in bed. What the fuck is happening? "Please, Lyla, more." She bobs and licks and squeezes and I have no hope of recovery. "Lyla." I try to pull her off me. "I'm gonna . . . I'm about to . . ." She sucks harder and that's it; I release in her mouth. She gags on the amount of it, but fuck if she doesn't swallow most of me. She sits back with soft *pop* as releases me, and wipes at the dribble on chin.

"You must have liked that," she says. All I can do is groan and let my head fall back into the pillows. When I manage to open my eyes again, she's still kneeling between my legs, a vision with her perky breasts and hard nipples. I lift a hand and crook my finger.

"Come here." She crawls up my body and lies down next to me. My limbs feel like lead, but I put an arm around her and pull her in close, kissing her soundly. "You literally took me down at the knees," I say as I trail my fingertips along her jaw. "Give me a minute to get the ability to use my limbs back, and I'm going to put you through your paces."

"You better," she says. "I left my vibrator at home, and my fingers aren't long enough to go as deep as I need it right now." I groan. No one would ever think this woman capable of the words that come out of her mouth when we're in bed together. "Besides, that little display just now was purely self-interest." She shifts so she's on her side and starts tracing the swirls of the tattoo over my heart. "I've figured out if I get you to come before you get your hands on me, you last longer once I get you hard again."

"You think you're clever," I say.

"I'd like to think I am," she confirms as she kisses my neck, her hand trailing over my chest. I lift her leg over my hip to open her up some and start to stroke her. I have her squirming and asking me to take her in minutes.

"I'm not ready yet," I say as I move her onto her back. Even as I say it, my cock is starting to stir once more. "Let me taste you. Trust me, nothing makes me harder than having my mouth between your legs."

That's not true. She walks into the room, and my pants get tight. She smiles at me, and I'm stuck with a tentpole between my legs. She said she used her vibrator while daydreaming about me, but I'll never admit just how many times I've jerked myself off to thoughts of her.

I work my way down her body, taking the time to kiss, lick, and nip as much of her as I can. She's all I want, all I need. I settle between her legs, and she spreads her legs wider, pushing herself into my mouth. It encourages me, makes me commit to getting her off like this all over again. It broke my heart and filled me with rage in equal measure that she had never had a man pleasure her this way. This woman should never be denied. She should have an altar built in her honor and damn if I might be the one to do it.

I make her come on my tongue.

Then my fingers.

Then my tongue and fingers.

By the time she's coming down from that third orgasm, I'm so hard I hurt.

"Need a minute?" I ask her as I stretch out next to her.

"Please," she pants. She's all loose limbs, messy hair, and damp skin. I'll need to change my sheets before we sleep, but this view is absolutely worth it. She has her arms thrown overhead, her legs still spread wide, and her lips are swollen from the times I broke away to kiss her.

"Tell me when," I say, content to wait until she's ready. I hold her close, peppering her skin with soft kisses. "You know you can tap out whenever you want."

"I don't want to." She shakes her head. "I need you in me, Kage."

"Whatever you want," I promise. "How do you want me to take you?"

"However you want," she says.

"This isn't about me." I shake my head. "How do you want it, Lyla?"

He who shall not be named didn't give her what she needs in the bedroom. He expected her to be meek, to be the girl on his arm, to—I hate the word—*serve* him. That's not who she is. She's strong and fierce and so brave. I asked her that second night we spent together at Kensington Manor if she was okay, if her EDS made sex painful for her because the last thing I want is to hurt her. She was honest, reminded me she's nearly always in some sort of pain, that she's likely sorer after sex than would be considered normal, but promised me that it wasn't anything I did or that she wanted to stop doing. I made her promise to always tell me if something was too much. She swore she would, and I fell a little deeper into whatever this. To know she deals with so much and yet is so *her* is just—incredible. I want her to embrace how strong she is.

"I told you, I want it however you want it." She moves so she's on her side, facing me. She cups my cheek and I turn my head, kissing her palm. "I like how you are with me, Kage. You ask me what I want and you make me tell you. You make me feel confident, strong."

She sees me as someone far better than I am. I don't deserve it. Worse, she makes me want to be the guy she thinks I am, and I just don't see how that's possible, not with my past, not with what being with me could cost her.

"Lyla, I—"

"Stop." She cuts me off with a finger to my lips. "I don't know why your self-confidence when it comes to me is so shitty, but I don't like it. You are good to me. You are good *for* me." Her fingers brush along my lips. I want to tell her I'm not good, that I'm not good for her. I want to tell her I absolutely ache to be the man she thinks I am. "I want you to take me however *you* want me. I trust you, Kage. I want to give you this."

Something deep inside of me cracks wide open. I bury my face in the crook of her neck so she can't read the emotions I can't hide. I don't know what this is, the way I feel. It's something I can't name, something I haven't felt before. It feels big and wide and terrifying and like something I want to hold onto forever. I can't form words, so I just hold her closer, beg any god, goddess, or mythical entity listening to please *please* let me keep her.

Another couple of minutes pass before she brushes her lips across my forehead.

"I'm ready when you are."

I stay as I am, an arm wrapped around her, my face still tucked into the safety of her, but I dip a hand between her legs to see if she needs a little more foreplay now that we've had a break. She's as slick as ever and after I work my fingers in and out of her a few times, I move us so I'm on top. I pour all I have into kissing her, then position myself at her entrance. I rest my forehead against hers, my lips hovering over hers, trading breath with her. I brace my weight above her to keep from crushing her.

"You have all of me," I promise. And, eyes locked with hers, I claim her with a roll of my hips.

I don't know how to put what I feel for her into words and I'm too fucking scared to label it. It's something I didn't think I was capable of feeling, something I didn't *want* to feel. So instead of fucking her like I intended to when I ordered her to my bedroom—hard, deep, and dirty—I show her how I feel about her. I give her the long, hard strokes I know she needs, but I take what I need, too. The connection. The care. Every little gasp, every little sigh of pleasure, every whimper, every whisper of my name, I store them all up in a place in my chest reserved for Lyla.

She begs for more, but I just can't. I need this to last. I compromise, adjusting our angle so my hips brush her clit with each stroke. Her hands are all over me, leaving trails of fire in their wake as she runs them down my back, over my shoulders, into my hair. Her hips rise to meet mine and this —her—is all I'm ever going to want.

"Kage!" she breathes. "I'm . . . So . . . Close . . ." I open her legs wider so I can give her a little more. When she peaks, it's the most stunning thing I've ever seen, and it drives me over the edge. I chant her name over and over like a prayer as I spill into her. Then, I collapse on top of her, but not for long. I hitch her leg over my hip and roll us so we're on our sides. I'm still inside of her but I don't want to lose that connection just yet, even as I go soft.

"That was life-altering," I declare.

"I . . . Agree . . ." She breathes as she cuddles into me and I hold her tight. "That was something entirely different."

I felt it, too. Whatever just happened between us, there's no going back from it. I don't *want* to go back from it. I eventually slip out of her, but we continue to lie there, me holding her, her cuddling into me. A thought occurs to me, and I try to dismiss it, but I can't. It won't leave me alone.

"Lyla?"

"Hmm?"

I'm uncharacteristically nervous as I trail my fingertips along her spine. "Are you . . . That Ken doll you went out with. Are you planning to see him again?"

The words come out rushed. I hadn't thought about him when we were tucked away from reality at Kensington

Manor. Now, back in the city, I've thought about that guy way too much.

"I was planning to." My insides seize up. I go to pull away from her, not sure how to navigate this, but she stops me with a gentle touch, then moves her hand to my cheek so she can turn me to look at her. "I was planning to," she says again, "but this guy I've had a thing for for a while got off his ass and asked me to give him a chance, so I let the other guy down easy."

"You did?" I hate how vulnerable I sound.

"The morning after your confession in the library, while you were in the gym with Luke and Theo, I called him, told him I'd met someone. He asked if it was 'that big guy at the bar,' and I told him it was."

My relief is palpable. I pull her to me, kiss her, vaguely think about how I need to tell her about Brynn, but I don't, not yet. Why ruin this moment?

We stay in bed a while longer before she finally pries herself out of my arms and heads to the shower. I consider joining her but behave myself and change the sheets instead. I toss the ones that smell like us into the washer, then check the gym's security footage. The car is gone, and all is quiet. I check my building's camera's next—hacked into those a while ago—then Bradley's, Kensington Enterprises, and finally, Theo's building, just to be safe. For now, everyone is leaving me the hell alone and the people I care about are safe.

I make good on my promise to let Lyla order whatever she wants for dinner and that turns out to be takeout Chinese. She takes it upon herself to invite Luke over, even offers him use of my shower if his plumbing is still on the fritz. He plays it off, she's none the wiser, and I feel like shit for lying to her. The folder Theo gave me taunts me and finally, after I've evicted Luke and we've actually managed to watch *Fight Club* all the way through after a few false starts at Kensington Manor, I decide it's time.

"I have something for you." I stand and retrieve the folder. I sit down next to her and offer it to her. She looks at me curiously before she opens it. I anticipate the gasp she lets out once she realizes what she's looking at.

"Kage! This is my dad's autopsy report! How do you have it?"

"It's your father's *official* autopsy report," I correct as I take the stack or papers from her. I shuffle a few papers. "This is his actual autopsy report." She looks at me, eyes wide. "This." I continue shuffling. "Is the official accident report." More shuffling. "This is the actual accident report." She stares as I sit back on the couch. "You will find that they aren't the same."

"How . . ." She shakes her head, dumbfounded. "How, Kage?"

"I told you, Lyla." I take her hand. "I have resources. I'm not afraid to use them."

"But this . . ." She waves the folder around. "This is—How?"

"I'd prefer you not know the details. My dad didn't build Kensington Enterprises to be what it is without making some enemies. He also made some friends. Friends helped me get this." I watch her. She's struck dumb, a phrase I never thought I'd use for Lyla. "Tell me what you're thinking."

"I . . . Don't know . . ." She shakes her head. "It's been just a few days since I told you I suspected something wasn't right and now you have this . . ."

"We can get rid of it," I tell her. "I can set it on fire, and we'll never have to see it again. It's up to you. You want the truth about what happened to your father, though, and while I think this might leave you with more questions, it's also going to give you some answers."

I allow her space to reel, even as I sit next to her. It takes her a long time to work up the courage to look through the papers I've given her, but then she takes a deep breath and starts to read. She starts with the official autopsy, the one regurgitated to the public. She breezes through it, likely because she already knows exactly what it says—that he had a massive heart attack while operating a motor vehicle. Then she gets to the actual autopsy, the one purposefully hidden from the public.

"This isn't remotely the same," she says as she reads. "It says nothing about a heart attack. It says all his vital organs appeared to be healthy." I stay quiet, let her keep reading, listen as she rattles off bullet points like *clean toxicology* and *no known history of illness*, even a note that says he was wearing his prescribed eyeglasses and his seat belt at the time of impact. "Cause of death: drowning." She looks at me, eyes wide. "My dad drowned." I nod confirmation. "Because his car went into the Potomac . . . They told us it was a heart attack."

I have a follow-up question for her, but I hold onto it for now. "Read the accident report."

She spares me a long look before she resumes her reading. Like last time, she goes through the official report quickly. That one will tell her the aforementioned heart attack killed him instantly, and that he drove off the bridge into the Potomac as a result. I hold my breath as she moves on to the actual report.

"Kage . . ." Her voice trembles. I'm still holding her hand, so I squeeze it in support. "It . . . This says . . ." She can't put words to it, so I do it for her.

"It says he was pursued at a high rate of speed and eventually ran off the road," I say as gently as I can. "Except, there was no shoulder. He went off the bridge, into the Potomac. His car was submerged in icy water. He drowned. He was likely gone before rescue vehicles arrived on scene despite a witness calling in the accident and them arriving within minutes." I watch her eyes fill with tears. "There were no signs of the vehicle that was chasing him. Or answers as to why he was being chased."

She breaks.

I pull her to me and hold her close, letting her sob into my chest. I feel powerless and there is *nothing* I hate more than feeling powerless. I can't take her pain away. I can't make her forget what she read. I can't tell her who was responsible, although I have a good idea. I can't fix any of this and it wrecks me. I'm always able to fix things for the people I care about. The one thing I haven't been able to figure out is how to fix death.

"I'm so sorry, Lyla," I whisper. "I'm so sorry."

I debate if this was the right thing to do. She wanted the truth. She knew something was amiss. I've given her what truth I know about her father's death, and she holds a few key pieces I don't have yet, like whatever is in those papers she found. I'm not going to make her give them to me, but I hope she will. I hope she'll share them so we can get to the bottom of this. But now she knows the truth, and it's crushed her. I hate this.

Worst of all, I've opened the door.

Her father's death is just one part of an intricate web of secrets, lies, and cover-ups. It's a web so complex, so layered, that it's impossible to truly know what's true or who to trust. All sides are guilty, none are innocent. At the end of the day, it will come down to who is the guiltiest, and there will be consequences aplenty. There already have been.

And I've invited Lyla into the heart of it.

She cries for a long time and I hold her—be the rock she needs me to be. There's a lot I can't be for her, but this? I can do this. I rub her back, kiss her hair, but I don't talk, don't offer her empty promises like "it's going to be okay." When she finally sits up, her beautiful eyes are swollen and bloodshot. I reach out and wipe away a stray tear.

"I'm sorry," she apologizes.

"For what?" I ask, frowning.

"Falling apart like that."

"No, Lyla." I shake my head. "You don't apologize for being upset. You're allowed to be upset. Sad. Angry. Confused. All of it. I don't know who made you feel like you can't show your emotions, but that's bullshit. You're allowed to cry."

This goes for everyone but me. I can't afford to let emotions get the better of me.

"My mom." I lift an eyebrow in question. "My mom doesn't like it when we show emotions. She says it shows weakness and as a leader, you have to be strong. Bradley is good at keeping his emotions in check, he has to be. He sees awful things in the ER. Alice is so good at it that we joke that she doesn't even have feelings. I've always worn my heart on my sleeve though."

"And I love that about you," I say, tucking a strand of her hair behind her ear and skipping right over the use of a very specific 'L' word. "You are not your mom, your brother, or you sister." The smile she gives me is faint but there. "What do you need right now, Lyla? Name it. I'll make it happen."

She could ask me to bring her the planet formally known as Pluto preserved in a snow globe and I'd find a way to make it happen. Anything to bring some semblance of a smile back to her face.

"Hold me?" she asks.

"As long as you need me to." I pull her back to me and she settles against my chest. She lapses back into silence, and I let her, tabling my follow-up questions for later. My own thoughts drift, thinking through what tomorrow could bring, what else I can do to help her on her quest to find the truth about her dad, and what I need to do to make sure no one knows she's poking around.

"Hell of a thing to have in common, isn't it?" she asks a while later. "Losing our fathers by drowning?"

It takes me a moment to put the pieces together. Car crash. Plane crash. Bodies of water. Drowning. "Yeah," I agree as I ghost my lips along her hairline. "It is."

"Let's not tell Bradley yet," she continues and I nod my agreement. He already knows, of course, but I'd rather him not know she's does. Not yet. "Or Alice. Or anyone, really. I need to figure out what to do next."

"Any idea what that is?" I ask.

She shakes her head. "Not yet." She sits up then and looks at me, serious now. "How did you get this stuff, Kage? I've looked for this kind of information everywhere. I couldn't find it."

"I called in some favors." A half-truth. "I was discreet. No one is going to know you have this unless you tell them." No one except me and Theo. And Will and Luke. "Promise me that you won't do anything rash? That you'll come to me, and we'll navigate this together?"

She considers me and I wait. I'm not going to back down on this. I need to be wholly and fully involved in this.

"Why does what happened to my dad matter to you?" she asks.

"Because it matters to you." I brush her hair back again. It's the truth, even if I have other reasons for wanting to know. "That's enough for it to matter to me." She nods, and I lean forward to press a kiss to her hair. "I'm here, Lyla. I'm going to help you figure it out." Another nod. "Please, promise me you'll come to me?"

"I will," she agrees. "Promise." I breathe a sigh of relief, and she lets out one of those full-body shudders people have after they've cried hard for an extended period of time. "Could we . . . Go to bed?"

I send her to get ready for bed while I take Sadie out. I make it quick, eager to be back with Lyla. I do one last check of the security cameras, then check that I locked my door even though I know I did. I text Luke, ask him to sweep my car tomorrow morning, just in case, and then join Lyla in bed. It takes us both a while to fall asleep, but she eventually caves, and once I'm sure she's going to sleep for the remainder of the night, I reach for my phone.

Me: Gave her the papers.

Theo: How is she?

Me: Devastated.

Theo: What about you?

I don't answer. And that's all the answer he needs to know I'm not okay at all.

20

KAGE

Lyla and I wake up slow the next morning. We have sex, although it's not wild and unbridled. It's on our sides, her leg thrown over my hip, the penetration shallow, but the connection what we both need. After, I take her out to breakfast and bring her back to get her things. The only mention of her father is my asking if she has the folder and her confirming its well-hidden among her things. On the way to Brooklyn, I bring up another issue.

"So, Bradley . . ." I start.

"He's going to be pissed," she says. "He's always been protective over me. He likes you, but you're dating me . . ." She trails off and bites her lip. I smile. That's another thing I guess we should discuss.

"We're together," I inform her. "You're my girlfriend. Unless, of course, you say differently." I don't have time to hold my breath because she smiles and nods.

"We're together," she agrees. "You're my boyfriend."

Boyfriend. That word sounds even more foreign to me than girlfriend, but I like it.

"As for Bradley," I continue, "he is, in fact, going to be pissed." I lace my hand with hers as I drive. "I want to be the one to tell him."

"I should tell him," she argues. "It will be better coming from me."

"Trust me, Lyla, it won't be. I'm his friend. You're his sister. His *baby sister*." She snorts at that term, which makes me smile. "It's basic guy code at the end of the day. Let me be the one to tell him." She looks doubtful. "It's been a while since we sparred. I'll get him in the ring with me and break it to him there. He'll want to fight, and we'll already be in a place to do it. Safely."

She worries her lip as she considers the proposal. "I don't like the idea of you two fighting."

"Trust me, Lyla, it will be the best possible way for this to go down. And it's not fighting. It's boxing."

"Fine," she agrees begrudgingly.

"It might take me a few days to get him to the gym with his schedule," I tell her. "But I'm not going to beat around the bush. I want him to know I'm with you because fuck sneaking around—I'm not doing that. You deserve more than that."

She smiles at me, and I've won this particular disagreement. When we turn onto Bradley and Gabe's block, I pull up to the curb—in front of a fire hydrant—and put the Bronco in park.

"What are you doing?" Lyla asks. "We can't park here. And surely there's something closer to home—"

"I'm kissing you goodbye," I say. "Can't risk getting caught on all those cameras at Bradley's, can we?" That makes her laugh and then I'm moving in and we're making out in my Bronco.

I use a substantial amount of self-control to pull back a few minutes later.

Dropping her off is painful. This feeling is layered. I've had her all to myself for five days, and now I'm going back to an empty condo tonight and I don't like it. I don't like not knowing the next time I'll get to be with her, even if I know it will be soon because I doubt I can stay away for more than twenty-four hours. Then there's the fact that I have to go to this meeting soon and who knows what the hell will happen there.

There's a lot of worry, too. I've always worried about her, but now she's mine. She has plans to meet up with Cecily for a late lunch and errands so they can catch up because apparently grocery shopping is a great way to spend time with a friend. Will is going to tail her, make sure nothing happens to her, and that she stays far away from the gym until I can clear it. I make a mental note to have her come in tomorrow for her first self-defense lesson. Maybe I can take her to dinner after. Or take her to lunch on her break from work. Fuck, I'm needy.

We act like we haven't been fucking every chance we get for the last few days when I walk into Bradley's with her. He and Gabe are both at home. Bradley hugs her long and hard, and Gabe acts like she's the second coming of Christ, which I can't blame him for. I take her bags upstairs which earns me a curious look from Gabe. I look around Lyla's room, think it's not really her, all things considered, seeing as she's not meant to stay at Bradley's long term, then I find a stack of sticky notes on her desk and scrawl out a note.

I'll call you later. Call or text if you need me. – K

I leave it on her pillow where I know she'll find it, then head downstairs. She's in the kitchen negotiating evening plans with

Gabe. She wants to have dinner with her friends, he's begging for her attention, and it sounds like she's agreed to meet him and Bradley for ice cream when I announce I'm leaving. She's polite, formal, as she thanks me for the weekend, and I feel all twitchy inside when I say she's welcome and I can't kiss her like I want to. I'm going to have to tell Bradley immediately because fuck if I can stand to be in a room with Lyla and not be *with* Lyla.

Bradley walks me out.

"Thank you for looking out for her," he says. "I know she didn't go quietly."

Quiet is not a phrase I'd use for his sister, but sure, let's go with that for now.

"She settled in." Into my family home. Into my friend group. Into my arms. Into my bed.

"You sure you know what you're doing?" he continues.

Not a fucking clue, but he's not talking about my newly-minted status as half of a couple.

"I have it under control." I look at him. "Sure you don't want to join me?"

"Not a fucking chance." He shakes his head. "You have someone on Lyla?"

"Will," I answer. "He'll tail her while she's out with Cecily. Can I trust you to look out for her when she's back with you and Gabe?"

"Of course you can," he says, like he's challenging me. "I'm the one asking you to watch out for her, remember?" Not anymore, he's not. "Will can go off duty once she's back with us. Just make sure someone is there to watch her on her way to work tomorrow."

It's Will's day to meet her after work. I wonder what it will take to talk him into meeting her to go *to* work. He'd have to kill a few hours before his private lesson—that part of his story isn't made up at least—but it would make me feel better if she had an escort.

"She's covered," I tell him. "I'll let you know what happens after it happens."

"Be smart," he warns me.

"I always am." I nod toward the house, where my woman is. "Keep an eye on Lyla."

He narrows his eyes at me. "You're rather concerned about my sister's well-being."

"You asked me to be," I remind him. I'm trying to play this off and failing miserably. "I'm doing my job by reminding you to do yours. Especially now." He doesn't look entirely convinced, but I don't have time to deal with him—it's closing in on three o'clock. "I'll check in later."

We part ways.

Now, it's quarter to three and Luke has let me know my guest is already waiting. I do the asshole thing and waste forty-five minutes. I drive to a coffee shop out of my way, get an iced latte, and text Will.

Me: Let me know when you have eyes on her. She's supposed to meet Cecily at 3:30 outside The Black Dragon. She should be leaving her place soon, if she hasn't already.

Will: You're going to be an overbearing asshole, aren't you?

Me: Fuck off. Keep her safe.

Will: You know I will.

When I finally make it to the gym, it's three-thirty, and Theo and Luke are leaning on the wall outside my office.

"She inside?" I ask. They nod.

"She's pissed," Luke supplies.

"Something about punctuality," Theo adds. "She got here early because your ass is always early."

"I'm right on time," I say as I look around. The hall is empty aside from us. "Where . . ."

"Made them stay downstairs," Luke answers as his lips twist into a smirk. "With Scarlett."

I snort. I bet her guards like that.

"He's with them," Theo tells me, and my gaze flicks toward him, cataloging that bit of information. I don't like that Cosse is here, but I'm not surprised by it. "He wanted to be in the room. She sent him with the others."

"Good." I nod. "Keeps me from having to do it."

"Want us to join you?" Luke asks.

"Not yet." I shake my head. "You'll know if I need you." I push open my office door with a flourish. "Veronica Adler," I state. "Can't say this is how I'd like to spend my Monday afternoon."

"You're a half hour late," she informs me, rising from the chair behind my desk. "And it's Senator Adler."

"You're not my senator," I remind her as I move behind my desk, forcing her to move back to the correct side of it. "I'm also not late. I told you I'd be in my office after three o'clock. It's after three o'clock." She is unimpressed. I settle in my chair. "What do you want?"

"You're not going to offer me a drink?" she questions. "No refreshments? It's a long trek from D.C. to New York."

"Offering a drink would imply I want you to stick around," I say. "Besides, I'm not exactly known for my hospitality." I fix her with a steady glare. "What do you want, Veronica?"

She sizes me up. Most people would likely cower under her cold stare. Not me. She might have three decades on me and a hefty dossier of political maneuvering under her belt, but we both know I hold the right cards.

"He's on the move."

"I'm aware." I nod once.

"You're supposed to be handling it."

"I am."

"Are you?" she counters. "Sinclair tried to kidnap my daughter."

"I took care of that. If something would have happened to Lyla, it would have been on you. We had a plan. You went rogue."

"You know I can't let their policies pass," she says. "If I would have stuck to our plan, it would have made it through the Senate."

"It wouldn't have made it through the House," I counter. "You're more concerned with your own political career than you are with preventing massive fallout."

"I stand by my decisions," she states.

"At the expense of your daughter?" I ask. "No one is ever going to call you Mother of the Year, but even I wouldn't think you were that low."

"Sinclair was reckless and rash," she says. "His plan would have never succeeded."

"It damn near did," I argue. "Lyla was fast enough to get away, and Scarlett was at the right place at the right time." My grip tightens on the armrest at the idea of something happening to Lyla that afternoon. "You've made your choices, Veronica, but it's your kids who suffer the consequences." I hold her eyes. "And your husband."

"Don't you talk to me about him," she hisses.

I've hit a nerve. Good. Because her lack of concern for her daughter has certainly hit mine.

"Just reminding you of what your actions have cost you," I say. "Tell me, will you be visiting with your kids while you're in the city?" She only glares at me. "They're doing great," I continue. "Bradley has an attending position all wrapped up and waiting for him after this last year of residency. He and Gabe are doing well, which I'm sure grinds your gears given the fact that it flies in the face of your platform." Her temper is boiling, but I keep going. "As for Lyla . . ." I pause to look her in the eye. "She's an absolute fucking wonder and you can't take an ounce of credit for it. She's thriving here, and I strongly recommend you keep your distance."

"Are you threatening me?" she asks.

"You know I don't make threats." I don't look away. "Learned that from my dad." It's all she can do not to lose her composure. "I'm doing my part," I continue. "You fucking do yours."

"I'm doing what I need to do," she states. "This is bigger than a few individuals."

"Not to me."

I let her ponder what I mean by that. I hate her for being willing to sacrifice a few—in her case, her children—in favor of the many. Since I have her, though . . .

"What's Marshall up to?" I ask, just to see what she'll tell me. "Why did he hire Perrin?"

"Marshall is planning a presidential run," she reports. "You know that. You also know that Perrin has a history of putting men in powerful positions."

"Keyword there?" I ask. "Men. He damn sure isn't going to help a woman out." Veronica grinds her teeth at the truth of that statement. "If Marshall gets in the White House, world leaders will be pushing nuke buttons all over the fucking globe within weeks of Inauguration Day."

"You have a filthy mouth," she informs me, and I bite my tongue to keep from making a comment along the lines of "your daughter likes my filthy mouth." But I will not disrespect Lyla. She's had enough of that from the woman across from me and the so-called man she shared a bed with before me. "We can't let Marshall in the White House."

"Are you implying you want to rig an election?" I ask. "That's not in my wheelhouse." Even I have some limits.

"We dig up dirt on him before he ever gets the nomination," she says. I open my mouth to begin to list just how much dirt we have on that man, and Perrin too. She holds up a hand. "Dirt we can prove." I simmer. She's right. Everyone knows Randall Marshall is filthy. No one can prove it, though, and he's one run through the primaries away from a presidential nomination. If he gets the nomination, history and statistics say he's going to be in the Oval Office. We have some time—a year for him to set the wheels in motion, a year for him to campaign, but time is a tricky mistress. You think you have plenty of it. And then it's gone. "Tell your minions to double down."

"Tell yours to do the same," I fire back. "Speaking of minions. What's your aide up to?"

"Cosse?" she asks.

"He's been having meetings all over D.C. Seems to be a pharmaceutical theme to them."

"I'm sure he has his reasons." Her gaze shifts away from me.

"I didn't think you knew," I say, my suspicion that she had no idea confirmed. "You might want to question why."

"He often takes meetings with lobbyists and other parties on my behalf," she reasons. "He sifts through the muck and brings me what's worth my time."

"Hmm," I hum. "I'd keep a close eye on him." My phone chimes with a text, and I don't look at it, but I intuitively know it's from Lyla. Everyone else who would text me knows what I'm in the middle of. I fight the urge to pick it up and see what she said, trusting that there's nothing wrong, and if there is, Will has it covered. "He's up to something."

"I know who I can trust," she informs me. "You'd do well

to remember the same." She starts to stand, and I make sure I get to my feet first. "Handle Sinclair."

"Do your part," I sling back. "On all fronts."

"You did us no favors by ending your engagement to his niece," she informs me.

"Did myself one hell of a favor though," I inform her, thinking of Lyla. "Trust me, Veronica, Brynn Sinclair was never meant for me."

She looks like she might say something further on the matter. Instead, she shakes her head and angles toward the door.

"Remember your place, Kensington."

"I'll tell your children you said hello," I counter. She gives me one more death glare before she opens my office door, where Luke and Theo are waiting

"I'll see you out," Luke says.

"No need," she snips.

"There is absolutely a need," he informs her. "Let's go." He boxes her out of my doorway and down the hall. Theo waits until they disappear into the stairwell before he steps into my office.

"Well?" he prompts.

"That could have been an email." He snorts in amusement. "She did what I thought she would do—puffed out her chest, issued a few empty threats, threw a few digs around. She thinks Cosse is loyal, but I'm hopeful I managed to sew a seed of doubt. Coming all the way up here was an attempt at a power flex, but she fell short."

"You think he's loyal?" Theo asks.

"What do you think?" I counter.

"Not a fucking chance."

I check my phone. Sure enough, the text is from Lyla. It's

a selfie of her drinking an Oreo milkshake, no caption. I smile and tap back a response.

Me: I can think of a better use for those lips.

Her reply comes quick.

Lyla: Behave. I'm in public.

I chuckle and put the phone down to find Theo watching me.

"Lyla?" he guesses.

"Yeah." I nod. "She was devastated." I know he knows what I mean.

"What's next?" he asks.

"We need to get proof of what Paul Adler knew," I say. "Getting our hands on proof will knock down the first domino. If we can knock one down, the rest will fall." I don't tell him that Lyla has at least some semblance of proof. Photocopies aren't going to do much for us, but they will help me understand what I'm looking for.

It hits me like a ton of bricks then. So much so I have to lean forward to brace myself with my elbows on my knees.

The key to ending all of this could damn well be *Lyla*. What she has in her possession could be the death blow we need. Six months ago, that knowledge would have excited me. I would have done anything to get my hands on whatever she has, anything to get justice, the consequences be damned.

Now though? I'm scared to fucking death.

Lyla could end this.

It just might cost her her life.

POLITICAL CAPITAL

Kage Kensington swore he'd never fall in love—then he met Lyla Adler. As their connection deepens, the threat to Lyla's life grows as secrets surface, trust is tested, and love proves to be the greatest liability of all.

Kage and Lyla's story continues in *Political Capital*, Book Two of the *Political Gain* series in which power corrupts, love is used as leverage, and secrets are the price of survival.

Available Spring 2026

ACKNOWLEDGMENTS

In July 2023, I finally got my hands on a book called *Fourth Wing* after somewhat patiently waiting for it to be restocked. I heard about it from Jamie on *The Popcast*, after she gave it a green light, and thought, "I need to read that." I flew through it, recommended it to everyone I came into contact with, and thought about our favorite characters all the time. An enemies-to-lovers story set at a war college with dragons would inspire me to write *Political Gain.*

Political Gain was not supposed to be anything special. When I put my fingertips to the keyboard, it was going to be 5-6 chapters of brother's best friend spice. It very quickly took on a life of its own. It became something unique, original, and intricate.

I often tell people the story fell out of me. I can't emphasize that enough. I wrote most of what I call "Draft Zero" of *Political Gain* in my office at my full-time job, toggling between conference calls and a Google Document. There was no plot, no plan, no outline. It was Kage and Lyla, sitting on a bench in my mind, telling me what to write. I was merely the scribe, and surprised right along with my readers who read Draft Zero in real time on Ao3, exposition, grammatical and spelling errors, and all, at how this story unfolded. I didn't see the twists in what will be *Political Capital* (book two) coming. I definitely did see the depths of *Political Damage* (book three). I had no idea that I'd be inspired to give Luke and Scarlett their own story (book four), and then Andie a book of her own (book five). All because I thought it might be fun to write a one-night stand.

I've spent the last year making *Political Gain* the best it can be. It's been reworked in places, tightened up, edited multiple times over. This series is, to date, my favorite thing I've ever written. So naturally, as I prepare to publish it, I think it's terrible, awful, no good, and everyone will hate it. Such is the life of an author.

I owe immense gratitude to Rebecca Yarros. Not only has her catalog of contemporary romance and romantasy inspired me as a writer and set my imagination spiraling on everything from flight class to ballet, it was seeing her on a stage in Philadelphia on a frigid January night that made me finally say, out loud, "I want to do *that*." Until then, I'd kept my writing dreams quiet, publishing my debut novel *Off The Record*, quietly and actively avoiding telling anyone outside of my immediate family and closest friends that I wrote a book. Seeing Rebecca on stage gave me courage to say, "I'm an author," and to believe that one day, I might get to be on that stage, too.

Rebecca - thank you. For not just inspiring me to chase a dream, but for modeling such grace under pressure. Maybe I'll see you on stage one day.

Daddy - you've never read one of my books, but you have them all (signed) on a shelf for everyone to see. That means the world to me. Thank you for believing I'm capable of flying to the moon, roping the stars, and making them do whatever I want them to do.

Libby - thank you for telling everyone you know that "my sister writes books." I promise I'll hire you to film my content one day.

Logan - thank you for sending me jobs like "Pepperidge

Farm snack tester" so I can "move to L.A. and write all day." You owe your big sister a drink at Cecconi's.

Hanna - thank you (and Nick) for driving me to that Rebecca Yarros event, then walking around downtown Philly for three hours while I lived my best life. I think about that Levain Bakery cookie often. Mostly though, thank you for always reminding me "you're already doing it" when I get overwhelmed by the size of my dreams.

Tracey - thank you for reading *Political Gain* in the back of classrooms and sending me your scandalized reactions in real time. And for always reminding me that it's "WHEN" I get to do this full-time, not "IF." I'll see you on set.

Cait - *Political Gain* wouldn't be what it is without your touch. Your line edit commentary gave me life. I can't wait to "come back here and explain yourself" with book two. Thank you for putting your heart and talent into this book, and for loving Kage as much as I do. Let's do four more of these.

And finally, to the OG *Political Gain* readers. This book is yours. Your love of this story is what inspired me to pour countless hours into edits and re-writes into it and get it into your hands as an original work. Thank you for reading, for showing up, and for being friends with me on social media. I couldn't do this without you, and one day, I hope I get to say thank you in person.

As Faulkner said, "if a story is in you, it has to come out." This story desperately needed to come out. And now... on to the next.

ABOUT THE AUTHOR

Sarah Wyland writes romance with heart. She lives in Knoxville, Tennessee with her dog, Griff. When she's not writing, she's probably reading, teaching or taking a Pure Barre class, or cheering on the Tennessee Volunteers. She is also the host of the This Might Be A Draft podcast, writer of Between The Pages on Substack, and co-founder of A Novel Weekend.

Learn more at sarahwyland.com.

ALSO BY SARAH WYLAND

Off The Record

Strictly Business

Of Gingerbread and Snow Globes